Ephemeral

def p. 153

Andie Andrews

This book is a work of fiction. The names, characters, places, and incidents are products of the writer's imagination and are not to be construed as real. Any resemblances to persons, living or dead, actual events, locales, businesses, or other institutions are purely coincidental.

Cover design by Jillian O'Connor (www.jocreativeconsulting.com)
Cover photo by Lorenzo Beer (www.lorenzobeer.com)

Published by Flying Chestnut Press
ISBN: 0692936629
ISBN 13: 9780692936627

Dedication

To my real-life college sweetheart and beloved husband,
who allows me and my imagination to run wild
and keeps the home fires burning until I return . . .

To my daughter, my creative kindred spirit,
who inspires me to be authentic and fearless in all that I do . . .

To my soulful, little chestnut horse,
my partner on this journey and my muse,
who makes me want to be a better human
and gives me wings to fly . . .

To Jesus Christ, the Lord of my life,
whose divine mercy is new each day . . .

my heart is yours.

1

A swirling, cackling, black cloud touched down and took flight half a dozen times, hopscotching across the paddocks and flashing flamboyant patches of red that made Clarissa—or Claire as she preferred to be called—gasp aloud on my back. I hated when she did that, programed as I was to be on the lookout for mountain lions hiding in the spring-loaded thickets that bordered the hundred-acre farm.

"Look, Sonny, red-winged blackbirds! Aren't they magnificent?"

I lowered my head and snorted, annoyed by the false alarm. It felt good to release the adrenaline her excitement produced when she sucked in the air that filled her lungs and traveled through her belly into her seat bones where they pierced the saddle and connected with my back like a plug into a live socket and electrified my body and made lightening bolts out of my legs. In such split seconds, she curses and wonders why I'm running in a blind panic, somewhere far away from whatever is about to make a hearty meal out of us. Out of me. Me first. I'm the one they blood thirst for. And so I typically run and ask questions later.

But this time I keep my feet in check, if only because she's done this ride after ride since we've been together. Will she ever learn?

"Sorry—did I scare you?"

She runs her hand down the side of my neck and scratches my withers. I instantly forgive her and throw her an ear, waiting for her next command.

"Let's trot to the end of the white fence," she telegraphs to me with her mind and the slightest brush of her heels. I pick up a lazy Western jog with just enough velocity to qualify as not-a-walk.

"Really, Sonny, is that all you've got? Can't you go any faster?" she chides.

There's dewy grass under my feet. I'll slip. She'll fall. Both of us will feel horrible about it. I love Clarissa, most of all on days when she gives me carrots and clarity. But sometimes I just have to say no. We finish our twenty-minute hack around the farm and she dismounts gracefully from the saddle. I like the way she rubs my face and gives me a peppermint the moment her feet hit the ground. She tells me I'm the best horse in the whole world. I'm coming nineteen years old. This isn't my first rodeo. Still, I believe her every time she says it.

As she leads me back to the barn, I notice the hitch in her hip is getting worse. Clarissa's getting older too, but you wouldn't know it by her energy field. She's perpetually twelve. Believe me, I know twelve. I was a lesson horse for twelve years with twelve-year-old, pony-tailed, pony-crazy girls clambering on and off my back every day at summer camp till twilight came; that dim, ephemeral hour when they would whisper their darkest secrets in my ears and bury their tears in my chestnut mane.

Clarissa has told me her secrets too, in words and images and quantum whorls where nothing is unknown between us. In fact, do you know what led Clarissa to me in the first place? Writer's block. That's a lot like colic in a horse, when you just can't get your crap out. At least that's what she told me. But it wasn't until her father died—three months from the day he was diagnosed with cancer—that the chance to have a horse of her own was born. For thirty years, she was his right hand in his hardware store and real estate development company; his faithful daughter, his loyal scribe, who taught him "the pen is mightier than the sword." He was her fearless leader. She was his secret weapon.

But the pen, like the sword, is double-edged.

As an English major at the University of Miami, she'd sprawled on the beach for hours, crafting stories and screenplays for master classes that tested her resolve to be a writer. For inspiration, she immersed herself in the dark worlds of Dostoyevsky and Kafka, then feeling depressed and overcome, she'd allow herself to be swept up in the romance of the Brontë sisters, soak up the folksy wisdom of Isaac Bashevis Singer, or steep her soul in the modern-day parables of Flannery O'Connor. Their ink spread on the pages before her like blood drawn from the sharp point of a pen, and she longed to prick her finger and be one with them and their literary genius.

Instead, she graduated and became a hack copywriter for a manufacturer of office equipment, then toiled as a book editor, helping other writers look brilliant. After she married and had a baby, she went to work for her father, using the English language as a clever instrument to circumvent municipal ordinances, woo investors, and wiggle out of the tight corners her father recklessly backed into with maddening regularity. She said he kept her busy and he made her laugh. Except when he made her cry.

I never met her father, but he sounds a lot like my Old Man, the first human I ever met on the farm in upstate New York where I was born to an off-the-track Thoroughbred, a sorrel mare with the same diagonal white socks as me. My dam was a real looker, people used to say, sleek with high withers and a winning streak that didn't last, even though she descended from the illustrious racehorse, Man o' War. She was covered by a flashy, Hall of Fame Quarter Horse who sired a long line of winning show horses, including a few world champions. My owner had high hopes for me until I came up shy of fifteen hands with faulty conformation. I am hopelessly cow hocked. Still, the Old Man thought he might make something of me yet. He worked me early and hard; I was green broke at two and ridden rough at three, with plenty of time spent hobbled or chained to a patience post in between local rodeos. The Old Man thought I'd be a good cow horse with my stocky build and my sturdy cannon bones. Never mind that I wanted to run fast and free like my predecessors; what I wanted, what I was bred for, didn't matter. I wasn't the one calling the shots. Clarissa says I'm built downhill, that's why my hips and stifles hurt, but I can tell you with certainty it's from bending around poles and chasing flags and 180 pounds of old-man-ass bearing down in the saddle and kicking up dirt in spectacular sliding stops for three years straight. All to make him look cowboy tough. Yep, her father sounds a lot like my Old Man.

Every now and then, Clarissa stole some time to work on her own projects—romance novels, and scattered poems and short stories written to revive her creativity as the fangs of domesticity sucked the India ink from her veins. When her daughter, a singer-songwriter, recorded some demo tracks of country music, Clarissa had an idea for a screenplay that could potentially get both of them noticed. I've met Gabriella a couple of times. She can barely refrain from plugging her nose with two fingers when she walks into the barn. She's slightly cow hocked, just like me, and her high-heeled shoes over dirt and gravel make her wobble like a newborn filly. She looks at me with curiosity but she never touches me. Still, her gaze is loving and indulgent as she recognizes her mother's dream living and breathing in me. I am the thundering freedom her mother feels in her chest until panic rears and a copper-and-steel bit bangs me in the mouth. She doesn't mean to do it. Her hands need to catch up to her heart.

Clarissa roughed an outline and charged into the first scene. She typed ten pages, then crashed into a writer's block—or should I say a mounting block? The story, a country-western romance, revolved around a dude ranch. The dude ranch was filled with horses that were central to the plot, horses she knew nothing about!

She figured if she was going to write with authenticity—or even write at all—she'd have to get her forty-something buttocks on a live horse. So began the search for a local stable where she could learn what it looked like, smelled like, and felt like, to ride a horse.

While there are more than a dozen horse farms within a twenty-mile radius of her house, Clarissa had never noticed a single one. So Clarissa did what she does best: she Googled until she had a sticky note brimming with addresses on it and sprinted to her car.

The first farm she visited that morning turned out to be a busy lesson barn. She approached a vast, sunlit paddock where more than thirty-five horses were too busy grazing to give her more than a cursory glance and snort. A battalion of workers, mostly young women in navy blue shirts, pushed wheelbarrows almost twice their size. Some were filled with hay, others with mounds of what looked to her like sawdust and mud. She pressed the side of her finger to her nostrils. It smelled like—ugh, she said.

"Feel free to take pictures of them," said one of the workers. "Just don't feed them. Some of them bite."

"Actually," Clarissa said, slowing her down just enough for the wheelbarrow to tilt. "I'm here to see about riding lessons."

The worker set the barrow on its hind feet and wiped her brow. It was too hot and humid for early June, everybody thought so. Especially the horses, whose sleek hair coats were already blotchy with sweat.

"English or Western?"

Clarissa hesitated, knowing she had half a chance to get it right. She searched for a clue. Most of the horses in the field looked lean, brown, and elegant—nothing like the flashy Paints and stocky Appaloosas she'd seen in reruns of *Little House on the Prairie*.

"English?"

Clarissa thought herself neither lean nor elegant, but figured she could easily hop on any one of those fine-boned horses without breaking its back. I wish I could've told her in the beginning that it's not so much the weight but the way a horse is ridden that matters. Clarissa used to sit on my back like a lumpy, 130-pound bag of feed that shifts and rolls until it inevitably falls off. Now, most days—except when she's in a mental slump—she's more like a 130-pound bag of feathers. I like that. A lot.

"But I'm not opposed to Western. I'm new to horseback riding," she confessed.

"Well, Western is a little easier and saddles with a horn are more secure. We only have one Western trainer, though. The office opens at ten. Ask the barn manager about lessons with Lillian. She's great with adult beginners."

"Thanks," Clarissa chirped as the worker hoisted the wheelbarrow and lumbered off.

So I'm an *adult Western beginner rider* Clarissa repeated to herself. At least she knew what to say when the barn manager arrived. With forty-five minutes to kill, she decided to visit the next barn on her list—a small, family farm just a couple of miles down the road. As she strolled to her car, it occurred to her that of course she wanted to ride in a Western saddle. Her screenplay was set in Oklahoma on a ranch! Besides, she liked the idea of a secure saddle with a horn—what was a horn, she wondered?

She pulled into a gravel driveway and followed it to a parking lot flanked by a charming, yellow barn. A small herd of horses milled around its perimeter, picking at piles of hay in pastures that were more mud than grass. Still, they looked happy and well fed. She got out of her car and approached a warped screen door with a crooked "office" sign nailed to it. There was that smell again....

A petite horsewoman in a pink baseball cap burst through the door and sized her up before she had a chance to speak.

"Looking for lessons for your daughter?"

Clarissa smiled and extended her hand.

"Hi, I'm Claire. I'm an *adult Western beginner rider.*"

The woman stifled a laugh as she grasped Clarissa's hand.

"I'm Meredith. And we mostly ride English here. I have a couple of Western saddles but it's more important that you develop a balanced seat before you worry about what kind of saddle you're sitting in. Ever been on a horse before?"

Clarissa shook her head. She said she'd been on a sedate, nose-to-tail ride on the beaches of Jamaica twenty years earlier, but that it hardly qualified as horseback riding. I always pitied the poor string horses who occasionally showed up at barns where I resided, largely used up and broken down. They were zombie horses, all the light gone from their eyes as a result of one too many idyllic sunsets burned into their corneas.

"Truth is, I'm doing research for a screenplay. I guess it doesn't matter if I ride English or Western, it's only a couple of lessons," she conceded.

"I only offer beginner lessons in packages of ten. It takes at least that long for a rider to find her seat—no point wasting my time. Or yours."

Meredith stared her down and drummed her hand impatiently against her skinny thigh.

Clarissa didn't blink. There was comfort in knowing where she stood with people; she said too much sugar made her heart race and her eyes twitch. I know what she means. I'd rather be ridden by ten Old Mans than by a dressage queen with killer hands cloaked in white gloves. And then there are the rodeo sweethearts who kick and spur and whip the stuffing out of their steeds and then turn on the sparkle and shine for the crowd. There's something about women, always working out their deepest angst and control issues on the back of a horse. I am not a metaphor for a man. Luckily for me, Clarissa seems to know that.

"Okay, when can we start?"

"Any day but Sunday. You'll need a pair of riding boots—something with a one-inch heel so your foot doesn't get stuck in the stirrup if you fall. Oh, and you might want to get your own helmet too. I have ones you can borrow, but I wouldn't want to stick my head in any of them. The kids use them, you know what I mean?"

Clarissa only heard the words *fall* and *helmet* and the threat of head lice. She nodded and rubbed the gooseflesh on her arm.

"Can I wear jeans?"

"Breeches would be better, but yes, you can wear jeans."

"Great! How about Tuesday at eleven?"

"That works. Oh, and you should know, my barn is about natural horsemanship. We won't be using spurs or bits, and we're going to learn about how horses think and act in the wild and use that information to build good relationships both on the ground and in the saddle. You okay with that?"

"Perfect," Clarissa replied. It sounded like stuff she could work into her screenplay and she was eager to get home and start fleshing out her characters.

"It's fifty dollars for a one-hour lesson, cash or check is fine."

Clarissa thought it was a sporting price for inside knowledge. Besides, she relished the idea of buying a pair of cowgirl boots and feeling totally legitimate wearing them. So she did. They were red with hand-tooled scrolls and her feet hurt in their pointy toes. But they fit Meredith's marching orders and that's all that mattered.

On the heels of fashion comes confession. She'd have to tell her husband what she was about to do. She knew it wasn't going to be easy. Kind of like giving a horse peppermint-flavored deworming paste. We all know it's not real peppermint no matter how sweet it might taste at first. Soon enough, the bitterness sets in and stuff starts to spew.

"You signed up for *what?*" George said as he set down his latest issue of *Wine Enthusiast* and furrowed his tidy eyebrows.

"Ten horseback riding lessons. It's research for my screenplay," she replied, sure he was already likening this newest adventure to her last pricey experiment creating matching jewelry for house pets and people.

"Can't you just Google this stuff? Or watch some videos?"

"No, I have to get on a horse myself. Otherwise, it won't ring true."

"Who's teaching you?"

"A lady at a barn on Swamp Road. She's a little gruff, but I feel safe with her."

"How much will it cost?"

She hedged, knowing this was just the sort of thing he'd find frivolous. But the advice her mother gave her as a newlywed had never let her down. "Clarissa," she'd said, "if you don't want to fight about money, always keep a little cash set aside in an account with your own name on it to use at your discretion." She didn't make much money working for her father, but every once in a while he'd hand her an extra fifty or hundred-dollar bill and she'd squirrel it away for times such as this.

"Don't worry, it's covered."

"Then have at it. Just don't get hurt," was all he said, but Clarissa knew what he was thinking. His oldest brother had been in a car accident at the age of fifteen that left him blind and traumatically brain injured for the last thirty-eight years. They both knew what that had done to a family that had once been as seamless as glass; now, they were hopelessly shattered and deeply disfigured by sharp accusations and jagged regrets that cut them to the bone. I know a little bit about such accidents; I crashed head-on into barbed wire fencing when I spooked the first night at my new barn, having just been rescued from kill buyers at the auction. I still have the scars above and below my left eye and a saw-toothed notch over my eyelid. The vet said it was a miracle my eyesight was spared. I wish my new owner had taken the time to desensitize me to the sights and sounds of the local airport next door. Little planes tilted and whirled and practically skinned my ears as they approached the runway. I was sure the monsters in the air were chasing me. Later that summer, they launched hot air balloons from the same airfields, kaleidoscopic masses that hovered over my head and breathed fire like horse-eating dragons.

By the time autumn came, I was over it.

George absently turned the page of his magazine. Clarissa bit her lip and fiddled with her wedding ring, a simple, gold band with a small cross engraved in the middle. She made a mental note to Google the patron saint of horseback riders and invoke his or her protection. She would not get hurt. She would not get hurt. She would not get hurt! She chased the thought from her mind and gave George a kiss. "I won't get hurt."

He nodded, willing to believe. But there was already stuff spewed all over them. They couldn't see it, but it was there.

The following morning, Clarissa walked into her first saddle shop. It was as large and well stocked as any sporting goods store she'd ever seen, though she had no idea what foreign objects hung on the walls or on the dozens of revolving racks that surrounded her. She recognized articles of clothing as such, but still, they looked elegant and exotic. The dark, woodsy interior had the feel of a rich man's library and she hovered just inside the doorway.

"Can I help you?" a young woman coaxed from behind a mahogany counter.

"I need a helmet."

"For your daughter?"

"I'm an adult Western beginner rider."

"Oh! Okay," she said and smiled. "Come with me."

Clarissa followed her toward a glossy wall that displayed a variety of riding helmets. Some looked as dull and ugly as construction hard hats. Others were sleek and covered in black velvet, though she instinctively knew those were out of her league—and price range. She inspected a basic, brown helmet with a sixty-dollar price tag. She thought it might blend in with her brown hair and she wouldn't feel like such a dork wearing it.

"How about this one?"

"That's a nice schooling helmet," the clerk replied. "Let's try one on and see how it fits. I'll be right back."

Moments later, she emerged from the stockroom with two boxes. "Let's try the small size first." She unwrapped the helmet and set it on Clarissa's head, then fastened the chin strap.

"How does that feel? Too loose, too tight?"

"I'm not sure."

"Well, you don't want it to wiggle around or it won't protect your head if you fall."

Ugh. There was that word again.

"Turn your head upside down and shake it," the clerk said. "Like this!" She demonstrated the maneuver with wild abandon. Clarissa isn't that kind of girl but for fear of flunking Helmet 101 she did as she was told. The helmet shimmied off her head and hung by the chin strap.

"Hmmm. Let's try the extra small."

They repeated the exercise, but this time, the helmet stayed put.

"Perfect! Do you like how it looks on you?"

The sales clerk pointed to a mirror and Clarissa peered into it. No, she hated how it looked—like she had a big, brown, bowling ball on her head. Her extra-small pinhead, that is. The experience was affecting her self-esteem—dangerous territory for a forty-something woman.

"It's fine. I'll take it." Clarissa forced a smile and paid sixty bucks plus sales tax to protect her head at the expense of her ego. Then again, it was better than head lice!

She went home that day and scoured her closet for blue jeans she could move in. She didn't know what kind of moves she'd be making but she knew that if she didn't find the right pair of jeans, Meredith would force her into a pair of high-waisted, tan, polyester breeches that would show every roll and dimple in her body. She simulated the motion required to mount a horse by throwing her leg over a giant exercise ball. Her elastic Calvin Kleins would have to do.

She didn't tell anyone else about her "research project" except for Gabriella, who didn't blink twice. As a musician, Gabriella understands that creativity breeds a certain amount of madness. She's had her own mad dashes to places of inspiration—and regret—throughout her twenty-five years. "Good luck with that, mom. Don't fall off."

"Hey, what doesn't kill you makes you stronger, right?"

"That's not funny."

Clarissa shrugged and smiled. Little did she know that in the days to come, her strength would be tested from the inside out, on the ground, and in the saddle, in ways she never could've imagined in her wildest romance novels.

2

The following Tuesday, Clarissa arrived at Meredith's barn at eleven o'clock looking every bit like an adult Western beginner rider. The glare of sunlight across the sand arena made her squint and wish she'd remembered to bring sunglasses. There were already visible ripples of heat hovering over the sand and she wondered if it would be too hot on a horse's feet. She'd never seen the bottom of a hoof before, but that was about to change.

"Good morning!" Meredith crowed as she rounded the corner of the barn holding what looked to Clarissa like a toolbox in one hand and a halter and rope in the other. She performed a quick body scan as she approached.

"Good morning!" Clarissa replied, sucking in her belly and her breath.

"I see you have a helmet. Let me see your heels."

Clarissa torqued her knee and lifted her foot for inspection. Meredith nodded.

"Can you squat in those jeans?"

"I can."

"Let's see"

Clarissa squatted.

She thrust the toolbox into Clarissa's hands. "I'll get your horse. Meet me in the barn."

Clarissa exhaled as Meredith charged toward the pasture. She secretly hoped she'd pick the pretty, white horse who had nodded as if to greet her as she lurched down the mud and gravel driveway in her pristine, white car. Her car was no longer pristine or white. Turns out, neither was her horse.

This horse, a mare, was yellowish-brown and caked in dried mud. Worse yet, Clarissa sensed she came with a sizeable attitude given the way Meredith had to repeatedly yank on the rope to get her to walk from the pasture to the barn. Meredith clipped the horse's halter to the cross-ties. Immobilized, the mare looked at Clarissa with a condescending eye.

"And you are who?"

"Claire, this is Jenny. She's a 23-year-old palomino mare."

Meredith's voice hushed with reverence, as though Jenny was of rare and noble rank. To Clarissa, Jenny seemed little more than a funky-smelling farm animal. But as she drew closer, she felt it; that powerful, penetrating pulse of energy that is Horse. It struck her like a seismic wave and within seconds, the scales fell from her eyes and Jenny morphed from muddy mess to magnificent. She couldn't wait to mount her sleek, long back and gallop toward the blue horizon as a brisk wind whistled in her ears—at least in her imagination!

Instead, Meredith rattled off a hasty explanation of the tools at hand and how to use each one to groom Jenny before their first ride. Clarissa balked at how long it would take to get Jenny clean. After all, she reasoned, if she was buying an hour of horseback riding lessons, shouldn't she get to spend a full hour on the back of a horse? Being a fairly good sport, however, she set about grooming the mud-crusted mare exactly as she was taught. Knowing Clarissa as I do, the conversation went something like this:

Clarissa: Hey, pretty girl! (Reaches out to pet Jenny's face.)

Jenny: Lady, you're in my personal space. Back off.

Clarissa: Oh, I get it. You need to look me over, right? Want to sniff my hand?

Jenny: Nope.

Clarissa: So, I'm supposed to groom you before we ride. How about it, sweetie, do you want a free makeover? (Starts using the curry comb as instructed.) What a good girl you are!

Jenny: Flattery will get you nowhere. Let's just get it done.

It would take time for Clarissa to discover the mystical properties of the curry comb. The slow, gentle rhythm of circles over circles, traveling length and girth while being attentive only to the circle one is in at that moment can be transcendent—for humans and for horses. Back then, she didn't quite know what to make of it, or of the way the power-of-now is at the heart of both horsemanship and relationships. After all, she was a woman on a mission, bound and determined to ride a horse and then get back to the business of writing. Did she really have time for this?

Clarissa studied the tools that looked to her like shoe buffing brushes, a stiff one and a soft one. Meredith had demonstrated how to use the stiff brush in forceful, little sweeps over the horse like a broom; and with each rhythmic sweep, Clarissa found herself stirring up the dust of marital strife and anxieties that had collected in the corners of her mind, then let them scatter and drift away. Thereafter, she commenced a soft, tender brushing that polished Jenny's hair, and in doing so, created light. And Clarissa was immersed in it.

She breathed deeply, set aside the brushes, and then stepped back to admire her work. Sunlight bounced off the cement floor and intensified Jenny's natural golden hue. Clarissa grew teary at the sight of mare's true beauty revealed. She swiped her eyes with the back of her hand, leaving streaks of dirt across her cheekbones. The last thing she needed was to get sappy in front of Meredith. It was bad enough that Jenny was casting a suspicious, round eye on her.

She had yet to learn that horses are mirrors—reflections of human hearts, souls, emotions, thoughts, memories, and intentions; Clarissa's inability to discern the beautiful truth about herself is a cross that has bedeviled her from the time she was a young girl who was sorely disappointed by Sister Mary Aloysius, her second-grade catechist who was beautiful and kind and holy, and who made her want to be a nun; who then left the convent the day after Clarissa's First Holy Communion to marry a mere mortal and henceforth, Clarissa went to work pricing nuts and bolts in her father's hardware store. If she wasn't to be a nun (oh, what was the point if it could be so easily undone?) but a clerk in her family's business (her destiny, she supposed), she vowed to scorn the world in her own way: by cloistering herself as a reader and a writer and perpetually imagining herself anywhere-but-here.

Eventually, she allowed herself to fall in love, to get married, and to have a child. Every now and then she attended Mass, hoping to make herself feel less earthly and profane. Then one day she stopped going to church all together. The disconnect lessened her disappointment in the God who had silenced her calling once and for all with a fleshy hand over her ten-year-old mouth, the God whom she wouldn't invite inside lest His glory shine through like it did when she was seven and she first felt the consecrated Body and Blood of the Lamb of God on her lips, in her mouth, in her soul, and she might glow—in vain—with supernatural beauty.

Now, plunged in a pool of light, her lips parted to inhale awe and her soul stirred in such a way once more as she basked in the glow of a thousand-pound mare who tossed her massive head and demanded attention—now! Clarissa jumped as the cross-ties rattled and shook her from her reverie. Good thing, too. If you ask me, ask any horse, daydreaming is for sissies. Every day, we get up, show up, and demand that our humans do too. Otherwise, there's a fairly good chance they'll end up covered in dust and regret with a panoramic view of the sky and a broken tailbone.

"Okay, let's have a good ride!" Meredith shouted as she rounded the corner.

"Amen!" Clarissa hollered and winced. What was *that* about?

Welcome, Clarissa, to the Church of Horse.

Thus began Clarissa's journey, a thirty-minute exercise that exasperated Meredith and the temperamental mare who cared nothing for being fawned over like a puppy and everything about the leadership ability of the human on her back. Of that, Clarissa demonstrated precious little. She had owned and trained dogs most of her life, but without biscuits in her pocket, she had no idea how to ask for what she wanted. And so she sat. And sat. And sat some more.

"Raise your energy!" Meredith ordered.

"Woo-hoo!" Clarissa shouted internally. "Giddy up!"

"Did you say something?" the mare seemed to reply as she twitched her ears ever so slightly and hung her head. Clarissa pondered the shapes of the clouds drifting by as her enthusiasm vaporized over burning sand.

"Walk on!" Meredith finally interceded. Jenny dutifully raised her head and took a lumbering step forward; then another and another until they were halfway around the arena. Clarissa murmured a steady stream of encouragement and sat taller in the saddle. After a few more laps punctuated by effusive whispers of thanks and praise, Jenny walked to the center of the ring and stopped at an invisible taxi-stand.

Jenny: So, this is where you get off.

Clarissa: Yep. Got it. Thanks for the ride.

She slid awkwardly out of the saddle and marveled as Meredith removed Jenny's tack in sixty seconds flat. Clarissa shuffled her feet and fished in her pockets. She had nothing to offer Jenny to reward her for her time and attention. Not that it mattered. The minute she was turned out in her paddock, Jenny spun her big Quarter Horse butt toward Clarissa and trotted off without a second glance.

"Next time, bring some game," Clarissa thought she heard her say. It was her first tiptoe into animal communication.

She turned to Meredith, who casually leaned against the fence with her arms propped on the top rail. "I think Jenny hates me."

"Nah, she just doesn't respect you." She patted Clarissa's shoulder and then set about her barn chores.

Clarissa stood alone at the gate and contemplated the difference between her effortless relationship with her dogs (fellow predators), and this strange, new paradigm that required her to elicit trust and respect from a prey animal hard-wired to flee from the likes of her. It would take more than sweet talk and liver bits. Just how much more, she had no idea.

She waved good-bye to Meredith, who whistled aimlessly as she hauled a muck bucket and fork from stall to stall. It was high noon; the wind was picking up and the smell of sunbaked manure drifted into her nose. Clarissa raced to her car—her poop-colored car that George was going to scold her for when he saw it—but she didn't care! She'd ridden a horse, a gorgeous, golden, palomino horse! Once inside, she breathed deeply and reached for her phone. Fourteen phone calls. One number. No messages. Clarissa knew exactly what that meant:

Clarissa! Where the hell are you?

She found her father seated behind his desk with his reading glasses perched on the tip of his bulbous nose and a dog-eared paper in his hand. He peered over the rim of his spectacles as she entered through the glass door to his office.

"Boy, am I glad to see you. Read this. Tell me what you think it says."

She took the paper from his hand and began reading a memo from the DEP regarding some land he planned to develop. He briskly tapped the tip of his pencil on the desktop as he waited for her to finish.

"You lose your hairbrush?"

"What?"

"Did you lose your hairbrush? Looks like you forgot to brush your hair this morning."

"No, I brushed it."

"You sure?"

She ran her fingers through her hair. Helmet hair!

"Oh," she said. "I was wearing a helmet." She didn't feel ready to confess it but she didn't want to hide it either.

"Motorcycle?" He seemed mildly interested. In general, her father wasn't one to plumb the details of her life, but anything fast and furious appealed to him.

"Horse."

He chuckled. "You were on a horse? Why?"

"Research for something I'm writing."

"Looks like you fell off."

She suddenly noticed her own pungent smell and the streaks of dust and dark dirt—horse manure?—ground into her tee shirt and jeans.

"Nope. I was spectacular. And I'm riding again on Friday."

"Next time bring your hairbrush. And some lipstick."

"Thanks for the advice."

"So? What does the letter say?"

She gently lifted the glasses off his face and buffed away the smudges that clouded the lenses.

"You might know if you could actually read with these things. Let's just say it's not going to be easy, but we'll make it happen." She put the glasses back on his face.

"The pen is mightier than the sword!" he crowed and grinned. It was a catchphrase she'd taught him that made them both laugh. When he smiled, he was as handsome and energetic and roguish at seventy-nine as he was at seventeen, the result of years spent as a quarterback, coach, and lifelong fitness buff. But during the last year, he had lost weight and seemed to be slowing in the race against time. He began to rely on Clarissa a little more each day for advice and consolation, especially when the doctor told him that the spots on his lungs were suspicious. A few months later, when his arm became too painful to move, tests revealed a cancer that had eaten though the bone. He needed to have it surgically repaired before he could even begin radiation. Now, a month later, he was still in a sling but it didn't stop him from driving his Mercedes convertible coup. Or chewing on cigars. Or drinking expensive red wine out of clear plastic cups. Preferably chilled, the Italian way. He picked up his keys.

"I gotta go, can I see a draft tomorrow?"

"Sure. See you tomorrow."

He got up and ambled stiffly toward the door, then turned around to face her.

"Do you think I should do it?"

"Do what?"

"The radiation. Your mother says I should do it. And maybe the chemotherapy, too."

She sighed, wishing she knew what he wanted to hear. She would say it, whatever that was, if it could restore his swagger and his peace.

"It's up to you, Dad. Don't let anyone make that decision for you."

"But if it was you," he persisted, "what would you do? Would you get it?"

"Probably not, but that's just me. You know I like to try holistic things first."

"Tell your mother."

"I'll try, Dad."

"Get that letter done. I don't want to lose any time."

She nodded, knowing that in his world, everything had become equally urgent. And rightfully so. Three months later, just after her final lesson, her father succumbed to the ill effects of chemotherapy and died. Amid a crushing recession, the family business folded like a castle of cards. Clarissa's fortress, where she wielded her pen like a sword, was in ruins, and in its place was a dusty and fallow field. She was faced with a life-changing choice: She could shuffle her feet in meandering, meaningless circles, lamenting the loss—or she could ride.

3

Clarissa didn't know if there was such a thing as cheating in the horse world, but she felt pangs of guilt when several months later she decided to take a few lessons at the busy lesson barn on the side. She wanted to see what other trainers were like in comparison to Meredith, who wasn't so gruff after all. Over the course of their lessons, Clarissa came to understand that Meredith simply wasn't one to suffer fools gladly, and having decided Clarissa was no fool she allowed her to become a friend. Clarissa was lucky to have found her. I've known a lot of trainers in my life and I can tell you that Meredith's sanity, honesty, and innate goodness is a rare trifecta. But winter was coming, and the idea of a large, indoor ring and lessons from a variety of instructors on a variety of horses appealed to Clarissa who was, in the vernacular of horses, starting to feel her oats. There was something bubbling up in her, a bounciness in her soul that came from riding Jenny every week. Yes, she was getting better. But Jenny was also a good babysitter and gave Clarissa far too much confidence for her own good.

She signed up for six private Adult Beginner lessons and met Patricia just moments before their lesson. She was youthful and chatty and barely took a breath as she told Clarissa about the horse she would be riding that day—Prince—and what to expect. Lo, Prince appeared, tacked up by the stable hands and ready to be mounted. All majestic, black-and-white, seventeen hands of him. She'd balked when she learned she wouldn't be allowed to groom and tack him herself. She likened it in her mind to kissing a stranger. But she didn't have a choice and dutifully walked him into the grand, indoor ring where she mounted him and sat atop what felt like Mount Kilimanjaro. Her confidence leaked out of her in a slow but steady dribble. Her heart fluttered and her legs felt like jelly. But when Patricia walked to the center of the arena, sized her up, and gave her the green light to walk, she was delighted to find little difference between her fifteen-hands mount, Jenny, and this mammoth Percheron-cross who dutifully picked up his feet in a royal, marching walk and made her feel like a little princess. She liked that he made her butt look small and her abilities large. After all, she seemed to be moving 1,500 pounds of mass with a flick of her heel. She had no idea such schoolmasters as Prince and Jenny and I run on autopilot and our currency is confidence.

That first lesson with Prince was followed by many more rides on Apache, a spirited Paint horse, and Tikki, a temperamental Warmblood. Clarissa's attempts to post the trot made her feel about as graceful as a gorilla on a pogo stick. "Up, down, up, down!" Patricia called out. "Sit a beat, find the correct diagonal!" *Really?* Clarissa thought to herself. *I can't find my other shoe most mornings. And you want me to find something as elusive as the correct diagonal?* Yet she continued to try—and to look foolish—in the name of progress. In the arena, nobody knew or cared how accomplished she was in other areas of her life. There, she was as green as the first blade of spring grass. She hated that she could quote Shakespeare and Austen and Winnie-the-Pooh at length and she still couldn't keep both feet in the stirrups for an entire lesson. She'd drop one or the other and scramble to find it, hopefully before Patricia noticed. She wanted to be good at riding horses. For some strange reason, it mattered.

That's why when someone at the barn told her she wouldn't have to post the trot or perch in a precarious, two-point position if she rode in a Western saddle, she eagerly traded her half-chaps for the chance to advance her skills—and her screenplay! Somewhere down the long side of the rail, she'd lost her focus and creative drive; her eyes were trained on riding horses, not writing about them. Nor was her mind on making dinner or vacuuming the floors. George was being patient, but she could tell he was reaching his limit. She hoped the more relaxed world of Western pleasure would balance not just her life, but also her buttocks in the saddle.

Lillian, the only Western instructor on staff, was a salty, old cowgirl. She looked like an airy, copper-haired pixie, but there was nothing delicate about her demeanor. She reminded her of Meredith in her blunt delivery and sparse concern for a rider's feelings. She yelled at Clarissa every time she attempted to tie the cinch *("not girth, that's English tack!"* she reprimanded), and no matter how much Clarissa tried and fumbled with the leather strap, she couldn't get the "rabbit" in the right "hole" without Lillian's help. She'd cluck her tongue and roll her eyes at Clarissa's incompetence. Clarissa laughed it off, but Lillian never did. Lillian took that cinch very seriously and for good reasons. Too tight, a nasty bite or a buck or a sore—too loose, a slippery slide over the barrel and into the dirt. I know firsthand about such things. The

Old Man was ruthless with the latigo strap; the way he'd thread it through the D-ring and then yank it upward and crank it as tight as he could in one fell swoop was a brand of torture horses never forget. That's why we blow ourselves up with anticipation. Our breath is our only defense against callous hands and merciless hearts. Truly, our breath is power and life! We can snort in protest, fill our lungs and bolt halfway to tomorrow, or use it to whinny sounds of danger and distress. In the best of times, we use it to sigh with contentment when a rider gets it right and the pain, for a moment, is a distant memory.

Clarissa's reward for finally learning to tie the cinch properly was a trail ride. She was excited to venture beyond the walls of the indoor ring and Lillian had chosen the perfect early-spring day for a walk-trot excursion into the fields behind the stable. That day she was assigned to ride Shooter, a ten-year-old Appaloosa whose name made her feel like she was living the Western dream. This is the stuff great screenplays are made of, she thought to herself, though somehow she knew she wouldn't find time to write that day. Or the next. If she wasn't riding a horse, she was reading all about us—how to groom and care for us, how to keep us "naturally," and how to become a better rider and leader. Leader? Clarissa? That wasn't in her repertoire yet. Dang if Shooter didn't know it too. Moments after they left the stable and entered the trailhead, Shooter jerked the reins out of Clarissa's hands and snatched a mouthful of scrubby grass.

"Don't let him do that!" Lillian barked.

Clarissa tugged on the reins and pulled Shooter away from the underbrush.

"If he does it once, he'll do it a hundred times if you don't stop him cold. Don't let him get away with that again!"

"Yes Ma'am," Clarissa replied. Seconds later, Shooter dove in for another bite. He managed to get a long stem or two in his mouth before she yanked his head up.

Lillian clucked and sighed.

"Sorry," Clarissa muttered. She made a mental request to Shooter to give her a break. It went something like this: *Listen, Shooter, I know you have me pegged as a pushover—and for the most part, I am. But it means a lot to me to have this chance to ride on a trail, and if you're as smart as I think you are, you'll behave. Unless, of course, you'd rather trot in mind-numbing circles around the indoor ring for the next forty minutes. Your choice, my friend.*

Shooter flicked his ears, snorted, and lowered his head—not to eat the grass, but to offer a nice, balanced walk with his eyes trained on the trail ahead. Was it possible that he heard her, she wondered?

"That's better," Lillian called from behind. "Now you have his attention."

So, horses can read minds? Clarissa pondered and grinned, feeling like she'd just won the lottery. It was a discovery that had the potential to make life with horses so much easier—unless one's thoughts were rife with negative self-talk, worry, and fear. The truth is, she never paid much attention to her thoughts. They were like wayward children in a playground, scattered here and there and everywhere with no real focus or discipline. She allowed them to run amok into light and darkness with equal access to both. But that day on the trail she glimpsed the power of words to change outcomes. Not necessarily words written on a page for all the world to see, but those secret ones humans whisper to themselves.

They walked for a half mile more, then trotted up a few steep hills and circled back to the barn. Clarissa could tell that

Lillian was pleased. She even offered a rare, thin-lipped smile as Clarissa handily dismounted and handed Shooter's reins to the stable hand.

"Good job, Claire. We just might make a horsewoman out of you yet."

Clarissa smiled softly and stroked Shooter's thick, powerful neck. *Thanks for the ride, Shooter. And thanks for listening,* she mentally telegraphed.

Shooter snorted again and walked off with his handler. But she was pretty sure she heard him say, *you're welcome, kid.*

"How was your lesson?" George asked as he loosened his silk necktie, dropped his ostrich leather briefcase with a thud, and kissed Clarissa on her ruddy cheek.

"Great, we went out on trail," Clarissa chirped as she hurried to cobble together a meal with precious few provisions in the house. As usual, she'd meant to go to the grocery store, but after her lesson she'd gone to a tack shop thirty miles away instead. It was the only one that carried Western gear and she wanted to see if there were helmets that looked less English. After all, she was officially an *adult Western beginner rider.* Her first trail ride had clinched the deal! She was disappointed, however, to find that a helmet is a helmet is a helmet. Worst of all, she was dirty and sweaty and had no dinner on the table to show for it.

She was thankful for the carton of eggs and the couple of red potatoes she had on hand. What might look like a meager meal in someone else's house was an Italian delicacy and legacy in hers: potatoes and eggs. Not just a random coupling, but a precise culinary creation with just the right amount of potatoes, sliced razor-thin, and fried to just-short-of-crisp in olive oil seasoned with salt, pepper, and oregano. Later, at least six eggs would be beaten into lightness, poured into the same pan, and stirred long over low heat until everything married together with no major clumps of potatoes or eggs. When she slid the mixture onto a plate and placed it in front of George alongside a glass of Chianti, he smiled at her like she was the best wife in the whole world. She breathed a sigh of relief. *Thank you*, she offered up to her long-gone Italian aunts and uncles who had taken her under their wing as a new bride to ensure that George would be well fed with the kind of simple, hearty, Italian fare that nourished the body and soul.

She'd come to their marriage with few skills that didn't involve a cash register or a computer. Called to work in the family hardware store at seven years old and barely able to see over the countertop, she was relegated to the task of bagging. With great precision, she'd drop nuts and bolts and washers into little brown bags and carefully seal the top with staples. They sold a lot of nuts and bolts and washers. Back then, everyone did their own handiwork and home repairs. She worked from nine until five on weekends and every day after school. Even when she grew older, there was no time for extracurricular activities, weekend football games, or playtime with friends. She'd never even heard of kids riding or showing horses!

Her mother, Grace, didn't dare to buck her husband's expectations. She never asked Clarissa to do a lick of housework or to learn how to cook or sew. Clarissa's quick mind and nimble fingers destined her to work shoulder-to-shoulder with her father, without the distraction of what he called "women's work." The only potential escape was college. So when Clarissa was accepted to the University of Miami, she jumped at the chance to pack her bags and hang up her scarlet work apron. She found it fitting that her uniform was the color of blood. Every single, monotonous minute of working in the hardware store sucked the life out of her and drove her deeper into a quiet state of rebellion. It was by her own clever design that it took her five and a half years to graduate with a four-year degree. The fear of donning that apron again kept her on a long course of academic probation, except when it came to English or Creative Writing, where she excelled and was admitted into master classes.

She was in grave danger of failing Marine Science 101 when she first met Geórgios Stamos. He was a Marine Science major, a tall, dark, curly-haired, foreign exchange student from Greece who came to Miami for its famed School of Oceanography. Clarissa was an English major who was forced to take a science class to graduate. She chose Marine Science, assuming they'd study and hang out at the beach. George, as he called himself in America, was annoyed he had to take the same class over to satisfy credits that didn't transfer from his Greek university. They were both in the wrong class. But in the Universe's wisdom and plan, they were in the perfect place at the perfect time.

George offered to tutor Clarissa in plate tectonics the day they got back midterms; she barely pulled a D while he got a handy and predictable A. The truth is, she didn't much care about passing the class. She was "that girl" who was just having fun. Nevertheless, when George glanced across the aisle and saw the sorry mark on her paper, then approached her with a proposal to help, she took one look at his ocean blue eyes and said yes. Two years later, she said yes to his proposal to marry him.

He knew from their second date on a Saturday afternoon that she was a lousy cook. In an attempt to bake her mother's famous game-day, pigs-in-a-blanket, she used too much quick dough and produced twelve pigs-in-a-football. But George didn't blink and she didn't bother to explain. He happily sawed through them and she knew he was a keeper.

After the wedding, they moved into a tiny house in New Jersey, a refurbished chicken coop located behind the hardware store on the same lot and block. It was so close to the store that when her father needed her, he'd simply bellow *"Clarissa!"* into the microphone behind the counter where pick-up orders for bags of sand and concrete were communicated to the outside yard. Her aunts and uncles took an instant liking to George and generous pity on Clarissa's lack of culinary skills. Aunt Mila immediately set about teaching her to make spaghetti and meatballs, the kind made with lunchbox bread. Clarissa crinkled her nose at putting her hands in the fleshy mound of meat to squish everything together. "Miss America!" Aunt Mila screeched in a coarse, pitchy voice that carried on the breeze to far-off places. "How you gonna make it right if you don't put your hands in the meat!"

Her Uncle Carmen taught her to make pasta fagioli, a hearty Italian soup with chicken broth and plum tomatoes and "Only Redpack!" tomato sauce if one didn't have the requisite homemade sauce in the cupboard. There were lots of tips and tricks and Old World recipes that they offered in the name of "Poor Geórgios!" Potatoes and eggs became a Friday night staple, especially during Lent. It was comfort food in the first degree and they both felt younger and happier when they ate it.

"So?" George persisted. "How was your trail ride?"

"Fabulous!"

"Fabulous?"

Clarissa seldom used such flamboyant language, accustomed as she was to her meek, little life. It caught him off guard and he laughed.

"That's great, honey, I'm glad you enjoyed it."

"How are the eggs?" she countered.

"Fabulous," he gushed and smiled.

And for a moment, they were supremely happy.

4

A few years earlier, George and Clarissa had purchased a lakefront cottage in the mountains of Pennsylvania. The two-hour drive each weekend gave them a chance to catch their breath and iron out midweek wrinkles in their marriage before they reached their destination. Clarissa thought it was as good a time as any to make the pitch for something she'd been thinking about for the past few weeks.

"So, I saw this ad for training to become an equine massage therapist."

George tapped his fingers on the steering wheel in time to the music and waited for Clarissa to tell him what she'd already made up her mind to do. But this time it was different; she craved George's input and approval. Starting new writing projects, even though they diverted hundreds of hours from their time together, never fazed either one of them. The risks were predictable and small. But the risk of starting a new career had the potential to change much more than dinner—or not—on the table. In a way, she hoped George would talk her out of it on the spot. She was looking for a reason, any reason, not to move forward, not to risk failing. It wasn't in Clarissa's nature to take risks, especially ones that might make her adrenaline pump and her heart beat faster and awaken the sleeping giant that was her soul. And yet, riding had already done that and made her want for more...more of what she couldn't name just yet, but more of something that included horses.

"It's seven hundred dollars for a five-day course, plus hands-on training, to learn how to massage horses therapeutically so that they move and feel better. Show horses, racehorses, other kinds of sport horses. And backyard horses, too."

"Can you make any money at that?"

"I think so. The going rate is sixty dollars per massage."

"If you want to do it, then do it."

"But what if I don't like it or I'm not good at it? That's a lot of money!"

"What if you like it and you're good at it?"

George took his eyes off the road just long enough to cajole her with a wink and a smile. Clarissa sighed and rolled down the window and put her face into the breeze. It was almost too much to contemplate that she could be anything but the hack romance writer she was. Besides, the construct of her stories had become her refuge and security. It was scary enough to try something new, let alone something new with twelve-hundred-pound animals who seemed to read her mind and know her heart.

"It's up to you," George added. "But I say go for it. If it doesn't work out, it's okay."

She nodded, wishing he'd balked at the idea, but the thought never did go away. She took the course that summer and started massaging horses that fall at the busy lesson barn where she took some of her first riding lessons. She wanted to give something back to those hardworking, forgiving, "beginner" horses—Prince, Tikki, Apache, Shooter and others—who had carried her dead weight on their backs without complaint. She couldn't bring herself to charge a dime. She loved making horses feel better. She said it was the least that she could do for God's ambassadors of freedom, a discovery she made about us in the coolness of autumn mornings as she offered the gift of slow, deep, soothing massage into overworked, knotted, equine muscles and watched and listened for signs of relief and relaxation: long blows of breath, lazy yawns, licking and chewing, as her hands swept away the stress, pain, and tension from overburdened backs and crooked bodies. She yearned to unlock them so that they might experience the fullness of the freedom for which horses are made; the same freedom to which we call Clarissa and others like her who somewhere along the way forgot that this is the human's natural state of being too.

She spent the next six months massaging and test-riding horses in every size, shape, and color and as she gained confidence and speed, she recalled the giddy, wind-in-her-hair sensation she first felt as a teenager behind the wheel of her first car, a 1972 Mustang convertible that her father impulsively traded one day for a backhoe and a beat-up Ford Pinto. Yep, from that very first walk on Jenny, she knew she was onto something. Something big. Something she loosely recognized as freedom that was magnified at the trot and exploded at the canter. If and when she gallops, if she ever finds the courage, she'll know the untamed heart of a horse.

One thing, however, was becoming clear: riding a horse demanded that she live in the moment—if for no other reason than the focus it required to keep from hitting sand and pea gravel. Right-here-right-now was both an anathema and a magnet as she began to drift out of the slow lane on horseback. Deep down, she knew her journey wouldn't—no, couldn't—stop there.

The first anniversary of her father's death had come and gone without fanfare, except for the memorial Mass that was offered on his behalf by the pastor who heard his last confession and anointed his pale, furrowed forehead with oil. While she'd never be privy to what he might have confessed—or not—Clarissa knew he was burdened with an overwhelming sense of guilt and bitterness stemming from a family feud.

Three years earlier, when his relationship with his brother soured over money, her father vowed to buy out his brother's shares in their real estate company. In his anger and pride, he paid far more than they were worth. When her father died soon afterward, he left Clarissa and her siblings millions of dollars in the hole. Their only choice was to liquidate some assets to relieve the crushing debt and prevent foreclosures.

That first year, they surrendered two commercial properties—as well as their childhood home—to the bank. Clarissa helped her mother pack the remnants of fifty-four years of marriage into two dozen boxes, then moved her into a condo in the housing complex her father had built, setting aside a unit should she ever need it. Clarissa's father exercised both tremendous wisdom and tremendous folly throughout his lifetime. The problem was, no one ever knew which would rule the day.

By the end of winter, Clarissa's business-savvy sister had managed to breathe new life into the company. She also kept the books and did everything she could to make sure Clarissa never lost heart—or hope. To that effect, on the first day of spring, she presented Clarissa with a dividend check for ten thousand dollars.

It felt odd to hold the check in her hand and to see the name of the family business emblazoned at the top. After forty years of working with her father, of building dreams and schemes and kingdoms together, this was her fair share and a stark lesson in investing in all the wrong things. After all, *what does it profit a man if he gains the whole world and forfeits his soul?*

She couldn't get that biblical warning out of her mind. She had ten thousand dollars in her pocket and a lot of soul-searching to do. She and George could pay down the mortgage, pay off Gabriella's student loan, or invest in their own retirement. George assured her he was taking care of all those things. "Do what you want with it," he urged her. "It's your money, Claire, you earned it."

She gave a portion to an order of religious sisters who were in residence nearby, faithful handmaids and poignant reminders of a path she didn't take. She set the rest aside and then prayed for what would benefit her soul. There was only one answer, no matter how many times she asked the question:

Buy your own horse!

She knew nothing about keeping horses, she chided herself. Sure, she could ride them, massage them, walk them, and sometimes if she was very quiet, hear them. That hardly justified buying one! Nevertheless, the thought of having her own horse made her feel hopeful and utterly consoled. She told George what she planned to do with the money. He nodded and gave his blessing, as though he'd known the answer all along. She took it as a sign that that there was a horse somewhere out there waiting for her. Immediately, she set about finding him—or her—with the help of Google and a winged prayer.

Horses with little or no training under saddle are called green. Riders with little or no training in the saddle are also called green. *A green horse plus a green rider equals black and blue.* But no one told Clarissa that when she set out to find a horse. Maybe they simply thought she already knew. And she was just green enough to be swayed by appearances; a glowing copper, a dreamy dun, a chocolate brown, a dappled gray, a flashy black-and-white—never mind that they all might be green on the inside and she could get seriously hurt.

She found the first horse she wanted to meet on a website that promised to match a rider with the horse of her dreams. The mare's name was Dolly—a show-stopping, six-year-old palomino, just like Jenny. But the horse she met a few days later was no Jenny. The mare repeatedly barged into Clarissa's shoulder as they walked and whipped her head around to bite her when she put a saddle on her back. The seller assured her that was Dolly's only vice. Instinctively, Clarissa thought it was too big a vice for a novice and politely declined to buy her.

The second horse she looked at came from an online classified ad posted by a local trail association. The photograph showed the head of a pretty, bay mare peeking out of a stall. Her eyes were dark and luminous and Clarissa liked her kind expression. She made an appointment to meet her, even though the ad said she was for light riding only. She didn't know exactly what that meant but she didn't care. She had no plans to jump her or to run her into the ground like some of the used-up athletes she massaged. Light riding sounded just right.

She instantly liked the woman who owned Cheyenne, a midlife rider who had broken her back in a skiing accident two years earlier. She wanted a safe landing for her beloved mare, a fifteen-year-old trail horse who hadn't been ridden in over six months.

"Do you want to ride her?" she offered.

Clarissa hedged. Not ridden in six months?

The woman looked like she might cry. Clarissa touched her lightly on the arm.

"Tell me a little more about her," Clarissa coaxed. "Your ad mentioned light riding."

The woman explained that Cheyenne had permanent damage to the navicular bone in one foot that made strenuous riding painful or impossible. Clarissa liked Cheyenne immensely. The mare had a sweet disposition and a desire to please. She had only moments to think about her own riding goals, skills, and desires, and knew she was in grave danger of making an emotional decision.

"I'm sorry," she finally said. "I just don't think it's a good match."

The owner's face drooped with disappointment. She stopped just short of offering to give the mare to Clarissa, believing she'd provide a kind and loving home. But Clarissa was sure she'd feel it in her bones when the right horse came along. All she felt then was sympathy and regret.

She drove straight home and scanned the same site where she'd seen Cheyenne listed. A new ad popped up. This one touted a seventeen-year-old gelding, an Appendix Quarter Horse who resided at Misty Acres, a local barn with a small lesson program. A younger Quarter Horse mare was also up for sale there. Clarissa grabbed her phone and made an appointment to meet the horses and their owner at noon the next day....

From my pasture, I watch with mild interest as a white car slowly approaches, bobbing over the uneven driveway and diving in and out of mud puddles and potholes. The windows are cracked and

I can hear the person inside saying the kind of words people say when they come off a horse. I've learned they're not very polite words, best said quietly or not at all. Unless of course, you're on the ground and something's broken. Then you can say them as loud as you want.

I see the driver careen her neck to admire Corona, the huge, black-and-white paint horse in the pasture next to mine. He's a looker all right, and people always ask if he's for sale. What they don't know is that he throws a good buck when it suits him—which is roughly every third time he's ridden. Still, people are hopelessly attracted to his flashy horse flesh. Ordinary chestnuts like me can't compete for attention and I stopped trying a long time ago. But if anyone really wants to know the best color of a horse, I'll tell them it's gold. An old horse is a gold horse. Yep, that's me. Takes a special eye to see it, though it's of no consequence to me. I'm not for sale. Nope, I'm Beth's forever horse. At least that's what she told me.

The driver parks on the far side of the barn and is temporarily lost to my view. I hear Zelda-the-chocolate-lab barking, making her typical commotion over an interloper inside the barn.

"Calm down, Zelda!" Beth yells. "This is Clarissa, she's here to meet Sonny."

Did she say Sonny? I trot down the fence line, my ears pointing like satellite dishes. From a distance, I see my tiny person, Beth, with her choppy, black hair spiking in all different directions and her glasses askew on her nose. She never did get them fixed after the last time Corona bucked her off.

"And the other horse, the mare," this Clarissa says, though she's still largely hidden from view. I can, however, see one foot shod in a red boot that shifts uncomfortably in the silence that follows.

"Oh! I'm sorry, Clarissa. Darla, the mare, is spoken for," Beth says. "My ex-boyfriend decided to keep her."

"Please, call me Claire. It's fine, I understand," Clarissa says, but I sense her disappointment. If this Clarissa person is as small and timid as she sounds, Darla would be a great match for her. She's a pleasant, buckskin mare, a packer and a people pleaser who takes good care of her charges. She's only been in Beth's lesson program for a couple of years, having been rescued by Beth from an auction house in Pennsylvania. Darla hadn't been homeless long enough to lose the light in her eyes and spent the next two years showing Beth her gratitude in willing strides and inexhaustible patience with the lesson kids. She knew she was one of the lucky ones, the ones whose feet would never suffer the cold, steel floor and cramped confines of a trailer bound for a slaughterhouse in Mexico, nor the piercing, steel bolt blasted between the eyes that would drop her dead—if, and only if, the Mexican was a good shot and got it right the first time. As it turned out, Beth's ex-boyfriend, Will, had fallen for Darla about the same time he fell for one of the young vet techs that tended to the lesson horses. Darla is safe in Will's hands. He's a good man, despite the fact that some people think he's a jerk for what he did to Beth. Strangely enough, they're still friends and he still helps out around the barn. I think that's what makes them good horse people. They're quick to forgive and move their feet forward, just like us. It's that simple.

"So why are you selling Sonny?"

Wait, what? What did she just say?

"I have no choice but to sell the farm, can't keep up with the payments. I have plans to move out west where it's more affordable. I can only take two horses. Sonny's a semi-retired schoolmaster. I wish I could take him with me, but I can't."

I had felt this coming, this shifting ground beneath my feet. Still, I couldn't believe that Beth would actually do what I had felt her saying and doing in her head, and so I'd stuck my own head in my big, round hay bale and refused to think about it. Until now.

"Come with me," Beth says to Clarissa.

I turn and amble back to the round bale in the center of the pasture and hover behind it, chewing away my anxiety as Clarissa comes into view.

She's as brown and plain as a field mouse; light brown hair, a brown jacket, and a skittish little walk that screams *don't notice me!* I pretend not to as she draws near.

"That's him, over there, on the far side of the hay bale."

My pasture mate, Daisy, trots to the gate to say hello. She would be going out west, wherever that was, with Beth and Marigold and Zelda, leaving me behind. I never let on just how much I like Daisy. She's a mare but not the uppity kind. We've been pasture buddies for twelve years. Twelve years! I wonder what's going to happen to the miniature donkeys, Joey and Flip and Macaroon. My mind races even though my feet are standing still. How can this be happening?

I keep my head down and my eyes locked on Beth and Clarissa's faces.

"Sonny!" Beth calls to me. I flick an ear but refuse to lift my head. I know what comes next. That head-to-hoof appraisal that will make me feel like horse meat. My only consolation is knowing that Beth would never—no, never!—send me to auction.

"He's a little food obsessed," Beth confesses. "Guess we'll have to go to him. You okay walking through the mud in those pretty boots?"

"Sure," Clarissa says, but I can tell she doesn't mean it.

Slosh. Slosh. Slosh. An unfamiliar hand touches my neck and I brace and absorb a wellspring of information that feels like a flood washing over me. This is Clarissa. This is my new person. I turn and glance at her face and feign supreme boredom, but in massive, quantum waves I have already discovered everything about her. The most important thing I know is that she's kind. I open my nostrils and blow a snort of relief all over her. She laughs as she wipes my snot from her arm.

"Nice to meet you too, Sonny."

She gives me a once over. I return the favor.

She finds me rough coated and caked with mud. I have a hay belly and runny eyes from the dust embedded in these bland, round bales. But it's all Beth has ever been able to afford. The Old Man used to give me rich, green alfalfa hay that made me feel tingly and alive all over. But not this hay. It makes me feel like I'm eating bricks.

Clarissa finds me solemn and bored and aloof. Funny, I think the same thing about her. But her hands are soft and her face is sweet, pleasing to look at with wide, green eyes flecked with gold. She is dappled sunlight. Yes, that's what I think.

"So he's seventeen?" she asks.

"Actually, he's eighteen," Beth says sheepishly.

Clarissa nods and suppresses a frown.

"How tall is he?"

"Just shy of fifteen hands. But trust me, there's a lot to him and he's steady on his feet. By the way, he's barefoot. All my horses are barefoot. I prefer his new owner keep him that way."

"How is he ridden? English?"

"English, Western, doesn't matter to him. He's a solid citizen and a great horse for an adult beginner. He's been in my lesson program for twelve years. Walk, trot, canter, he'll even jump if you want him to. He's good on trail, especially with other horses. A little pokey though. You'll need a lot of leg to keep him going out on trail. Oh, and we practice natural horsemanship. You know what that is, right?"

"I know a little bit," Clarissa replies, thinking back to her early lessons with Meredith.

"Well, for me, it's about using so-called games to build stronger, more natural relationships with my horses, first on the ground, and then under saddle. It appeals to their natural instincts to play and to recognize leadership when they see and feel it, just like they would in the wild. Makes for a more respectful and cooperative partner. I'll teach you what I know so that you two get off on the right hoof, so to speak."

Clarissa tilts her head. I sense her indecision.

"Is he easy to catch?" she asks, as if mentally ticking off a list of important questions.

"What do you think?" Beth quips as she handily clips a purple lead rope to my frayed, purple halter.

"C'mon, boy, let's go into the barn and say a proper hello."

Clarissa backs up and I brush past her. I won't deliberately step on her foot like some horses would do to humans who don't give way fast enough. She doesn't know how lucky she is. Yet.

I feel her eyes on my butt as Beth leads me though the springtime mud. I wonder if she notices the hitch in my gait that comes from my right stifle and makes me track up short on that side. Beth hasn't said anything about that but she knows it's there; she knows how my stifle locks up and freaks me out until she eases me backward, which unlocks the joint and brings me back from the brink of panic whenever it happens. She parks me in the center aisle of the barn and drops the lead rope onto the ground. Clarissa scrambles to pick it up and Beth chuckles.

"It's okay, I've taught him to ground tie."

Clarissa grins and I stand extra still, trying to convince Beth that she should keep such a fine, obedient horse.

"Sonny doesn't cross-tie. If you cross-tie him, there's a good chance he'll pull back and break the ties. That can be dangerous for you, for the horse, and anyone else in the way. Never figured out what sets him off so I taught him to ground tie instead. Don't worry, he won't move."

She's right, the pressure on my poll when I'm attached to the cross-ties makes me feel anxious and trapped and all it takes is the rustle of a bag or a falling muck fork or an unfamiliar scent in the air to crank up the pressure and suddenly I'm a twelve-year-old girl with a daddy-longlegs in her hair. I can't help it. They ogle me with a mixture of sympathy and reproach. The weight of their stares make me want to hang my head and take a nap. And so I do.

Clarissa puts her hand on my soft, squishy shoulder. I don't mind. It's warm and vibrates tenderness.

"May I palpate him?" she asks.

I'm not sure I like the sound of that. I pick up my head and toss her a hairy eyeball.

"Sure, have at it."

Soon, I hang my head again and relax as Clarissa's hands sweep over my body, stopping every now and then to explore the knotted muscles and twists of tension that have accumulated over time. I feel her probing for more information, something that will tell her who and what I am and as she palpates longer and deeper, she discovers my sweet spots and my resistance and the strength of my will. It's all there for her to read like fingertips over Braille and when she's done, she knows I'm an old man set in my ways, just as I know she's an old woman set in hers. How will this ever work?

"So what do you think?" Beth says.

"I don't know," she murmurs. "Is there anything else you can tell me about him?"

"Well," Beth pauses and elevates her dark brown eyes in thought. She has too much integrity and love for me to lie. "He's really tough to load, he travels best in a stock trailer. He has a locking right stifle. It gets hitchy every once in a while and the only way to unstick it is to push him back on his hindquarters and then move him forward. But it gets better with work. Oh, and don't ever hit his butt with a crop or he'll buck. Don't know where that came from either, must go back to his early years. Other than that, I can't think of anything else except to say he's a good horse—he'll keep you safe."

Clarissa recalls her promise to George that she won't get hurt. She lightly traces the blaze over my eye that ends in a pronounced hook. I try to project my good mind and steady disposition.

"You said he's an Appendix Quarter Horse?"

"Yes, he has Thoroughbred bloodlines on his dam's side. His registered name is Hotter Sonny Dee. Never been raced as far as I know, but there's a lot about his first six years that I don't know."

Clarissa does the math. She wishes I was anything but eighteen years old. She doesn't know if I can go the distance with her and I don't know any other way to tell her that I can but to toss my head proudly. At the same time, she moves in closer to my face and the next thing I know, she's crouched on the floor holding her nose. There are big, red drops on the concrete floor and I hear her say one of those words.

Beth says it too, and rushes to get a towel.

"It's my fault," Clarissa manages to say. "I know better than to get into a horse's space. I'm fine, it's just a bloody nose. I think." Her voice is thick with pain.

"Let me see it," Beth says as she helps Clarissa to her feet. She stares intently at Clarissa's face and breathes a sigh of relief. "Straight as an arrow. Definitely not broken."

Clarissa presses the towel to her nose and as the bleeding begins to subside, she musters a valiant smile.

"That's one way to make a lasting impression, Sonny."

It wasn't what I was going for, but I'll take it.

"You okay, boy?" she whispers and draws near. She wants to know if I'm okay. I'm a horse, of course I'm okay. Just the same, I feel a little mushy around her. How can this be?

"I have an idea," Beth says. "Why don't you come back tomorrow and I'll ride him for you? Then you can take a couple of lessons on him and see how he feels to you. I'll teach you some groundwork, too. No charge. I want you to get to know him better before you decide."

"Really? That sounds great, thank you!" Clarissa gushes.

"Better get some ice on that," Beth says.

"Good idea. See you tomorrow, Sonny."

She scratches my withers and I drop my head for a nap. Clarissa steals a backward glance. What was she expecting? A parade?

I hear Daisy whinny for me in the pasture. I lift my head and whinny back to her. Beth sees Clarissa off and then walks me back to the gate. I prance in place as she unclips the lead rope from my halter and I bolt into the field to join Daisy, who invites me to play with a swish of her tail and a whirl and a buck. I back up to her and kick out, knowing there's just enough distance between us to prevent a strike. She runs down the fence line and I chase her into the corner and back again. Then together, we drop our heads and graze, gingerly picking at little tufts of spring grass that poke through the dirt. The sun feels warm on my back and the air is cool in my panting lungs. The moment is ephemeral—and it is enough.

"Geez, Sonny, you couldn't do that when Claire was here?" Beth laments and shakes her head. "You need to bring it tomorrow, buddy. Not many takers for an eighteen-year-old horse."

I take her words—and her warning—to heart.

When sunup comes, I'm ready. I wait at the gate for Beth to bring her special concoction of flax and black sunflower seeds and oats and apple cider vinegar with a little bit of beet pulp mixed with some grain. She makes it warm and wet and frothy for me, and I slurp it up and down into my belly where I feel how much she loves me.

Then she leads me from the pasture into the barn where she fawns over me forever, starting with the shedding tool that rakes my coat and pulls out the long, coarse, muddy hair that has kept me warm all winter. Beth sputters as my hair flurries everywhere, into her nose and into her mouth and all over her clothes. She looks like a mini-me and I'm amused. Then she brushes me until shiny copper emerges and glints in the morning sun. She wipes my runny eyes and trims my ears and geriatric whiskers, and then gravitates to my feet, rasping away the overgrowth and polishing my hooves until they glisten like black and white pearls. Finally, she picks up a brush and pulls it through my long, auburn tail and my shaggy mane until all the tangles and unruly strands are gone. She gives my forelock a tender swipe with the brush and traces the whorl on my forehead with a finger. Her eyes are wet and glisten in the sun.

"Beth?"

"Hey, Claire, I'm in the barn giving Sonny a spring makeover. Come and see!" she calls out merrily, dabbing her eyes with the same rag she uses to wipe mine. I can feel her heart fluttering. It makes mine flutter too.

"So, what do you think?" Beth chirps as Clarissa comes into view.

I can tell by the look on Clarissa's face and in the mirror of her mind what she thinks. I am magnificent. I am the wild mustang on the grassy plains of old. I am the noble warhorse of a thousand generations. I am the industrious plow horse and the elegant carriage horse whose hooves over cobblestone make way for pageantry and kings. I am the pack horse, the racehorse, the show horse and the dream horse of young girls in every place and time. I am the trail horse, the therapy horse, the abandoned horse, the rescued horse—and the slaughtered horse. I am earth horse and spirit horse, untamed and uncontainable. I am the Alpha horse. I am the Omega horse, that last one who will ever live. She knows, and I know, I am every horse. I am gleaming copper and dewy-eyed with liquid hope and promises and she sees it, she knows it.

I am Clarissa's horse.

"He cleans up real nice," is all Clarissa says. Seriously, Clarissa? You can run but you can't hide, I want to tell her. I merely snort my displeasure.

"I think we'll go Western today. You want to tack him up?" Beth asks.

"No, I'll just watch, that way I'll know how you do it."

Beth sets a fleecy, purple saddle pad on my back and I flinch. I know what comes next, that flimsy, old saddle that tips and rocks and squeezes. It's the only Western saddle in the barn and I try not to mind. But when she sets it down and threads the latigo strap, I blow up in expectation of the pain.

"Come on, Sonny, breathe!" Beth cajoles, but Clarissa frowns. She eyes the cinch and my distended barrel. She places her hand on my croup and gives me a little scratch. It distracts me enough with its nice, tingly feel that I instinctively blow out all the air I'm holding in. Foiled by a good scratch on the butt. Will I ever learn?

"Good boy," Beth says as she tightens the cinch two more holes. The points of the saddle tree dig into my shoulders, right on cue.

She unstraps my pasture halter and puts on a purple rope halter in its place. She attaches purple-and-gold braided rope reins and makes sure that the knots over my nose aren't too tight. Forget my nose, look at my shoulders, I want to shout. Instead I stand stoically and still. She hands Clarissa the reins.

"Why don't you lead him into the ring?"

Clarissa hesitates.

"Never mind," Beth says, sensing Clarissa's reluctance. "I'll take him if you don't feel ready. It's important that Sonny senses your leadership from the start."

I can already tell that Clarissa is a buttercup. It will take every magnanimous bone in my body not to exploit her weaknesses. But that is true only in this moment. It may be different in the next. I hope so or I'll have to take charge.

Beth steps in the direction of the sand arena and I lag several steps behind. She tugs lightly on the rope, asking for more energy. I comply by speeding up an infinitesimal degree. Clarissa trails behind us, inspecting my stride and the way I track. I know it's not perfect, but it's the best I can do.

Beth parks me in front of the mounting block where I stand like I have cement feet. I'm very, very good at standing still.

She takes one last swipe at my cinch, climbs the mounting block and then handily swings herself into the saddle. She bumps her legs against my side and I dutifully begin to walk. Beth calls it my chain-gang walk. I'm no spring colt. My joints and muscles need time to loosen up.

"He just needs a couple laps to get going," Beth shouts to Clarissa, who watches from outside the split rail fence. Her arms are casually folded over the top rail and sunlight spills on her hair. She radiates kindness and expectation. I like her enough to want to impress her.

We take several spins around the ring and weave through orange cones and around colorful jumps that no longer hold any appeal to me. In my mind, I can jump 3'6 with my eyes closed, but my flaccid, achy stifles betray me.

Beth closes her legs around my barrel and asks for a trot. I'm unhappy to oblige and toss my head and swish my tail—but I'm obedient. Once I get going, I'm happy for way my body extends and loosens up and I drop my head with relief. As we trot by Clarissa, I pick up my head and my energy. I want her to see how good I can go when I try.

I can feel her as I pass by. Yes, I know my trot is a little choppy. And yes, Clarissa, I cut corners shamelessly, it's just a silly game I play with the kids—and sometimes with Beth—to make them work for my respect. She has no idea what it's like to have kids flapping and banging their legs against me and pulling my face into the corner when all I really need is a look, a thought, a whisper. Is it really that hard?

Clarissa watches intently as Beth moves my feet forward, backward, and sideways in flawless half-passes. I can tell she's impressed because she smiles. The next lap around, Beth exhales a whoa and I offer a perfectly square halt, directly in front of Clarissa. I am very, very good at stopping, too.

Beth dismounts and waves Clarissa into the arena. I'm panting and not used to the work. She hands Clarissa the reins.

"You want me to ride him?" I sense a hint of panic.

Beth unclips the reins and attaches one end to the loop under my chin.

"Nope, I just want you to walk him around the ring, then hand-graze him in the pasture. Just spend some time getting to know him. It'll be good for both of you."

Clarissa takes hold of the rope and shifts her feet, not sure where to point one or the other. I make the decision for her and step to the left.

"And there you go!" Beth says as we stroll toward the top of the ring. Clarissa finds her feet and offers me a nice, energetic walk. I turn, backup, and stop on a dime and she giggles with surprise and appreciation.

"Nice, Sonny. Very nice!" she coos to me and my heart swells in my chest at the sound. She picks up a trot-in-hand and I can't help my excitement at the chance to show off. I throw a little buck and accidentally bump her in the arm.

Now, it's Clarissa who stops on a dime. She looks at me sternly.

"That, Sonny, was not very nice."

I hang my head.

"You're in my personal space."

Yes, Clarissa, I get it.

She perks up and grins at me. "Come on, let's try that again."

She leans slightly forward; I pick up my feet and keep perfect time with hers. I can feel her smiling, even though I can't see it. She shows me in images rolling through her mind what it would be like to be her horse. A new, green halter. A saddle that doesn't pinch. A canter in a broad meadow where the sun casts an amber glow and turns it into a field of gold.

"Much better, Sonny, thank you!"

She stops and I stop; she faces me and rubs my face and twirls my forelock. She's in my personal space. But she's docile and kind and I don't mind. She leads me from the arena to a place outside the muddy paddocks where the earth is soft and green, and the blades of grass are sweet. Just like Clarissa. My Clarissa.

Moments after she takes her leave with a promise to come back, a red pickup truck hauling a long, silver trailer rolls up the driveway. I watch from the side of my big, round hay bale as a man and a woman step out of the cab and Beth comes out to greet them. They shake hands and the man tips his hat, just like the Old Man who first owned me used to do. The woman glances around the farm, taking in every shape and size of horse. I can hear her crunching numbers and pounds in her head. She smiles sweetly at Beth, who points in my direction.

A breeze blows by, and that's when I smell it. That distinctive smell that every horse knows, the lingering odors of sweat and adrenaline and terror wafting from slits in their trailer where horses for sale—horses like me!—are carted to the auction house, then off to the slaughterhouse if the kill buyers win the day. The three of them chat and laugh as the man cocks his hip with confidence and the woman's brain continues to crunch.

They meander toward me and I freeze in place. Daisy presses up next to me.

"So, that's Sonny, he's the chestnut Quarter Horse."

"He's how old again?" the woman asks.

"Eighteen. But he still has a lot of miles to go."

"That's the perfect age for our program," the woman says wistfully.

"He'd be an awesome therapy horse," Beth nods. "He's a semi-retired schoolmaster and knows how to take good care of the kids."

"He sounds perfect," the woman says, "doesn't he, Joe?"

"How much do you want for him?" Joe says.

"Twelve hundred."

The man shakes his head. "We're a small non-profit, Ma'am."

Beth takes a deep breath but she can't smell what I smell and so she merely exhales and shrugs. "It's more important that he finds the right home. He's a great horse, I want him to be happy. If it doesn't work out, I'll take him back, no questions asked."

"I could take him off your hands right now for four hundred."

Beth rests her gaze on me and I feel the same pressure she feels. The seconds tick by. I finally breathe when she does.

"Listen, I have a real nice lady looking at Sonny. At this point, I feel obligated to give her the first right of refusal. But if she doesn't want him, I'll sell him to you for four hundred—for the sake of the kids. Can you wait a day or two?"

Their annoyance ricochets all over, bouncing off trees and shredding the air, but the man merely nods and the woman smiles. She's all teeth and her mouth is bright red.

"Sure, we'll come back for him," she offers. "Call us as soon as you know."

They shake hands on the deal and as the horse traders drive off, I hear the man's voice rise and the woman's voice sour and long after they're gone, the smell hovers in the air and the herd—all of us—grows very quiet.

On the way home, Clarissa stops by the fieldstone chapel on the hill. It's where she goes when she can't hear herself think and she crouches low in front of the corpse on a cross and she asks for a sign, any sign at all, that will point her in the right direction. She hasn't learned to trust her instincts or her feet to take her where she needs to go. That's something horses do naturally; it's the thinking that slows us down and makes a meal out of us. When we flee, it's only as far and wide as the immediate threat itself. Then we rest and drink and graze as though it never even happened. But Clarissa hasn't figured that out.

She keeps on running this way and that, looking for the very signs that she mentally passes by at sixty miles an hour. At that speed, everything is blurry. No wonder she can't make a decision. Maybe when she comes back—if she comes back—she will see me.

She picks up groceries and then lays them out on the table at home like a jigsaw puzzle. She sighs and then throws everything together in a pot: carrots, celery, little gold potatoes and some pre-cooked chicken. She adds some broth and some spices and calls it dinner. She's smart enough to pick up some fresh, warm bread. George is a sucker for fresh, warm bread.

"Hey, you're home early," Clarissa says as George closes in for a kiss.

She offers a cheek and then turns back to her computer screen where she's still looking for a sign. Any sign.

"What are you doing?"

"I'm looking for something."

"What?"

"I'm trying to figure out how to fix a locking stifle."

"With a stifle key?" George banters and grins. But Clarissa doesn't see him smile. She doesn't even look up. "What's a stifle?"

"It's the part of Sonny's anatomy that doesn't work so well. Could be a deal breaker."

"I'm sorry to hear that. I know you really like the horse."

"There are other horses out there. Younger horses with no issues," she says roughly and shrugs. Still, she knows there are no guarantees, having massaged 26-year-old horses who move like they're twelve, and 12-year-old horses who can't move at all.

"At this point, I'm not even sure I want a horse."

"Sure you do. You're just commitment shy."

"I married you, didn't I?"

"Yeah, but that was a fluke."

Clarissa stops Googling long enough to gaze at George. She still finds him as handsome as she ever did, maybe even more so now that his ocean-blue eyes are framed by deep lines at their outside corners that crinkle when he smiles and remind her of how long he's been devoted to her. Only her. At least that's what she prefers to think.

"Soup's on the stove and there's warm bread in the oven. Help yourself."

"Aren't you going to eat with me?"

Clarissa gnaws on a pencil and stares at the screen.

"I have to figure this out by tomorrow. Beth texted me and says she needs an answer."

"Claire...take a break. Have dinner with me."

At sixty miles an hour she can't see the plea in his eyes. Horses are far better than humans at that. We read our person's face like a map and know where she is and where she's been and more importantly, what kind of ride we're about to have. But Clarissa sees none of that. Only one thousand and forty-seven Google results on locking stifles.

"Suit yourself," he finally says.

"Don't be mad," Clarissa calls out after him. She's mad that he's mad. It's a mad, mad world where computers are king and men have wanderlust in their veins and blue-ribbon horses are sent to slaughter. I have some blue ribbons pinned to my stall door. But Clarissa doesn't see them. She's too busy looking for a sign.

5

"Okay, Claire, I'm gonna lunge Sonny before you get on him to get his yahoos out. I'll show you the basics, then you can try."

"Sounds good," Clarissa says.

Beth doesn't say anything to Clarissa about the other buyers, and Clarissa doesn't mention Beth's text. But they both know this is the day. I can feel the tension in the 22-foot cotton line that Beth attaches to my rope halter and detect traces of adrenaline in Clarissa's choppy exhales. Her normally soft, round eyes are slits of expectation as she looks at me differently today. I offer an obedient, marching walk, just the way Beth likes it. I round the circle with my head long and low and stretch out my back, preparing to trot. Beth clucks to me and raises a long stick with a string attached; I rev my engine and get my back legs under me and trot and trot and trot.

"He looks good, doesn't he?" Beth says.

"Yes, he's tracking nicely," Clarissa confirms with an authoritative hand on her hip.

After several more rotations, Beth kisses for a canter and I toss my head, surprised by the sudden ask. She usually gives me more time to warm up, but today she's in a rush. I plant my right foot firmly under me and strike off with my left foreleg. I feel the drag on my rear toes as I go around and around, but it's the best I can do.

"I read that trotting over ground poles and uphill work can do a lot to strengthen his stifles," Clarissa says.

"Wish I had the time for that," Beth sighs. "But you're right, he'll probably improve with steady work."

Beth swooshes out a long exhale and I transition to a trot, and then to a walk. She peers at my hind end and I immediately yield and face her. Beth hands the lunge line to Clarissa along with the stick and string.

"Ok. Ask him to walk to the left."

Clarissa lifts the stick and then raises and points the hand holding the lunge line to the left. She's clumsy and out of order, but I know what she means and agree to walk on. She asks for a trot and then for a canter. I'm growing tired and achy and I start to slow down, offering half my original effort.

"Good job!" Beth says. "Let him rest a minute and then we'll tack him up."

I pant. Clarissa nods. Beth leads me back to the barn and hoists my Western saddle onto my back. She rushes about the tasks of cinching and bridling me. I don't know what the hurry is. Or maybe I do.

Beth needs me gone.

Clarissa leads me to the mounting block and I stand perfectly still for her. She surprises me when she sits in the saddle deeply, but very gently. She asks me to walk and I dutifully pick up my feet. I'm weary from running in dull circles on the lunge line.

I cut the corners and pull myself with my forelegs. Beth hands Clarissa a crop. I get the message and pick up a trot, but only for a few strides. Clarissa bounces a little too much for my liking, but she smiles all the way down to her butt cheeks. I feel happy and try harder. We weave through orange cones and trot down the center line where I stop flawlessly at X.

"Good job, Sonny!" Clarissa strokes my neck and dismounts.

"You guys look awesome together," Beth gushes. "How did it feel?"

"It felt good. And I felt safe."

"Told you," Beth says and finally smiles. She walks over to me and rubs my face.

"I was hoping to give Sonny a massage today, would that be okay?"

"Sure," Beth says. "But you know—"

"I know. You need an answer."

Beth nods. "I'll keep Zelda inside so she doesn't bother you."

"That would be great. Give us an hour?"

"Take your time." Beth whistles for Zelda who charges in from the field dragging the leg bone of a deer. Beth makes her drop it and shoos her toward the house. As soon as they leave, Clarissa's eyes grow soft and round again. I can feel her slow, rhythmic breath on my back as she places her hands over my sacrum where her warmth diffuses and penetrates deeply. I sigh and cock my hip and lean into her. She sweeps my whole being with her hands, not the heavy hands she sports on the reins but hands like a summer breeze, infused with heat and refreshment. And then she begins. Fingertips touch and spiral and prance and dig and caress. At first I resist, but she only goes slower, and deeper, and I feel myself uncoil and lengthen and soften. I blow out the last of my resistance and allow Clarissa access to memories entwined in muscles and she feels them, she feels me, and she knows I am weary but still willing. She works her way down one side of me and then the other; eventually, she finishes with another long, leisurely sweep of her hands and says, "There you go, Sonny."

She gives me a carrot and combs her fingers through my forelock as I munch slowly, feeling slightly dazed by the endorphins surging through me.

"So, you're too cool for school, huh?" she whispers.

I snort again and come to my senses. More carrots please.

"Trust me, I get it," she muses.

Perhaps she misunderstood my request. I snort again.

"Oh, you want another carrot?"

I'm delighted that she's teachable. She fishes into her pocket for the goods.

"Easy, buddy. There's plenty more where that came from."

Her eyes are dewy and sparkle in the sun. I like the way she whispers sweet nothings as I scarf the morsel from the palm of her hand. Beth appears at the entrance to the barn and watches us. I'm pretty sure she has dew in her eyes too.

My gaze wanders. Clarissa follows it to Beth.

"I'll take him," Clarissa says softy.

"I think the two of you are going to be very good for each other," Beth declares. "Let me grab his paperwork. I'll be right back."

I paw at the ground. Clarissa smiles and feeds me another carrot. At this rate, I'll have her trained in no time.

Clarissa and Beth exchange all sorts of chatter and notes and paper and before I know it, I am what I knew I would be all along.

I am Clarissa's horse.

And George's by default. After all, if he was going to object, he should've been there when the deal went down.

"Congratulations," he says when Clarissa shows him the bill of sale that night. He kisses her on the lips and makes a vain attempt to rearrange her helmet hair. "So when do I get to meet the new man in your life?"

"This weekend."

"I thought we were going to the lake house this weekend."

"Um, hello? I just bought a horse." She waves the bill of sale under his nose.

"So?"

"So, I need to spend time with him and get to know him. He needs to understand that I'm his new owner. Otherwise, he'll think I'm just another student on his back. Go without me if you want, it's okay."

George sets down his glass of wine and draws Clarissa closer. "You know I don't sleep well without you."

"You sleep like the dead and you know it."

Clarissa lowers her gaze. They had both taken to pretending to sleep when they were really both wide awake and wondering how the fault line in their bed had grown so deep, so fast, that they duck under the covers and tremble at the shifting ground beneath them.

"Okay," George concedes, "but I'll miss you."

"I know," Clarissa says and rests her head on his chest. She takes note of the half-empty bottle of wine on the kitchen counter and flinches. George recently joined a wine club that meets every Wednesday evening on the grounds of a posh, farm-to-table restaurant nestled in the surrounding highlands. The sommelier, Yvonne, is a young, burgundy-lipped Frenchwoman transplanted from the vineyards of the Southern Rhône Valley, full of pomp and luxury and thirst. From that very first night, George raved about her vast knowledge and discerning palate and soon, very soon, Clarissa begins to suspect that George has a crush on more than the hallowed grape. In self-defense, Clarissa clings to the ancient creed of *summa summarum*, roughly translated by first-century monks as: I do not care that I do not care. Sweet acedia, as sweet to Clarissa as any wine—which in this case is a 2012 Châteauneauf-du-Pape Rouge that goes by the name of *Solitude*. How fitting, she thinks to herself. After all, she had urged him to find a hobby so that she could pursue her own without feeling guilty. If she ended up alone, it would be her own fault. *C'est la vie!*

She delicately uncoils from his arms. George tightens his grip around her waist and whispers in her ear.

"So...wanna horse around?"

Clarissa exhales a breathy sigh and doesn't care that she doesn't care.

George sweeps her off her feet but she's secretly thinking about mine. She's going to need to schedule a barefoot trim very soon. My toes are much too long for her liking.

When daylight comes, Clarissa throws off the sheets, gets dressed, and races to the kitchen where she whips up an apple-and-banana smoothie. She reserves the core of the apple for me and tosses it into the chic, equestrian tote bag Gabriella bought her for Christmas. If her mother was going to be smelly and dirty, Gabriella was at least going to make sure she was fashionably so. After all, in Gabriella's world, fashion covers a multitude of sins—and less-than-civil smells.

I know Clarissa's coming. I park myself beside my hay bale with one eye on Daisy and an ear cocked to the dirt road. The distinct tick-tick-hum of her car reaches my ears before she does and by the time she turns off the engine and steps out of the compartment, I already know why she's here. She has come to make a prince out of me.

Her arms are laden with bags. Scary plastic bags that rustle in the spring breeze and set every horse's teeth on edge. She's oblivious to the tension she's creating in the herd. Daisy raises her head and pitches her ears on high alert. It's never a good sign when Daisy does that. She's the boss mare and if she says run—well, we run.

I stroll to the fence line to investigate. Maybe Clarissa will put down the bags and feed me some carrots. I'd like to spare her the drama of a stampede. But in the end, it's Clarissa's choice.

She sets the bags at her feet. I snort at them even though they're playing dead. I stretch and twist my neck and poke my head beneath the top rail looking for a treat, careful to miss the electric tape that teaches us our boundaries. It's an artifice that makes humans think they're in control of our feet. But the truth is, if we wanted to, we'd break loose and run free and nobody could stop us. The mild jot of the fence isn't half as annoying as the flies that are just now starting to show their ugly green heads and torture us to death. Or nearly as irritating as waiting for Clarissa to give up the goods.

"Hi, Sonny!"

She reaches out to pet my face. I pull back and her smile fades. First things first, Clarissa. She glances around the barn, embarrassed by my snub. That's when she realizes we're truly alone, horse and rider, on a twenty-acre farm. It's the first time Beth hasn't come down from the house to greet her and she vibrates anxiety. In fact, Beth has gone to visit Daisy's new barn out west and Will is in charge. I like Will. He doesn't put bitter herbs in my feed like Beth sometimes does. Just straight grain, drizzled with molasses. But it's our dirty little secret.

Clarissa fishes into her tote bag and produces the core of an apple. It's not a carrot, but it'll do. I take it gingerly with my lips and taste the love. I look at her expectantly. Clarissa takes a deep breath and sighs. The air is rife with the pungent aroma of onion grass underfoot, mixed with the earthy smells of moist clay and orchard hay and the musky adrenaline Clarissa produces at the thought of riding me. She stoops and rifles through her bags and pulls out a new, green rope halter and matching lead rope, just like she promised. She opens the gate and steps inside my paddock. I lower my head and offer my face. She knots one side of the halter and attaches the rope to the loop at my chin. I follow her out of the paddock. Clarissa grabs the plastic bags and clenches them in her other hand. I try not to mind the crinkle of them. Daisy lifts her head from the spring grass and nickers a weak protest at my departure, then continues to graze. I'm curious to see what Clarissa has in mind. There's a faint echo in her head, a voice I don't know but Clarissa does:

"Where have you been, young lady? For all I know, you could be lying dead in a ditch!"

Clarissa's adrenaline spikes again and now I'm nervous too. I settle down as she grooms me with a brand new curry comb. When she's done, she reaches for a saddle pad and lays it gently on my back. Before I know it, I'm tacked up and being led to the outdoor ring. I can feel the saddle shifting over my back; my cinch is loose, too loose, but Clarissa doesn't notice.

She climbs the mounting block and I move off before she has a chance to mount. Check the cinch, Clarissa, I telegraph to no avail. She clambers down the block and jockeys me back into position. "Ho!" she says, and I stand still at her command. She grabs my mane and steps into the stirrup. I feel the saddle slip sideways and Clarissa sinking with it. She cries out and manages to avoid tumbling off the mounting block. She balances precariously on one knee and holds onto my mane for dear life. I'm a lesson horse. I've seen much worse. If I just stand still, chances are nobody gets hurt. She extracts her boot from the stirrup and scrambles for her footing on the block. Eventually, she lets go of my mane and breathes. She scoots down the mounting block and glares at the cinch.

"Thanks a lot, Sonny!" she says, and I feel the sting of her consternation. "That's what happens when you blow up like a balloon."

That's what happens when you don't check the cinch, I snort. She's mad but not for long. She repositions the saddle and tightens the cinch three holes and the next time she tries, she mounts with grace and ease.

"Walk on," she says.

I'm happy to oblige and offer a slow, meandering walk, but when she asks for a trot, I balk. She bears down in the saddle and nudges me with her heels. Nope. There's no one in the center of the ring clucking to me and driving me forward and so for that reason alone, I have to politely decline.

"Sonny, trot-trot!" Her voice is girlish and thin. Her gaze is on the ground.

She clucks to me. It's an odd sucking sound. I reckon she'll get better with practice.

"Seriously, Sonny, don't make me beg."

I would prefer she didn't. I would prefer she simply ask me with conviction.

She bumps me harder with her heels. If Beth were here she'd shout, "More leg!" I seek the pulsating energy of legs that simply ask and give me a chance to answer, but Clarissa's legs feel like wet blankets draped over my sides. She drives me forward with her seat and I speed up just enough to get out from under the grind.

"Trot-trot!"

I lift my head. But not because I'm about to trot. I lift it because Daisy has lifted hers. And so have all the other horses in the herd. They're frozen stiff and eyeing the hilltop beyond our fields. The mares start to whinny and trot along the fence line. Our collective distress increases by the second and Clarissa finally looks up from her focus on the ground. I jig and spin around for a better look, vaguely aware that Clarissa is managing to stay on. A lone, rogue gelding perches like a statue on the hilltop. The sight of him—an escapee who has breached the fence—is upsetting and exciting all at once. I can barely contain my desire to run the fence line with the others, but I'm trapped in the ring. I am trapped.

Clarissa clambers off my back. The fugitive whinnies and races back and forth over the hill, urging us to join him. I feel Clarissa grab the reins, grab my face.

"Please Sonny, wait till I get the reins off, then you can run. Please don't run with the reins on!"

I don't want to but I walk with her, barging into her shoulder as I look around, look behind, look anywhere but where we're going. Once at the paddock gate, I prance with wild impatience as her shaking hands untie the knot in my halter and slip the reins over my head and off; I am off, and I shoot though her hands like a cannon ball and join Daisy and my other pasture mates as they run and call to our displaced brethren. At once, we are a wild, stampeding herd of mustangs, horses who have never forgotten no matter what humans might have us forget.

As shaken as she is, Clarissa marvels at how fleetly and fluidly I move. She's grateful for my supreme act of obedience. Beth's voice echoes: *He's a good horse—he'll keep you safe.*

A good horse indeed, and a mighty fine mover too, she thinks! Now, the gig is up. Not only does she know what I'm capable of—she's intrigued. She begins to wonder if I'm neither depressed nor lazy but rather, after twelve years of schooling, as beset by acedia as she is. She wonders if my round hay bale is the equivalent of her writing desk, which she craves only because it's where she's left to her own pleasure—which is none. That is to say, nothing pleases her. And nothing particularly displeases her.

There's revelation in this moment of wild instinct. There can be no more sleepwalking. Or sleep-trotting. Life strikes by the heartbeat and the hoof beat. I gallop alongside Daisy and dip my head and throw a buck. Pay attention, Clarissa! It's all happening. Right now!

"Mom!" Gabriella reprimands. "I've been calling you for hours. For all I know you're lying dead in a ditch somewhere!"

Clarissa cradles her phone between her ear and her shoulder as she brushes off the saddle pad and returns it to the rack. "I'm fine, I'm at the barn. And please stop channeling my mother."

"You have to keep your cell phone on you, Mom. What if something happens?"

"Nothing's going to happen," Clarissa says, deciding not to tell Gabriella about her stumble on the mounting block or the spectacle of a herd of wild horses. Will had showed up just in time to corral the rogue horse and repair the breach in the fence before things got entirely out of hand. Later, Clarissa removed my saddle and thanked me for not running her over. She surprised me with a fat, chewy, molasses cookie as an extra special treat and laughed when my eyes grew round with pleasure.

"In fact, we're barely trotting. Sonny makes a slug look supersonic."

"Are you wearing a helmet?"

"Yes, I'm wearing a helmet."

"You're not alone there, are you?"

Clarissa glances at the barn cat. "No, I'm not alone."

"You better not be. So, can I come over for dinner? Brandon's working late."

Clarissa glances at her watch. If she hangs up the phone this very minute and races to the grocery store and allows thirty minutes of prep time she just might get dinner on the table by six.

"Of course! I have to go, we'll chat later, okay?"

"Okay," Gabriella barely ekes out before Clarissa hangs up and tosses the phone into her tote bag. She hurriedly scribbles a check to Beth to cover the cost of board for another month, but before she even finishes the flourish of her name, she knows what she has to do. Our barn is full of horses suffering benign neglect from absentee owners; besides, Beth herself is busy with a new lover of her own, too busy to babysit Clarissa and me. The perilous events of the day remind Clarissa of the hazards of riding alone. She thinks a new barn, a bigger one with more boarders and more horses, would be better—and safer—for both of us. She envisions rolling, green pastures dotted with oversize run-in sheds handcrafted in Amish country to withstand the elements and provide generous, cooling shade for me as the summer approaches. She knows it will come at a price, but the sight of me standing in the mud mindlessly chomping at my hay bale has become an anathema to her, a metaphor of sorts for her own existence. As for me, I'm content with my pasture and my beloved Daisy who protects and leads us with fairness and confidence. But as much as Daisy and I know our days at Misty Acres are numbered, we both know we're natives of a collective soul that is indivisible and everlasting. We will never be separated. And so, where Clarissa goes, I will go.

She's barely halfway down the driveway when she prompts her cell phone for directions to the nearest boarding facility, the same one where she'd briefly met Dolly, the nippy palomino mare. She thinks she can squeeze in a visit and still get dinner on the table—maybe a few minutes late, but she'd get it done!

When she arrives at Two Step Farm, she likes what she sees. Rolling hills. Acres of pastures and miles of trails. She's delighted by the distinct Western vibe that will save her from having post the trot in a slippery English saddle. Best of all, there's a huge indoor arena with six-inch-deep footing, overhead fans, and sunlight streaming through a row of skylights. Clarissa strolls into the barn. A few young riders mill about but none pay her any mind. She admires the varnished stall doors with shiny steel bars and then peers into the stalls themselves. She's seeking pasture board for me, but if there's a stall to be had at a fair price, she thinks it just might suit an old lesson horse who has paid his dues.

As luxurious as the stalls appear on the outside, she notices that the water buckets are dirty and wanting, the shavings are thin and heavily soiled, and the horses are on lockdown at four in the afternoon without a shred of hay on the ground. Some are pacing. Some are cribbing. Some are sleeping. Given the glossy photographs and ribbons on the wall, most are Western pleasure horses who don't appear to have any pleasure at all. No, such a place would never do!

She hurries to her car before anyone notices her. On the way out, she spots a rundown barn on the property and drives by slowly enough to peer inside. There, the bread-and-butter trail horses are kept for hack riders, prisoners in straight-in stalls with barely enough room to turn around, let alone to lie down. They're tethered to the walls with frayed cotton ropes and their misery wafts through the rolled-down windows of Clarissa's car and makes her teary with regret. She wants to massage away the strain in their necks and give them carrots and comfort and company. But she can't. Dinner has to be on the table by six. It's what she said she'd do and by God, she'd get it done.

She stops at the grocery store and shops like she's on a game show with two minutes to fill her cart. She heads straight for the produce section to grab apples and carrots for me. Then she fills her basket with shortcuts: pre-made bison burgers, freshly baked buns from the bakery, coleslaw from the deli counter and corn on the cob. An intentional picnic, that's how she'll sell it, she decides. Perfect for a temperate spring evening and a harbinger of long weekends on the lake. George will be happy to taste summer on his lips.

She barges into the kitchen where Gabriella perches on a counter stool and leafs through a glossy catalog from Bloomingdales. She doesn't look up.

"Dad called."

"What did he say?"

"He has to work late. He said he couldn't reach you and not to bother making dinner. I couldn't reach you either, what's wrong with your phone now?"

Clarissa reaches into her tote bag, rummages for her phone, and glares at the dark screen.

"It's dead again. What's the matter with this thing?"

Gabriella cocks her head and reprimands her with her eyes.

"Really, Mom? It's not that hard. You look at the battery symbol and if it's low, you plug it in. You know you're making everyone worry about you, right?"

"Dad doesn't worry. It's not in his DNA."

"Oh yes he does. That's why he called me. He said your new hobby is turning him prematurely old and gray."

"Your father is half-bald. He wishes he was gray!" Clarissa begins to unpack her groceries and sets them on the countertop. Slams them, actually.

Gabriella's expression softens.

"Don't be mad. My husband's working late too, it's what men do. So let's do what women do...." She grins mischievously.

"Oh. You want to go shopping?"

"I thought you'd never ask."

"Give me a minute to change out of my barn clothes."

"Take your time. And don't forget the perfume."

"Very funny. Channeling my father now?"

The two women pause and the air thickens with dormant grief. Gabriella recalls her Poppy's belly laugh and zest for life. Clarissa remembers how many dinners her own father missed, the odd hours he kept, and how her mother looked the other way as women of her generation were taught to do. Clarissa had met at least half a dozen of her father's mistresses over the years; some she only recognized as such much later in life—like the weird, artsy woman who sewed tartan-plaid skirts for her and her sister when they were teens. And the ditzy, blond florist who made lavish bouquets that her father brought home to her mother twice a week—long-stemmed roses in the winter, peonies in the spring, calla lilies in the summer, and late sunflowers in the fall—until the affair was over and then she mostly got humble bunches of white carnations, symbolic of her wedding bouquet and reminders that in his own reckless way, he loved her still.

The women shop. The men do what men do. And when George comes home that night and gives her a kiss, there's wine on his breath. She doesn't know the vintage or the provenance, but she knows betrayal when she tastes it.

The next morning she rises and decides to visit a barn in the hill county where price tags climb with the landscape. But Clarissa doesn't care about the price today. If she has to dip into the household coffers to offset the difference, it's the least George can do. After all, he's *working late* and can afford it.

She finally reaches a farmhouse at the end of a steep, gravel road whose owner had advertised space for a quiet gelding. Clarissa's enamored by the long stretches of spring-green grass that covers rolling hills and dales. A copper fox-and-hound weathervane catches glints of sunlight as it whirls at the whim of a warm, southern breeze. It's picture perfect and Clarissa smiles as she imagines me meandering in acres of contentment.

"So what do you do?" the barn owner asks with a tilt of her head as she not-so-subtly inspects Clarissa for a clue. She has cascading blond hair and a Scottish lilt that makes her sound charming and friendly.

"I'm a writer," Clarissa answers.

"No," she says, tossing her nose into the air. "What do you do with your horse?"

"Oh, I just ride for pleasure."

"You don't jump?"

"No."

"Fox hunt?"

"Oh no, I ride in a Western saddle. I think I'd like to trail ride though."

The barn owner gazes at the weathervane as her interest in Clarissa dwindles.

"All of our boarders ride English. Would that bother you?"

"I haven't bought a saddle yet. I could buy an English one if I had to," Clarissa concedes.

"Do you have any interest in Eventing? I prefer that my boarders take lessons in the sport."

The barn owner has a foxy gleam in her eye and Clarissa suspects she's being set up for a fall. She peers into a distant field where logs, hay bales, and other natural jumps are strategically arranged. She knows it's useless to pretend.

"Frankly, I don't see myself ever wanting to jump over tree trunks or run through rivers."

Just when Clarissa thinks the barn owner's nose can't tilt any higher, it does.

"But thanks for your time," Clarissa adds politely, not wanting to burn any bridges. She'd learned from her stint massaging horses just how small the horse world is; no sense pissing off the natives.

"Good luck with your search," the barn owner replies and sniffs.

"Thank you," Clarissa says. But her reply hangs in the empty space where she stands. To the barn owner, Clarissa is already dead.

The next barn on her list is just a couple of miles north and west. She hopes it's as pretty as the one she's leaving and blasts the radio to distract her from the unruly thoughts that romp in her head like kids on a playground. *She should be home cleaning or doing laundry. Or writing! She hasn't worked on her screenplay in weeks, it isn't going to write itself. Dammit, she forgot to say her prayers this morning. No wonder this day feels doomed! And what about George? God, she can't even think about George right now. Did she remember to pack the carrots? No, she forgot the carrots! Now her horse is going to hate her too, just like the women in high horse country with magnificent Warmbloods and charming accents and long, well-toned legs sheathed in tall, gleaming riding boots. She's out of her league, she's out of control, she should turn around and go home where she belongs....*

The last remaining child on the playground stomps his feet and storms off.

I don't care!

Clarissa hesitates at the regal, blue-and-gold sign that hails her arrival at Crown Ridge Equestrian Services. She mumbles one of those words and steers her car up a newly paved, serpentine driveway. It's lined with pear trees and surrounded on both sides by lush pastures with horses grazing so contentedly that they don't even lift their heads as she drives by. She feels like Dorothy approaching Oz, sure she's leaving New Jersey behind and about to enter a gentleman's farm somewhere in Kentucky. Or the English countryside.

Surely she can't afford this place, she thinks, as she continues to climb and marvels at endless stretches of pristine, white fencing bordered by thousands of daffodils. The run-in sheds are bedded with straw and bigger than some of her college apartments. There must be a mistake in the price of board that was advertised online. She sighs and braces for disappointment.

Upon reaching the crest of the hill, Clarissa parks under a towering oak tree whose branches splay and twist toward the sun. She steps out and scans one hundred acres of bliss. There are two barns: a stark white one with black trim, big enough for at least two dozen horses, and a small, dark blue one set off to the side. She takes several strides downhill and pauses at the peculiar sight of a short, pudgy, bald man with a sharp goatee chatting with a glamorously tall woman outside of the little blue barn. It appears they've just finished riding and from the way they dress and gesture and laugh, they're charter members of the high horse society. The chubby little man is dressed in black riding pants and a black polo shirt with the collar artfully upturned. He holds a massive, gray draft horse by the reins with an enviable mix of authority and ease. The woman flaunts a sleek, black Thoroughbred as though he's just one more expensive accessory. She too is dressed in black, in well-tailored English riding clothes accented with a rhinestone belt that makes Clarissa's eyes squint. Her caramel hair is as long and straight and lustrous as her horse's tail, and her plump lips are meticulously colored with bright fuchsia lipstick. Clarissa rolls her eyes and reaches for her car keys.

"*Hola!* Can I help you?"

Clarissa freezes at the sound of gravel crunching underfoot. She glances behind her and into the face a stable hand whose wide, white smile against his dark bronze skin seems genuine. He's short and stocky with bulging arms that flex as he jerks the reins to keep a high-spirited Thoroughbred mare in check. The horse scrambles several steps backward and settles down.

"Oh! I was just..." What is she doing, anyway? Snooping? Lurking? The right word escapes her.

"You want to talk to Bridget about boarding your horse here? She's down there, in the ring." He points further downhill. The outdoor arena is hemmed in on three sides by a dense hedgerow that's immaculately trimmed.

Clarissa hesitates.

"Tell her Miguel sent you. She's the barn owner." Miguel smiles again and leads the Thoroughbred toward the little blue barn and the beautiful people hobnobbing outside of it. Moments later, a tall, elegant, Dutch Warmblood emerges from an opening in the hedgerow, led by a statuesque, sixty-something woman with silky white hair that drapes her broad, athletic shoulders like an expensive, fringed shawl.

Clarissa meets her halfway down the pea gravel path.

"Bridget?"

Bridget's artic blue eyes slam Clarissa's face. She's stiff and frosty and porcelain-pale and Clarissa mentally dubs her the Ice Queen. She half expects crystallized breath to curl from lips that flatten at the interruption of her day.

"Hi, I'm Claire. Miguel said I should speak with you about boarding my horse here." Clarissa reverses direction and strives to match Bridget's long, gliding stride.

"I'm afraid I don't have any stalls available at the moment but I could put you on the waitlist." She has an off-putting accent. Not British. Not Irish. Not Spanish. Clarissa can't quite pin it down. Maybe it just sounds cold.

"Actually, I'm looking for field board. I have an eighteen-year-old Quarter Horse who's been on pasture board his whole life."

"Mare or gelding?"

"Gelding."

"I have room for one more gelding in that five-acre field over there."

She points in the direction of the little blue barn and the beautiful people. Clarissa has already nicknamed them The Bluebloods. She cringes at her royal predicament and struggles to keep up. As they reach the top of the hill, Miguel appears like a well trained minion to take the horse from Bridget and lead him into the wash stall.

"Let me show you around," Bridget says with a flourish of her hand.

Clarissa can't keep from grinning as Bridget points out the various amenities at Crown Ridge: six hot and cold wash stalls, two bathrooms, climate-controlled tack rooms, trailer parking, a bridle trail around a forty-acre back field that connects to a nature preserve, spacious indoor and outdoor arenas, a sixty-foot round pen, and sprawling pastures to ride in. Bridget greets The Bluebloods as they approach the barn.

"Bernie, Natasha? This is Claire, she's thinking about boarding here. Her horse would be in Merlin's field."

"Marvelous," Bernie says, and Clarissa thinks he might actually mean it. "What kind of horse do you have?"

Natasha stares at Clarissa blandly. Her fuchsia lips are frozen shut. Clarissa's not even sure she could move her face if she wanted to, puffy as it is with fresh injections.

"Sonny's an eighteen-year-old Quarter Horse."

"Oh, very good," he replies with a distinctly French accent. "Merlin's a Percheron. Did you know some villages in France still use Percherons to transport their children to school?"

He grins an elfin grin and Clarissa's instantly charmed by his merry disposition. Maybe Natasha's nice too, she thinks, once her face unfreezes. And maybe, just maybe, she could be comfortable at Crown Ridge, Western saddle and all.

"How much did you say the board was?" she asks Bridget.

"Five-hundred and twenty dollars. That includes tax."

"When could we move in?"

"Whenever you want," Bridget replies. "Do you need help trailering?"

"I think Sonny's former owner will help me with that."

"So do you want to sign a boarding contract?"

"Yes," Clarissa replies. "Yes, I do."

"Okay, let's go back to the office."

Clarissa waves goodbye to Bernie and Natasha. Bernie eagerly calls out after her.

"Clarissa! Do you trail ride?"

"Not yet, but I'd like to!"

"We'll have to arrange a day to ride together."

"I'd like that, Bernie, thank you!"

She feels happy and hopes I'll be happy there too. She thinks the horses look healthy and content, as content as captive horses can be. Bridget seems to be warming up, and there's a mild bluntness about her that Clarissa finds comfortable and familiar. Once in the office, however, Bridget's eyes frost over.

"We deworm here every eight weeks. Board is due the first of the month, no exceptions, no grace period. We charge five percent interest for every day you're late. We require a deposit of one month's board and thirty-days notice of intent to vacate. If you default on that, we keep your deposit. You supply your own supplements, there's no charge to administer them. But we don't do blanket changes. We don't pick feet. It's all in the contract."

She pulls a four-page document from a desk drawer and shoves it in front of Clarissa.

"Bridget, I'm a little uncomfortable with the deworming program. I'd like to have a fecal count done twice a year. Would you be agreeable to that?"

"We deworm every horse, every eight weeks, no exceptions. We have some very expensive show horses here and we cannot take chances with them. What's your horse's name, anyway?"

"Sonny."

"That's it?"

"Actually, it's Hotter Sonny Dee."

"Then that's what we'll put on his nameplate. All the horses get brass nameplates for their halters. No charge. It's our welcome gift to you."

"That's very nice, thank you."

"You're welcome. Any other questions?"

Clarissa has a dozen questions but she only dares to ask one of them.

"Can I bring him on Saturday?"

"Sure, I'll tell Miguel you're coming. Do you have a trainer?"

"No, not yet."

"I offer lessons for sixty dollars an hour. I have a distinguished colleague who gives lessons here as well. His name is Sebastian Bergalo. Perhaps you've heard of him?"

Clarissa shakes her head. He sounds exotic and totally out of her price range.

"Does it matter if I ride in a Western saddle?"

"I can't speak for Sebastian, but as for me, you can ride in whatever you like. I want you to feel happy and safe here."

Clarissa grins and immediately writes a check for the security deposit. She hopes that Will is willing to help with transportation. She expects Beth to be upset by the news of our departure, even though she knows it's inevitable. And she's right. Beth is not only upset, she's mad. She doesn't understand the hurry; worse yet, she needs the money. She stops coming down to the barn in those last days. Just the same, Will offers to trailer me to the new stable for twenty bucks and a case of imported beer.

Clarissa has been sending me mental images of my new home and feeding me apples and fat, molasses cookies outside of Will's trailer for the past four days. I'm pretty sure she thinks it will help me make peace with the big steel box that will take me away from Daisy and Beth and Will and every familiar sight and smell I've known for the last twelve years. But it doesn't. When the day comes for me to step onto the trailer I go only because Will asks me to. He has coveted and won my trust with his consistency and calmness and blackstrap molasses drizzled over my grain and in whispered confessions in my fuzzy ears. He is honest. Honest enough to leave a relationship that doesn't work anymore. A horse appreciates honesty, even when it's not pretty.

The ride is bumpy and the bends in the road, which I can see through narrow slits, make the trailer sway and I sway inside of it. Will hung a hay net in front of me, but I can't think about eating, I can only think about getting out of this cold, steel trap. When the trailer finally slows and rolls to a stop, I smell other horses and snort loudly, making my presence known. Will opens the back door and unties me; I hastily back out and snort again and whinny for my herd. New faces appear. I stand very still and survey my surroundings, scanning and sniffing for mountain lions and other such predators who may be lurking in the thickets and woodlands beyond the manicured fields.

"Aw, he's cute!" someone says.

"Thank you," Clarissa replies.

"How old is he?" another asks.

"He's coming nineteen this summer." Clarissa strokes my neck and asks me to relax. Doesn't she see the horses barreling toward us from the pasture, two bays and a gigantic gray? They're full of bluster and making a big show of letting me know my place before I take another step.

"He looks much younger! What's his name?"

Clarissa smiles at the tall, raven-haired woman with the raspy voice who's well past sixty but seems more like a filly to me. She's lean and energetic and she vibrates authority and kindness. Horses like that. A lot. I think I like her already.

"His name is Sonny."

"Hi Sonny, I'm Carla. That big brown horse over there is mine. His name is Hershey. He's a very sweet horse, I think you'll like him. Did you get the joke, Sonny? Hershey is a sweet horse, ha! And what's your name, honey?"

"Clarissa—actually, it's Claire," she corrects herself.

"Nice to meet you. I hear Hershey and Sonny are going to be pasture mates, so we'll be seeing a lot of each other. Do you go out on trail?"

"I haven't yet, but I'd like to."

"Let me know when you're ready," Carla barks. "I gotta go get my horse. See ya!"

A stable hand takes my lead rope and walks me toward a dry lot next to the pasture where Hershey and the other horses stomp and paw at the ground.

"Thank you, Miguel," Clarissa says.

"Wait!" Will blurts.

He walks over to me and caresses my cheek. Then he leans down into me so that we are forelock to forelock. We linger for a moment, suspended in time. He doesn't say a word. He doesn't have to. In an instant we have relived twelve years.

He strokes my neck and steps aside, allowing Miguel to lead me away.

"Take good care of my boy," I hear him say.

"Of course," Miguel answers, but the truth is, he only sees another mouth to feed. His grip on the rope is tight and his hands telegraph unnecessary roughness.

"We'll put him in this dry lot for now so that the other horses can see and get used to him through the fence," Miguel explains to Clarissa. "That's the safest and best way."

He unclips my lead rope, throws several flakes of hay, then latches the gate behind him. Hershey snorts and paws at the ground on the other side of the fence. The big gray is next to him and a tall, gangly Thoroughbred hovers and paces behind them, each with a wary eye on me. I put my head down and munch on a mound of hay that's greener and livelier than any I've had in the last twelve years. It reminds me of the Old Man's hay and I wonder if he's here. Even if he is, so is Clarissa, and I don't care. I feel safe, even as the other horses shove their noses under the fence and pin their ears and make faces at me. It's raining hay. And I am happy.

"It's okay, Miss, you can go home, he just needs some time to settle in."

"I know, Miguel, but I'm worried about leaving him."

"Don't worry! Pedro and I will keep an eye on him."

I give Pedro a quick once-over as he comes into view pushing a wheelbarrow full of shavings and manure. He moves very fast, like a little beetle.

"Right, Pedro?" Miguel calls out to him.

"Qué?" he answers.

Miguel gestures to Clarissa and says something in rapid Spanish.

"Sí, mucho caliente!" Pedro replies and they both grin.

"He says yes, Miss Clarissa, we'll take the best care of your horse."

"Claire," she corrects with a smile, "just plain Claire."

But they've already christened her *Caliente Claire*. Hot Claire. It's what she is, and she doesn't even know that men think that way about her. In her mind, she's still a squat, ugly duckling to her younger sister's effortless swan; the girl who also ran in every girl race, the one whose college writing professor forsook her art in favor of the porn written by the sexy, long-legged redhead in the front row and gave her the last, coveted seat in the choicest master class.

No, she doesn't know. And George doesn't tell her. If he did, she'd laugh and tell him that he was growing old and sentimental. And blind.

But he doesn't tell her. And she doesn't know.

Later on, as the sun goes down, Clarissa comes back to check on me. I first hear the tick-tick-hum of her car and then see the dark outline of her body perched at the top of the hill. She has a sweeping view of the farm from there, and she stands as still as a fence post for a very long time. She radiates loss and loneliness. I invite her to be with me in the ephemeral blue of twilight. Still, she resists the urge to come down to my paddock. She wants me to be a horse, to do what horses do; she doesn't want to get in the way of the natural order that will place me in the herd where I belong. Already, even with the fence between us, I know that Hersey is the boss, followed by Merlin—even though Merlin towers over him by at least three hands. The other bay Thoroughbred, Moose, is a quirky character. His mind is a mash of impulses. He's young and foolish and far too cocky for a four year old. I already know I'll have to keep an eye on him and put him in his place. That's what happens when humans coddle their horses. They get spoiled and forget their manners.

I engage in a game of chase along the fence line. It feels good to run and play with the horses on the other side. By the time the chasing and bucking stops, I realize Clarissa is gone. Night has fallen. The farm sleeps.

But not Clarissa.

She lies awake in her bed, rehashing the argument she had with George as though it was happening all over again...

"So you're not coming to the lake this weekend either?" George sets down his knife and fork on the edge of his dinner plate and awaits Clarissa's reply.

"Will can only trailer him to the new barn on Saturday. I'm really sorry."

"Is this what our whole summer looks like?"

Claire answers with a listless shrug, loath to make any more promises she can't keep.

"Listen, if you want to spend your weekends at the barn doing your own thing, then go ahead and do that. But don't expect me to wait around for you to decide if and when you can leave your horse. Jesus, Claire, after all the time and money we've spent to get to this place in our lives, you're going to bail on me now?"

"I'm not bailing," Clarissa protests. She puts down her fork too. Their appetites dwindle as they fill their mouths with bitter words and fight to keep from saying them.

"It's a temporary situation, George. It's not like I've spent the last twenty years doing my own thing. I've been keeping a house and raising a family and trying to bring in some money when I can...Now that my father's gone, I have this tremendous void, this wasteland of time to fill, and I'm suddenly asking myself who and what I'm about and the truth is, I don't really know. I'm trying to figure it out...why is that so hard for you to understand?"

"So you're having a midlife crisis?" His tone is mocking. Her fingers clench the tabletop.

"Maybe. Aren't you?"

George doesn't answer. He pushes his chair away from the table and leaves a half-eaten slab of filet mignon behind. Claire had cooked it two minutes too long for his liking anyhow.

"Where are you going?"

"To the lake house."

"Tonight?"

"I don't have any meetings tomorrow. I can work from there. I'll be back on Sunday."

Clarissa doesn't try to change his mind. She can hear him stomping and muttering to himself in the walk-in closet. She plugs her ears like she did when she was ten and her father punched holes in the plaster walls rather than punch her mother, who had knack for goading him until he snapped. Moments later, George brushes past her, duffle bag in hand, and plants a lifeless kiss on the top of her head. She always hated when he did that, preferring that he not kiss her at all. She's of a mind that men should kiss their women on the lips with tenderness or passion or a heady mix of both—or not at all. She swipes the spot where he kissed her with the palm of her hand, dispelling the insult. The garage door opens and an engine revs and moments later, she's washing dishes and feeding the dog expensive table scraps from George's plate.

Later that night, just like this night, she curls up alone in her king-size bed with a book that lays open on her lap but she's not reading the words; in her mind, she's galloping somewhere far away as her hair whips the air and her eyes are drenched in golden sunrise and her heart rumbles and pounds in harmony with hoof beats that fleetly carry her to that sheltered place, that anywhere-but-here to which she's run since she was just a girl. Only now, she hastens there on the back of a horse, an old lesson horse whose gallop is feeble compared to what it once was. Still, I gallop when the need arises. I run for my life. Clarissa runs from hers. It's a wonder that horses and humans can coexist at all!

6

It's Sunday. Clarissa rises at dawn. She toys with the idea of going to church but can't bear the thought of going without George. The fieldstone chapel on the hill, the one with early Mass, is where she and George were married. The cold, hard, wooden pew would seem even colder and harder with altar memories bearing down on her. So many promises throughout the years. So many prayers for her marriage that she lifted to Jesus, who stared down at her from a crucifix suspended in midair, clad in a loincloth and eternal love. Now that's real commitment, she mopes, as she takes a coffee cup out of the cupboard, the red one George gave her for Christmas that confesses: *I'd Rather Be Riding*. She's sure he's out on the lake by now, trolling for bass with his lake buddies and swapping tales of wives and fishes gone wrong. She takes comfort in knowing he'll be back by dinnertime, that they'll have a chance to redeem themselves, at least until Wednesday comes and he goes where he goes.

She brews a cup of tea and powers up her laptop. In lieu of Mass, a string of Hail Marys springs forth from her lips as she waits for the screen to blink to life and when it does, she forsakes all for the gods of Google who will point her to the Western saddle of her dreams.

Undeterred by the distance of forty-seven miles, she heads to a part of New Jersey dotted with roadside farm stands and gentle hills grazed by Holstein cattle, sheep, and horses. She sits in the parking lot of Two Cowgirls, Four Horses for an hour before the tack store opens, reading a book by a self-proclaimed master of natural horsemanship. If a horse had written the book it would have only six words instead of sixty thousand.

Be a leader. Be here now.

Yep, that's it. But Clarissa's an information junkie and she'll fill her head until it explodes, or I do. Then, and only then, will she consent to keep it simple.

The shopkeeper finally turns the lock. Clarissa tosses her book on the passenger seat and hastens toward the old-fashioned, wrought iron door. Once inside the store, she marvels at all the bling: silver spurs, silver conchos, silver bits, silver jewelry, silver-studded headstalls, and rows of western saddles embellished with hand-engraved silver polished to a mirror-like shine.

"Good morning, what can we do you for today?"

"I'm looking for a Western saddle."

"New or used?"

The woman behind the counter is heavy-set, with curly, platinum hair and a showmanship smile, the last vestige of a long career in Western Pleasure that devolved into a business shilling western tack and trading horses. Those she couldn't trade or sell, she sent to auction, the dirty little secret of two cowgirls with no horses of their own.

"I'm not sure," Clarissa replies. "I'm open to looking at either."

"The ones along the wall are used. They're here on consignment. What size?"

"I don't know. I'm a size eight in jeans."

"I mean the horse, what size bars?"

Clarissa gazes blankly.

"How big is your horse? How many hands?"

"He's just shy of fifteen hands," Clarissa says, relieved to know the answer.

"What breed?"

"He's an Appendix Quarter Horse. His name is Sonny. He's my first horse."

"How wonderful," the owner coos and Clarissa thinks she's sincere. "Tell me about his withers and his shoulders."

"Well, he has big, blocky shoulders and he's a little high in the withers."

"His back?"

"Short. Very short."

The owner's face creases with concern. "Can you trailer him in for a fitting?"

"Not a chance, he doesn't trailer well."

"In that case, I'd recommend full quarter horse bars, a round skirt if we can find one, and I'd say a size fifteen seat for you."

"Okay," Clarissa says, scanning the wall. "Let's look at the used ones first."

The owner turns over tags and reads the notes on each one. Clarissa's naturally drawn to the saddles dripping in silver and the owner doesn't bother to tell her they're for serious show girls—the ones who wear yellow, rhinestoned shirts and bedazzled belts and expensive black or white felt hats and dark red lipstick so their teeth look whiter to the judges than they really are.

Clarissa doesn't even wear lipstick most days, and definitely not this day, but the owner doesn't seem to care. She wants those saddles gone. Just like the horses she keeps back at the farm, ten heads to a three-acre field.

"How about this one?" Clarissa asks shyly. She likes the crosses that are hand-tooled into the leather and thinks that maybe it's a sign.

"Go ahead and sit in it, sweetie. See how it feels."

Clarissa swings a leg over the saddle horse and lands in a rough-out seat that feels like cement. She winces and shakes her head. It was penance to sit in that saddle, and no amount of pretty would make up for the pain.

"Try this one," the owner suggests. It's generously trimmed in silver, only lightly used, and has a padded leather seat. Clarissa sinks into its softness.

"Ooooh, much better! How much is it?"

"Four hundred, a real steal. The lady got out of horses after a bad fall. Paralyzed from the waist down, poor thing."

Clarissa thinks that's bad juju and quickly moves on to another saddle. This one has four red roses, one tooled into each corner of the caramel-colored skirt, and a cantle trimmed in silver. The conchos are engraved with a circle of barbed wire, a pattern that's repeated on the worn, leather fenders and on the edges of the saddle skirt. There are deep scars on the leather and rubs on the horn, marks of a genuine horsewoman. Clarissa finds the combination of roses and barbed wire mildly disturbing and poetic and appealing. She likes the fit, even if the seat is a little on the hard side. She hopes it's in her price range.

"How much?"

"That one's special. I bought it on a whim on eBay, only because in all my years I've never seen anything like it. I don't know much about it except that it's a custom piece by some obscure saddle maker. Oh, it's seven-fifty, by the way. But I'll let it go for seven."

The saddle is at the top of her price range, but she's intrigued by its twisted beauty and finds it worthy of her imagination.

"I'll take it."

"Sure you don't want to check out the new saddles? I have some real nice trail saddles with seats that feel like you're sitting on a cloud."

"No, this is the one."

"Well, that was easy!" the owner crows and writes up a receipt before Clarissa can change her mind. She throws in a cheap pair of rope reins and a plain, brown saddle pad and sends Clarissa on her way.

"If that horse doesn't work out for you, give me a holler," the owner calls out as Clarissa clumsily barges through the door, catching one of the stirrups on the door handle. She whispers one of those words and yanks it free, then tosses back a cheerful reply.

"Thanks, but I'm sure we'll be just fine!"

"Bless her little green heart," the owner mumbles as the iron door clangs shut.

It's early afternoon by the time Clarissa reaches Crown Ridge. She hauls the saddle out of the trunk of her car and searches for me from the hilltop. My head is down and my mouth is filled with spring grass that's moist and sweet, but my eyes are on Clarissa, who doesn't know to look for me in the pasture with Hershey and Merlin and Moose. She vibrates anxiety as she stares at the vacant paddock. I snort loudly to deflect her negativity.

Clarissa's eyes migrate to the sound and she sighs with relief when she sees me. There's an easy peace in the pasture; when

I entered through the gate this morning to join my new herd, Hershey gave me a benevolent once-over, while Merlin stomped and pawed. I stomped and pawed back at him. He swiveled his massive butt to kick me but I moved off before he got too close. Merlin thinks he's the one in charge, but Hershey calls the shots. He's a fair and honest leader, and so I don't mind. Moose is gregarious but full of stealth and wiles. His approach was friendly until he got close enough to nip me on my face. I squealed and wheeled around to kick him and he trotted off. Back at the Old Man's ranch, wily horses were whipped and tied to the patience post until they sprouted manners. Could take hours. Could take days.

Some eventually got sent to a horse trader or directly to auction anyway. The Old Man always said it cost just as much to keep a good horse as a bad one. I was very careful not to be bad. Just the same, I was bound for such a fate, or worse, after my stifle gave out from working cows six days a week. But the Old Man didn't mention anything about it to the cowboys at the sale barn when he dropped me off. By the time Beth discovered my disability, she'd come to appreciate my sound mind and gentle disposition around even the youngest and clumsiest of her students. She called me her rainmaker. Parents paid good money to put their kids on my back. They knew I was beginner-safe and asked for me by name. My currency was confidence and Beth cashed in on it until my gait slowed and my stifle stiffened to the point where she took pity on me and put me out to pasture.

But this pasture is different. It's lush and sweet and energizing. Good thing, too, because all the horses here have jobs. They hunt or jump or *piaffe*, or go out on trail. There are even a few broodmares tasked with producing six-figure foals. The outdoor ring has been hectic since sunrise with Bridget's project horses, who she trains herself with whips and spurs and heavy equipment when no one's looking. Her exotic imports froth and groan as she pushes them forward—more forward! Sweat drips down their narrow, slabbed sides and when their training session is over and their saddle pads are removed, steam rises off their backs like prayers for deliverance. I munch the grass and put it out of my mind. There's nothing more urgent than green grass. Now.

Clarissa approaches the gate and calls my name. I lift my head. She calls again. I go back to grazing. That's how it works, Clarissa. You call, I stall. Have I not taught you anything yet?

She enters the gate with my new, green halter and a ten-foot lead rope in hand. I'm in the basin of the pasture and Clarissa has to walk two acres downhill to get to me. Hershey grazes in the farthest corner of the basin, Merlin hogs shade in the run-in, and Moose loafs somewhere on the plateau, out of my line of sight. Clarissa takes her time, appreciating the vista from the hilltop. Hershey snorts, acknowledging her presence. I snort back my knowing that he knows. By the time Clarissa reaches me, I have inched even closer to the bottom fence, my way of protesting the halter and rope that will lead me to whatever work Clarissa has in mind.

"Geez, Sonny! Could you make me walk any further?"

I lift my head and push her with my face. Her feet give way. I'm in charge.

"Sonny! Knock it off! I bought you a new saddle, let's go try it on."

Thanks, but I'm busy right now, I snort.

She leans down and manages to slip the halter on my face, then buckles the side clasp with conviction. Okay, Clarissa, you seem like you really mean it.

A heartbeat later, our heads pop up at the sound of pounding hoof beats. Moose suddenly appears at the crest of the hill, vibrating bluster and mayhem. Clarissa freezes at the sight. She's holding my lead rope and although I can breakaway any time I choose, I can't leave Clarissa behind. Moose tosses his big, brown head and begins the charge. I wish Clarissa would unclip the lead rope and let me take care of business. Instead, she aggressively twirls the end of it, hoping to scare him off. But Moose doesn't care. He's a rogue horse, I knew it from the start. Just then, another set of pounding hoof beats joins the fray. The sound comes from the opposite corner of the pasture, galloping closer and closer, but it's the hammering of Clarissa's heart that echoes in my ears. She gasps as Hershey charges towards Moose who continues his charge towards us. The two Thoroughbreds intersect a mere two lengths from where we stand. Hershey snakes his head and drives Moose into the fence line—then chases him with fury all the way back up the hill.

Clarissa says one of those words. A lot of them, actually.

Her body trembles and her breath is jiggy. Move your feet, Clarissa, I try to tell her. It's the only way to dispel the fear and get back to thinking happy thoughts. What's true for horses is true for humans but sometimes they get stuck.

I'm not exactly sure what an a-hole is, but that's what she calls Moose. She shouts the word into the breeze, gulps in air, and moves us forward. Once we reach the top of the hill, Clarissa gives Moose the stink eye. He feels her indignation and snorts it back. She stops short at the sound, unclips my lead rope, and takes it with her as she approaches Moose in a slow, thoughtful arc. He gives her a wary glance and flicks his tail, but continues to graze as though nothing ever happened. She breathes out her animosity and breathes in courage and peace. Keeping an eye on his teeth and his feet, she reaches out and strokes him lightly on the neck, then scratches his bony withers. The few words she murmurs sound gentle and forgiving. Moose blows out the last of his resistance. He's still a rogue horse. But Clarissa won him over that day with unexpected mercy and kindness. Clarissa's a bit of a rogue too, maybe that's why she doesn't hold it against him. She doesn't know that yet. But I do.

By the time we reach the gate, I'm already eager to get back to grazing, but Clarissa has other plans. She ground ties me in a patch of shade under the leafy oak tree, then lifts a saddle onto my back. It settles neatly into place, just behind my shoulders with light contact along the sides of my spine. She steps backward and inspects the way it looks from every angle. She pushes down on the seat, then rocks the saddle side-to-side and front-to-back. She seems satisfied and smiles. She does the same thing with a pad underneath, then attaches a fleecy cinch, pulling it just tight enough to keep everything in place.

"Riding today, sweetie?"

Carla pops out from the back of the little blue barn where riders with horses on field board keep their tack. She's dressed in beige riding pants that hang on her bony frame and a pink polo shirt that makes her skin glow like a teenage girl's. She fastens the strap of her hot pink helmet beneath her chin and grins at my fancy get up.

"Not today, we're just trying on a new saddle."

"It looks good on him. And look at those pretty roses on the skirt, I've never seen anything like it! Where'd you get it?"

"Two Cowgirls, Four Horses."

"Criminals, both of 'em. They sold my friend a horse last fall that was supposed to be beginner-safe. He was until the drugs wore off. Then he bucked her off and she broke her hip."

"Geez," is all Clarissa says.

"Well, they can't mess with a saddle the way they mess with horses so you'll probably be fine. It's gorgeous. Good luck with it."

"Thanks. Are you riding today?"

"Nah, I just like to wear my helmet around the barn 'cause I look so sexy in it."

Clarissa cocks her head and wonders if she means it.

"I'm just kidding, kiddo. Of course I'm riding, it's a perfect day to be out on trail. Wanna come? It's just Bernie and me. He should be here by now but you know those Frenchies, always fashionably late," she says in her best mock accent.

"I think we'll stick to groundwork until Sonny gets used to being here."

"He looks pretty happy," Carla argues. "You're not one of those people who never gets on her horse, are you?"

"No, we ride," Clarissa says defensively.

"Good. Then let's make a date to go trail riding. You free on Wednesday?"

Clarissa hesitates. That was only three days away. Would we be ready for the big show?

"I think so," she says. "Sure, why not."

"I teach Tai Chi in the morning. I can be here by noon."

"Sounds good, do I need to bring anything?"

"You mean like an apple pie or something?"

"I don't know what I mean."

Carla laughs and heads for the gate.

"Just bring your horse," she tosses behind her.

"Got it," Clarissa says and smiles. Carla calls out to Hershey, who lifts his head from the overgrown grass at the fence line and walks briskly toward the gate.

"See that, Sonny? That's how it's supposed to work. I call, you come, okay?"

She puts on my rope halter, takes off my saddle, and leads me down the hill to the arena where Bridget gives a jumping lesson to a teenage girl. There's not an ounce of tension or fear in the girl's mind or body as she crouches into position on the back of a majestic Warmblood and handily clears a 3'6 jump.

"Again!" Bridget commands.

The horse and rider circle around. The Warmblood huffs and hurls herself over the fence and in her excitement throws in a little buck on landing.

"Don't let her get away with that! Do it again!" Bridget reprimands as she traipses around the ring in a tight circle, following her charges. We hover by the shrubbery at the entrance to the ring, waiting to be invited in.

The Warmblood notices us first. Bridget follows her gaze.

"You can come in, we're almost done. Inside leg, outside hand! Leg, leg, leg!" Bridget's voice escalates into a raspy yell. The girl looks like she's about to cry but she doesn't dare to defy the Queen. She sails over the fence once more, sticks the landing, and curls her horse into a perfect twenty-meter circle at the canter.

"Thaaaat's better! Much better!" Bridget says and claps her hands. "That's enough for today. Cool her down."

Bridget turns her attention to Clarissa and me as we enter the ring.

"That's Gretchen. She's one of my rock stars," Bridget brags as we draw near.

"She's a fantastic rider for her age."

"No, the horse is Gretchen. The girl's name is Holly. She's okay, she'd be much better if she'd take a few more lessons a month. By the way, did you want to take a lesson with me?"

Bridget's gaze pierces her like the pointy end of an icicle.

"Yes, but I have no desire to jump. So, what would you teach me?"

"Jumping is like frosting on a cake," Bridget says. "First you have to bake the cake."

She smiles and Clarissa begins to relax.

"Besides, your horse is twenty years old or something like that?"

"He's eighteen."

"He's too old to start jumping. But I could teach you how to ride better, more balanced and secure in your seat. What do you do with him now?" Bridget studies me with a critical eye. I can tell she's not impressed.

Clarissa bristles at Bridget's references to me as though I'm little more than another piece of equipment in the ring. She was used to people fussing over me and offering carrots and high praise of the steady, old horse that I am.

"We mostly just walk and trot around the ring."

"That's fine, we can start from there. Let's meet Tuesday at nine. So," Bridget says with a twist of amusement on her lips, "what's the orange stick for?"

"Oh," Clarissa says, and holds it up for inspection. "It's for lunging and for playing natural horsemanship games."

"Games?"

"Yes, like to-and-fro and traveling circles and press-and-release..."

"I've never heard of games with horses, except for Olympic games."

"Well, it's kind of like learning to dance with a horse."

"Oh, you mean like in freestyle dressage."

"No, I mean like in a relationship."

"I don't get it," she says with a shake of her head. "Back in my country, there is not all this silliness. We just ride."

Clarissa nods and I rub my face on her, reminding her of my presence.

"Don't let him do that," Bridget says and intentionally bumps me as she passes by. "It's disrespectful. See you Tuesday."

"Okay," Clarissa replies. But she doesn't mean okay, I won't let him do that. She means okay, I just agreed to take a lesson with a master of unnatural horsemanship. She's already peeing in her paddock boots. I nudge her again and bring her back to now.

We have a marvelous time playing our games, Clarissa and me, as I reveal a little bit more about who I am and what I'm willing to do when she asks me correctly. A tall, lanky, masculine figure in tan breeches and a dark blue shirt watches us from the top of the hill. Clarissa doesn't notice him, but I do. She's too busy laughing and twirling the rope over my head for the desired no-effect, and stroking my neck with appreciation when I move off the lightest touch of her hand on my barrel. Truly, we are playing and she's silly and uncensored. She praises me profusely and feeds me bits of carrots. The man on the hill vibrates a confusing mix of amusement and disdain. I can't tell if he's friend or foe, but it doesn't matter. I lose myself in the dance into which Clarissa invites me. Me, a salty old horse, dancing! We're clumsy and unsure of our next step, but the moment is joyful and ephemeral—and it is enough.

At suppertime, George comes home as promised—neither one minute before nor one minute after six o'clock. Clarissa's still giddy from our day at the barn. He's greeted by her radiant smile and the comforting smell of turkey breast and roasted potatoes in the oven.

"Hi!" she says tentatively.

"Hey," George replies tenderly. It's what she had hoped for and she breathes a quiet sigh of relief. He looks relaxed and wrinkled and scruffy, like a boy who's been out building makeshift forts in the woods all day until the dinner bell rings and he slides into home plate with just enough time to wash his hands before supper. George closes the gap between them and gives her a hug and a kiss on the lips.

"I missed you."

"I missed you too. You smell like dirty worms and fish."

"You smell like a horse."

"Touché," Clarissa says and laughs. She steps back and inspects him more closely, looks past appearances, looks into his ocean blue eyes and she knows; knows he was drinking beer and working on building her flower boxes for the petunias and marigolds and trailing vines she plants every year at the lake, knows he was working on working it out, whatever it is, that has rooted in his soul and is watered with wine and wanderlust.

She can kiss him because there's lake dirt on his lips and they'll taste clean and pure like they did when they were young. And so she does and the dinner burns and neither one of them cares. They order Chinese and bask in Sunday. They go to bed fat and happy. He holds her hand until he falls asleep.

But she doesn't fall so easily. Once alone with her thoughts, there are prayers to pray and memories that taunt and spin until she's trussed in their orange-glow straightjacket. She reminds herself that she's never much cared what the morning brings; sunshine or rain, it was all the same—one day closer to heaven or to hell, or with her luck, terminally trapped somewhere in-between. In fact, she contemplates, maybe this life is purgatory itself. In a way she hopes that it is, that eventually the memories of her father's reckless nakedness and his hand up her skirt, tickling her with the wet end of a cigar in places no father should be will be purged from her eyes, from her brain, from the deep recesses in her body where shame still dwells. For years, she used that shame as hot fuel for the raging feminist whose body was so disconnected from her brain and from her heart that she could bring a man to his knees with spent passion and then flee without a backward glance. Then she met George, a man with no guile in him, a man who simply asked her to stay. So she did.

Twenty-something years and a child later, Clarissa clings to her little family like a castaway to a raft. Metaphorically or not, she's floating in purgatory, atoning for the sins of her father. Perhaps that's why she perpetually feels neither here nor there, ever anxious for her real life to start. Surely, she thinks, this can't be it—surely this can't be all! Oh, but if this is all of it, then she'll suffer it in the third person, like a swooning character in one of her romance novels who's swept along by tide and circumstance. Perhaps she'll yet be rescued by a dinghy bearing divine intervention. Or maybe she'll just slowly drift out to sea....

Either way, why should she care? No, she doesn't care at all, she says with her arms pressed to her sides and her hands clenched in little fists. Except she does care that on Tuesday she'll brave a lesson with the Ice Queen and on Wednesday she'll trail ride the kingdom with Carla and more likely than not, she'll be the court jester of Crown Ridge by the week's end!

"I don't care," she sputters into the night. She clutches at her chest. She thinks her heart is clattering with anxiety but actually, she's rattling like dry bones about to spring to life.

"What's the matter?" George murmurs and reaches for her in the dark.

"Nothing, sweetie, go back to sleep."

He sighs and rolls onto his side and obliges. She stares at the clock until it blinks dawn. The alarm shrieks. George staggers to his feet and gets dressed for work and kisses her good-bye on the forehead as she feigns sleep. As soon as the screen door shudders, she leaps out of bed and begins to write. She's not been inspired to write for months but this morning, her fingers fly across the keyboard. There's something bubbling up that she has to get on paper, this story about a girl on a dude ranch and a horse and a man. Who is this man?

She writes long into the morning, then forsakes her art to tend to me. But instead of riding or playing games, she merely offers me a carrot and picks my feet, and sends me back into the pasture to laze and graze in the afternoon sun. She admires me from outside the fence and sends me images of hearts and stars. I catch them floating along streams of consciousness, at that special place where ours merge and become one.

Eventually, she stirs in preparation to take leave. Before long, she jigs up and down and hollers my name and waves goodbye like she's never going to see me again. Don't spoil the moment, Clarissa! I don't want to encourage her and so I keep my head down. She needs to learn that to a horse, a whisper is better than a shout. And a well-thought thought is even better.

When Tuesday comes, she leaps out of bed again and races to the barn. She's eager to pay homage to the Queen and hopes the frothy caramel latte and double-chocolate donut will curry favor in and out of the arena.

"Good morning!" she chirps as she pops into Bridget's office. She mentally curtsies and places her humble gift on the massive, golden oak desk. A silver Olympic team medal is pinned to the royal blue wall.

"Good morning," Bridget says, eyeing the booty before her. "Thanks, I didn't have time to make coffee this morning. I've been up since dawn with Gretchen. She colicked overnight."

"Oh no! Is she okay?"

"Vet came and tubed her twice already. Miguel's been hand-walking her and she seems a little better."

"That's scary."

"And expensive," Bridget adds. "Good thing she's insured."

"I didn't know horses could be insured for colic."

"She's a six-figure performance horse. She's insured for everything."

"Gee, maybe I should get insurance for Sonny."

Gretchen pops the top of her coffee cup and takes a sip.

"No papers, no point."

"He has papers. He's an Appendix, out of Man o' War."

Bridget laughs and fishes the donut out of the paper bag. "That doesn't really mean anything. It not what's in the genes. It's what's in the training."

"Maybe so. But you can't totally dismiss his DNA."

Bridget grins and tilts her nose.

"Let's see what happens in the ring today. Bring me your racehorse."

"Yes ma'am," Clarissa says, then bolts out the door and calls me in from the pasture. I come because it's already hot this early summer morning; I'm thirsty and a bucket of cool water and carrots await me at the top of the hill. And Clarissa. Sweet Clarissa. Today I will come and say hello and go wherever she leads me, as long as she leads me with kindness and confidence. Hershey cocks an ear and monitors my moving feet. Moose follows closely behind me, too close for my liking and I pin my ears and toss my head in protest. One step closer and I'll kick.

He gets the message and veers off before we reach the gate. I stop for a hearty drink because I can, because Merlin isn't hogging the run-in and his conspicuous absence allows me to take a long, satisfying drink from the trough. His person came early this morning and took him out on trail, along with the gleaming, black Thoroughbred and the sparkly lady with the pink mouth that doesn't move.

I come to the gate dripping sweet spring water. Clarissa strokes the blaze on my face and laughs, and lets me wipe my floppy lips on her sleeve.

"Listen Sonny, you need to bring your A-game this morning. We have an audience with the Queen and you need to move those feet. No chain-gang trots, okay?"

These are the words she says. But she telegraphs a picture of me dragging my feet across the sand and I'm confused. She vibrates anxiety and suddenly I prefer to go back to the pasture and graze. She slips on my halter and tugs the lead rope. She moves off several steps before I do.

"Come on, Sonny!"

I dutifully pick up my feet. She leads me to the area outside the little blue barn where she grooms me and tacks me up in my new saddle. I like the way it settles into place and the open spaces behind my shoulders—but I don't like the cinch. Never have, never will. The Old Man used to thread the leather straps through the rings and then yank hard with a fisted hand until the air rushed out of me in a swoosh that left me breathless. Clarissa cinches me in bits at a time and whispers apologies every inch of the way. Somehow, I think she knows there are memory cells in my skin that rebel at the mere sensation of leather against my hide. I wish they'd go away, but they've become a part of who I am.

She knots my green riding halter, attaches my rope reins, and leads me into a sandy arena that already gives rise to ripples of heat. She silently asks me to yield to the lightest pressure of her fingertips in every direction. Forward, backward, sideways. She draws me in then pushes me out with her energy. I like this Clarissa. I will follow her anywhere, I will walk and trot and canter, even with the pain that hobbles my stifle. All she has to do is ask of me the way she asks of me now. The same man in tan breeches watches us dance from the same hilltop, sheltered under the brim of the oak tree. I can feel his gaze hover and circle like a hawk; it's lofty and keen and curious, but not in a predatory way. He cocks his hip and tilts his head, and his mirrored sunglasses reflect our whirling and lightness of being. Who is this man?

Bridget appears through the gap in the hedgerow and I feel Clarissa stiffen.

"Are you ready for your lesson? I won't baby you, you know."

"I'm tough, I can take it," Clarissa says with a wink.

"Where's his bit?"

"Sonny goes bitless. It's all he knows."

"You have no control over a horse without a bit," Bridget snaps. Clarissa's shoulders sag at the reprimand—but only for a moment.

"Sonny's different. He's well broke and he has good brakes, you'll see."

"Okay, but if I don't think you'll be safe, I can't let the lesson proceed."

Bridget checks my cinch. Granted, I've let out some air and Bridget takes up the slack in one tidy pull. I swish my tail and pin my ears but she doesn't seem to notice.

"Are you planning on showing Sonny?"

"I haven't given it much thought, but probably not. He doesn't trailer well."

"Then why did you buy a show saddle?"

"I bought a show saddle?"

"Yes, this silver needs to be kept polished. And I assume the roses are for show as well. Didn't anyone tell you it's a show saddle?"

"No, but I thought it was unique and pretty and classically Western with the roses and the barbed wire motif and the exquisite leather tooling..." Clarissa's voice wilts as Bridget yawns.

"There's nothing to stop you from schooling in it, it's perfectly fine. It's just—different, that's all."

Clarissa sinks into the awkward silence. Bridget walks off and arranges several cones in a twenty-meter circle.

"Go ahead and get on," she shouts behind her.

Clarissa leads me to the mounting block and I stand perfectly still until a fly lands on my leg and I shift my feet.

"Make him stand still!"

Clarissa marvels at the eyes in the back of Bridget's head, or perhaps she has little minions planted everywhere, watching her every move. She finds the thought creepy and mounts with no small measure of dread. The sun beats on her shoulders and on my poll and I begin to sweat before we even move off the mounting block. Clarissa steers me to the center of the ring where Bridget awaits.

Bridget starts to melt too, and shields her pale eyes from the sun with an ice-blue visor. She orders Clarissa to walk around the ring, once in each direction, then to pick up a posting trot.

"I want to see a nice marching walk!" Bridget warns as we head toward the rail.

Clarissa cues me with her legs to quit plodding and pick up the pace.

"That's better. Let me see him stop."

Clarissa asks with the reins instead of her seat, a maneuver that fails to escape Bridget's critical eye. I stop short and unbalanced.

"So, he does have good brakes but he's sloppy. Next time ask with your seat and get him to square up. Go ahead, walk on... more leg, Clarissa, make him go!"

Clarissa squeezes me and I walk forward with a bit more energy. We cover the arena in both directions. She chatters incessantly in her head, all kinds of stuff and nonsense and there's nothing but noise between us. I cock an ear behind me, waiting for her to dial me in.

"Okay, pick up a posting trot!"

Clarissa barely asks, so Bridget does. She charges towards me with a whip in hand and clucks with sharps ticks of her tongue. I trot because of Bridget. I take Clarissa along for the ride.

"He's lazy!" Bridget pronounces and shakes her head disdainfully.

"I know," Clarissa replies as we circle the ring for the third time. The sunlight begins to sear my skin and we both drip sweat and misery.

"That's your fault too, not just the horse's."

"Okay, so how do I fix it?" Clarissa sputters as she posts past Bridget on the wrong diagonal. We look and feel clumsy. I know she can do better but for some reason, she quit riding. I string out my hind legs. My stifle hurts. It feels all wrong.

"Okay, stop. Just stop!"

"Whoa!" Clarissa clenches the reins and I stop. Bridget approaches and strokes my face.

"He's a nice horse, Claire, but he's super lazy and dead to the leg."

"He was a lesson horse," Clarissa says and sighs.

"I understand, but that's no excuse. If you want more from him, you're going to have to work for it. He needs re-training. And he needs a job."

"Just tell me what to do."

"First of all, you'll never ride correctly with that foolishness on his face. Put him in a regular headstall and a bit, a snaffle bit will do. Second, I think he's ring sour. Maybe he'll do better in an open field."

"I think that's a great idea."

Bridget pats me on the neck and sends us off to the rail again.

"Trot around the ring one more time, then circle him around the cones.

Clarissa bumps her heels against my barrel and I pick up a trot. As we finish our lap, she steers me toward the cones.

"That's not a circle, that's an egg! We have a lot of work to do."

"I know," Clarissa concedes as she brings me to a halt.

"That's enough for today. It's too hot and he's out of shape, and I've seen what I need to see. Meet me back at the barn in thirty minutes. I'll get him in a bit. Your homework is to practice twenty-meter circles and square stops during the week. Remember to use your seat, not your hands. Soften those hands, Claire, that way when you really need to use the reins, he'll listen."

"Thanks Bridget," Clarissa says and dismounts.

"You can leave cash in the lockbox or add our lesson fees to your board. Your choice. Oh, and polish that silver!"

"Yes, ma'am."

A teenage girl riding a leggy, flea-bitten Thoroughbred tacked in German apparatus enters the ring. Her eyes are flinty and her posture is impeccable. She wears a fancy insignia on the breast pocket of her white polo shirt and her shiny steed exudes strength and nobility fit for a lesson with the Queen.

"Okay, Heidi, let's see what we've got today. Baron looks fantastic!"

Clarissa takes me by the lead rope and together we trek uphill to the little blue barn. She's mopey and sweaty and hardly looks at me. I'm mopey and sweaty too, but I look to Clarissa to tell me I'm the best horse in the whole world.

Silence hangs in the air, a sopping curtain of defeat and self-recrimination. But it doesn't last long. When we reach the barn, Clarissa lifts the saddle from my dripping back and sets it down. She hoses me off with cold water and scrapes the excess off my back and leads me under the shade of the oak tree to graze on sweet grass and stealthy dandelion leaves.

"Apparently we have some work to do," she says and sighs. I feel the anxiety leave her body and invite her to breathe in the intoxicating fragrance of the earth underfoot. She hears me and inhales deeply. She puts one hand on my shoulder and scratches my withers with the other.

"Did I tell you today that you're the best horse in the whole world?"

My nature never changes, I offer, only the eyes through which I am seen. I hope Clarissa never loses sight of me. The soul of me is here, present in every moment, hers to enter into and commune with at will.

She can put me in a bit. She can tie me to a post. She can ride me in a silvery Western saddle or none at all. She can put me out to pasture or she can ride me into the ground. No matter what has been or what is or what may be, here, in this moment, I am the best horse, I am every horse, in the whole world.

7

"What are you Googling now?" George asks as he hunkers down in the brown recliner Clarissa's been trying to get rid of for the last two years. A creature of habit, he sips a glass of scotch before bedtime and watches half an episode of a sitcom in perpetual reruns that Clarissa finds offensive and banal. By the fifteen-minute mark, his glass will be empty and he'll saunter off to bed with a perfunctory goodnight kiss. Until then, he makes idle conversation between the canned laughter.

"A bit."

"Of what?"

"Not a bit of something, just a bit. For a horse."

"You mean that thing in a horse's mouth?"

"Yes, that thing."

"What kind of bit are you looking for?"

She's annoyed she has to answer questions he won't remember or care that he asked come morning. She glances up and pays him enough mind to get to ten-fifteen without a fight.

"A magic one."

"Huh?"

"One that will turn Sonny into a racehorse and me into Velvet Brown."

"Who's Velvet Brown?"

"Really, George?"

George chuckles and shrugs.

"National Velvet? With Elizabeth Taylor and Mickey Rooney?"

"Never heard of it."

"It's a book turned into a movie, a classic movie."

"Sounds like a chick flick."

"Totally," Clarissa says dryly.

He turns his attention back to the television and the last few sips of scotch in his glass. The ice finally clinks and signals the end of a long and silent night. Clarissa's first lesson with Bridget has driven her into an acute state of melancholy. The last thing she wanted to do when George got home was to rehash the details of her epic failure to perform even the most basic maneuvers on horseback with any semblance of grace or skill. Instead, she claimed a queasy stomach, opted out of dinner, and retired to the sofa to scribble the same words in her journal she's written a dozen times before: *I have no business owning a horse!*

Yet each and every morning, she begins anew with the mantra from still another classic movie that her mother introduced her to when she was a just a girl, the story of Margaret "Molly" Brown, a Denver neo-socialite and philanthropist who survived the sinking of the RMS Titanic. Tragedy turned musical, the so-called unsinkable Molly Brown would shake her fist at every indignity life threw her way and belt out the same cheeky refrain: *I ain't down yet!*

That's my Clarissa. Stubborn. Kind. Courageous. Unsinkable. She just doesn't know it yet.

It's two in the morning by the time she settles on a popular Western Dee snaffle bit with copper inlays that will taste tangy in my mouth. She shuts down her computer and scurries to bed, knowing that in just four hours, her feet will hit the floor all over again. This night, however, exhaustion has its way. She's too tired to whip herself into a sleepless frenzy over the fact that it's already Wednesday and that later, this very day, George will meander off to wine class and it will take three days before the wanderlust fades from his eyes. No, her last waking thought is of Velvet Brown fearlessly jumping fences to win the Grand National steeplechase. She drifts off with a smile on her face, twelve years old at heart and crazy in love with her very first horse. Just like Velvet. And I am her Pie.

"Boy, am I happy to see you! I thought you might not show up!" Carla crows. She's already putting the finishing touches of fly spray on Hershey's legs. She accidentally sprays her own face and sputters and says one of those words. "Excited for our trail ride?"

"Mostly," Clarissa hedges as she grabs my halter and lead rope from the fence post.

"You've been out on trail with Sonny before, haven't you?"

"Just once, on a quick hack around the property where he used to live."

"How was he?"

"He didn't spook or anything. I was told he's the pokiest horse on the trail so I'm not too worried. "

"Well, just to be safe, we'll take it nice and easy. We'll hack around the field, go through a little bit of woods, and then we'll circle back."

"Sounds good!" Clarissa says as she heads into the pasture to halter me. I watch the spectacle of humans catching horses without the least bit of interest in engaging Clarissa in the sport. If humans would just stand still when they enter our space and give us a chance to volunteer to join them, we just might. Instead, most approach us like mountain lions, some with stealth or misplaced aggression; others trudge toward us with trepidation and a colossal fear of failure and then expect us to follow the leader—ha! We already know our human's general intention and disposition before they even unlatch the gate and decide if we'll keep our heads down grazing, move off, or join up. Today, Clarissa radiates nervous energy, but she's excited and happy and I think I want to know more. I offer to meet her halfway and she smiles at the sight of me marching toward her.

"Good boy, Sonny," she calls to me. "Thanks for coming to see me!"

Ripples of heat hover between us; I'm already sweaty and thirsty but I expect Clarissa will give me a bucket of cool water and carrots and shade. She doesn't disappoint.

Carla has left Hershey tacked up and tied to the split rail fence while she gabs with a group of boarders across the way. Clarissa slips Hershey a carrot and hurries about the task of tacking me up. She grimaces at the snaffle bit that Bridget loaned her. She doesn't have a headstall to attach it to, so she buries it at the bottom of her grooming bag for now. She's becoming quite proficient at tacking me up. Nothing too loose, nothing too tight. Nothing upside down. Clarissa tells me we're ready to hit the trail. I get the picture she sends me and I jig excitedly in place.

Come on, Clarissa, let's go!

She walks me to the top of the driveway and back down again, then checks my cinch. She tightens it two notches and I huff in protest.

"Sorry, but the saddle can't slip when we're out on trail. That would be bad. Very, very bad." She winces as she contemplates the wreck it would cause, then banishes the thought from her brain. She steps back and inspects me from head to hoof. She likes what she sees and nods.

"Okay, Sonny. Off we go."

She leads me toward Carla, who sees us coming and waves us over.

"Come here, I want you to meet some boarders from the swanky barn. The show girls, I call 'em."

"Jesus, Carla, you make us sound like snobs," one woman says.

"Because you are!" Carla replies and guffaws. They laugh too because Carla dared to say it aloud. Only Carla can say such things and get away with it.

"This is Camilla, this is Penny, this is Regina, this is Margaret," she says, pointing to three gorgeous blonds and a redhead, all dressed in show barn uniforms: neatly tucked-in, tailored riding shirts, beige breeches and expensive, leather belts. There's not an extra ounce of anything on their bones, not a single wrinkle or a dimple of cellulite, and Clarissa shrinks into my shoulder.

"Ladies, this is Clarissa—or just plain Claire as she likes to be called."

Indeed, Clarissa has never felt plainer.

"And this fine specimen is Sebastian. He's their trainer," she explains with a sweep of her hand toward the tall, lanky man standing in their midst. He effectively rebukes Carla with an arch of his dark brow, then turns his attention to Clarissa. His eyes are a burnished bronze and I feel her teeter as they glance her skin. He extends his hand.

"It's a pleasure to meet you, Clarissa."

He flourishes her name with a gentle roll of his Spanish tongue and she drops my reins to shake his hand. The loop of them brushes the ground and the quartet of show girls stiffens and gasps.

"Pick up your reins, sweetie, before your horse gets caught in them!"

"It's okay, he won't move," Clarissa says and puts her hand in Sebastian's.

"Claire. Call me Claire."

"Why?"

"Because it's my nickname?"

"That would be like calling me Seb. Very unappealing, no?"

The show girls giggle and Sebastian smiles. His teeth are white and straight and impressive, even to a horse, and seem even whiter against his tawny skin. I recognize him as that man, the one who stands at the crest of the hill and watches us dance. Clarissa, let's go, let's dance! I prance in place.

"Your horse is moving," one of the show girls deadpans.

"Fine, then call me Clarissa." Clarissa shrugs and withdraws her hand, unsure if Sebastian is making fun of her or not. Her hand is warm and tingly; I know because I feel what she feels when she picks up my reins. "But my friends call me Claire."

He flinches at her impertinence. He didn't see that coming. The sharp angles of his face return as his smile disappears. His tall frame grows taller and he crosses his lanky, muscular arms for effect.

"I'm nobody's friend, isn't that right, ladies?"

"Damn straight, at least not in the ring!" Carla replies before anyone else can. "I took one lesson with you and I wanted to kill you. Or myself."

"Perhaps. But you learned something, didn't you?" Sebastian parries.

"Yeah," Carla says as her feet start to move in the opposite direction. "I learned that Argentinian men are misogynists—but damn good trainers," she concedes. "The real problem is, I can't afford lessons with you, Sebastian. You're like a drug pusher. The first one's for free, and then we end up hooked!"

The show girls laugh and nod in agreement. Sebastian shakes his head and waves his hand as though to say he's done with this frivolous conversation.

"Come on, Claire, let's hit the trail!"

"Nice meeting y'all," Clarissa says as she turns to follow Carla back to the little blue barn. It's a bit like being sent back into the unwashed masses after a fleeting encounter with royalty. She's glad to be in training with the Queen after meeting the King of Crown Ridge. No, not the King, she decides. The Grand Duke, dressed for a sporting day with the resident elite in his tan breeches and Italian leather riding boots and navy blue polo shirt with crisp, white piping.

She isn't sure she likes him much, if at all. Still, she finds him intriguing, fodder for a character in one of her romance novels. But she thinks of him as neither dark nor brooding, like her typical, medieval hero. In fact, she finds him droll and intelligent and if her hand is not mistaken, vibrant with warmth and passion. Perhaps he's just the man she's been looking for to plug into her screenplay, the man who has yet to fully materialize and steal her modern heroine's heart! To that end, she could use a little more face time with Sebastian Bergalo. And yet, she know that while they occupy the same space, they don't breathe the same air; his is higher, purer, and beyond her bourgeois reach. She'd be surprised if they ever spoke again!

Hersey stirs from his nap in the shade as we approach. He nickers to Carla and stretches out his neck for a treat.

"Good boy, Hershey," Carla says as she fishes into her belly bag. She produces four peppermints. She gives one to Hersey and one to me.

"Want one?" she says to Clarissa as she pops a red-and-white disc into her own mouth.

"Sure," Clarissa says.

We share a happy, minty moment, then mount up and head out down the grassy side of the paddock fence to the open field in the distance. I snort as we enter the field; it's open and broad with no protection at all from predators. Clarissa startles at the sound and makes me even more nervous. But soon, Carla starts to chatter and draws Clarissa into her tall, animated tales where Clarissa relaxes—and so do I. Before long, we're steeped in the shade of acres of woodland. There's sweet relief under the dense canopy of trees that line the well marked, wood-chipped trail underfoot. The smells are different in the woods; musty and moist from the bogs the river creates on both sides of the trail. We walk at an easy pace meant for beginners. Clarissa strokes my neck every now and then and I lower my head and stretch. It feels good to move long and low, without the constant pressure of more leg, more leg!

We reach a clearing—a mowed field with a gentle incline.

"Wanna trot?" Carla asks.

"Sure!" Clarissa says, her confidence rising.

"Okay, follow at least one length behind us. I won't let Hershey go too fast, I promise. I'll raise my hand to signal when we're going to slow down to a walk. Got it?"

"Got it," Clarissa says.

"Okay, let's trrrrrrot!"

Hersey picks up an easy trot but his stride is long and I have to go faster than usual just to keep up.

"Easy, Sonny!" Clarissa says and clamps on the reins. I try to slow down, but horses don't like to get left behind. The last one in line is dinner.

"Easy!" she repeats, and I try, I really do try. At my age, the hill slows me down just enough to make Clarissa feel comfortable. When we reach the top she laughs out loud.

"That was great! Good job, Sonny!"

"Nice riding!" Carla exclaims. "Sonny has an engine, you know."

"Thank goodness Hershey kept a steady pace. I think Sonny wanted to race!"

"They all do," Carla says as she twists in the saddle to give Hersey a scratch on the butt. "It's how they are out here. They feel free, you know? Like nature intended."

Clarissa nods and I feel her heart swell. She's proud of me, proud of herself, and in that hilltop moment, her acedia flees and my stifle doesn't hurt and we are as we were made: unbroken and unbridled and fully alive.

"You want to keep going?"

"Yes, please!"

Carla laughs and points to the yellow marker on the left. "That trail is the long way home. We'll have to cross a stream. You okay with that?"

"Yes, I think so."

"You'll have to be, there's no way around it once we get there."

"We can handle it."

"That's what I like to hear. Okay, let's just walk."

As we enter the woods, Clarissa breathes deeply of the moss and pine and moist bark. My foot falls sound like hushes, soft and rhythmic, and her hips move in harmony with mine as we glide through patches of fern and dappled sunlight. It is all too sublime for words, and even Carla falls silent. When we get to the stream, Carla merely tosses back a smile and nods her head to urge us on. I follow Hershey's lead. Cool water ripples over my fetlocks and the stream is lined with smooth stones embedded in clay that feels firm yet forgiving under my feet. When we reach the other side, we scramble up an embankment and merge into a sunlit field. The little blue barn looms in the distance.

"Good job, cowgirl!"

"Thanks, Carla! That was awesome!"

"Glad you enjoyed it. Now you're not a trail virgin anymore."

Clarissa laughs. "And you make a mighty fine trail pimp."

"Ha! I like that, I'm gonna use that!"

"Actually, you're more like my fairy horsemother."

"Aw, that's sweet."

"It's true. Thanks for taking me under your wing."

"You're welcome. That's what real horsewomen do. It's not supposed to be a catfight. By the way, what did you think of the show girls?"

Clarissa shrugs. "They seem nice."

"I don't know if I'd call them nice, but they're not so bad once you get past the bling. As long as you're not competition, in or out of the ring, you're safe from their backbiting."

"What do you mean, out of the ring?"

"Didn't you see the way they swoon over Sebastian?"

Clarissa's heartbeat quickens and her fingers flutter on the reins at the sound of his name. I pretend not to notice and keep plodding toward the barn. I think it might be close to feeding time and I'm getting hungry.

"What's so great about Sebastian?"

"I call it TLC—Trainer Lust Complex. He trains them to be better riders but they think he has some magical power that makes them jump higher and keeps them in the ribbons. They idolize the man to the point of—well, you know. Of course, it doesn't hurt that he has an exotic accent and that he's so good looking he makes my eye twitch. Oh, and he's a chef, too. How sexy is that?"

"He's a what?"

"A chef! He's been known to cook a delectable dinner for two, if you know what I mean.

"That's crazy. He sounds like a character in a romance novel."

"In the flesh!"

"So, is he—"

"Single?"

"No, I was going to ask if he's a jerk. He seems like a bit of a jerk."

"He's single and he's—different. I don't know, Claire, I don't live in that world."

"Me neither."

"Guess we should head back to our lowly little barn. These guys are hungry and thirsty, and so am I. Shall we trot?"

"Yes!"

"Okay, let's go!" Carla bumps Hershey with her gangly legs and he leaps into an energetic trot, much more energetic with the barn in sight. I follow his lead, but his stride is long and fleet. I'll have no choice but to canter to keep up!

As we round the bend in the trail I pick up my left lead and canter forward. I hear a yelp and a thud and feel an incredible lightness on my back. Clarissa? Clarissa, where did you go?

"Claire!" Carla yells and spins Hershey like a top. He stops and so do I. I hang my head and grab a mouthful of weeds, but my eyes are on Clarissa, who lies motionless in the tall grass.

"Claire! Are you okay?"

Clarissa stirs and uncrumples her body, rolling from her side onto her back. She stares at the sky and slowly lifts her head.

"I'm okay—I think."

She sits upright and rubs her right hip, which has taken the brunt of her fall. She's suddenly grateful for the few extra pounds she carries there. Carla dismounts and hurries to her side. I ground tie where I am.

She peers down at Clarissa and her eyes narrow.

"Are you okay or not?"

"Yeah, I'm fine."

"Then get back on your horse. Right now."

"I'll just walk him back. I can't mount from the ground anyway."

"I'll help you. It's really important, Claire. You have to get back on. Right now."

"Okay, okay!"

Clarissa stands up and brushes herself off. She doesn't even notice that she's shaking.

"I lost my crop. I have to look for it."

"You can come back and look for it later."

"Oh! And my sunglasses," Clarissa says, patting her face with alarm. "I just bought those glasses, dammit!" She chokes back a whimper.

"Come on, let's go!" Carla barks. Clarissa doesn't understand why Carla has turned so mean, but I do. I've seen dozens of riders come off and never return to the barn. Carla knows if she doesn't get Clarissa back in the saddle, there's a chance she'll sell it next week and never ride again. Fear is like that, like a snake in the tall grass that winds around your chest and chokes the love of riding out of your heart. Get out of the grass, Clarissa!

She appears to hear me and steps back onto the trail. I stand perfectly still while Carla gives her a leg up. She lands in the saddle with a thud. She feels heavy, inside and out. I mosey forward, hoping she knows I didn't mean any harm. I was pretty sure I heard my feed bucket rattle; the food here is rich and plentiful and I need to get to my bucket before that fat, old draft horse eats my share!

Carla mounts Hershey and we walk side-by-side. She keeps a watchful eye on Clarissa, prepared to pony us if she needs to. But Clarissa's on the rebound and she lets out a giggle.

"Well, at least I got it out of the way!"

"What's that?"

"My first fall!" She sounds giddy and Carla laughs.

"So, your first trail ride and your first fall. This is a red-letter day!"

"It wasn't as bad as I thought it would be," she muses.

"They say it takes seven falls to make a real horsewoman, you know."

"What happens after the seventh one?"

"You earn your wings."

"Oh crap, like heavenly wings?"

"Nope, that's when you get to fly with your horse."

Clarissa smiles at the thought.

"Come on, let's trot around the ring a couple of laps just for fun."

"Okay," Clarissa says and I'm happy to oblige, eager to prove I'm still the best horse in the whole world. Carla is a wise, old horsewoman. We trot and we laugh and we all feel better.

Just as we're about to leave the ring, Sebastian and Margaret, the redheaded show girl, appear at the break in the hedgerow. Margaret clutches Dante's reins and the horse tosses his head. They enter stiffly, like equestrian royalty. Sebastian studies us and I feel Clarissa squirm.

"That's an interesting saddle," he says.

"Thanks," Clarissa replies.

"Wait, is that an insult?" Carla chimes in. "I think it's very beautiful."

"I merely said it's an interesting saddle, I know of such saddles from my country."

Clarissa's intrigued. She wants to know more but she's having trouble finding her vocal chords.

"It looks like an Argentine saddle, crafted from Argentine cow hide and perhaps used by a gaucho—or one of his women—on parade. The Spanish roses speak of our tradition."

"What's a gaucho? Aren't they ladies pants?"

"A gaucho in Argentina is the equivalent of the American cowboy. They work as horse trainers on *las estancias,* our ranches."

"Huh!" Carla says. "I thought they were just pants."

"Why am I not surprised?" Sebastian teases. "May I have a closer look?"

"Sure," Clarissa says and prepares to dismount. Sebastian holds up his hand.

"No need, stay as you are."

With two strides of his long, muscular legs, he reaches my flank and inspects the saddle more closely. He runs his hands over the leather, peers under the skirt, and glides his fingertips over the rim of the cantle.

"No doubt, this fine silver is from our Argentine mines. Where did you get it?"

"Two Cowgirls, Four Horses."

He stares at her blankly.

"It's a Western tack shop."

"What did you pay for it?"

"Seven hundred."

"You did well. It is a work of art."

"I thought so too," Clarissa says and smiles.

"Should you ever wish to sell it, let me know." His eyes cloud with a distant thought, then he catches himself and squints into the sunlit arena. He watches Margaret mount Dante and scowls when the horse moves off the block before she's seated. He shakes his head reproachfully and turns his attention back to Clarissa. He frowns and then reaches out and touches her on the back of her neck. She flinches with surprise.

"Don't move!" he commands, then pinches his fingers closed. "Deer tick," he explains, as he plucks it from her skin and crushes it between his fingertips.

"Ew!" Carla wails and crinkles her nose. "That's disgusting!"

"What did you want me to do, kiss it?"

"You probably got that when you came off," Carla says to Clarissa. "You're lucky he got it before it bit you."

"You came off?"

"Yeah, she did! But she got right back on," Carla says proudly before Clarissa has a chance to answer.

Hershey starts to jig and I definitely hear the rattle of the feed cart in the distance. I careen my head around and look for Merlin. I blow out my worry and impatience.

"Are you hurt?" Sebastian asks.

"I'm fine," Clarissa says, her voice shrinking with shame. But her subsequent blush isn't from embarrassment; it's from the sensation of a man's fingertips brushing the nape of her neck, just behind her ear, a man who isn't George, who isn't anything like George, and whose touch she feels still, like a phantom caress. He seems amused by her discomfort and she can't decide if she hates him or herself.

"Next time you're in trouble, keep your heels down and your eyes up. If you look at the ground, that's where you'll end up. You must look where you want to go and believe that you can get there, even if you're barely hanging on." He pats my hindquarters and steps toward the center of the ring.

"I'll try to remember that," Clarissa says but he doesn't seem to hear her. He's already focusing on Margaret and the massive, gray Thoroughbred held captive by her titan grip on the reins.

"You can't just take, Margaret, you have to give back to the horse too!" he shouts and says something under his breath in Spanish. "How many times will I say this to you?"

"Sorry, Sebastian," Margaret calls out as she whizzes by at an extended trot, kicking up sand and sweating profusely.

"Don't apologize, just fix it!"

Carla and Clarissa exchange winces and steer Hershey and me out of the arena. We trudge uphill, stifled by a glaring sun that burns too hot for early summer.

"I hope you know you just got free advice from one of the top trainers in the country."

"Really? It sounded more like common sense to me."

"If it was so common, no one would come off. The thing about Sebastian is that he doesn't so much correct your body as he corrects your mind and how you think about riding. Then, the body follows naturally."

"If he's so great, why does Margaret look scared to death?"

"She's totally over-mounted. Sebastian has tried to get her to sell that horse, he's too much for her to handle. He has to be twice as hard on her to keep her safe."

"Do you think that's my problem too? Am I over-mounted?" Clarissa says as we reach the top of the hill and she slides down the side of my barrel until her feet hit the ground.

"Nah, you're just over-thinking. You have a real nice horse, but you gotta ride every moment like it's the only one that matters. Truth is, it doesn't get any better than this!"

Carla dismounts and removes her helmet. Despite the heat, she looks sleek instead of sweaty, not like Clarissa, whose fine, brown hair hangs in limp, wet sections plastered against her skull. I'm dripping sweat too, and anxious to get to my bucket of grain before Merlin does.

"I'm gonna give Hersey a quick bath and then I gotta pick up my dog from daycare. You sure you're okay?"

Clarissa nods as she goes about the business of untacking me. "Yep, I'm good. Thanks for inviting me to ride, it was great!"

"So you'll do it again sometime?"

"Of course!"

Carla throws her arm around Clarissa's shoulder.

"You did good, kid."

Carla slips me a cookie.

"You too, Sonny. Nice canter!"

Clarissa grins and removes my saddle. She draws water from the well and sponges off my sweat. I instantly feel cooler and refreshed. She tops off my sponge bath by feeding me a tasty carrot, leafy stems and all, and turns me loose in my pasture. Luckily for me, Merlin has yet to return from his own trail ride with Bernie and the sparkly lady. I eat my afternoon grain in peace and then doze in the abundant shade of the run-in where no one chases me out. Clarissa watches, satisfied, then rubs her hip and winces. Her gaze drifts to the arena and she wonders what it would be like to take a lesson with Sebastian Bergalo. She rolls her eyes at the absurdity of the thought. He's out of her league, just like the show girls, and black velvet helmets, and the regal, gray gelding who trots on air. Besides, she reasons, who wants to take lessons from someone who scares people half to death? If she were to ask me, I'd tell her someone who would consent to anything, anything at all, just to feel alive.

Later that day, long after Clarissa's gone, Sebastian comes to the little blue barn and slips inside the dimly lit tack room. I can track his movement through the open Dutch doors that line the run-in shed. We field boarders like to stick our heads inside and pin our ears at the horses stuck in the box stalls on the other side of the aisle. Sometimes we taunt them in their captivity. Other times, we envy their soft, rich, alfalfa hay, especially when our meager, shared piles of brittle grass hay dwindle and our water buckets go foul or empty. The grooms at Crown Ridge pander to the show horses at Bridget's bidding. Those of us on pasture board are relegated to sloppy seconds in time and attention. It's okay, I don't need much in the summer—just green grass and plentiful, clean water. I hope Clarissa catches on to the neglect.

Sebastian locates my new saddle hanging on the wall and runs his fingers over the grooves in the tooled, barbed wire and engraved silver plates and the scalloped conchos that adorn the skirt. His fingertip hovers over a Spanish rose and traces the capricious curve of its petals while a mourning dove on a copper cupola sings its last song of the day. It's a fleeting moment of contemplation, one that makes his broad, square shoulders sag; he runs his fingers through his dark, wavy hair as though trying to deflect the thought, the memory, that has settled below the surface of him. He feels my curious stare. It jars him from his melancholy and he approaches me and tousles my forelock.

"What's your name, boy?"

He searches the wall where our halters hang for a clue. Most of the horses have their names stitched or engraved on a brass plate on their halters, but not me. I have no name on mine just yet; only a medal of Saint Anne, the patron saint of equestrians, clipped to the buckle. He seems to know which one belongs to me. He inspects the medal closely.

"Good Saint Anne," he says. "Were you sleeping when Clarissa fell today?"

He shakes his head dismissively. He doesn't believe in angels or saints. Not anymore. Not since the accident on *la estancia....*

Nightfall approaches. He takes his leave and in the blue of twilight, the horses graze and close ranks and breathe stillness and peace. The moment is ephemeral. But even if it were to be our last, for us—it is enough.

There's no such peace in Clarissa's heart or home this night. When George returns from the office and finds her lying in bed with a bag of frozen peas on her hip, he gazes at her with a chilling mixture of disinterest and contempt.

"What happened?" he says blandly.

"Sonny went right, I went left," Clarissa says and smiles. She wants to assure him she's not hurt too badly, even though the softball-size, speckled bruise on her hip says otherwise. He doesn't smile back. He doesn't ask if she needs some liniment, or a cup of tea, or if she wants to talk about it. All he can think about is the twisted wreckage of his father's American-made Buick wrapped around a cypress tree, and his older brother's brain, damaged beyond repair. Fifteen at the time of his joyride, he was now a perpetual eight year old with the look and libido of a grown man. In a single, careless moment, George's *Opa!* had exploded into a mass of chaos and comas and medical waste. Clarissa had promised him she wouldn't get hurt. He's angry, but he doesn't know if he's angry at her, or at his brother, or at his father, who left the keys in the car.

"I have to go."

"Where?"

"Wine Club."

"Oh yeah. I forgot."

"Did you hit your head?"

"No, I just forgot, that's all."

"You need anything?"

"I'm fine," she says gruffly.

He nods, ignoring the tone in her voice. He has his own panacea for his brokenness inside, for the way the wife of his youth seems to have slipped through his fingers over the years in pursuit of some elusive something more...not more of him, the aging, balding man he sees in the mirror who secretly wonders if he ever really won Clarissa's heart in the first place—and if he did, if he could ever hope to keep it. To his own dismay and self-loathing, he's evolved into a blue-suited, international finance guy who's terminally landlocked in a plush, corner office. To that effect, broken too is the dream of ever becoming the intrepid marine scientist who had hoped to set sail with Clarissa in pursuit of discovery and adventure. He would tend to Mother Ocean on a thirty-foot sloop amid the Greek Isles and the Florida Keys while she wrote poetry and novels in the cabin down below, and they both agreed they would be poor but stupendously happy. It has since become clear they won't be sailing anywhere any time soon; rather, it seems to George that Clarissa has traded the dream of growing old together at sea for *terra firma* and a quest for something she still can't name but chases with a vengeance, this time on horseback. If he'd had any idea it would go this far, he never would have encouraged her to buy a damn horse—to buy me! But she was stricken and dull and detached in the wake of her father's death and the void it created, and he would've consented to anything at all if it would bring the light back into Clarissa's eyes. If not upon a fair, blue sea, he could always find a home in the luminous, emerald valley of her eyes. Now, they seem to shine only when she speaks of me; of riding, and the way she feels when she's on my back and we're traversing the landscape of loss and gaining ground and she thinks she just might be running toward her life instead of away from it for the very first time.

George doesn't realize he has gifted her with sacred space. He doesn't understand that as a result, she's never loved him more than she does right now, curled into a comma with a bag of frozen peas on her hip. She's never felt more alive, but all he sees is more brokenness—and so, he seeks solace in another woman's arms and in her rare Pinot Noir wines from Cotês de Nuit that are only accessible to sommeliers of beauty, beguilement, or worldwide repute—and the occasional, wealthy fool.

"You promised you wouldn't get hurt," he blurts as he hovers in the doorway and fidgets with the doorknob.

"Honey, I'm not hurt, I'm just a little bruised. Nothing some frozen veggies can't fix." Clarissa holds up the bag and grins but the horse is already out of the barn. Not just out of the barn but halfway down the road and stomping and cavorting in the vineyard. She doesn't understand his cold expression, which far surpasses the icy numbness in her hip.

"It's a food-and-wine pairing night, they tend to run long. Don't wait up."

Clarissa nods and her smile fades. Moments later, she hears the screen door shudder. She thinks they really have to get the hinges on that door repaired. It's enough for a door to slam once. Twice or even three times is just plain cruel.

She adjusts the pillow behind her neck. She touches that place just behind her ear where she was touched today in an unexpected way by an unexpected man in a bold and unexpected gesture of kindness. Who is this man, she wonders. Is it enough to probe him on paper, to make him spring to life and do her bidding on the pages of a half-written screenplay that no one, including herself, thinks she'll ever finish? Or does she really want to know him? She had made a living inventing life. Maybe, just maybe, she wants to jump into the fray and feel for herself the stuff of romance novels; from the dark, mysterious attractions to the heady interactions to the long-awaited consummations that make a woman weep. Wednesdays make it easy to think that way. She expects to be over it by sunrise and goes to sleep with the light on, hoping she'll sleep lightly enough to hear George come home. But he doesn't come home for a very long time, and by then, despite the steady, incandescent light, she's enveloped in shades of longing that even the pristine shafts of Thursday morning can't dispel.

8

"Sonny!" Clarissa calls to me. The sun climbs in the sky and sweat already drips down my sides. The flies are merciless for early morning and grub around the inside corners of my eyes until they're rife with sticky, gray sludge. They flock to me, the oldest and the slowest and the weakest one in the pasture. Yes, I know what I am, the laws of nature define me. If it was a matter of will, I'd be a prince among horses; but my body betrays me and my only defense is the fly spray the grooms neglect to apply. Clarissa hasn't bought me a fly mask, but she will when she sees me. And so I come.

As I approach the gate, she gasps. There are fly welts on my barrel and my neck. Just wait, Clarissa, there's more.

"Sonny! What happened to you? Oh my goodness, look at your eyes!"

I can tell by her expression that she hovers between horrified and pissed off. But there's something different about her eyes, too. They're thick-lidded and glassy and sad. She fastens my halter and rope and leads me out of the pasture into the cool shade of the oak tree for closer examination. She rummages through her tack bag for a rag, runs some cold water over it from the well pump, and dabs my eyes until they feel clean and bright again. Then she opens a jar of pungent, waxy salve and applies it to the bites on my body with tender, circling fingertips. I really wish she'd scratch them long and hard but she's doing the best she can.

"I guess no one bothered to put on fly spray," she mutters, searching the grounds for Miguel. "But look here, Sonny!" she says, brightening. "I bought you something!"

A fly mask, I presume. It's about time! But it's not a fly mask that she produces from the bench by the little blue barn. It's some kind of instrument of torture and I back away at the sight of it. She holds it out for my inspection and I balk once more at the crop-like handle and what appears to be the tail of another horse tied to the end of it. I wonder what horrible end came to the horse who lost his tail. My eyes grow round with worry but Clarissa merely laughs and holds it out to the side and shakes it up and down and the horse tail dances.

"Silly horse, it's for the flies! I can swat them away when we ride on trail so they don't bother you!"

I see the image she projects to me, succor from the flies and a happy trail ride, but I still find it worrisome. Then she puts the horse tail over her own head and swishes it in front of her face. She leaves it there like a veil for a moment, then giggles and lifts it and her face reappears. I get it, it's a game, and I consent to play.

She reaches forward with the swisher and touches me with it on the shoulder. I flinch but I don't move off. It feels silky against my skin. Then she puts the horse tail over her own head again and laughs.

"Where's Sonny? Sonny, I can't see you!" she sings. She lifts the swisher and peers at me. "Oh! There you are!"

She does the same thing to me, this time on my face, and I flinch again, but I'm starting to like this game—mostly because it makes Clarissa vibrate with joy.

"Sonny, where are you? I can't see you!" she sings again, then lifts the veil from my face.

"Oh! There you are!"

If horses could laugh, I would. As it is, I feel a happy bubble rising in my chest. I love this version of Clarissa. She drapes the horse tail over her face one more time but I'm distracted by the sound of approaching footsteps on gravel. Clarissa doesn't seem to hear them. She's still singing and swishing and playing the game.

"Sonny, where are you? I can't see you!" Her face is buried in horse hair, but only until another voice speaks.

"Hello, Clarissa."

She slowly lifts the horse tail and turns her face aside. Sebastian doesn't offer the relief of a smile. He simply gazes at her with stern curiosity.

"So, you think owning a horse is fun and games?"

She feels the sting of his reproach and shrinks from it. I urge her to keep playing, we were having such fun—me, an old horse having fun!

"I was desensitizing Sonny to a fly swisher so we can ride on trail."

"Perhaps your time would be better spent learning how to stay in the saddle."

"Maybe," Clarissa says. Her spine stiffens and she grows a little bit taller. "But I'm taking lessons with Bridget and I'll get better. You know, there's nothing wrong with having fun with your horse."

"There is if you don't have his respect first."

"Sonny respects me."

"Of course he does. That's why he bolted to the barn and dumped you in the weeds."

"What's your point?"

"That's how riders get hurt. They think their horses are house pets. Sonny's not a pet, he's a partner. There's a big difference."

"I know that, I know he's not a dog. He doesn't even bark."

Sebastian nods his head thoughtfully; the humor isn't entirely lost on him but he keeps a lock on the corners of his mouth.

"So, what gives? Why aren't you at the show barn?"

"I'm here for Moose. His owner is putting him in training with me."

"Now there's a horse that needs some manners. While you're at it, can you teach him not to get in my space? Every time I get Sonny from the pasture he runs interference."

"He does it because he can. You control the space, Clarissa, not the horse. It's all about what you project. If you project weakness, the horse will dominate. You're not a person out there, you're just another horse."

Clarissa sidles close to me and strokes my neck. I lower my head and rub my itchy face on her hip. I press into her deeply. It feels so good!

"Ouch!" she exclaims and steps aside. She rubs the bruise hidden below her new black breeches, the kind the sparkly lady wears. Sebastian's eyes are drawn to her hand on her hip and linger there, taking in the gentle curves accented by her form-fitting pants.

"It's going to take more than fancy pants to make a horsewoman out of you, Clarissa."

Clarissa turns and fusses with my crooked halter to hide the threat of tears she feels behind her eyes—more tears!

"But you have real potential. Don't let your emotions get in the way."

Sebastian brushes past us and unlatches the gate. Clarissa watches and says one of those words under her breath. It's full of hisses in the middle and I'm pretty sure she means it.

"Come on, Sonny, let's go for a walk."

She doesn't want to be there when Sebastian returns from the pasture with Moose in hand. She watches him approach Moose with the kind of authority that makes Moose plant his feet and surrender before Sebastian even gets close enough to halter him. Out of spite, Clarissa mentally telegraphs, *run, Moose, run!* I sense Moose's confusion as he receives the impulse and although he shifts his feet, he yields to the strength of Sebastian's will and stays put. I don't know why Clarissa dislikes Sebastian. He's strong and straightforward and fair—admirable qualities to a horse but apparently not so much to humans. Especially not to Clarissa.

She tells me we're off for a walk but we're standing still too, just like Moose. She can't seem to take her eyes off Sebastian and her head cocks to the side as she contemplates the sight of him taking the time to give Moose a friendly rub on the muzzle and a scratch on the withers before placing the halter on his head. She wishes he was half as solicitous of her and marvels at the way Moose follows him so willingly. She's pretty sure that even if a lead rope weren't attached, Moose would follow him anywhere. At 16.3 hands, Moose is a tall, leggy keg of dynamite. At the moment, however, he looks more like a docile, elegant Thoroughbred, a mirror image of the tall, leggy, elegant man who leads him with such confidence that Moose doesn't even think to balk or pull back. But there's nothing docile about Sebastian Bergalo, she gripes with a shake of her head. He's arrogant and rude and just plain mean. In fact, he's not even worthy to be in one of her romance novels and she mentally scratches him from the line-up.

"Come on, Sonny, let's get out of here." She tugs on the lead rope. She doesn't need to do that. I would follow her anywhere too.

We walk down the hill, down the long, serpentine driveway and I feel her start to relax as the steady clop of my hooves on the pavement creates a soothing, four-beat rhythm. Tall, yellow flowers surround us on every side and their sweet smell enters my nostrils, along with the fragrance of fresh-cut grass. I miss the carpet of dandelions at my old farm. There's hardly a dandelion to be found in this vast, green place and I long for their bittersweet taste on my tongue. Just the same, I lower my head and sneak a few bites of the dense, dark green grass neatly lining the driveway. Clarissa yanks my head.

"We're not allowed to graze here!" she reprimands. "You want to get me in trouble?"

I look at her blankly. Grass is meant for grazing. The world has gone mad.

I lower my head for another bite. This grass tastes exotic but very good!

"Sonny!"

"*Señora!*"

Clarissa spins and sees Miguel hovering at the top of the hill with a wheelbarrow and a rake. She smiles and waves. I continue to feast.

"There's no grazing allowed along the driveway," Miguel yells to her. "If you want to graze him, go into one of the pastures."

"I know, I'm sorry!" Clarissa shouts and yanks my head from the grass again. "Thanks a lot, Sonny," she grumbles.

I gaze at her sullenly but feel no shame. It's just not in my nature. She instantly forgives me and strokes my fly-bitten neck, reminded of the neglect. We turn and trot up the hill until we reach Miguel, who's hunched over grooming the mulch around a bevy of rosebushes.

"By the way, Miguel? Can you please remember to put fly spray on Sonny before turning him out? I found him eaten alive this morning."

She smiles but all he offers is his back.

"No problem," he grunts and goes about his business.

"Thanks, I really appreciate it. They say that chestnut-colored horses attract the flies and their skin is much more sensitive..." Her voice trails off. He doesn't appear to be listening. Clarissa dallies but a moment, then moves us toward the little blue barn. If she was sad when she first arrived this morning, she isn't anymore. She's vibrates irritation, like I feel when there's a fly crawling around my eye. Only much worse.

Clarissa drops the lead line and allows me to graze while she perches on the wooden swing that hangs from one of the oak tree's craggy limbs. From there, she observes the activity in the arena down below. Sebastian sits in the saddle like royalty while Moose carries him in a floaty trot down the long side then curves into a perfect crescent moon orbiting a twenty-meter circle. Sebastian doesn't appear to move a muscle and yet Moose seems to know exactly where to go now and where to go next. In an eye blink they transition to a canter that leaves Clarissa steeped in envy and awe. And in an eye blink Sebastian is back in the line-up and back in the dim corners of her imagination where she wonders what it would be like to be subject to such authority. But is it really authority, or the foundation of a partnership being formed with Moose—Moose! No longer a rogue horse but a royal steed!

A gallery of show girls adorns the benches at the mouth of the arena and ooh and ogle horse and rider. Sebastian knows they're there, but every time he approaches the bottom of the circle, his eyes surreptitiously lift and alight on the woman perched on a swing like a little, brown wren. He finds her delicate and yet brave in a foundling kind of way; his instinct is to protect her and he doesn't know why. Or maybe he does, but he hasn't allowed more than a fleeting thought of Sofía since he came to America ten years ago. A memory of barbed wire and roses and Sofía, his raven-haired, dark-eyed bride, assaults his mind and his body braces against the thought, against the impact. Moose skids to a stop and toggles Sebastian in the saddle. The show girls gasp. He was only doing what Sebastian subconsciously cued him to do but Sebastian taps him with a crop and sends him forward. He doesn't look up from the circle again.

As Moose's training session comes to an end and the show girls swarm, Clarissa hops off the swing and returns me to my pasture. She wants to be gone by the time Sebastian arrives with Moose. She offers me sweet bits of apple and a promise to ride soon, then mists me with fly spray before turning me loose. I'm free to go, but I linger. She thinks I want more apple but what I want is more connection. Clarissa's mind is anywhere-but-here. Don't you feel it, Clarissa? It's all happening, right here, right now!

"Have a good day, Sonny. Make good choices." She rakes her fingers through my forelock and walks away. I turn and meander to the water trough. It's low and dirty and it hasn't occurred to Clarissa to inspect it. I drink from it anyway on this morbidly hot day. I think to take a nap under the canopy of the run-in but Merlin sees me coming and chases me out. I'm relegated to roaming patches of shade thrown by random, small trees bordering the pasture. It's meager relief, but it will do. I save my strength and my energy for the battles worth fighting. I wish Clarissa would do the same but she's been watching me scavenge for shade and is already storming toward the office. She raps on the trim of the open door and peers inside.

"Hi Bridget, got a minute?"

Bridget glances up from a stack of papers and swivels sharply in her chair. Her snow-white hair, gathered in a neat ponytail, switches like a horse tail. Her office smells like vanilla cupcakes, courtesy of an air freshener she keeps on the corner of her desk. It's far too sweet for Clarissa's nose and she grimaces without knowing it.

"What's the matter, you look unhappy."

"I'm not unhappy, I just have a couple of concerns."

Now it's Bridget who grimaces, but she knows full well that she's doing it.

"Hopefully I can address them."

"Well, I noticed this morning that Sonny's covered in bug bites. I'm pretty sure he wasn't fly sprayed last night."

"Do you know that for a fact?"

"No, but it's pretty obvious."

"The guys know to fly spray all the horses, especially the ones on field board. Maybe they couldn't catch him."

Clarissa can't help but laugh. "Sonny? No, Sonny is definitely catchable."

"Well, if he was anywhere near the run-in, he got sprayed. You can't expect the guys to go into the bottom of the pasture to spray a horse, especially one who doesn't come when he's called. We have over forty horses here. They don't have time for that."

"I guess I understand that. But that leads to another problem. Well, not a problem exactly but another concern."

"Go ahead," Bridget says and sighs as she rises from her chair and stretches her arms across her chest like a wrestler before a big match. She's Olympian tall and sinewy and incredibly fit for a senior human, and Clarissa feels dwarfed in more ways than one.

"The run-in is big enough for all four horses. But Merlin stands sideways and he lets Hershey in, and occasionally Moose, but there's no room for Sonny—even if Merlin didn't chase him out."

"That's herd dynamics, Claire, you can't expect me to change that."

"But it's ninety-three degrees and a thousand percent humidity. There's no other shade for Sonny and he's sweating bullets."

"So what do you want me to do?"

It dawns on Clarissa that she doesn't have an answer. She knows Bridget's right, the herd has its own language and structure, but she can't bear the sight of me frothy with sweat.

"Maybe move him to another pasture until this heat wave is over?"

"All my pastures are full, except the one with the mares. I won't put a gelding in with the mares. It's a recipe for trouble and then you'll really be unhappy."

"I'm not unhappy," Clarissa repeats. "Just concerned about my horse. Maybe I could rent a stall for a few days."

"The only empty stalls are in the show barn. And I don't rent them by the day, only by the month. You can rent one for twelve hundred dollars."

The heat wave was expected to last four more days. Clarissa does the math. She feels hot and annoyed and reckless.

"Okay, I'll take it."

"What?"

"I said I'll take it. He has to be able to get some relief from the heat in the middle of the day. He's an older horse, he doesn't thermo-regulate like the younger ones do. I'll turn him back out in his regular pasture at night."

Bridget sniffs and chuckles. "Whatever makes you happy, Claire. And don't worry, I can have the guys turn him out at night, no problem."

"That would be helpful, thank you."

"It's the least I can do."

Clarissa agrees but she doesn't dare to say so.

"You can leave a check in the lockbox. I'll have Miguel get the stall ready and move him over after lunch," Bridget says. "And by the way, please keep Sonny off the grass along the driveway. We like to keep it looking nice for our boarders and visitors."

Clarissa bristles at the thought of Miguel tattling tales. She makes a mental note to be careful what she says when he's lurking about—and it seems that he's always lurking about! The Queen of Crown Ridge has her minions, and in Bridget's eyes, Clarissa is just one more.

"Have you been practicing your circles?"

"What?"

"Your circles. I'm looking forward to seeing your progress."

Clarissa sees where this is going. There's a price to pay for Bridget's time and indulgence!

"I can come early tomorrow morning for a lesson—if you're free, that is."

"I can fit you in. But don't forget to put him in the snaffle bit."

Clarissa mentally curtsies and thanks Bridget for her time. Her body is pumped full of adrenaline and trembles from the confrontation—but at least she has something to show for it. She heads to her car to fetch her checkbook and passes the wash stall on her way. Sebastian gives Moose a good hosing off and Clarissa wonders why he doesn't relegate the task to one of the grooms, like most of the show girls do. She tries to sneak by. He pretends not to see her and she thinks she has succeeded. By the time she comes back down the hill with a check in hand, he's leading Moose back into our pasture. Moose calls out to me with a low nicker. In our own way, we're becoming buddies, united in our quest to topple Merlin from his throne.

Clarissa drops a check in the lockbox and calculates how many pairs of shoes she could buy with that money. Oddly, the thought doesn't bother her much. She has need of only one pair these days; not swanky designer shoes, but clunky, black paddock boots that have stone dust in the creases and pine shavings and manure stuck to their thick, treaded soles.

Three hundred dollars a day for four days. It was the cost of a nice hotel room in Napa, California, where she and George had vacationed last fall, before she bought Sonny and before he wet his whistle with French women and wine. She leaves Crown Ridge with a hole in her wallet and a trickle of tears provoked by the insults of the day. She rebukes herself for caring one whit about any of it and taps into a rising tide of indignation that makes her feel vibrantly alive and brave and slightly reckless all at the same time. It's a precarious state for a woman unaccustomed to claiming her power to influence the universe; she'll either harness it and use it to reach new heights of freedom and glory, like a racehorse, like my own kin, War Admiral and Man o' War...or she'll wear it like a yoke, like a plow horse who toils under the sun with all his might, digging ever deeper furrows of discontent.

I watch her slumping shoulders lift and her stride lengthen as she transitions into a marching walk, the kind of walk she expects from me. I think I know what she will choose. And no one will see it coming, not even Clarissa, who fumbles for her car keys and wipes the sweat from her brow and sighs. Sebastian stands beside me, chomping on an apple. He offers me the core of it, perhaps in consolation for my lowly status. No one dares approach him—or us—to beg for a share. Moose and Hershey and Merlin watch from the shade of the run-in as Sebastian glides his hand over my sweaty back. His fingers lightly press into my muscles, testing them and assessing their strength. He knows I'm assessing him as well—the palm of his hand against my skin speaks of a man who has been gentled by time and circumstance. Not broken, but made soft and bendable like the new branches on the giant oak whose shade I covet; soft and bendable like the hundreds of ranch horses he started and trained in Argentina became, before his whispering ways became local legend and tickled the ears of wealthy land barons who courted his talent for their fancy ranches and polo ponies. And yet, to the eye, he appears neither soft nor bendable, but rigid and hard like the old, craggy limbs of the giant oak whose shade I covet. I covet. Can someone bring me some shade?

He eyes me with curiosity, the same way he eyes Clarissa from afar.

"She doesn't know there's a racehorse in there, does she?"

Yes! He feels me and all who have come before me. Like Clarissa, I lift my back and stand a little taller.

"*Hola, Señor Bergalo!*"

Miguel stands at the gate with my lead rope. They exchange words about me in a language that's rapid and rolling and at the end of it, Sebastian shakes his head and chuckles softly.

"Looks like you're moving up, my friend. Take it from me, don't let it go to your head."

He scratches my withers and steps aside as Miguel fastens the lead rope to my halter. I don't know where he's taking me but Sebastian isn't worried, and so neither am I. Before I know it, I'm in the brassy land of Show. Burnished nameplates grace every stall and every halter and the horses themselves are polished to a shine and the air is funky with artificial smells, chemical smells that I can only guess make everything seem cleaner, whiter, or brighter. But there are rotating fans overhead that bring relief to my nostrils and burning hide, and best of all there's a stall just for me. It's bedded with pine shavings up to my fetlocks and topped off with green hay that's soft in my mouth and I'm covered in glorious shade. I eat and lie down and roll onto my side as cool air swirls over me and all that I need, the universe provides.

Sebastian makes his rounds, inspecting each horse for comfort and care. He barks a few orders to the hired hands, who scurry to bring fresh water or pick manure or replenish a dwindling pile of hay. When he's finally satisfied, he turns to leave, but not before peering into my stall and grinning at the sight of me splayed diagonally on the ground. I look up at him adoringly, moving only the muscles of my eye.

"Don't thank me, thank Clarissa. If I had my way, I'd be working you in the round pen every day to move your feet and strengthen your topline and bring you back to your full potential. You're better than this...this," he says, sweeping his hand through the air, "is a fool's paradise."

He arches a dark brow at my indifference and continues down the aisle.

"Sebastian!"

Sebastian halts mid-stride and turns at the sound of his name.

"I'm having some problems with Dante's saddle and I was wondering if you could take a quick look at it. I think his body's changing shape and it's not fitting him quite right." Margaret closes the distance between them and gazes up at him with doe-like eyes that he finds pleasingly dark and adoring. But he's in no mood for Margaret's neediness today, today of all days.

"What's wrong with it?"

"It keeps shifting to the right when I ride."

Sebastian nods and presses a manicured fingertip to his lips as if to hold back a curt reply. He knows it's not the saddle. He knows nine times out of ten that it's the rider who's crooked, but his livelihood depends on keeping show girls happy.

"Is he tacked up?"

"Yes, he's on the cross-ties in the outdoor wash stall. I was going to take him for a hack around the farm, but now I don't know if I should."

As they walk toward Dante, Margaret sidles closer, close enough to brush his arm with hers and she steals a glance at his face to see if he feels what she feels. He pretends not to notice her subtle overtures. There have been many such advances, not just from Margaret, but from other show girls at other barns where he has been in residence through the years. Ten years ago he could think of no other woman but Sofía and such overtures were easily dismissed. Eight years ago, as the mourning of her death gave way to natural longings, he began to indulge in the pleasures offered to him by neglected housewives with expensive horses and too much time. He has since resolved not to stay at any given barn for more than two years. That's about the time it takes for things to get complicated, with tearful declarations of love, or divorce proceedings, or both. To his credit, he won't make promises he can't keep, and therefore he promises nothing. Still, the women come to him. Some for lessons. Some for love. All for nothing but the chance to feel beautiful and talented and utterly consumed by an exotic Latin lover whose way with woman is as masterful as his way with horses. He finds the women very beautiful, but lacking the deep soulfulness that draws him to horses, that drew him to Sofía and her once-feral Baguales mare on a remote *estancia* in the foothills of the Andes. She and her horse, Rosalita, were kindred souls, wild roses with no boundaries, with thorns that drew blood like barbed wire and yet possessed of a deep and ethereal softness that gradually unfurled and blossomed in his calloused, gaucho hands. But his hands have since become soft with money and privilege and his own soul has grown as cold as the steel buckle of the girth he now grasps. He had found—and lost—his *espíritu de inspiración.* Without it, he is much like a Grand Prix horse whose airs above the ground are elegant and impressive but whose eye is dull with repetition and the artifice of it all. Oh, to be as his is! To break loose and gallop full speed into here, into now! But instead he merely tightens Dante's girth a couple of inches to keep Crooked Margret from rolling the saddle and biting the dust.

"That should do it," he says.

Margaret gives him a hero's smile and thanks him with her eyes.

"I knew you'd make it right."

"It's my job," he says dismissively as he ruffles Dante's silvery mane and offers a silent apology for the unbalanced ride ahead. Dante curls his head around just enough to lightly brush Sebastian's arm in a subtle gesture of mutual affection.

"Nonsense! Don't you know you have the magic touch?"

"That all depends on who you ask."

"Well, I think you do!"

"Thank you, Margaret."

She puts her hand at the top of Dante's neck and slides it down until it reaches the edge of Sebastian's palm.

"Care to join me for a quick trail ride?"

He's pretty sure she's not talking about a trail ride, but he feigns ignorance.

"I don't trail ride," he says gruffly.

"Why not?"

"I like wide open spaces. And so do horses."

He knows horses need room to run, to see and to escape any real or imagined threat that may cross our paths and spook us into bolting somewhere, anywhere, in a blind panic. Even so, there are some threats that can't be outrun, like the rogue thunderstorms that sweep in over *Las Pampas* in the early spring, with cyclonic winds that flatten the prairie grass and obliterate the landscape with blinding rains. Such was the storm that overtook Sofía and Sebastian one early April morning. What began as a merry adventure to search for and photograph the dwindling herd of feral Baguales horses that roam the fertile steppes of *Las Pampas* turned into a maelstrom that left his beloved bride of three months crumpled in the grass with a broken neck and her mare, Rosalita, hopelessly tangled in the barbed-wire fence that bordered their neighbor's cattle ranch half a mile down the road.

He flinches at the memory of the searing thunderbolt that struck the ground just a few feet from Rosalita's hooves as they galloped toward home, trying in vain to escape the storm that chased them with a vengeance. From twenty feet behind, Sebastian felt the current of electricity charge the air and skim over his body and heard himself scream Sofía's name as Rosalita reared and Sofía tumbled and the boom swallowed them both in one ravenous bite. He held her broken body in his arms and shielded her from the stinging pellets of hail that followed. Then, he carried his bride home, his cheek clinging to the crown of her long, black hair and his mouth whispering anguish and eternal love into her shuttered ears. His grief was magnified by the sight of Rosalita, whose horse flesh was mangled and tangled in twisted barbed wire from her poll to her tail, surrounded by uncharacteristically somber gauchos who had mercifully spared him the task of ending her misery.

"Well, if you ever change your mind, I'd love to trail ride with you."

Margaret coyly tucks a glossy red curl behind her ear. Sebastian wavers. She's a pretty woman with an exquisite, alabaster complexion and flirty freckles across her nose—and he has need of something that will vanquish the pain that squeezes his chest like a girth pulled to the last hole.

"I have eight horses to train today," he says tersely. "Pleasure is not an option."

Margaret looks stricken and fumbles with Dante's reins, eager to escape before the embarrassment she feels creeps into cheeks already flush with desire. Sebastian softens at the sight and grasps Margaret's hand.

"Thank you for the invitation. Perhaps another time?"

He smiles at her and she exhales relief and collects her pride from the wash stall floor.

Margaret nods. "Sure, just say when and I'll be there." She pulls back her shoulders and tugs on the reins and takes a few steps forward. Sebastian can't help himself.

"Remember, sit evenly on your seat bones!"

"I will," Margaret promises. Dante snorts as he passes by. He knows it's hogwash, too.

Sebastian proceeds to halter a boisterous, three-year-old colt in the back pasture and leads him into the round pen where he deftly moves his feet in both directions with subtle gestures of pressure and release, teaching him not to resist, but to enter into the dance. Today he'll introduce the colt to his first saddle, and he has allotted all the time it will take to make the saddle a bridge that connects this horse and his first human, rather than a barrier between them. He gently slides the saddle on and off the colt's back, and although the colt stiffens at the sensation, Sebastian has already won his trust. It's not the kind of introduction I had at the Old Man's ranch. There, rough stock cowboys carelessly threw a forty-pound, double-skirted Western saddle on my back and cinched it down real quick, then let me buck and run and buck and run until the fright and the fight drained out of me. It would never be our seat of connection; it was my Old Man's personal recliner, where he'd lean back and jam his boots forward and chaw and spit tobacco at my feet. I have a permanent bump on my spine from the constant pressure of an ill-fitting saddle that no one cared to check. It's chock with calcium and the collective memory of men who dominated, not danced, with ranch horses like us whose flanks needed only the lightest, kindest touch to respond with the fullness of our nine-pound hearts. Nine pounds that pulse with an innate desire to run free. And yet we consent to the bridle and reins, the saddle and the crooked seats and so much more because if nothing else, we crave relationship in this unnatural world into which we are thrust. It is an anathema to a horse to be without a herd, even if it is a herd of two, horse and human. We can only hope for one who is mindful of our wild instincts to run, to play, to self-preserve, and to dance the dance of sun and heat and cold and wind and yes, the dance of love. We love!

Right here, right now, I love my stall.

I listen to Sebastian train the colt in a tone of voice that is as smooth and whispering as the gentle breeze that swirls over my head. I wait for Clarissa to come back and see me and grin at my cool and obscene pleasure. She says it all the time, but today I have extra assurance: I really *am* the best horse in the whole world.

9

"Hey Claire! How's Sonny?"

Clarissa's no longer a stranger to the college girls working at the local tack store. They're all equestrians themselves, mostly hunters and jumpers with the occasional student of dressage. Over the course of her last twenty shopping trips, they've come to adopt her as a sort of quirky aunt who's every bit as horse crazy as they are.

"He's doing great. How's Bella?"

"She's getting better. We still have a month of rehab to go."

"She'll come back stronger than ever. I'll keep praying for her."

"Thank you, I appreciate that. How can I help you today?"

"I need a fly mask. One with a nose to protect him from sunburn. The end of his muzzle is turning pink."

Clarissa follows the clerk to the back of the store and snatches a jar of horse muffins from a shelf on the way. She knows I'm a fool for the dark, chewy ones that make my teeth stick together and my tongue roll in my mouth with sweet satisfaction. She's in a hurry today to get what she needs. She also has to shop for a new dress, maybe half a dress after what she just paid for my stall. George is taking her out to dinner tonight. She assumes he wants to make up for his callousness the night before and she's eager to make things right between them. She wishes she'd never let on that she'd taken a fall and vows never to wear her peas on her hip again.

She catches a glimpse of herself in the mirror as she passes the wall of helmets. She smiles at the image reflected back, no longer a stranger in an exotic world of velvet and leather and metal and tan and fleece accouterments that adorn equestrians and their horses. She was proud of having survived those first, awkward visits; her too-tight breeches, her extra-small helmet head, her sweeping ignorance of bits and girths and reins and supplements. The tack shop had become her second home, her guilty pleasure, and she's thankful George never sees the monthly bill. She even smiles at the sight of her dun-brown hair pressed down from the heat and humidity. It's only that way because she has a horse. She has a horse! It's all she can do to contain her joy at the thought that there's something—no, not something—but a living being who allows her to be as she is, without judgment or expectation of anything but kindness and cookies. Clarissa's very kind. And she always brings me cookies. I am never disappointed!

The clerk selects a fly mask from several different styles and hands it to Clarissa.

"This one has a long nose and darts around the eyes so it'll be more comfortable for him."

"Perfect!" Clarissa exclaims.

"Anything else?"

"Not today. I'll come back when I have time to browse."

"Going riding?"

"No, shopping."

"Bummer."

"I know. But it's too hot to ride anyway."

"You can always just hack the trails."

"Yes, but I have a dinner date."

"Someone special?"

Clarissa laughs. "Yeah, my husband."

"Oh, I thought you meant *date*, like a romantic date."

Pangs of regret and longing grip Clarissa's heart. It had been over a year since she and George had gone on a romantic date, one that actually made them remember what drew them together in the first place. Where had the time gone? Where had they gone? That girl in the mirror, the one who once thrived on domestic bliss and the hum and drum of everyday life, where had she gone? I know. Clarissa knows.

She's gone riding.

"Don't forget to pray for Bella," the clerk says as she hands Clarissa her bag.

"You got it," Clarissa says and she means it. Prayer is the one thing Clarissa can offer back to the young women who welcomed her into their pony club. She lacks their breath of experience and knowledge, but she can pray for the horses they train and ride and love with a devotion that drives them to work long hours at the local tack store to help afford their keep. It's also the one thing that keeps her hope alive that she might someday feel what they feel—passionate and vibrant and free—not just on riding days, but every day.

For now, that hope is ephemeral, something she fleetingly holds in her heart like the smallest of birds in a soft hand, whose heartbeat quivers and thrums with the anticipation of being released into the wild, blue sky.

She leaves the tack shop with a quiet resolve to try to rekindle the romance between her and George, the boy who carried her books and ate her scorched meals and first loved her with a tender passion and intense devotion that made her blush and sigh, and so God-awfully happy she hadn't become a nun.

When she arrives at the mall, it feels as foreign to her as the tack store once had been. She doesn't know where to shop for a dress for a grown woman; the clothing on the walls and racks seems skewed toward school girls or quietly despairing housewives who don't seem to know they've aged out of plunging necklines and elastic fabrics that hide nothing—least of all their fear of being unbeautiful on the inside. She darts in and out of the expensive boutiques, then heads to the dress department in one of the big anchor stores that promises twenty percent off just for crossing the threshold. George has always been a tactile man—he craves the feel of softness on his fingertips and so she shops with hers, plying the fabrics and drawn to anything in blue, the color she knows attracts his eye and heart and admiration.

She eventually tries on a breezy, pale blue dress with aquamarine flourishes stamped on a delicate overlay of silk. She twirls in the mirror and the fabric swirls around her like the sea, and she smiles contentedly. This is the one. She pins her hope on it and pays ninety-nine dollars less twenty percent, a bargain for a chance to resurrect sunken treasure from the cool, dark depths of indifference and neglect.

She dashes to the cosmetics counter and selects a lipstick in a lush shade of pink that reminds her of the peonies that bloomed in the front garden of the little house she and George lived in as newlyweds. She doesn't know where the memories are coming from, this floodgate that has suddenly burst open as she stands on shifting sand with a blue dress and a golden tube of lipstick in hand. Perhaps it's that intuition that all humans have, just like horses, when our lives as we know them are endangered. The difference is that most humans will stand still and take the fall, like paralytics or martyrs or hapless heroes, while horses will rear and kick and fight or flee lest we perish before our time.

Her subconscious mind thinks a blue dress and a tube of pink lipstick might save her. She collects an arsenal of memories to bring to the table. She doesn't even know she's doing it, but that's the way of instinct, of survival. The will to live is as natural as the air we breathe; whether she'll fight with all she's got or just stand there looking pretty is ultimately Clarissa's choice.

That evening, she dresses with great care, mindful of every button, every seam, and the way her diamond-and-sapphire earrings hang from the lobes of her ears. George had surprised her with them on their last night at sea on a cruise around the eastern Caribbean. He said they reminded him of the ocean and the way the stars shine on the water at twilight—and that whenever she wore them, he would remember that night and how much he loved his nautical bride. That was just over three years ago. She hadn't worn them much since then, and not even once in the past year. The barn was no place for diamond earrings that dangle and can get caught on helmet straps or lead ropes or look just plain silly when mucking stalls. Clarissa knows this from experience. She's already lost one diamond earring and a gold hoop. She hasn't fessed up to George just yet, knowing it will make him regret giving such extravagant gifts in the first place. He never did do well with things that get broken or lost. Clarissa is no exception.

She gives her hair, plumped with hairspray, a final smoothing over and forces a smile at her reflection. She wishes she'd had time to polish her nails; they were dull and ragged with tears at the cuticles but at least they're clean, she consoles herself. She heads out the door and drives twenty minutes to a trendy French restaurant near George's office. She didn't like having to meet him there. But he warned her he might have to go back to work and she was loath to bicker about it before the night even began. Clarissa had never been to *Chez Amelie*. It had a reputation for being swanky and modern and stupidly expensive. But it was George's pick and she didn't want to seem ungrateful.

Diminutive chandeliers cast a seductive, golden glow over each table. The *maître' d'hôtel* escorts Clarissa to a round booth in the corner where George greets her with an appreciative grin. She gives him a moment to look her over before shimmying into the booth beside him.

"You look beautiful," he says. The words hang wistfully in the air between them. He leans over and kisses her on the cheek, then creates a little more distance between them than there was in the first place. "I like that color on you. New dress?"

"Yes. It was on sale," she feels compelled to add.

George laughs. "It's okay to shop for yourself instead of Sonny all the time."

From the glimmer in his eyes, she's pretty sure he means everything he says. Just the same, there's an unexpected surge of adrenaline pumping through her veins. She takes a sip of water and tries to relax and bask in his admiration.

"I try not to be frivolous. We have how many more years on Gabriella's student loan?"

"I paid it off last month. I meant to tell you that."

"Good thing, because this place is outrageous. Nineteen dollars for a salad with some goat cheese sprinkled on it?" Clarissa shakes her head as she peruses the prices on the menu. George reaches out and gently takes the menu from her hands.

"How about if we just order a nice bottle of wine and a shrimp cocktail to start?"

Clarissa smiles. "Sure, why not."

"Red or white?"

"Whatever you like. I'll drink anything after the day I've had."

"Tell me about it," George coaxes as he gives the sommelier a discreet nod.

"First of all, I get to the barn this morning and it's already ninety degrees and there's not a single drop of fly spray on Sonny. His eyes are a gunky mess and he's standing in the sun dripping buckets of sweat because the other horses won't let him in the run-in."

"Why is that?"

"Well, herd dynamics I guess, but still...."

George swirls and inhales the ruby-colored wine the steward has just poured, then takes a sip and rolls it back over his tongue. He nods his approval and the steward pours the wine into two crystal glasses with deep, round bowls.

"And then," Clarissa continues, "I get reprimanded—twice!—for letting Sonny graze on the grass along the driveway. I shared my concerns about the run-in and the fly spray with Bridget. Let's just say she wasn't very nice to me, but hey, at least I know where I stand! So—"

Clarissa stops short of saying anything about moving me into a luxurious stall that's fifty times the price of a goat cheese salad.

"So, what?"

"So—that's why I had a bad day."

"Sounds traumatic."

Clarissa laughs. So does George.

"I know, it's ridiculous. Let's just forget about all of that. How was your day?"

George hedges and his jaw flutters. "I just found out I'll be in charge of a new project overseas. I might have to do a bit more traveling than usual to meet with global investors."

"Where?"

"Paris. Want to come?"

"No. But invite me to Yellowstone and I'll be there."

"You wouldn't leave your horse for that either."

"Try me," Clarissa teases. "I like wide open spaces."

George rolls the stem of his wine glass between his fingertips. He stares at the wine in the bowl and swirls it and watches curvy legs of liquid trickle down the crystal in languid streams. He holds the glass up to the light of the chandelier and gets lost in the ruby glow.

"What's the matter?" she probes.

"How's your hip?" George counters.

"It's fine. How's yours?" She fidgets with the napkin on her lap and confronts George with her eyes.

"Clarissa,"

"What, George?"

"How's the wine?"

"It's fine, too."

"Cheers," George says, and extends his glass toward hers.

"What are we toasting to?"

"Clarity," he pronounces.

She thinks he might be referring to the wine, but she's not sure.

"What do you mean?"

Clarissa takes a long, deep sip, longer and deeper than fine wine allows. The sommelier glares at her disapprovingly.

"I couldn't handle seeing you hurt last night."

"It was a stupid accident, it's not going to happen again."

"That's why they're called accidents, Claire. You don't know when they're going to happen. Or happen again."

Clarissa sighs. She can't argue with his logic.

"You know how I feel about people I love getting...damaged. I've already had too much of that kind of heartache in my life."

"George, I ride at a lurch. That's not nearly fast enough to get brain damaged."

"Horseback riding is more dangerous than riding motorcycles, did you know that?"

"So I've heard. But you've met Sonny, you know what kind of horse he is. He's very sweet and gentle and he wants to take care of me."

"He took really good care of you yesterday, didn't he?"

"That was my fault, not his."

George arches a brow and waits for an explanation.

"Apparently you're not supposed to trot back to the barn. Now I know better."

"You were trotting when this happened?"

"Actually, we were cantering. But only for a hot second."

"Until you fell off?"

"Pretty much." Clarissa bites her bottom lip and looks away.

George shakes his head. He takes a lusty sip of wine but the sommelier gives him a pass. He gazes into Clarissa's eyes. His focus shifts to her earrings as they catch a flicker of candlelight. He pauses, mesmerized by the sight of them.

"This isn't working for us," he finally says in a distant whisper.

Clarissa's eyes sting with the threat of tears.

"I love you, Clarissa. But I miss you and I'm lonely and I can't stop worrying that something's going to happen to you and ruin everything we've planned. I keep hoping this is just a phase you're going through, something you need to get out of your system, like your violin lessons and your antique book collecting and making jewelry for dogs, but instead you seem to be getting sucked into this horse thing deeper and deeper and it's a bottomless pit. I feel like it's only a matter of time before something bad happens."

"But what if something good happens? What if I get really good at riding horses and I become ridiculously fulfilled and live happily ever after?"

"And you can't do that with me?"

"I didn't say that. What I mean is, it's—it's like wine," she says, caressing the rim of her glass. "It's beautiful and complex and it makes you feel happy to drink of it and learn about it and share it with people you love."

"But I don't share your love of horses."

"I don't share your love of learning about wine," Clarissa says pointedly. "But I put up with your Wine Club."

George flinches. His expression hardens.

"Maybe there wouldn't be a Wine Club if there wasn't a horse."

A waiter brings a shrimp cocktail to the table. The shrimp are outlandishly plump and hang on the rim of the bowl of cocktail sauce like fleshy flower petals. For a moment they both stare at their mutant size.

Clarissa finishes her wine in two gulps and sets the empty glass on the tablecloth. A droplet escapes and bleeds into the fabric, saturating the fibers and turning them pink, the same deep pink of her lipstick that glosses her mouth with useless prettiness.

"What do you want me to do, George?"

"It's up to you."

"No, you have to say it. Say you want me to give up my horse."

"No, I want you to give up *riding* your horse. You can even bring Sonny home if you want. I'll fence in a pasture and build you a run-in. We have plenty of room. And he'll never want for fly spray or shade or green grass."

Clarissa shakes her head. The very thought of never riding another horse—of riding me—is an anathema to every bone in her body. Every bone that might fracture or break. Every bone that moves her flesh and every bone that enables her to trot with joy beside me or grips the reins that guide me or sits in a pair astride me as we cover vast territories of grief and shame and yearning for a place to be free of memories George knows nothing about; long-repressed memories of being prey, the same way horses are, to the desires of predators who are fleeter or stronger or both. She knows what it is to be ambushed in the night, to have ravenous flesh bear down on her and take what is hers alone to give; to not make a sound for fear of endangering others in the herd, to sacrifice her body to save them from a similar fate. She knows the one who came for her would have come for her younger sister as well had she not stood in the breach. After that first deed was done, she knew she could never be a nun, a pure and holy virgin bride of Christ; in the same way, I knew after six years with the Old Man that I would never again be sound enough to race the wind like the sires and dams who came before me.

Whether or not she realizes it just yet, we're kindred spirits, Clarissa and me. She knows what it is to be manhandled and used up and cast aside. She knows what it is to startle and spin and bolt at the merest threat. She knows what it is to exist in spooky silence, unsure of what might spring forth and attack her next. If you ask me, she's more horse than human; skittish and flighty and prone to run. Our Old Mans were brutal, with hard hands and inhumane hearts. But she can't tell George that. She can only do what horses do to escape pain and violence and the feeling of vulnerability: move her feet—or mine—as fast as she possibly can.

"I can't do that. I want to ride. I need to ride!" She hears the panic rising in her voice but can do nothing to stop it.

George nods slowly and somberly. He finishes the remnant of wine in his glass and scoots to the edge of the booth.

"I'm sorry to hear that, Claire. I really wanted you to say yes."

Clarissa pleads with her eyes for him to stay, but he rises to his feet, peels two fifty-dollar bills from his wallet, and sets them beneath his empty glass.

"I've been given the option of living in Paris for a couple of months to get this project off the ground. I think maybe it's a good idea."

Clarissa swallows hard and forces herself to lift her chin.

"I'm sure they have fabulous wine clubs there."

"*Bien sûr!*" George says. But of course!

And then he was gone.

She forces herself to sit still, even to pour herself a second glass of wine lest she incur the pity of her fellow diners and the disdain of the sommelier by trailing George out the door. Of all things, she will not allow herself to be pitied. She prefers to let them think she's married to a very busy man who has been called away on a very important matter. And so she lingers for over an hour in her pretty blue dress and pink lipstick, settles the bill, and lets the waiter keep the remaining twenty-four dollars in exchange for his complicit silence regarding the mascara stains on her starched, white napkin.

She leaves with her head held high and nods goodnight to the sommelier, who by now has softened at the sight of her. He pretends not to know what has just transpired, though he's seen hundreds of such breakups over the course of his career. The more expensive the wine, the more likely the husband is to leave. He may be a liar and a cheater, but at least no one will accuse him of being cheap.

Far from intoxicated but not entirely sober, she drives to the only place she can bear to be. I hear the tick-tick-hum of Clarissa's car as it churns up the driveway. Evening has ushered in a gentle breeze and I clamber to my feet, feeling cool and refreshed and eager for turnout in the field. Soon, Clarissa appears at my stall door.

"Well look at you, Mr. Fancy Pants," she coos. "You're up to your knees in hay and bedding, how do you like that, huh?"

I nicker to her, anxious to bust out of this little box and to run free and eat moist, green grass. My feet prance at the doorway. Grab my halter, Clarissa, let's go!

"I thought Miguel was supposed to turn you out," she mutters, already dreading having to speak to Bridget about that in the morning. "Come on, buddy, let's go."

I lower my head and shove my face into the halter. It's all I can do to stand politely while she fastens the buckle and clips on the rope. She leads me down the barn aisle as other horses, the show horses, voice their complaint. They want green grass and freedom too. But their owners will hear nothing of it lest their glossy show coats turn muddy from a good roll or their feet bruise on stones or they come up lame from too much horseplay. Clarissa telegraphs an apology to each one of them as we pass by. It's meager consolation but they accept it and go back to cribbing or weaving—the vices of too much energy and confinement—or simply resume munching on hay.

Her ankles twist and bend in her high heels as we walk over gravel to my pasture. She smells like flowers and her hair is bigger too, but I'd know my Clarissa anywhere from the kindness she vibrates and the breaths of wonder she takes whenever she's with me. Still, she exudes an air of sadness that lends a quiver to her voice when she sets me free at the gate.

"There you go, Sonny. Have a good night. Make good choices!"

It's what she used to say to Gabriella when she was a teenager on the loose. She wonders how she's going to tell her that her father has chosen to take an extended leave of absence...are they separated, she wonders? Is that what she is, newly separated? And how will she ever tell Gabriella that she chose a horse over her father? What kind of choice is that! What makes a choice good, she wonders? Good for whom and for what noble purpose? Her head swims and she's not sure if it's from the wine or the bedlam in her brain.

"Hello, Clarissa."

Sebastian is close enough to smell the flowers on Clarissa's exposed skin. She startles. I watch with a wary eye even as I graze, making sure no one else steps from the dusky shadows the way that he just did. Clarissa spins, prepared to bolt.

"Oh my God, you scared me!" She clutches her chest and glares at him. "What are you doing here?"

"I always do night check on the horses. Miguel and his hombres are usually a six-pack in by this time. They can't be counted on to get the job done."

"I didn't know that."

"Let it be our secret then, yes?"

Clarissa nods and exhales adrenaline and relief.

"Surely you're not riding dressed like that." His eyes graze over the landscape of her body. Clarissa's breath quickens but she stands perfectly still. "You look very pretty."

"Thank you. I went out to dinner with my husband."

Sebastian merely cocks his head and studies her face. He notices the smudges of mascara at the corners of her dark green eyes and a pale, jagged line where a tear has cut through rosy blush.

"I wanted to make sure Sonny got turned out. I was afraid they might forget about him, seeing that he's just an ordinary horse in a barn full of show horses."

"There's no such thing as an ordinary horse," Sebastian says and smiles. It's not the cocky, practiced smile she's used to seeing and she's struck by the difference. "I would have noticed and turned him out."

"I appreciate that. I have a lesson with Bridget in the morning and he needs to get his yahoos out. The last thing I need is another rodeo."

They hover in a moment of silence. He senses her vulnerability. He has sweet Argentinian wine in his cottage at the far end of the property where rows of privet hedges hem in his indiscretions. If it were Margaret, or Camilla, or Penny, it might be different. But it's Clarissa. She smells like jasmine and acts like prey and his head is swimming too, swimming with choices.

"Well, have a good evening, *Señora*," Sebastian says as he takes a half-step backward.

"*Señorita*," Clarissa corrects him.

"Excuse me?"

"*Señorita*. First my horse dumps me. Now my husband."

Clarissa shrugs and smiles weakly. She can't believe she just said that, but for some reason, she doesn't care. Saying it aloud makes it a simple fact of life, one she has to deal with.

"I'm sorry." Sebastian stuffs his hands in the pockets of his jeans, fighting the urge to touch the curve of her tanned shoulder in a gesture of sympathy. "Give it some time. Maybe he just needs time to think."

"Maybe," Clarissa allows, even though she knows better. She's surprised and intrigued by this alternate version of Sebastian, the one in frayed blue jeans and scuffed boots and a black tee shirt that clings to his muscular chest and is tucked into a narrow waistband. His dark, wavy hair ruffles in the warm breeze and his eyes have lost their dark conceit. He looks like a ranch hand. If she didn't know better, that's what she'd think he was. Not just from the way he's dressed, but by the casual way he moves and speaks and looks at her with chivalrous concern. It makes her want to cry. No, it makes her want to run.

"I gotta go," she blurts.

"So do I," he says. "Don't worry, I'll make sure Sonny gets turned out at night."

"Thanks, but I got it. You have show horses to handle."

Sebastian bristles.

"Is that all you think I'm about?"

"Umm, yeah, pretty much."

"So you think you know me?"

"I didn't say that, I just know they say you're a famous trainer. And that you have quite a fan club...of women."

"I'm just a horseman."

"If you say so."

"Don't be so quick to judge—me or the horses," he growls as he begins to walk toward the show barn with a lengthy stride.

"What are you getting so mad about?"

Sebastian stops in his tracks. He has no idea why he's so riled, or maybe he does as he recalls how far he's come from his humble beginnings as a carefree gaucho on the grassy plains of Argentina. Life was simple. Horses were horses. Women loved their men and men loved their women in cozy beds or under the canopy of stars on nights just like this one, ripe with the scent wild roses wafting on a sultry breeze and jasmine rising from Clarissa's tanned skin. There were no blue ribbons or bragging rights or brassy nameplates or rhinestoned women begging his time and attention. There was but one extraordinary woman, a horsewoman, kind and humble and brave and beautiful—like the jilted *señorita* who stares him down this very moment. Only Clarissa has no idea that she's any of those things.

Sebastian turns on his heels. Clarissa's eyes are wide with the expectation of a cool and biting response. Instead, Sebastian's voice is soft and mild as he fleetingly turns to face her once more.

"In every show horse is the horse that nature intended. What is true for horses is also true for humans." He feels no need to explain himself further. "*Buenos noches, señorita.*"

"Good night," Clarissa says in a voice that's drowned by the whinnying of horses in a neighboring field. One of their own is lost or missing. She knows the feeling and can't help but wonder if Sebastian knows it too.

By the time she gets home, everyday traces of George are gone. His razor and shaving cream, gone. His weekend ball cap, gone. His multivitamins, gone. His cell phone charger, gone. His favorite Chateau Lagiole corkscrew made from the horn of the African Zebu, gone. He's left behind a sheet of paper with contact information for the hotel where he's staying until the end of the week and for *Les Jardins de la Villa*, his Parisian home away from home. He promises to keep in touch. She stares at his messy penmanship, something she never did understand about a man as meticulous about everything else. She thinks back to how she used to type his research papers for him in college and extract a kiss for every word she couldn't decipher. They kissed a lot in those days. She can't remember the last time they kissed like they did then....

She tosses her car keys on the table and powers on her laptop. She wants to know more about the hotel where George will be staying, what it looks like, where it's located, and the decor of the rooms, if only to imagine him safely tucked in at night.

Preferably alone and miserable without her. Really, George? Is this necessary?

But what if he's not alone? Or miserable without her?

She works herself into a quiet frenzy and before long, her fingers wander along the keyboard and type in the address for Crown Ridge. She migrates to the *About Us* tab and scrolls past the picture of Bridget holding her two Pomeranians astride her six-figure dressage horse, Angus. She notices the squinty tension in Angus' dark brown eyes and scrolls back up for a closer look. I can tell you about Angus just from living across the aisle from him for one day. Luckily for him, he's merely a head weaver, as Bridget would never stand for a horse that cribs on her varnished walls, or a horse with sawed front teeth that might look less than picture perfect when she hauls back on the reins, seeking just the right contact; pounds of pressure that cause his mouth to gape and his teeth to flash as they *passage* in elegant circles. He weaves to release the pressure that never seems to be released, pressure that builds up in his head and neck after being held with his nose pinned to his chest for too many practiced hours. He weaves to relieve the life-sucking boredom he feels at never being allowed to break loose and run in the fields like we do. The view outside his Dutch door is spectacular. Rolling fields and dark green grass and an occasional dandelion that creeps in when Bridget's not looking. He wants it all, Angus does. What horse wouldn't? And so he weaves, the motion itself a denial and refutation of his daily grind. It is a shout from the depths of his equine soul that says: I can't believe this is happening to me!

Poor Angus. He is pleased to perform. He will do whatever is asked or required of him. All he begs in return is a taste of the freedom that belongs to the horse.

And so he weaves.

Clarissa scrolls further down the page to the place where Sebastian's photo appears in a tidy square with a short biography below. She reads it slowly and carefully, searching for a clue that might explain his passion for horses over people, the way his gaze turns distant at the most unexpected times, the odd mix of cockiness and awkwardness he displays around her, but not around the show girls who bring him expensive bottles of California wine and home-baked cookies and three-course meals in search of his guilty pleasure, all the while wishing it was them. But all it says is that he hails from *Las Pampas* in Argentina, and trained polo ponies for some of Argentina's most prestigious farms for fifteen years before coming to the United States ten years ago. She scrunches her nose at the last sentence: in his spare time, he likes to work leather. She finds it an odd bit of trivia, but supposes it's akin to cribbing or weaving for stress relief in the high-stakes world of performance horses.

She sinks backward into the sofa and stares at his photograph. Upon closer inspection, his eyes are squinty with the same kind of tension she sees in Angus. She lowers the lid of her laptop and quietly snaps it shut. Raindrops from a rogue summer storm begin to pommel the skylights overhead and although they're black with night, she raises her eyes and searches the darkness. Only then does she allow her tears to fall freely, accompanied by sobs that are drowned out by the pounding rain. She had learned from the time she was a young girl to never let her cries be heard. Cajoling words and a manly hand across her mouth had trained her well for such mortification. A quiet girl was a very good girl. And now, she supposed a quiet wife was a very good wife. Only she doesn't feel like being quiet. She feels like galloping full speed on the back of a horse with a wave of her hat and a mighty yee-haw into a vast, open field that leads to nowhere and everywhere at the same time. So this is the price extracted for seeking such wild abandon. Abandonment for abandonment. The irony isn't lost on her and she smiles a rueful smile and tastes her tears.

Eventually, she falls asleep where she is as the moon rises and remnants of raindrops glint on the glass panels above, just like the grass where I graze glistens under moonlight. I feel Clarissa's pain as it spirals into the whorl of our connectedness. I lower my head and move my feet toward the sweet clover that will be even sweeter for the rain. Just keep moving your feet, Clarissa. The sweetness is there. It is yours for the taking!

10

"You've got that horse in the snaffle bit, right?"

"Yes ma'am!" Clarissa says as she leads me through the opening in the hedgerow and into the freshly dragged arena. The rainstorm from the night before has created near-perfect footing. Soft, but not too soft. Deep, but not too deep. I like the way it feels under my hooves. It's excellent footing for trotting and cantering, if I were inclined to trot or canter. But I'm not.

Bridget gives me a thorough going over with a sweep of her eyes and stops at my bitted mouth, just like I hoped she would.

"Claire!"

"What?"

Bridget throws her hands on her narrow hips and frowns.

"The bit is on backward."

"What do you mean backward?"

Bridget sighs and begins to undo the buckles and straps on my headstall. She takes a lead rope and loops it around my neck.

"Hold him while I fix it."

Bridget doesn't explain what Clarissa did wrong, she has no time for that. Her hands flurry and twist and moments later, the headstall is back on my face and the bit is in my mouth and I feel better—for now.

"Okay, today we're going to see how your twenty-meter circles are going. You've been practicing, right?"

"Well, not so much in the heat."

"Horses get used to the heat, Claire. You have to stop babying your horse."

Clarissa doesn't disagree; for a moment she wonders if it might even be true. She simply nods and climbs the mounting block, then sits in the saddle with a lightness that makes me happy to carry her. She fumbles with reins that are now connected to my mouth. I feel her reluctance to lift and use them, but I trust her to be gentle.

"Don't throw away the reins like that, Claire. You have to take up contact."

I flinch at the word. I know exactly what it means.

"Take him down the center line and turn left."

I'm all too happy to walk forward, away from Bridget's shrill voice.

"He's walking like he's drunk! Straighten him out!"

Clarissa closes her legs and tries to ride me between her knees. I do my best to please her but I'm slightly crooked by design, my body having compensated over the years for being ridden by beginners like a bicycle.

"Okay, let's take up a rising trot."

Clarissa cues me by lifting and giving the inside rein, just like one of her favorite Western clinicians on television taught her to do.

"Stop throwing the reins away! Why are you doing that?"

"That's how Western riders cue their horses for an upward transition," Clarissa calls back.

"Well, today you're practicing classical equitation. Shorten your reins and send him forward with your legs! Not your hands!"

I can feel the temperature rising, both in the air and in Clarissa's body as she puts her legs on me to drive me forward into a trot. I respond with a handsome Western Pleasure jog, long and low, like Beth taught me to carry myself many years ago. Clarissa smiles and I feel her seat bones sink and relax. She finally starts to breathe.

"What is that?" Bridget yells as we approach.

"It's a jog. A Western version of the trot."

"That's unacceptable. Pick up his head. Add leg. More leg!"

Clarissa does what she's told. The bit bangs me in the mouth. I toss my head with displeasure. Western displeasure. I feel a rodeo coming on...

I quicken my step but it's clumsy and erratic as I pull myself along with my forelegs.

"Circle at letter A!"

Clarissa bends me around her inside leg and holds me in with her outside leg. I do my best to keep my balance; I have no choice but to drop my shoulder. Our circle disintegrates into a spiral.

"Okay, halt!"

Clarissa tucks her seat and brings me to a stop. Bridget closes the distance between us. She peers at me from below her ice-blue visor and shakes her head vigorously. The crows in the trees around us squawk like Bridget's handmaids.

"This horse has no engine—and he's definitely ring sour! Let's get him in the field like we talked about last week. Have you ever ridden Sonny with spurs?"

Clarissa blots the sweat from her forehead.

"No, I haven't." She stiffens like a stick at the thought. The mental picture she projects makes me stiffen too.

"Follow me," Bridget commands.

The three of us traverse over a winding path of woodchips and gravel until we reach a pasture that's mostly flat and bordered by a split-rail fence.

"Let's see how he goes in here, first without the spurs," Bridget says as she folds her arms over her chest. "Go ahead and walk one lap, then pick up a trot when you get to the gate."

Clarissa nods and sends me forward. I like the openness and the smell of grass and I naturally move out with higher and longer steps.

"That's better!" Bridget nods her approval. "Now ask him to trot!"

Clarissa cues me and I trot with more energy than before. But not much more. It's hot and it's buggy. I swish my tail in defense against a greenhead that dive bombs my flank.

"It's okay if he gets annoyed. He has to learn that when you say trot, you mean it! More leg!"

More leg gets us nowhere fast. Bridget intercepts us and fastens a pair of spurs to Clarissa's riding boots. She gives her a short lesson on how to use them, taking her by the ankle and pressing the prickly spur against my side in rhythmic pulses.

"Okay, let's see if this works. Go!"

Clarissa asks for a trot and I comply. But this time, she doesn't wait for me to volunteer more energy. She defaults to the spurs and as I feel them dig into my sides, I am all at once in a rough stock barn with the Old Man flapping his legs against my barrel, then mercilessly digging with long, sharp rowels that rake my skin and break open my flesh while he pushes me harder and faster...faster...faster!

"Faster! Make him go!" Bridget yells.

Pressure builds. Sensations deepen. The cellular memory of my skin erupts.

And then it happens. A greenhead attacks my underbelly and as it lands and bites amid the already rising chaos of my right brain, I buck and spin. Clarissa yelps and Bridget shouts.

"Heels down! Sit back! Grab that horn!"

Clarissa does all three things and manages to stay on.

"Hey!" she bellows as I come to my left-brain senses. "What the hell, Sonny!"

Bridget rushes over and takes Sonny by the reins.

"You okay?"

"Yeah, I'm okay." Clarissa breaks into a grin. "I stayed on!"

"Give me those spurs," Bridget says and grabs Clarissa's ankle. "He doesn't like them."

Bridget removes the spurs from Clarissa's boots and I snort with relief. She steps back and eyes me with aversion. Her voice is sweet but her teeth are bared.

"I'm sorry, Claire, but I can't teach you anything on a horse like this. He's lazy and he bucks. You need a more suitable mount. I have a nice mare you can lease."

Clarissa's jaw drops. "But this is my horse!"

"I'd get rid of him if I were you. He needs a more experienced rider and a firmer hand."

"I'm not getting rid of my horse. Who does that?"

"Plenty of riders who want to move up in their career and abilities. He'll be a good horse for someone, just not for you. I can give you the name of a good horse trader."

Clarissa scratches me on the withers and dismounts.

"Are you saying you don't want to give me lessons anymore?"

"Of course I do, but not on this horse. No trainer wants a student to come off on her watch. It's bad for business." Bridget mindlessly spins the rowel of a spur like a pinwheel.

Clarissa squints at Bridget. She can't fathom how a woman who spends so much time with horses could actually dislike them so much.

"Feel free to use the wash stall in the show barn to cool him down. Technically, you're entitled to use it for the next thirty days."

Bridget bares her teeth again and Clarissa manages a tight-lipped smile.

"Oh, and let me know if you want to meet my mare. I think you'd like her." Bridget glances at her watch. "I have another lesson in the ring in five minutes. Sure you're okay?"

"I'm fine. I'm gonna hang out and let him graze for a while."

"Not in the bit!"

Clarissa bristles. "I'm pretty sure it won't kill him."

"You'll be sorry."

"I doubt it."

Now, it's Clarissa who bares her teeth and gazes boldly into Bridget's scandalized face. She doesn't see Bridget flinch but I do. Body language is my specialty. And for once, I actually like seeing Clarissa act like a predator instead of prey.

As soon as Bridget stomps off, she turns her attention to me.

"Wanna tell me what that was all about?"

I lower my head to graze. She sighs and allows me to reach for the tall grass at the foot of the fence. Without Bridget's shrill voice saturating the atmosphere, we can hear the sound of rushing water just beyond the stand of white trees at the edge of the property. The river is high from last night's deluge, and with the river come greenheads—torpedo-shaped flies the size of human thumbs with colossal, green eyes and greedy fangs that shred horse flesh with just one bite. Clarissa has never seen one before. Beth's farm was high and dry, not like Crown Ridge, whose lushness in the lower pastures is a gift from the river—a gift bundled with a host of bloodsucking things.

Another greenhead appears and buzzes around my belly. Clarissa has me by the reins so I swat it with my tail. It darts to the other side where Clarissa stands with a hand on her hip, ready to school me on proper horse-and-rider etiquette.

"Ooh! Ooh! Ooh!" she squeals as the drone of wings fills the air and a greenhead dive bombs my flank once more. I swish my tail and stomp my feet and throw a buck as it lands and bites. Clarissa drops the reins and slaps my ribs.

"Got it!" she says, then glances at her bloodied hand. "Ew!"

She wipes her palm on the grass, then tilts her head and studies me. "Is that it, Sonny? You bucked because you got bit?"

She runs her hand over my barrel, then glides it underneath, stopping at the welt. It's already the size of a horse muffin and throbs with heat. She drops to one knee and peers at my belly, just to be sure. There's a telltale, bloody hole where fangs punctured my skin.

"Geez, you got nailed!"

Thanks for noticing, Clarissa. May I please go back to grazing?

"Come on, let's get some salve on that. Oh, and by the way—looks like we're gonna need a new trainer."

I snort with pleasure as she sends me a mental picture of Bridget blotted with a big fat letter X. She clucks and pulls me off the grass and we march uphill with purposeful strides. As she leads me into the wash stall and hoses me off, she decides we need an authentic Western trainer, maybe one who can school her in showmanship as well. She sprays a steady stream of cold water over my bug bite. It helps to dull the pain. I snort again with relief and nudge her with my head. A carrot would make my world complete.

"Not now, Sonny, let me finish! You'll feel better, I promise." Despite the overhead fans, the show barn is hot enough to melt the peppermints in Clarissa's pocket. She scrapes the excess water off my skin and washes my face with a cold, wet towel. When she's done, she offers me a hot, gooey peppermint. Still, it feels smooth and cool in my mouth.

She leads me into my stall and opens the top half of the Dutch door so I can look out over the arena if I choose. I swivel my butt around and take a long drink of water from a pail that hangs from the bars of my stall. There's a fresh pile of hay in the corner. I'm in no hurry to eat it, knowing it's mine. All mine!

"I'll come back to see you tonight," Clarissa says and kisses me on the cheek. She ruffles my forelock and tells me I'm the best horse in the whole world, no matter what Bridget thinks. There's determination in her footsteps as her boots click down the center aisle of the barn. It isn't long before I drop to my knees and roll onto my side in a cushy nest of pine shavings that cling to my damp hair. I sprawl and inhale their woodsy fragrance as the pounding rhythm of horses jumping fences drifts into my ears. I rest easy knowing my work is done for the day. But Clarissa's is just beginning.

She steps out of the barn and notices a clutch of show girls huddled outside of Bridget's office. Their voices are hushed but excited, like a brood of hens scratching and pecking at their feed. Clarissa hopes to slip past them until Carla pops out of the poor man's wash stall with Hershey in hand and makes it impossible for her to avoid being seen.

"Claire!" she bellows, "Where have you been? And what's up with Sonny's new digs?"

The show girls stop clucking and twist their necks in Claire's direction. They're as eager for her answer as Carla is, who waves her over as she hitches Hershey to a fence post to dry.

"Come over here, I want to talk to you," she says sternly.

Clarissa has no choice but to run a gauntlet of beady stares on her way to Carla's side. She thinks it would be rude to not acknowledge her fellow boarders—though they don't seem the least bit interested in acknowledging her. They're scratching for tasty morsels, and today Clarissa is fodder for a whole meal.

"Good morning, ladies," she musters as she lifts her chin and flattens her stomach.

One twitches a smile. Another bobs her head. A third offers a hello so thin she barely moves her bright pink lips. Only Margaret returns what sounds like a friendly greeting.

"Hi, Claire!" she says with a toothy grin.

Claire quickens her pace and scurries past them before they can peck.

Carla plops on a sunlit bench and pats the space beside her. Clarissa sits and wilts as the sun beats on the top of her head and Carla's big, brown eyes squint with displeasure.

"You know I like you, right?"

"I think so. Yes, I do."

"So I'm gonna give it to you straight, okay?"

"Okay."

"What's this I hear you're making trouble around the barn?"

"Me? I'm making trouble?"

"I heard you had words with Miguel. And that you got caught hand-grazing Sonny along the driveway. And that you've been complaining about the care and the other horses in Sonny's field."

"Oh my gosh, that's so not true. I mean, parts of it are true, but it's not like you make it sound!"

"So, what's not true?"

Clarissa rubs the base of her throat in an effort to dispel the lump that threatens to rise and burst into a sob. It doesn't take much to unravel her today. She shakes her head and grips the edge of the bench with her fingers and barely resists the urge to flee.

"I found Sonny with fly welts all over his body yesterday morning. I simply asked Miguel, and then Bridget, to see that he gets fly sprayed before turnout. It wasn't a big deal, at least not to me. And as far as the grazing goes, it was a mistake. Sonny got out of hand and I corrected him as fast as I could. But Miguel thinks I ratted on him and now he has it out for me.

Carla nods and her eyes begin to soften.

"Barn drama," she declares. "Doesn't take much to start it."

"As for the horses in Sonny's field, they're all wonderful, even Moose, once you get to know him. It's just that Sonny is the low-man in the herd and he can't get into the run-in for shade. All I'm trying to do is take care of my horse!" Clarissa's voice catches as she tries to hold back the tears.

"So that's why he's in the show barn?"

"Bridget made me lease the stall for a whole month. I only wanted it for a few days, till the heat wave is over, but she wouldn't hear of it."

"Shame on her!" Carla gripes and shakes her head. "That's just mean."

"You said it, not me!"

"Yeah, but they expect it from me. I've been here long enough to speak my mind without getting a black eye. You, on the other hand, need to lay low and go with the flow for awhile."

She pauses and takes Clarissa by the hand.

"Don't get me wrong, you have to be your horse's advocate, sweetie. But you also have to be smart about it. You know, pick your battles."

Claire nods and sighs. "I can do that."

"One more thing."

"Oh God, now what?"

"I heard Bridget kicked you to the curb this morning."

"What do you mean?"

"I heard she doesn't want to give you lessons anymore."

"At least not on Sonny. She says he's the wrong horse for me. She has a mare she wants me to try."

"Who? Ruby?"

"She didn't say."

"It's Ruby, I know it. That mare kicks and bites like Mike Tyson. Don't you get anywhere near her. And there's nothing wrong with Sonny, by the way. He's a good horse."

"I know. But thank you for saying so."

"What are you going to do about a trainer?"

Clarissa shrugged. "Look for another one. A Western one, I think."

"I know someone."

"You do?"

"Yeah, I rode in a clinic with him a couple of years ago. He's a genuine cowboy, the real deal. If that's what you're looking for."

Clarissa nods and brightens and squeezes Carla's hand.

"You really are my fairy horsemother."

"I've been called worse things," Carla chortles and springs to her feet. She reaches Hershey's side and strokes his sinewy neck. "Look at you, my big, sweet hunk of chocolate! Are you ready to ride?"

Hershey pokes his face under Carla's armpit and curls around her torso.

"Look, Claire, he's giving me a hug!"

"He sure is," Clarissa says and laughs. It feels good to laugh, even if it is in the wake of George's desertion and Bridget's rejection and the show girls' condescension. Even if it is for the briefest moment, it gives her hope that she's still—unsinkable.

"Excuse me, can Hershey have a carrot?"

Clarissa hadn't noticed Margaret's approach from behind and is equally surprised by the shyness in her lilting Irish brogue.

"Sure!" Carla replies.

Margaret offers Hershey a chunky bit of carrot. He pulverizes it in his massive jaws and nudges her for more.

"Sorry Hershey, that's all I have," Margaret says and holds up her hands.

"Come on, big fella, let's get you tacked up!" Carla crows as she leads Hershey toward the little blue barn. "I'll text you the cowboy's number!" she tosses behind her.

"Thanks!" Clarissa says, then sinks into the uncomfortable silence created by Margaret's presence.

"We heard you had a little tussle with Bridget this morning," Margaret finally says.

Clarissa brushes at specks of pine shavings on her black breeches, trying to buy some time. If she confirms, she'll fuel the fire. If she denies, she'll be lying....

"She doesn't like me either," Margaret confides in a low voice.

"What's not to like about you? You have a magnificent horse and you're a fantastic rider. Geez, you're practically the poster girl for this place."

"I fired her so that I could take lessons with Sebastian."

"Oh. That explains it," Clarissa says and grins, but only because Margaret grinned first.

"So why did you choose Sebastian over Bridget?"

Margaret glances at the sky and ponders the question. Her dark eyelashes flutter with anxiety.

"I guess I just never really felt safe with Bridget. It's like the horses are machines to her. They either shut down around her—or they explode. And besides, she harps on me constantly, picking on every little thing!" Her eyes dart to Clarissa's face for commiseration. "But Sebastian, he seems to know what the horses are thinking and feeling, and he has a way with them that makes them want to give their best. Then I perform better, too. Does that sound weird?"

"Not at all. But I'm surprised she keeps Sebastian around if she's losing clients to him."

"She'd lose a lot more money if she let him go. In case you haven't noticed, he's a hot commodity."

"Oh, I've noticed."

"Then you also know that any gorgeous girl who comes to the barn is going to have a hard time fitting in. The ladies here are pretty territorial."

"Good thing I'm not gorgeous. I'm having a hard enough time as it is."

"Oh, but you are! That's why they shun you. Don't you even know how pretty you are?"

Clarissa mulls the question.

"I guess I just don't think of myself that way. And no one's told me that for a long time."

"Well, I just did. And it's mostly because I want you to know I don't have anything against you at all. Except maybe the way Sebastian talks about you."

"He talks about me?"

"Yes, when we're having a lesson and I get all nervous and hunched over, he says I should spend time on the ground working and playing with my horse, like you do. He says you have a great relationship with Sonny. And that you have the heart of a true horsewoman."

"He said that—about me?"

Margaret nods. "So I was hoping you might teach me how to play with my horse."

"I'd love to!"

"What will I need?"

"A sense of humor."

"Oh God. You're gorgeous and you have a sense of humor too?" Margaret rolls her eyes and throws her hands in the air. "Well, at least you're married! Finding a single man willing to date a woman over forty is like trying to find a horseshoe in a hundred-acre field!"

Clarissa instinctively reaches for her wedding band and squeezes it, the same way a dreamer might pinch herself to see if she's sleeping or awake. It feels tight on her finger this morning, more like a vise than a vow. Still, it beat being forty-something and single!

"Can we meet tomorrow? I have a lesson with Sebastian at ten, but I'm free after that."

"Sounds good."

"Great, see you then!"

"Margaret—"

Clarissa can't help herself. She has to ask.

"Did Sebastian say anything else about me?"

Margaret averts her eyes and purses her lips.

"It's okay, you can tell me."

"He said he could never give you lessons. You're too..."

"Too what?"

"Well, he calls you a *pequeña mula*."

"What does that mean?

"I asked my housekeeper. Apparently, you're a—little mule," she says apologetically. "Maybe he means stubborn? I don't know."

Clarissa tosses her head and laughs. It sounds exactly like something Sebastian would say and she finds herself oddly flattered by the comparison. The last thing she wants is to be perceived as a sniveling woman. No matter how sniveled she is on the inside, she prefers to appear as sure-footed and rugged as a Spanish mule. She clutches the metaphor to her chest and sighs with amusement.

"That's hilarious."

"You're not offended?"

"I'd rather be a mule than a—nag."

They exchange conspiratorial grins as Bridget strolls by without acknowledging either one of them. In that moment, they each became the friend the other needed, sort of like when a pair of rescue horses are thrown together in the kill pen and instantly become each other's comfort and protector. There's a certain magic that brings souls together, a gift of the cosmos to compensate for all the bad stuff that happens in between.

It's a fact that the universe has its own system of checks and balances. When I lost my worth at the Old Man's farm and was sent to the auction, I was rescued by Will and Beth and lavished with kisses and giggles and baths from adoring little girls for the next twelve years. There was even a little girl I had learned to love, who leased me for two years and took me to horse shows and together, we jumped fences and dabbled in Western Pleasure, and won all different colors of ribbons, mostly blue. I thought we'd be together forever, but then she grew taller, much taller, and went away one day and never came back. I got older, and the days got duller, and hay grew scarcer and the winters too cold for me to be out in a frozen field with my sticky stifle and arthritic knees. That's when Clarissa came along and put a soft, fuzzy halter on my face and led me to green pastures and a luxurious stall that protects me from every element under the sun. I've learned that for every clod of manure on the heel, there's a pristine puddle that washes it away. The trick is to not sink further into the crap, but to keep moving forward in search of that which cleanses and quenches and revives. When Clarissa finds it, I hope she flops on her side and immerses in it. Like me, in my cozy nest of pine, where the sound of her laughter makes my ears twitch with happiness.

"See you tomorrow, Margaret."

"Maggie. My friends back in Dublin call me Maggie," the redhead says as her eyes alight on the dwindling circle of show girls who have turned their attention to the sight of Sebastian's black pickup truck winding up the driveway.

"They're not so bad, they're just jealous, that's all."

Clarissa rolls her eyes and chuckles softly. "Of my utter greenness and my odd Western saddle and my stocky, little Quarter Horse?"

"It takes guts to be who you are. I wish I had that kind of confidence!" Margaret shrugs and offers a parting wave.

Clarissa waves back and stands a little taller as she reflects on Sebastian's praise. Maybe she does have the heart of a horsewoman; a fledgling one at that, but maybe, just maybe, it could grow wings and she could fly, fly with me, past the clouds and the stars to that lofty, weightless place where all is exceedingly holy and well. For now, she's tethered to the earth, but if nothing else, I am faithful; I will yoke myself to her until she's able to fight both gravity and fear. She did it today in an impressive display of horsemanship on my bucking back. She wasn't afraid, and she didn't come off. If she did it once, she can do it again—and again! Yee-haw, Clarissa, that's how to get it done!

"Good morning, *Señoras*."

A chorus of demure hellos greets Sebastian as he ambles toward the show barn, dressed for a day of lessons in tan, fitted breeches and tall boots and a white polo shirt that accentuates the bronzed glow of his Argentine skin. He stops short at the sight of Clarissa standing under the oak tree, her face upturned and gazing into a cerulean sky. She feels him before she sees him; his dark eyes glance over her skin and it tingles with the knowing that he is here. Before she turns around, she breathes deeply of air that floats on the cusp of hope that she didn't make a complete fool of herself the night before—that he might feel anything for her but sorry!

"Hi," she ventures as he closes in.

"Hello," he replies and offers her one of the two cups of iced coffee he holds in his hands.

"For me?"

"Yes, for you. You mentioned you were having a lesson with Bridget this morning. It's a cup of consolation." He winks as she takes it from his hand.

She senses the deeper sympathy behind the gesture and stares at the toes of her boots.

"Listen, about last night, please don't feel sorry for me. And don't be mad at me either. I was just rambling."

"I'm not mad, and I definitely don't feel sorry for you."

"You don't? Why not?" She lifts her gaze and furrows her brows.

"I've seen you stand your ground with Sonny enough to know that you've got a strong will. Whatever you want to happen will happen."

"Oh, so you think I'm—*stubborn*?"

Sebastian merely cocks his head and gazes at her, allowing her to answer her own question. She takes the opportunity to appreciate how rich and dark his eyes are, darker than the coffee in her cup, and filled with a tender concern that her wounded pride briefly allows.

"I have a little something else for you." He reaches into his back pocket and produces a thin packet wrapped in white tissue paper. A clumsy, crushed red bow holds it together and he stares at it awkwardly.

"I guess I shouldn't have stuffed it in my pocket," he says.

Clarissa sets her coffee cup on the bench outside the barn. She takes the packet from his hand and eyes it curiously.

"Go ahead, open it."

She unties the ribbon and peels back the paper and studies a thin strip of leather, the same size as a nameplate, with my name tooled into it. Not just my name, but my name surrounded by four red roses, similar to the ones on my saddle.

"Sebastian, it's lovely. It's a nameplate for his stall, right?"

"A fancy brass one seems wrong for a Western Pleasure horse."

"You made this? When?"

"Last night. I thought it might cheer you up."

He doesn't know where the inspiration came from; he only knows that after leaving Clarissa last night, he felt drawn to his mallet and awl and an urge to create something that transported him to another time, another life, so different than this one. His hands have a memory of their own; the curves and lines and flourishes he produces are traces of the past, rising from his fingertips like the dead. Clarissa's smile is bittersweet. She grieves her separation from George, and yet the universe seems to be offering one check and balance after another.

"Thank you," is all she says lest she break down and snivel.

"So? How did your lesson go?"

"Let's just say I'm three for three."

Sebastian's crunches his eyebrows and tilts his head.

"First my horse. Then my husband. Now my trainer."

"Bridget dumped you?"

"Apparently my horse is unworthy. And so am I, by association."

Sebastian raises a finger to his lips in contemplation and restraint. He doesn't want to speak too soon, to offer something she's not ready for. She has too much pride, too much fear, too much resistance, to be teachable. If she were ever to be his student, she'd have to trust him enough to surrender all of those things. Besides, if last night was any indication, she merely sees him as a shallow, show-barn trainer with a following of women who idolize him and vie for his time and attention. Little does she see or know that he's still a gaucho at heart, one with an increasing fascination with the jasmine-scented cowgirl whose level gaze sears him like a branding iron on the flank of a steer.

"So now what?" is all he says.

"Carla knows a Western trainer. She says he's a genuine cowboy. I'm gonna give him a call."

"I see."

Clarissa doesn't notice the way his shoulders square off and stiffen. She's too busy examining the nameplate in her hand and runs her fingertips over the expert tooling.

"This is beautiful. Thank you."

"You're welcome," he answers coolly. "Good luck with the cowboy."

Clarissa frowns.

"Do you have something against cowboys?"

Sebastian chuckles. She mistakes it for scorn.

"Oh, I get it. They're not really horsemen, are they? Just a bunch of rednecks, right?"

"Did I say that?"

"No, but that's what you're thinking."

"That's not what I'm thinking."

"Well, I'll tell you what I'm thinking. I think maybe you're a snob."

Sebastian nods somberly. It's bad enough that he despises his own duplicity when he awakens each morning to dress and act the part of an elite dressage trainer. Apparently he does it so well that other people have come to believe it too. Perhaps it is, in fact, what he has become. The thought makes him reel with self-doubt and recrimination. He takes a long sip of iced coffee to buy some time to rebound.

"Again, it seems you know everything about me."

"I'm just trusting my instincts."

"Or maybe you're afraid."

"I'm not afraid of anything."

"You should be."

"Of what?"

"Of me."

"Why?"

"The cowboy can give you Western lessons. But I can teach you softness, and feel, and connection that will change not only how you think about riding, but how you think about yourself."

Clarissa's knees weaken at the way his words, spoken with tenderness and conviction, tunnel in her ears and rumble like thunder in her chest and flow through her body like hot, liquid steel. She struggles for breath, but manages to speak. She forces herself to sound cavalier.

"Okay, then teach me," she challenges.

She glances down and feigns interest in a barn cat scampering by.

Sebastian reaches out and lifts her face by the chin. Her cheeks turn warm and pink at the sensation of his hand against her skin.

"No."

"No?"

"You're not ready, *señorita*."

He turns sharply on the heels of his polished boots. Clarissa watches him walk away and shakes her head and whispers one of those words.

Actually, a lot of them.

Silly Clarissa. All she had to do was say please.

11

"Okay, Sonny, let's make a good impression on Clint Eastwood."

The Western trainer's name isn't really Clint Eastwood; his name is Clint Markowitz but he sounded like a cowboy on the phone with lots of *y'alls* and *ma'ams* and so she's taken to calling him Clint Eastwood in her mind.

It took him a week to find the time to squeeze her into his training schedule. Good thing too, because it took that long for Clarissa to find the nerve to approach Bridget and ask for permission to bring an outside trainer on board. When she did, she was dealt a withering look and a piece of paper that guaranteed Crown Ridge indemnity and a thirty-dollar ring fee per lesson. Clarissa signed the paper and mentally calculated the skyrocketing cost of learning how to ride. She wasn't happy. But she was determined, now more than ever, to become an accomplished rider if for no other reason than to show both Bridget and Sebastian that she could do it damn well without them!

Other than the hour she'd spent with Margaret showing her how to play games with Dante, her daily visits to the barn have been shorter, her mood less buoyant, her face subtly creased and stoic, like a horse in pain. To show pain is to display weakness. To display weakness is to invite any predator within a ten-mile radius to pounce. And so a horse internalizes pain and ends up with an ulcer or a sour disposition or no other choice but to separate from the herd and eventually lie down and die. But sometimes, just sometimes, a horse gets better. I hope Clarissa gets better. My life depends on it.

She's heard from George only once in the week that he's been gone. He sent her a text message saying he arrived in Paris safely, and that he'd taken it upon himself to reach out to Gabriella and take the blame for their separation. For whatever reason, he chose to fall on the sword and spare Clarissa the risk of being seen as a crazy horsewoman by a daughter who believes her mother is bombproof in matters of the heart. The fact is, no living creature is bombproof; certainly not horses, certainly not me! Even if it were possible for a bomb to go off on the outside with little or no reactivity, that doesn't mean that under the right conditions, a horse or a human won't explode from the bombs within.

I hear Clarissa's heart...tick, tick, tick. She can only hold back so long, and just like a horse will throw a buck, or rear, or bolt, I watch for subtle signs that she's going to blow. The routine of polishing the silver on my saddle and picking my hooves and washing my face with a bristly washcloth is balm for her soul. I, on the other hoof, wish she'd just pitch a fit and get it out of her system so we can get on with the business of learning how to dance in the rain.

This misty, Saturday morning rain guarantees a traffic jam in the indoor ring. In the summer, the lesson horses start early, just after sunrise if they're lucky enough to belong to Sebastian. Bridget, on the other hand, nurses her morning coffee and donuts until just shy of eleven, when the sun is already high in the sky. Then she'll mosey to the outdoor ring with one or more students and their horses and stand in the cool shade in the corner of the arena while her charges drip sweat around twenty-meter circles. But on rainy days, it's a rodeo as the jumpers jump and the dressage horses circle and halt and salute at X, and the remaining horses and riders hug the rail, waiting for their turn to dominate the ring.

This is the mob scene into which Clarissa and I enter with Clint Eastwood and his jingly spurs announcing our arrival. Her eyes flit to Sebastian, who stands at an angle to us with his sinewy arms crossed over his chest as he watches Margaret and Dante perform a flawless side pass. He nods his head approvingly and flashes a smile. Margaret beams and pats Dante on the neck, then glances up and waves at Clarissa. Sebastian follows Margaret's distracted gaze. He sees Clarissa and me in my new western get-up and his face flinches with concern.

"I really don't mind riding outside," Clarissa offers tentatively. "It's only drizzling."

"Nonsense," Clint Eastwood says with a voice that carries throughout the arena. "Don't worry, they'll make room for us. Go ahead and get on your hoss."

Clarissa walks me to the mounting block and pauses, stymied by the rawhide rope dallied around the horn, then wound into a coil and fastened to the front saddle strings. Fringed tassels hang from my leather slobber straps, which connect the thick, braided mecate reins to my bosal-style hackamore. I keep looking for the cows, surely there must be cows! I have sported this rough stock equipment before and cut the wiliest cows from the herd with lightening speed in my youth. I prance in place, excited for the cows to come. But I don't smell cows. Just anxiety. Clarissa's anxiety.

"I'm confused by all this—stuff," she says, as she puts a foot in the stirrup and throws her leg over the cantle. She sits and picks up the reins. Clint Eastwood tips back his white cowboy hat and narrows his eyes and studies her posture. His lips frown under his speckled, handlebar mustache.

"Sit on your pockets," he growls.

"I am."

"Deeper!"

Clarissa slouches and squiggles her seat. She mentally laments her posture. *Ear, shoulder, hip, heel!* She can't possible keep them all in line and sit on her pockets too! She gives up and thrusts her feet forward.

"Lookin' good, cowgirl!"

His voice booms and the activity in the arena slows as riders lose their focus and turn their eyes toward us.

"Okay, let's walk a lap around the ring. Let me see how he goes."

Clarissa picks up the reins and squeezes her legs and off we go, a one-horse parade with a dozen humans on horseback ogling us, some more blatantly than others. Bridget murmurs *pfft* as we walk by. Clarissa doesn't hear it, but I do. I snort my rebuttal and stretch out long and low. I feel pressure on every side as critical eyes bore into my barrel and my muscles twitch and tense. I veer off the rail, seeking the relief of open space. Clarissa grabs my face and steers me like a bicycle back to where I was. She knows better, but today she's as green as spring grass all over again. Her breath spills out in shallow, little puffs and her seat bones squirm uncomfortably. I speed up and dart out from under her going into the bend. Someone has to take control!

"Sonny!" she reprimands me. She sits up straight in the saddle and in an instant, the Clarissa I know is back in charge. *Ear, shoulder, hip, heel!* A balanced ride is a quiet ride.

"On your pockets!" Clint Eastwood bellows. "Take up the slack in the reins and push him forward!"

Clarissa collapses and squeezes her legs. I lift my head and quicken my gait, but not enough to satisfy the cowboy.

"I'm going to have to put you in spurs."

"No spurs!" Bridget chimes in from across the arena. "He gets fresh."

Clint Eastwood laughs. "Let him get fresh. We'll show him who's boss."

Bridget says *pfft* again and turns her back on the spectacle we're creating, while Sebastian simply pretends to ignore us. But I notice the ever-so-slight shift in his dark eyes when we come around the corner. He sends Margaret and Dante into a trot and comments on her elbows, flapping like a duck, he says. He tells her to give the inside rein and as she makes the adjustment, he steals a glance at Clarissa's hands. Like me, he senses the quiet panic in fingers that curl too tightly around the braided rope. Her nervous energy travels down the reins like so much noise. I can't hear a word she's thinking.

When she finally completes her lap around the ring, Clint Eastwood says *whoa!*

I grind to a stop. He looks at my feet.

"Nice square stop," he says.

Clarissa sighs with relief. She glances through the gap in the arena doors. The rain has stopped and a sun-washed haze seeps in.

"Why don't we finish our lesson outside?"

"I'd like to try him first. I want to see for myself how much horsepower's in there and school him a little bit."

"You mean you want to ride him?"

"Yep, come on down."

Clarissa dismounts and hands Clint Eastwood the reins. Her fingers uncurl slowly. She hesitates to let go.

"I ain't gonna hurt him, Ma'am."

Clarissa drops the reins into his calloused hands.

He mounts from the ground and my back drops out from under him. He's not heavy, just hard. The difference is in the intention.

He sends me forward a couple of steps then clucks and spurs me into a trot. He reclines in the saddle and jams his feet like the Old Man, and prods me with his inside leg into a circle, then another, and another. I drop my shoulder with fatigue and pull with my forelegs. He yanks my shoulder up and kisses and kicks and spurs until I canter and bend around his inside leg like a crescent moon. My stifle jams and I falter. He picks up the tail end of the rope that's dallied around the horn and slaps my shoulders with it. I canter and bend, faster and tighter as he cranks my head all the way to the inside. The long muscle of my back twists and burns. I break into a trot and head sideways to the rail. He spanks me hard on the buttocks with the tail end of the rope and makes a loud, guttural sound in his throat. I throw a buck. He stays on. I buck harder and I feel his weight shift but he sticks the buck and jerks my head up and around to the side in a virtual headlock

"Stop! Just stop!"

Clarissa darts through the gauntlet of riders to the place where Clint Eastwood and I have come to a breathless standstill. The riding ring falls silent but for my own panting breath.

"Get off my horse!" she orders as she inspects me for harm. It is the memory, Clarissa, more than the muscles that twist and burn. She raises her eyes to Clint Eastwood, who seems amused by her long stride and clenched fists. Big mistake, Clint Eastwood.

She grabs the reins from his gangly hand and gives me back my head.

"Get off," she says again, this time in a ragged whisper.

"I'm just showing him who's boss, ma'am," he bellows.

"I'm the boss. And I said get off my horse."

She doesn't care who's watching. She doesn't care who hears. I lick and chew with relief as Clint Eastwood slithers off the saddle. His spurs clink as his alligator boots hit the sand. Clarissa reaches in her back pocket and produces a fistful of dollars. She thrusts it towards him. He glances at the face of his watch.

"Still got thirty minutes." He's taunting her now and she knows it.

"We're done, Mr. Markowitz."

"You say so," he says and shrugs and takes the money from her hand with a lazy grin.

"You gotta make him go, Ma'am, or he'll run all over you."

"The only thing that has to go is you!"

I can feel the tremble of Clarissa's hand traveling through the reins. Still, she stands her ground and looks the cowboy squarely in his rounded eyes. He can't believe she's sassing him this way!

Clint Eastwood bares his teeth and tips his hat and thrusts Clarissa's money into the back pocket of his high-waisted jeans. He nods and mutters to Bridget as he approaches the arena doors.

"Goddamn hoss needs spurs. Maybe a good whippin' too," he growls.

Bridget smirks and rolls her eyes indulgently, until she realizes she's being watched, too; by her students and by the horses whose minds absorb the sounds and images of whips and spurs against horse flesh and the inhumane roars humans make when driven by fear or domination.

"He's a nice horse," she offers weakly as the cowboy brushes past her.

"They're all nice—until they're not. Just like most women I know."

"*Pffft*," Bridget says again as he slips through the crack in the door and disappears, and the jingle of his spurs gradually falls silent. "Hey!" she yells to her charges. "Let's get those horses moving!"

The arena springs back to life. Clarissa loosens my cinch and strokes my neck and kisses my face and leads me toward the door. She vibrates regret and remorse and I nudge her shoulder ever so lightly, almost imperceptibly, as we move forward. It's not your fault, Clarissa. Kicks and kisses. It's the story of a domesticated horse's life...but oh, how a kiss on the muzzle from tender lips has the power to make our burdens light. It's bright and breezy and the sun feels good on my overworked hide. Come on, Clarissa, let's lose these silly riggings and ride!

I snort with pleasure as Clarissa's mind meets mine. She exchanges my rodeo gear for a simple rope halter and reins and we amble along the greenways between paddocks, inhaling the heady fragrance of wet grass and fresh rain. Her breath slows. The sting of tears behind her eyes dissipates. The ache in my back disappears. There is light and peace and no point. No point at all. Just two souls floating on a summer breeze. It is ethereal and ephemeral—and it is enough.

By the time we return to the show barn, it's quiet with the aftermath of Saturday morning lessons. The parking lot has emptied out, the horses have been hosed down and returned to their stalls, and filtered sunlight creeps through the Dutch doors lining both sides of the aisle. Clarissa untacks me and leads me to my stall where a pile of soft, green hay awaits. I lumber in and stick my nose into the fragrant mound and snuffle it enough to separate it into loose clumps. She stands beside me and runs her hands over my spine and my sides and my stifles. I flinch when she touches my right stifle, and stamp my foot when she touches it again.

"Hey," she implores, "let me help you."

She swipes at the gadget she carries in her pocket and music fills the air. The other horses hear it too, and we breathe a collective sigh as she begins, slowly and gently, to massage my nearly nineteen-year-old muscles that bunch and tighten and ache in a dozen hidden places. She finds every knot and as she does, I stop eating and lick and chew and release the pent-up pain I've learned to hide so well. Every so often, I give her a big, hairy eyeball, a warning sign it's too much, too soon, and she backs off and rests her hand and lets the heat of her palm seep into my skin until the soreness gives way to her healing touch. She's in no hurry. There's no one waiting for her at home. No messages to read. No dinner to cook. No place to be but here. With me.

And Sebastian.

"Clarissa," he says quietly, not wanting to startle her.

Clarissa peers over my withers.

"Is Sonny okay?"

"I think so," she says, then continues to massage my shoulder, deeply and intently. She focuses on the fibers that run down into my forearm and avoids Sebastian's gaze.

"What about you?"

"I'll live. I've suffered worse humiliations in my life."

"You impressed me."

Clarissa pauses as his words sink in, then continues to massage me.

"How so?"

"You were fearless in there."

"I can stand up for myself when I have to."

"But you didn't—"

Clarissa stops massaging me and looks into Sebastian's eyes. They're dark and probing and coax her to hear him out.

"You stood up for your horse. Most women would've shied away from making a scene, but you didn't. You did what you had to do to protect Sonny."

"And made a fool of myself besides. Bonus points for me."

Clarissa reaches for my pectoral muscle, the one that gets sore from perpetually dragging myself on the forehand. She practically disappears under me, a calculated move on her part.

"One must be willing to become less so that another can become more. In this, is love. And true humility. Today, you demonstrated both."

Clarissa feels her breath catch in her throat at the sound of the words rolling off his tongue with ineffable sweetness and conviction. She struggles for something to say, but all she can muster is a thoughtful harrumph.

"Clarissa?"

"Yes, Sebastian?" Clarissa moves her hands to the mound of my withers and gently rocks it back and forth, loosening the muscles on either side. She smiles at the way my eyelids droop in response.

"I will teach you."

Clarissa's hands momentarily rest on my withers as she contemplates the offer. She immediately resumes massaging me, not daring to glance at Sebastian. If she did, she'd see the nervous way he shifts his feet and the slight twist of discomfort in his ruddy lips and the spark of hope in his eyes that she'll say yes. There's something in her soul that he recognizes; just as horses are mirrors, so too can the human eye reflect the soulful yearnings of another. Not since Sofía died has he felt his native heart stir with such desire to share his vast love and knowledge of horses with another. Not just any other, but Clarissa, who is one of the least naturally talented riders he's ever seen yet whose passion for horses rivals his own.

"Okay," she says.

Clarissa glances at Sebastian for a split second, just long enough to catch the glint of satisfaction in his eyes and the fleeting curve of his lips. She shifts her attention to the long muscles of my back and glides the heel of her hand from my withers to my loin, pressing into my flesh and creating waves of heat that make me lick and chew the tension away.

"Monday afternoon. Four o'clock. Meet me in the field behind the ring."

"Why in the field?"

"You'll see. Tack him up. And keep it simple, a rope halter will do," he says with a wink.

Clarissa can't help but smile. There's a lot of equipment she's going to have to return to Two Cowgirls, Four Horses. She still hasn't figured out that their specialty is selling everything a rider doesn't need—and more. If word was ever to get out that all one really needs when working with a horse is love and humility and leadership, they'd go belly-up in no time.

I yawn and yawn, and yawn again. Clarissa giggles at my show of teeth, some discolored, some ground down, others etched with crevices that show my age. She finishes the massage with long strokes of *effleurage* that make me feel connected and whole.

In my world, Clint Eastwood is already a distant memory. My new trainer, Sebastian Bergalo, caresses me with kind eyes that invite me in and tell me he knows...he knows my language and he knows the soul of the horse and even now, as he takes his leave, I hear him whisper, without words, what he knows every horse needs to hear and believe.

You're safe with me.

Clarissa tops off my massage with a horse muffin and I turn and wander to the darkest corner of my stall to savor it and settle in for a nap. I cock my hip and rest on a toe. She gently rolls and fastens the stall door behind her as she steps into the aisle. She thinks I don't notice her departure, but what living creature wouldn't notice the absence of water, or air, or sunlight?

Clarissa is my world.

Not just my world, but my heart. Who would've thought a tired, old lesson horse like me could fall in love again? If it could happen to me, it could happen to anyone.

Clarissa tiptoes down the aisle, making sure her heels don't disturb the horses at rest. When she steps outside, she pauses to watch Sebastian retrieve his own horse from the farthest paddock. He's a blue roan gelding, known around the farm simply as Azul. Among humans, only Sebastian knows that his full name is *Mi Cielo Azul*, my blue heaven, his sole connection to that place where Sofía is; the horse that allows him to feel that he rides with Sofía still—in his mind, on the grassy, Argentine plains with the wind whipping her glossy, black hair—and in his soul, racing alongside her in the deep blue spans of paradise where she is forever young and fearless and free.

Only he has gotten older; only he, bound by gravity and guilt, is hunched with regret. He had always kept Sofía safe, no matter how daring she was by nature; he should've seen the storm coming. He should've urged them to turn back sooner. He should've ridden ahead and parted the storm for her to pass through unscathed. Instead, he chose to be her rear guard, and in doing so, it was she who was snatched from the earth; she whose spirit was sucked into the furor of the wind and rain and thunder. It should've been him. He curses and wishes it were him.

Clarissa watches as he hand-walks Azul onto the trail that leads deep into the dark green woods. She wonders why she's never seen him ride Azul in either of the rings; she wonders if Sebastian ever rides him at all.

What she does know is that in two days, she'll be Sebastian's student. She rolls her eyes at the thought. Her! The accidental student of a world-class dressage trainer—and the accidental ogler of a man who makes her want to write again, who has stepped from the depths of her tired imagination and onto the pages of real life. The lines of reality blur and she mentally rattles the thought from her head that he's anything but what he is: her riding instructor, and perhaps the inspiration for the hero—or villain—in her next romance novel...or screenplay!

For the next twelve hours, her fingers race across the keyboard, writing as though someone threw open the gate and she's free to buck off her inner critic like so much dead weight. She doesn't write just anything, but prose and dialog that's bold and romantic and lusty, the way she used to write when she was first married and George was the lucky recipient of the passion and frenzy she'd feel by five o'clock.

But George is working and wine clubbing in Paris and she's weighing the options if her screenplay doesn't sell. She could muck stalls or work in a hardware store or edit books for a living. She's never mucked my stall, but if and when she does, she'll discover it's not about the poop, it's about the grander purpose. There's a certain serenity in the soul of stall muckers. The act of creating order out of chaos is God-like and very good.

I hope she chooses mucking, but for now, she chooses writing and drinks George's most prized red wine and flops onto their king-size mattress, exhausted yet restless. The bed feels large and lonesome and she clutches at the coverlet and pulls it up to her chin like a nun, fending off useless urges. By the time morning comes and the telephone rings, she's slept off the worst of it and only the vague remembrance of her overindulgence in word-sex and wine remains.

It's an ironic remedy for the very thing that ails her; those cloistered feelings of guilt and shame that have resided in her body from girlhood. I'm pretty sure that if she had remained untouched and untouchable, she'd manifest as Sister Clarissa, barefoot and brown, secretly writing eccentric, dystopian novels or Potteresque trilogies to entertain the innocents in a cell slightly smaller than my stall. As it is, she slits a vein and lets dark, dysfunctional love drip on the page in the hope that the light and beauty and poetry of words can make it all wildly romantic and right.

The phone rings a third time. She rolls on her side and answers it.

"Claire?"

"George? I can barely hear you!" she bolts upright and presses the phone to her ear.

"I'm at *Au Petit Fer à Cheval* drinking *Château Léoube* from Provence."

"In English please, George!" she shouts above the din on the other side of the world and runs her fingers through her bird nest of hair as though he can actually see her.

"I'm at a bistro called The Little Iron Horse and drinking a glass of French rosé."

"That's what you called to tell me?"

"The bar is the shape of a horseshoe and it made me think of you."

"Sonny doesn't wear shoes." She sighs and leans against the headboard. If he'd even once paid attention to her concerns about the condition of my hooves, he'd know.

"There are lots of posters of horses on the wall. One actually looks like Sonny. Like I said, this whole place reminds me of you."

"You need to be reminded of your wife?"

She doesn't mean to be surly, but if she isn't, she thinks she might cry. She hears George sigh heavily and imagines he's toying with the thought of simply hanging up.

"Claire, I don't want to fight with you. I just called to tell you I miss you."

Clarissa throws the covers aside and scoots out of bed. She paces slowly and thoughtfully.

"Are you drunk?"

"Maybe a little."

Clarissa nods and pauses to glance at herself in the mirror. She's barely eaten a bite since George has been gone and it shows. She leans in and pinches her cheeks. They're dead pale and sinking fast.

"How are you?" she asks.

"Lonely."

"What, no wine club?"

George utters something in French to someone in the background, then takes a lusty sip of wine that gurgles in Clarissa's ear. She's not even sure he heard the question over the lively chorus of feminine voices.

"Come to Paris."

Clarissa laughs. "Come to Paris? I should just drop everything and come to Paris?" She throws a hand in the air and shakes her head vigorously.

"I just purchased a first-class ticket for you. Your flight leaves on Monday at four." He slurs his words and takes another noisy sip.

Clarissa mentally fast forwards to Monday. Four o'clock. She can ride an airplane or she can ride me. With Sebastian. In lush, green fields embellished with blue belts of wild chicory and patches of tasty, tingly, red clover that make my mouth drool.

"I can't. I have plans."

"What kind of plans."

"I have a lesson."

"Cancel it."

"I can't. If I do, I might never have this chance again."

"Bridget will understand."

"It's not with Bridget."

"With who, then?"

"He's a world-class dressage trainer."

"And he wants to teach—you?"

"Yes."

She hears the clanking of glasses and dishes and a concert of lilting French voices in the long silence that follows.

"Let me know if you change your mind, Clarissa," he finally says. "About Paris—or anything else."

He only calls her Clarissa when he's looking for her, when she's present but barely there, when he senses her trailing off like a wisp of smoke and all he can do is call out to her and grasp the air. This time, she's too far gone; he knows and she knows, she's too far gone to hear him.

"I'm not going to change my mind. I told you before you left, I can't...I won't..."

Her words fade into the memory of their last supper together.

"*C'est la vie*," he says in a near-whisper that brushes her ear with sorrow.

"*C'est la vie*," she echoes, knowing full well what the words mean: her damp, crushed, helmet hair; the fragrance of accomplishment and fresh-cut hay; the peace that comes from picking feet and combing knots out of my long, silky tail; the invigorating breath that courses through my barrel and rises and falls against her legs in perfect rhythm with her heart; the liberty she feels when she's on my back; this and so much more. *This—this is life!*

"I'll call you again, okay?"

"Okay."

He says goodbye in French. She doesn't say goodbye at all. She tosses her phone on the bed and perches on the corner of the mattress. He's more than a little drunk, she tells herself. The proof is in her first-class ticket. In all their travels, George never did see the value in spending three times as much to fly through the same airspace at the same speed. He'll probably regret having invited her to Paris once his fine, French buzz turns into a bourgeois, American hangover. Worse yet, he'll likely find some pretty French maid—or sommelier—to drown his sorrow with in the meantime. She lets out an angry yelp and springs to her feet.

Clarissa's a little hung over too. She clutches her forehead and shuffles to the kitchen table where her wine glass sits empty and her laptop sits open, the cursor blinking where her story leaves off. She skims the last several sentences and groans. She doesn't know if art is imitating life, or life is imitating art; she only knows she can't possibly entertain these—thoughts—about another man!

She highlights the scorching prose and hits the delete key. She nods with satisfaction. She hovers over the keyboard and loosely wraps her arms around herself. The embrace leaves her feeling silly and cold. Her fingers creep back onto the keyboard. She finds the command to undo and her words reappear on the screen. She reads them and sinks into them and loves them like wayward children. Unlike her typewritten text, this indelicate ache in her can't be so easily undone.

The phone rings again. Gabriella's face pops up on the screen. She has George's striking, blue eyes but hers still sparkle the way George's used to when they were young lovers; too young and too loving to believe they could ever be separated by half-truths and whole continents.

Clarissa breathes deeply, pushing past the pangs in her head and in her chest.

"Hi!" she chirps, glad for the distraction.

"Hey, Mom, I'm heading to the mall. Wanna come?"

"Yes, yes I do."

"You do? You hate shopping."

"I need to take my mind off my troubles."

"You mean Dad?"

"Him too."

"I'm so sorry, Mom."

"What doesn't kill you makes you stronger, remember?"

"Stop saying that!"

"I'll be there in twenty minutes."

"Don't speed."

"Stop mothering me!" Clarissa says and laughs as she hangs up the phone. As much as she hates shopping, she shudders at the thought of writing things that shouldn't be written by the light of day, let alone on a Sunday morning. If she wasn't going to church, then going shopping was surely the lesser evil. Besides, the tack store was just a couple of miles down the road from the mall. Her conversation with George reminded her that she's out of the wintergreen stuff she paints on the walls and soles of my hooves to give them a glossy shine and keep them from chipping. The smell tickles my nose but I like it.

That's the first thing she does on Monday when she arrives at the barn. She picks and paints my hooves and gives me a peppermint and the heat of the day dissipates in cool, minty splendor. I paw at the rubber mat under my feet. She glares at me and I paw once more before I stop. It's my way of letting her know that I cease and desist under protest. Really, what's one more peppermint?

She grooms me with special care today and I squirm under all the fuss. I shy away when she lifts the saddle pad towards me. There's not a horse I know who likes the sight of a big, brown blob approaching its flanks. It triggers a deep-seated, sensory alarm of bears and other wild beasts that lie in wait for meaty prey like me. Worse yet, after all of Clarissa's ministries, I'm shiny and bright right down to my toes and I don't stand a chance of being unseen by saber-toothed things. I snort as she places the pad on my back and then relax when it doesn't bite.

"Was that necessary, Sonny? Listen, you need to be extra good today, okay?"

She ruffles and combs my forelock, and I lower my head and gush when she kisses me on the muzzle. Her lips are puckered and very pink and make an unabashed smooching sound that confirms my status as the best horse in the whole world.

"Good boy," she says as she lowers my saddle on my back and I stand perfectly still. She gently tightens the cinch and I thank her by instantly moving when she picks up the lead rope and steps off the rubber mat. We head toward the outdoor ring and I feel her relax as we meander down the gravel path without incident. Mondays at Crown Ridge are the quietest days of all. The show horses are exhausted and the show girls are too tired to do anything but shop or drop. Best of all, it's Bridget's day off and the grooms take advantage of it by cracking their first beer at noon and disappearing until it's time to throw more hay.

Puffy clouds hang in the sky, a few with gray undertones that threaten a stray shower. They creep overhead, fanned by a breeze just strong enough to keep the greenheads at bay. The gravel crunches loudly under our feet. As we reach the end of the footpath and the barrier of the hedgerow, we emerge at the threshold of a fragrant, freshly mowed field where Sebastian hears us coming and greets us with a smile.

He leans casually against a fence post, his long, lanky body accentuated by a light blue tee shirt over faded jeans and topped by a black cowboy hat that shields his eyes from the late afternoon sun. Clarissa's nervous energy travels down the lead rope and zaps me in the chin. She had expected to see Sebastian in tidy, tan breeches and a navy polo shirt, his standard uniform for teaching the show girls and their horses how to half-pass and pirouette. She flinches at the sight of him and holds her breath. I exhale for both of us, a loud, nostril-flapping blowout that makes Sebastian laugh. I look at him with a big, round eye. Clarissa is spooky around him and I don't know why. Maybe I should be spooky too. I prick my ears and stiffen my neck.

"Maybe it's the hat," Sebastian says, and lifts it off his head to reveal waves of dark brown hair that tousle in the breeze.

I blow out again.

"Or maybe not. Are you nervous?"

Clarissa can't deny the flutter in her chest.

"How did you know?"

He points to me and grins. "Meet your mirror. It helps if you breathe."

Clarissa eyes Sebastian warily. She cocks her head and studies him from his black cowboy boots to the brim of his hat, stopping when she reaches his eyes. They register amusement at her boldness and she blinks and looks away.

"I'm sorry, I just didn't expect to see you—like this," she stammers. "It's kind of freaking me out."

"I thought you wouldn't mind if I ditched my formal attire. I promise to treat you with the same severity as everyone else."

"Oh God, please don't," she blurts and makes him laugh. She likes the timbre of the sound, more of a pleasing, low chuckle than a guffaw. If you ask me, it's clearly a nicker. I think he likes my Clarissa.

"Okay, let's get started."

Clarissa's eyes dart around the field.

"What are you looking for?"

"A mounting block. I can't mount from the ground."

"That's okay. We're not riding today."

"We're not?"

Sebastian shakes his head.

"Then what are we doing?"

"Walking."

"Walking?"

"Hand-walking. I want to see how you handle Sonny on the ground."

"You've seen me do groundwork before," she protests.

"Yes, I've seen you play your so-called games, but this is different. Go ahead."

"Just walk?"

Sebastian nods and resumes his stance against the fence post. Clarissa steps off and I fall in behind her, lagging a stride and a half behind. She shuffles her feet through the grass and I shuffle mine too. Clearly, we're not in a hurry.

"Where are you going?" Sebastian calls out behind her.

"I don't know," Clarissa tosses back. "We're just walking."

After several more strides, she stops and turns around. I take advantage of the moment to dive in for a mouthful of grass.

"Sonny, no!" She yanks my head and reprimands me with her eyes.

"Can I come back now?"

"It's up to you," Sebastian calls out. Clarissa thinks she's paying him far too much money to watch her stroll—to watch her ass! She reverses direction and leads me back to where we started.

"So?" she asks him with wide, green eyes that flash irritation.

"I see the problem. At least one of them," he drawls. He takes the lead rope from her hands and walks off with me, my nose in line with his shoulder. We head to the fence post with the little notch on top. After that, we turn and walk to the brown spot in the grass, then turn sharply again and head for the iron latch on the gate. When we reach the gate, he turns and trains his eyes and his thoughts on Clarissa. We make a beeline for her. I'm slightly out of breath from keeping up the pace. He hands my lead rope back to Clarissa. I hang my head with relief.

"Try again."

"I don't know what you did to make him go like that," she admits.

"Focus, Clarissa. Pick a spot to go to now, and then a spot to go to next. You can't wander when you're supposed to be leading. If you don't take charge, he will."

Clarissa nods. She steps off hesitantly. I barely move. Sebastian grasps Clarissa by the arm and stops her from moving forward. Her bare skin tingles where he touches her and she glances at him shyly. He pretends not to notice.

"Try again. This time, take a deep breath and step off in the direction of your focal point. Don't look at the grass or at Sonny. Keep your eyes up!"

She draws breath and her energy builds and travels down the lead rope. I match her lively step and we march to the well pump and then to the fence post with the missing cap. We turn and walk to the patch of tall, blue flowers then abruptly turn and head toward Sebastian. We walk a brisk, straight line until she starts to waver at the sight of him and her knees go slightly weak. We're walking...and weaving, like Miguel and Pedro after dark. Clarissa, where did you go?

"You did fine until the end. What happened?" Sebastian asks.

"I don't know. All of a sudden I lost my—focus."

"That's a happy fault," he says. "Now that you've felt the difference, I hope that's the last time I see you drag your horse around like a pet rock. He's your partner. Don't ever forget that."

Clarissa nods, dumbstruck by the sheer simplicity—and brilliance—of the lesson.

"What we learn on the ground, we'll take to the saddle."

"Now?"

Patience, *señorita*...shall I still call you *señorita*?" He tips his hat to shield his eyes. He can hide the apprehension he feels in asking, but he can't hide the way he vibrates hope. At least not from me.

She shrugs. "You can, but I prefer you call me *mucho caliente*," she jokes with a straight face. "That's what Miguel and Pedro call me." She doesn't mean to sound flirtatious, but she does. Sebastian tosses back his head and laughs, breaking the tension between them.

"So I've heard. Actually, they call you *Caliente Claire*. They think you're very beautiful."

"They do?"

She tucks a wayward strand of hair behind her ear and presses her lips together pensively.

"Why is that such a surprise to you?" he chides.

Clarissa lowers her eyes and replies with a faint shrug. She knows he isn't expecting an answer, that he's merely pointing out that she doesn't see or know herself at all. In that moment, I feel the whirl of her confusion as fleeting images of her body being used and abused float behind her eyes and she watches with the fledgling detachment of a free spirit hovering over the corpse it once inhabited. There's a quiet giddiness about her, something she only vibrates when Sebastian is near and his voice travels through her like a fervent Spanish guitar that rings across the wasteland and brings her back to life.

I toss my head as a dragonfly whizzes by. I know they don't bite but they're pesky and strange and make me nervous just the same. Clarissa turns her attention back to me, grateful for the distraction. I swing my neck and contemplate diving in for more grass. Sebastian points to the tree line and foils my plans.

"Let's move on," he says tersely.

His authority is such that Clarissa doesn't dare question him, and neither do I. She falls in beside him, and I fall in beside her. We trek briskly across the field and step onto a trailhead that leads into the dazzling, dappled shade of thick, towering oaks mixed with wispy, fragrant pines. A carpet of brown needles covers the trail and we sink into a spongy silence. Every now and then something scurries in the underbrush but I'm not the least bit skittish, not with Sebastian in the lead. Our pace is steady and energetic until we come to a fork in the trail. The massive trunk of a fallen oak tree lies across one path while the other plummets to the riverbank. Sebastian stops and turns to Clarissa.

"Which way?"

"I don't know."

He steps aside and yields to her. "Your choice."

"We're blocked either way," she reasons.

"Are we?"

"Is that a trick question?

Sebastian raises his dark brows and challenges her with his eyes.

"If we go that way," she points to the riverbank, "we'll have to wade through the water to get back on trail." She glances down at her red leather cowboy boots and groans. "I really don't want to ruin these boots, they're my favorite pair! But if we go the other way, we'll have to jump the log. Sonny can't jump. He's got a bad stifle!"

"So what are we going to do?"

"We're going to do what's best for Sonny. We'll have to cross the river or turn back." She looks at her boots again and sighs loudly.

Sebastian nods, satisfied. "Spoken like a true horsewoman. But know this: when Sonny truly sees you as his leader, he'll do anything you ask him to, including jumping over logs with a bad stifle. I've seen horses race through wildfire and flash floods and the most sudden, violent storms on the Pampas without a moment's hesitation for the one they love—even if it costs them their lives."

Sebastian's forehead creases in remembrance and his eyes narrow with bitter regret. He's tempted to share his secret with

Clarissa, whose green gaze is soft and intuitive and probing. She instinctively places her hand on his shoulder in a gesture of sympathy. He's never breathed a word to anyone outside of his hometown as to the circumstances of Sofía's death. What good could come of it? He needs neither judge nor jury to convict him of his negligence.

"I wish someone would race through wildfire for me," she says wistfully.

"You are the wildfire. You're *Caliente Claire*, remember?" Sebastian forces a carefree smile and she slowly withdraws her hand, but not before he feels the burn.

"Come on, Sonny, no jumping for you today," he says and turns in the direction from which we came. I'm happy to oblige. All these emotions ricocheting off the trees in the middle of nowhere makes me want to move my feet toward somewhere familiar and calm.

We walk in silence all the way back to the show barn. Clarissa's mind conjures images of horses running through fire and rain; they're vivid with color and motion and sound and speculation, as one might expect from a girl who retreats to the heights of her imagination when trouble rears—especially trouble that has dark, inviting eyes and tender, enlivening fingertips that brush her skin like dawn and beckon her from the pages of her virtual life. When we reach the aisle, my hooves clop on the hard cement and she tumbles from her lofty musings. She lands with a thud. No, really. She lands with a thud. A muck fork clatters to the ground and I jump sideways.

"Clarissa!" Sebastian exclaims, and says something in Spanish that sounds like it might be one of those words. I shuffle my feet to move out of the way, careful not to step on her buckled, little body. A moment later, she moans softly and then scrambles to her feet like a horse after a good roll in the mud. She clutches her wrist and definitely says one of those words.

"Are you all right? What happened?" Sebastian says, propping her up by the elbow.

"I don't know, all of a sudden I just felt—lightheaded."

Sebastian scans her for signs of injury. He presses his hand to her forehead.

"I'm not sick!' she says with an awkward laugh as she wipes the grit from her bottom lip. "It's probably just low blood sugar or something. Hey, who needs a horse to bite the dust?"

Sebastian doesn't acknowledge the joke.

"When did you eat last?"

Clarissa pauses to think. She'd had a cup of tea that morning and a salad at lunch with Gabriella the day before. Truth is, she's had no desire for food since George has been gone; her entire being rejects the idea of eating alone and her hunger pangs have morphed into cravings for something deeper and more satisfying. Not me, I walk myself into my stall, my lead rope trailing behind, and attack the mound of rich hay that awaits me. I munch with one ear cocked to the voices murmuring in the aisle.

"I can't remember."

"Let me see your wrist."

"It's nothing, see? I can bend it, it's just a little sore."

"Sit there while I take care of Sonny." He points to a green tack box across the aisle.

"I can do it," Clarissa protests.

"I said sit," Sebastian commands. "And eat this while you're at it!" He hands her a peppermint from the community treat jar. She shuffles to the tack box and perches on the edge of it. She unwraps the peppermint and pops it in her mouth. My ears perk at the crinkly sound.

Sebastian calls to me softly as he enters. He strokes my neck and proceeds to undo the latigo strap that holds my saddle in place. He meticulously binds it and puts up the cinch, then places both hands on the saddle to lift it from my back. I feel him as I feel Clarissa, his mind bending and his heart breaking as the saddle springs to life in his hands. He runs his fingers over it as though he's a blind man feeling the face of the one he loves.

"This is ridiculous," Clarissa calls out. "I'm coming in there. I have to pick his feet."

Sebastian emerges from my stall and Clarissa meets him at the threshold. She grabs my saddle and pad from him and marches toward the tack room. She has to admit, she already feels better.

"*Pequeña mula!*" Sebastian says under his breath and shakes his head.

Clarissa hears him and grins.

Sebastian picks my feet while she's gone and gives me a quick brushing. By the time she returns, he's casually leaning against the doorjamb, a tall, lanky silhouette carved into the backdrop of a golden, late afternoon sun.

"Come with me."

"Where?"

"To my cottage. I'm going to make you something to eat."

Clarissa laughs. "That's not necessary. I'm fine now."

"Tell me, Clarissa, did you learn anything today?"

She contemplates the question and offers a singular, thoughtful nod.

"Then return the favor and allow me to feed you."

"I'm not asking for favors. I intend to pay you just as any other student would. Eighty dollars per lesson, right?" She fumbles in her back pocket for the folded bills she'd inserted earlier. He raises his hand to refuse the payment.

"I have a different arrangement in mind. I'd like to barter lessons for your saddle."

"My saddle's not for sale."

"One day perhaps, you will sell it, and I will have the right to it."

"And what if I don't?"

Sebastian sticks his hands in his pockets and shrugs. "It's a risk I'm willing to take. Your saddle reminds me of where I came from...I'd like to have it someday." He holds his breath and doesn't even realize he's forgotten to exhale.

Clarissa considers the offer. She's already bleeding green from the cost of supplements and ring fees and my luxurious stall. She doesn't know how long the money from her father's estate will hold out. She'd counted on a year, and on George's help after that. She'd sell the saddle a thousand times over before she'd ever sell me—and ride bareback if she must!

"Okay."

"Okay to the saddle or okay to a meal?"

Clarissa shrugs. "Both, I guess."

Sebastian breathes out. He lifts his hat and runs his fingers through his hair to dispel the pent-up tension. The deepest creases disappear from his face.

"Follow me."

He turns and steps onto the sunlit driveway that tapers at the furthest corner into a narrow, obscure path covered with wood chips and bordered by mounds of leggy ferns. Clarissa ducks into my stall and kisses me goodbye on the cheek.

"You know you're the best horse in the whole world, right?" she murmurs into my ear. She doesn't ask me to acknowledge her affection. She gives it freely and allows me to accept or reject it at will. Today I offer a brief sweep of my muzzle over her chest and go back to eating my hay. There's no need to get mushy. She knows my heart.

Once outside, she glances furtively. It's the quietest hour of the day, just before feeding time when the grooms awaken from their late afternoon *siestas* and the air explodes with the sound of rolling carts and the rattle of buckets filled with grain and the nickers and stall kicks of hungry horses. Just the same, she walks hurriedly, partly to dodge any prying eyes, as well as to catch up to Sebastian, who seems not to harbor the least bit of doubt that she'll follow him—just like the horses do.

When they reach his secluded, straw-colored cottage, he pivots and waits for her to step onto the front porch. She sniffs the air, fragrant with the perfume of dark crimson roses that spiral and climb the rough-hewn porch posts then spill over the pergola in a reckless tangle of blossoms and thorns. She notices his tall, gleaming riding boots camped outside the door, and a trio of brass hooks upon which hang his gold-tipped dressage whip and a navy cap embroidered with the official logo of Crown Ridge that he wears on training days. After today, they seem to her like artifice, the trappings of a cowboy roped into a Rolex world where performance and prestige are paraded for all the world to see. He brushes the soles of his scuffed, cowhide boots against the cocoa mat outside the door, hangs his hat on the last hook, and turns the doorknob. He swings the door open and sweeps his hand before him, bidding her to enter.

She steps tentatively over the threshold.

"Don't be shy. I promise to leave the ruthless trainer outside the door."

Clarissa glances around a tidy space that hosts both the living room and the kitchen. A cozy, round table for two is tucked into a nook created by a large bay window that overlooks an unruly vegetable garden in the backyard. A bottle of red wine graces the table and two glasses with deep, round bowls anchor the head of each place setting. A petite vase of crimson roses picked from the front porch rests squarely in the center.

"Expecting company?" she bristles.

"If you're asking me if this is a set-up, the answer is no."

Clarissa arches her eyebrows and probes his face for the telltale twitch of a lie.

"In my country, wine is the lifeblood of the soul and the heart of every meal. Every Argentine knows that the purpose of wine is to bring people closer together—not to encourage solitary contemplation. My table is an open invitation and connection to the land I left behind."

Clarissa nods, satisfied with the explanation; not just satisfied, but unexpectedly moved by the sentiment. She finds it poetic and romantic, and just a touch sad. Her eyes sweep the rest of the room, seeking more clues about the man who doesn't seem the least bit unnerved by her presence in his home. The spartan furnishings reveal little more than a preference for leather, and the sole decoration on the wall is shadow box that encases a beautiful, western bridle embellished with silver conchos and diamond-shaped, turquoise stones across the browband. There are no glossy, ringside photographs, no blue ribbons, no bronze statues of horse heads or other typical equestrian accouterments. As she sinks into the seat he offers her at the table, she sighs with contentment.

"Thank you for the invitation. I admit I'm getting tired of contemplating my own navel."

Sebastian tilts his head and his eyes drift to her belly.

"Oh! It's just a silly, American expression. It means excessively thinking about one's own problems.

"Yes, it is silly," he says curtly.

He deftly opens the bottle of Malbec on the table. He pours out fragrant wine burnished with a sheen that looks like iridescent blackberries. She swirls it in the deep bowl of her glass. She can't help but wonder what George would say about it. He'd probably use terms like viscous and robust and tannic and spicy and acidic. But that's not what she says.

"It's sacrificial, isn't it?"

He questions her with his eyes as he pours himself a glass and sits directly across from her.

"The wine, it's sacrificial. You called it the lifeblood. I guess that's how I've always thought about wine. The grape is born to be crushed, to provide life for the soul. It's a story old as time."

Sebastian pauses, then offers just enough of a smile to keep his words from sounding cruel. "Such a tragic little thought. Perhaps you do spend too much time contemplating your navel."

Clarissa grins, amused by his bluntness. "Right. Never mind. I'm just channeling another time, another place—a long-lost passion. To Argentina!" she says and raises her glass.

"To Argentina," Sebastian replies, and as their glasses touch and he watches Clarissa raise the rim to her tantalizing lips, he too flashes back to another time, another place, a long-lost passion. His dark eyes cloud over.

"It won't take me long to pull something together. You shouldn't drink on an empty stomach, *señorita*."

She puts down her glass. He's right. After just one lusty sip, she already feels the liquid warmth diffuse throughout her face and into her chest. It feels like the heat of a campfire, the flush that comes from sitting too close to a throbbing flame.

"I have homemade chicken empanadas in the refrigerator. And some provolone I can fry on the grill. How does that sound?"

"That sounds like a lot of food. I'd be happy with some toast. Really Sebastian, please don't fuss over me." She fidgets with the stem of her wine glass. She wasn't used to being pampered, let alone by as manly a man as Sebastian. She'd just assumed he'd be full of bluster and machismo and everything she'd ever heard Latino men to be. But then again, the only Latino men she knew were the grooms at Crown Ridge and the landscapers George hired to mow the lawn when they moved into their new house on a seven-acre spread in the old part of town. She'd planned to grow mammoth zucchini and heirloom tomatoes and keep a few chickens for farm-fresh eggs. Four years later, the land is still barren and the lumber George bought to build a chicken coop lays in a heap outside the shed, a haven for chipmunks and the occasional scream-worthy garter snake.

"I'm not fussing. I'm just trying to feed you." His lips form a thin line. "Are you always this—what is the word? Stubborn?"

He shakes his head and strides into the kitchen. She watches him take a cellophane-wrapped plate from the refrigerator and place several puffy, fork-pressed crescents of dough on a baking sheet. He puts them in the oven to warm, then forgoes the grill and carves off several slices of cheese from a small wheel of provolone and arranges them on a plate alongside a mound of shiny, green grapes. He sets the dish in front of Clarissa, takes a sip of wine, and stares at her expectantly.

She pops a grape into her mouth, surprised by its sweetness.

"Oh my God, these are delicious!" she says, plucking another from the pile. "Try one!"

He smiles at her enthusiasm and sits across from her. He splashes more wine into his glass and leans back in his chair. His long legs stick straight out as he crosses them at the ankle, and Clarissa can't help but notice their muscularity. They're the legs of one who trains up to ten horses a day, not with whips and spurs, but with his seat and legs alone, teaching them to respond to ever lighter shifts in weight and pressure until the lightness is such that it appears as though he's riding on a cloud. We are born this way, with a natural lightness of being; it is a true horseperson who can buoy what has buckled under the egos of men and women alike.

"You're making me self-conscious," Clarissa says. "I thought we're not supposed to eat or drink alone."

Sebastian tugs a grape from its stem and eats it. Clarissa grins as the sweetness transforms his face and he nods in agreement.

"Told you so!"

She reaches for her wine. He stays her hand.

"Don't you think you should eat a little more first?"

"I promise, I'll eat whatever you put in front of me."

She isn't lying. It's as though someone flipped a switch in her brain that makes her hungry for everything. Food. Wine. Companionship. Affection. God only knows what else. She brings the glass to her lips and draws a sip of wine. It's rustic and lush and tastes like she imagines Argentina looks and feels.

"Tell me about Argentina."

"Argentina," he says wistfully, "is a land of many personalities." His gaze lifts to a distant, grassy horizon etched into his mind. "As for me, what I know best is the Pampas. It's our American West."

"So—you're a cowboy?"

"In my country, we are known as gauchos, descendants of Andalusians who intermarried with the natives of the land. Our heritage is horsemanship, it is in our blood. In fact, it's said that a gaucho without his horse is only half a man."

Clarissa leans forward and props her chin in her hands, her eyes round with intrigue.

"I was known as a *domador*, a horse trainer. I trained horses for the *estancieros*— ranchers who needed dependable cattle horses for their farms. Some *domadors* would break the horses in the most primitive ways, the old ways of our forefathers, using methods of stress and deprivation. But I searched for a better way, a more humane approach that honors the soul of the horse. I became known as a soft-touch *domador*, sought for my gentle but most effective ways. Before long, *estancieros* across the Pampas were lining up to have me start their most prized colts. When word of my abilities spread beyond the Pampas, I was recruited by the owners of Argentina's most elite stud farms to oversee their breeding programs and train their polo ponies."

"Are they really ponies?"

"In a sense. They're the offspring of our native Criollo horses, crossed with the English Thoroughbreds. From the Criollo comes endurance. From the Thoroughbreds come speed and grace. The ponies are no taller than fifteen hands but as big-hearted and bold as any horse. And certainly more agile than most."

"Sounds like a pretty good gig—so why would you leave?"

"Let's just say I needed a fresh start."

"Sounds like girl trouble."

"Excuse me?" Sebastian sputters, nearly spitting the wine from his mouth.

"Girl trouble. Who was she?"

Clarissa blames the wine for her boldness, but even if it were water, she would have begged to know. Sebastian's mouth sets in a thin, hard line and hems in his bitter response.

"Well, if it's not girl trouble, then it must be trouble with the law. No one leaves a charmed life for no good reason. Are you a criminal?"

"Some would say," he deadpans.

"Are you really?"

"Um...no." He stands and ambles into the kitchen and peers into the oven. "You do have quite the imagination, don't you?"

"I'm a writer. It's how I roll."

"What do you write?" he asks as he sets the baking sheet on the stovetop.

"Romance novels, mostly."

He transfers the empanadas to a plate and garnishes the edges with dollops of thick, green chimichurri sauce. He sets the plate on the table and resumes his stretch in the opposite chair. He lights a grassy-scented candle as the natural light fades into a dusty blue that sidles in and washes over them.

"So you're a hopeless romantic?"

"I suppose I am a romantic. And I'm *definitely* hopeless," she says with an embarrassed roll of her eyes.

"Hope breathes."

"What?"

"As long as you have breath, there is hope."

Candlelight dances in the darkness of his eyes. He places an empanada on her plate.

"Eat."

She presses her fork into the flaky, golden pastry and it gives way to the spicy aroma of the warm, moist meat within. She raises a bite to her lips and once consumed, she gushes with pleasure.

"Oh! This is amazing."

Sebastian refills her wine glass and points to the dollops of chimichurri.

"Try it with the sauce."

Clarissa swirls her next forkful in a vibrant, green fusion that's fragrant with fresh parsley, cilantro, and oregano in a silky olive oil base.

She slaps one hand on the table and moans with delight. "Holy empanada!"

"Now," he says, "take a sip of the wine."

Clarissa raises her glass to her lips. As the dark, shimmering tonic rolls over her tongue, she savors the exquisite, exotic blend of flavors in her mouth. She closes her eyes and slowly leans back in her chair and sighs.

"Welcome to Argentina," Sebastian says and smiles.

12

Clarissa groans and pulls the sheet over her eyes to shield them from the harsh morning light. She doesn't have to open her eyelids to know her head hurts. As the fabric scratches her cheek, she startles. This is definitely not the soft, blue, Egyptian cotton that lines her own bed! Her eyes fly open. She gasps and bolts upright and says one of those words with whispered gusto. She says the word over and over again as her feet hit the floor and she searches for her boots. She sounds like a clucking chicken.

Spying them neatly paired at the foot of the bed—Sebastian's bed!—she forces herself to be quiet and still. She glances around, taking stock of herself and her surroundings. The room is largely brown with a smattering of Aztec reds and golds. There's a single photograph in a weathered frame on the bedside table; not of a woman, but of a horse, wearing the same turquoise-studded bridle that now hangs on the wall in the living room as art—or perhaps a shrine, she ponders. But the pondering only hurts her head more and she turns her attention to the twist in her jeans and the wrinkles in her shirt. At least she's fully dressed, she consoles herself. Whatever happened—or didn't—couldn't be that bad. She leans over to grab her boots. Her brain bobbles and she's slightly nauseous and she clutches her forehead and moans. Damn Argentinean wine...so lovely yet so cruel!

She tugs her boots onto her feet and sighs with relief. At least she's prepared to bolt at the first sight or sound of Sebastian. She tiptoes to the door, but not before her eyes rivet on the work table in the corner. It's full of scraps of leather and an arsenal of tools that look sharp and primitive and masculine and remind her that she's in the dwelling place of a breathtakingly mysterious man.

She cracks open the bedroom door and tiptoes into the living room. There's no need for stealth. Sebastian slept on the sofa in the tack room last night. I know because he came to check on me and the other horses later than usual and never left, not until just before dawn. That's the slate blue, anguished hour when he ventures out with Azul and eventually returns in peace. Living in the show barn, I am privy to his comings and goings and secrets too.

Clarissa glances at the dining table, neatly reset for two. There's no trace of last night's encounter to be found, except for the stubby wick of the candle, which has burned down and drowned in a pool of hot wax. Realizing Sebastian's already gone, she stares hard at the table and tries to piece together memories that flutter behind her eyes. Hazy vignettes roll out like choppy scenes in her screenplay. Oh my God, did she really tell him she had once wanted to be a nun? Something about *wasted beauty*, he had replied, words so tenderly spoken that they sounded like resurrection and peace and made the call to be something other a happy fault. She glances out the bay window. Crimson roses brandish sunlight and dew and she recalls something he said about the roses...blood roses, he called them, the same color of the roses that climbed the walls of his *estancia* on the Pampas... where he lived with his wife. Yes, he confessed, he had once been married. She remembers the squinting discomfort in his eyes and the firm set of his mouth. There would be no more details. He had already said too much.

Girl trouble! She knew it from the start. And now she had girl troubles of an entirely different kind. If anyone was to see her leaving Sebastian's cottage—especially any one of the show girls—they'd bury her and her reputation alive! Mean girls are like that. They sport long, fanged memories and clawing grudges that maim their prey but never to the point of death. They much prefer to toy with the objects of their disaffection until their noses detect the scent of younger, fresher blood. Mean girls, especially single ones, are perpetually on the hunt, just like mountain lions. No wonder they're always wild-eyed and exhausted.

Not so with horses, whose maiming always ends in a meal. Being prey ourselves, we've learned to keep our feet moving and our ears ever attuned to the sounds of encroaching danger. For us, it's something as subtle as a footfall in the brush, a mere whisper of movement, the faintest crunch, the snap of a twig, the way the air vibrates with opposition. But for humans, the sights and sounds of danger are much less obvious. Often they come with toothy grins that lull humans into a false sense of security.

Clarissa barrels off the front porch and onto the pea gravel path outside of Sebastian's front door. "Claire!" Camilla says and smiles as they nearly collide at the first bend. "What are you doing here?"

Clarissa skids to a stop. She notices the picnic basket hanging on the show girl's tawny, well-toned arm and shrinks on the inside. Perhaps Sebastian has a steady rotation of guests at his table after all!

"I just stopped by to tell Sebastian I have to cancel my lesson today," she fudges, hoping she doesn't look too disheveled. "But he's not home," she says flippantly and attempts to smooth the wrinkles in her shirt.

Camilla scans her from head to toe; she nods, slowly and voraciously. "Of course not, he's in the arena giving a lesson to Regina. Didn't you bother to look there first?" Her delicate nose twitches at the scent of fear.

Clarissa's shoulders collapse as Camilla's shrewd smile reveals the gig is up. Clarissa has two choices: fight or flight. "I have to go," she blurts. "You two enjoy your picnic."

"Oh, this?" Camilla says, holding up the basket. "It's just some fresh-picked tomatoes and cucumbers and cilantro from my garden. I thought Sebastian might like something healthy to go with that gooey, fried provolone he likes so much. I suppose it's his guilty pleasure. We all have at least one, don't we?"

She drips emphasis on the word *guilty* and packs a punch into the word *pleasure*. Her dark blond hair gleams in the sun like the golden hide of a mountain lion. She's clearly toying with her now...move your feet, Clarissa, before you get hurt!

Clarissa flinches and shrugs. "I suppose," is all she says. She feels Camilla's slanted, gray eyes burn a hole in her back as she turns and heads down the path toward the parking lot. Her breath comes in shallow puffs as she walks as fast as she can without breaking into a run. When she reaches her car, she fumbles for the key fob in the pocket of her jeans and unlocks the door. She climbs into the driver's seat and checks her appearance in the rear view mirror. Ugh, she says, and leans back in her seat. She conceals the mascara smudges under her eyes with massive, black sunglasses and fires up the ignition. I raise my head in my pasture at the familiar tick-tick-hum that floats in the air then fades away. What? Not even a carrot for the best horse in the whole world?

She races through three yellow lights. Unwilling to fight, her flight instinct runs on autopilot. She barely comes to a full stop when she pulls into her driveway; she jams the car in park, then bolts into the house and peels off her wine-stained shirt and slept-in jeans at the threshold of the laundry room. She can't stand the sight of herself wearing her own folly. In what world was consenting to Sebastian's invitation a good idea, she berates herself? She tosses her clothes into the washer and slams the lid. She hears the muffled, double chime of her cell phone—then says one of those words and lifts the lid. She fishes out her phone just before the water rushes in and stares at the screen...

Come to Paris.

She sinks down to the floor, her naked back pressed against cold, stainless steel.

Come to Paris.

She knows it's neither a command nor a suggestion, but a tender invitation to bridge a distance greater than the ocean between them. She clutches the phone to her chest and closes her eyes and prays ancient prayers she stopped saying long ago; their slow, steady recitation replaces the rumble of confusion in her soul with waves of peace and inspiration. When she opens her eyes she knows Paris will have to wait...

She hurriedly showers and puts on fresh make-up and clothes. Then she eagerly sits down and writes until her hero reveals himself in flesh and blood and distinct features that reconcile the dueling passions within and elevate art to life and the one Love that matters in the end. It is her sacred offering, her hope that she is a still a pen in the hand of God; perhaps not a virgin bride, but a pen whose scratching may yet recover what was lost so many years ago to human hands who blackened her soul and profaned her blossoming body in the dark hallways of innocence. By the time she finishes typing for the day, she's thoroughly intrigued by the man that stares back at her on paper. She wants to know more. She has to know more! She gathers her resolve and a fistful of carrots and heads to the barn to defy her demons—or mountain lions, as they manifest to me.

I wait for her at the gate, knowing that the long shadows overtaking the pasture signal the end of my day in the field. Now that the heat wave is over, Clarissa makes sure I get turned out during the daytime too. I join up with my original herd—Hersey, Merlin, and Moose—and graze to my heart's content. But I'm not content. I look for Clarissa to dance and play at the end of the day, and when I hear her coming—I know she's coming from the slight hitch in her hip that makes one footfall heavier than the other—I nicker my eagerness to join in whatever silly game she invents for me. I nicker again, this time with impatience as she stops to chat with Bernie.

"Hello, Clarissa."

"Hey, Bernie. Did you ride today?"

"We went on trail with Natasha and Raven. Carla and Hershey are still out there somewhere. It was a spectacular day! You missed the best part of it," he says as he gestures to a cavalcade of clouds rolling in.

"It's okay. Sometimes I like to come a little later when the barn's not so busy."

Bernie smiles and nods. There's something in his sawtoothed smile that doesn't sit quite right with Clarissa. That's because he's not smiling. He's leering.

"Ah yes, when everybody isn't minding everyone else's business. We're all entitled to a little privacy, eh?"

Clarissa rolls back on her heels, creating a little more distance between them.

"Say, would you like to grab some dinner with me when you're through?"

"Oh! Thank you, but I—just ate. Yeah, I just ate."

"Maybe just a drink then?"

"I can't, I have to go back to work after this."

"Work?"

"Yes, I'm writing a story."

"What's it about?"

"It's about a guy on a dude ranch—and a girl."

"Oh, so it's a love story?"

He leers again. She half expects him to rub his little hands together like a creepy uncle in the attic. Instinctively, she folds her arms across her chest. I nicker and swish my tail in protest at the delay. She gestures in my general direction.

"Duty calls."

"Another time, perhaps?"

"Bernie..." Clarissa searches for the right words. "You know I'm married, right?"

He tilts his head and tugs at his salt-and-pepper goatee. "I heard that you were—dating. Perhaps I heard wrong. *Je regrette*, my apologies, Claire."

Clarissa nods dumbly, then makes a quarter-turn toward the gate. She doesn't run but she wants to. She fumbles with my lead rope, which is looped and tangled over the top rail. She frees it and attaches it to the ring on my halter, then leads me further into the pasture rather than out of it. She vibrates confusion and radiates heat. I nudge her with my head, unsure of her intentions. She caresses my face and releases a heavy sigh. I mimic her with a long, hearty blow. A soon as Bernie leaves, she turns us toward the gate.

"Come on, Sonny, let's go play."

I follow her through the gate and into the shade of the oak tree. Miguel and Pedro appear at the top of the hill with muck forks and wheelbarrows in tow. They spot Clarissa and rapidly fire words that sound bawdy and rude, and giggle like twelve-year-old girls. I feel her shrink back and I mentally urge her to move her feet forward—always forward!

We turn the corner onto the gravel path that leads to the outdoor ring and the riding fields beyond. She flinches at the sight of Camilla, Penny, Regina and Margaret nestled in a in a tight circle against the hedgerow as they hover over images on a tiny screen. They startle at the sight of us, too.

"Oh! Hello, Claire," Camilla says. "I'm surprised to see you back here today."

"I thought I'd do some groundwork with Sonny before our lesson tomorrow."

"So you were able to reschedule it?"

I feel the negative charge in the air and paw at the ground, eager to move on.

"Yes, Sebastian's very accommodating," Clarissa improvises.

Camilla raises a pale, blond eyebrow. "Indeed, he is. I think we can *all* agree on that."

The show girls exchange scandalized glances and at least one of them fails to hide their collective inner smirk. Clarissa inhales sharply as she realizes last night's indiscretion has eyes and ears and legs and is running loose throughout the barn. Even Margaret refuses to look her in the eye. Instead, she glances at her watch and gasps. "I have a lesson in ten minutes! See you later, girls. And congratulations on your new granddaughter, Regina. She's gorgeous, just like her Nana!"

"I'm not Nana, I'm Gigi!" Regina sniffs. "Nana is for fat Italian women with stubby, white beards and torpedo boobs."

"My Nana was very beautiful," Clarissa declares. She doesn't like Regina's smug assessment of her beloved Nana, who was truly the most beautiful human being she had ever known. She fixes her eyes on the distant field and inches toward it. I can't wait to get out in the open, too. This narrow, closed-in space is a playground for predators.

"You must have inherited her good genes, my dear," Regina replies. Her words don't sound the least bit haughty and Clarissa ventures a sidelong glance. Regina counters with a generous smile.

There's a certain respect that is garnered from living and speaking one's truth. Perhaps Clarissa has the show girls—or at least some of them—all wrong. Perhaps her own refusal to believe the beautiful truth about herself has created more angst and division and isolation than mean girls ever could.

"Thank you," Clarissa murmurs we step off and pick up the pace.

"You're welcome," Regina chirps and suffers a glare from Camilla.

"Well, she *is* very attractive!" Regina half whispers. "And she seems awfully nice, too."

Camilla merely rolls her eyes and says *pfft* in her best imitation of Bridget, who observes all from her throne on the hill and scribbles handwritten notes in her little black book of infractions committed by the unwashed masses. Even the show girls are not immune from her imperious eye—and Clarissa occupies several pages!

By the time we reach the parking lot where the trailers are arranged in neat little rows, Clarissa's boil over Sebastian's indiscretion bubbles over. It's all I can do to keep up with her without breaking into a trot. She doesn't even notice the stiffness of my ears until I leap sideways in a giant spook at a sudden movement detected by my left eye. It's the thinking side of my brain, but right now, it thinks I'm gonna die.

"Sonny!"

"Whoa, Sonny, it's okay," Sebastian says as he emerges from the side door of a three-horse gooseneck trailer.

I snort and release adrenaline. I snort again to express my irritation. Clarissa shushes me and walks me in a tight circle to help redirect my focus and excess energy. I have to admit it helps. I hang my head and lick and chew as Sebastian approaches. I'm over it.

"Sorry about the spook. I didn't know you were out there," Sebastian says. He admires the blush in her cheeks and the way the pink of them makes her mossy eyes glitter. But Clarissa's not blushing. She's throwing off a different kind of heat. "Did you sleep well?"

"Never mind that. I hope you're satisfied!" she sputters.

Sebastian tilts the brim of his hat to get a better look at Clarissa.

"As if it's not bad enough that every man around here now thinks I'm hot to trot—the show girls think I'm a hussy."

Sebastian grins. Bad move, Sebastian.

"Oh, you think that's funny? I knew last night was a bad idea! Waking up in your bed with a massive hangover was punishment enough. But I didn't think you'd tell the whole barn that you slept with me when you didn't," she hisses.

"I don't think it's funny. But I do think it's amusing that you care what anyone thinks. And for the record, I said no such thing—but maybe Camilla did. I understand she saw you leaving my cottage this morning. And your car parked in the same spot overnight *is* a bit incriminating." He arches one brow and shrugs.

"I can't believe you're being so cavalier about this. I'm a married woman, you know."

"Are you?" Sebastian thrusts his hands in the pockets of his breeches and artfully collapses into a casual stance. She flinches and gasps.

"Yes! As a matter of fact, my husband is begging me to come to Paris."

This time, it's Sebastian who flinches, but Clarissa doesn't notice. She doesn't see the bat of his eye or the subtle clench of his jaw or hear the way his breath catches in his throat—but I do. His dark eyes grow darker, like creeping shade over pasture.

"You should go," he urges, even as his weight pitches forward and his hands curl into fists in his pockets lest he reach out and grasp her by the arm. "Paris is the city of love, is it not?"

Clarissa furtively twists the gold band on her finger. He's right. She should go. Does he want her to go? Why would he suggest that she go unless he didn't care if she should stay or go? But his voice is tender and provocative with allusions to love; just the word on his lips takes her breath away—but not for long. The tension is too thick for me. I blow out a nostril-flapping whoosh of air that makes Clarissa gasp and wince as droplets spray her arm.

"Sonny!" she reprimands me again, then thrusts her hand on her hip and turns back to Sebastian. "What are you doing here, anyway? Don't you have lessons today?"

"I was replacing the bungees in Margaret's trailer with a breakaway tie. We're taking Dante to his first show on Saturday. He doesn't trailer well and if he panics, it won't be pretty."

Clarissa glares at Margret's massive gooseneck trailer, replete with cozy living quarters—and a bed! Her imagination flares and she rattles and shuts down like a broken furnace.

"Well, maybe you'll get lucky," she says coldly. "Listen Sebastian, I've been thinking. The last thing I need in my life is more drama. I just want to come here and enjoy my horse. Maybe it's best if we cancel our lessons for awhile."

Sebastian returns her cold stare.

"As you wish, Clarissa. Your horse, your rodeo."

"What's that supposed to mean?"

Sebastian glances at his watch.

"I have to go. I have a lesson in five."

"So go!" she snaps, but she's the one who turns away first. She leads me toward the field where we practiced walking in-hand under Sebastian's watchful eye. He's still watching; I feel his eyes follow like a rear guard and I swish my tail in protest. There's pressure on every side!

I drift toward the fence. Clarissa tugs on the lead rope and insists that I walk closer. She tosses a glance behind her and sees Margaret's fiery hair glowing in the sun as she marches toward the ring with Dante in tow. He's not moving any faster or more willingly than me. We are both members of the same chain gang today, only his invisible chain is spun from gold.

Clarissa tightens her grip on the lead rope when we reach the first fence post. She picks a point in the distance; I think I know what it is, but then our connection breaks as Clarissa's ears flood and her mind clouds at the sound of Margaret's girlish laughter cascading downhill to the place where we stand. Clarissa steps forward and I linger behind. She has no focus and therefore I have no inclination to follow her anywhere at all.

"Come on, Sonny!" she barks at me and tugs a little harder. "We did this perfectly yesterday, remember? Let's go."

I take a few reluctant steps forward. She tilts her chin down and gazes at the grass. I think it's an invitation. I dive down and snatch a bite. She yanks my head and smites me with a look of betrayal.

"Really, Sonny? Why won't you listen?"

She grimaces at my swiveling ears. I hear every little thing but Clarissa, whose vague intentions swirl into white noise. I want to please her but I don't know how. She sighs at my wide-eyed, worried expression. "It's okay, Sonny. It's all my fault—I'm the worst leader in the whole world! I'm so sorry you're stuck with me!"

She tosses the end of my lead rope onto the grass.

"Go on. Eat!"

She sinks to the ground and draws her knees to her chest where she rests her head. She begins to make pitiful, little sounds that make her back heave and her breath stutter. I watch her with a troubled eye as I bow my head to graze.

"Hey!"

Clarissa startles and pops up her head. She paws at her face with her hands.

"There's no crying in horsemanship!" Carla shouts as she emerges from the trailhead with Hershey. Clarissa scrambles to her feet. Hershey breaks into a high-stepping trot and I swish my tail excitedly. He's full of bluster and confidence and turns in my direction.

"Whoa," Carla says in a husky voice. Hershey halts and stands as still as a fencepost while Carla dismounts.

"What's wrong? Did you come off or something?"

"No, it's nothing like that. I'm just—so frustrated!"

Carla grins. "If riding was easy, everyone would do it."

"Forget riding, I can't even lead him! What kind of horse wants to be saddled with someone like me?"

"I didn't know we were having a pity party. Anyone else coming?"

Clarissa shakes her head and spills another tear.

"Nope, just you."

"So," Carla says as she reaches out and wipes the tear from Clarissa's cheek with her thumb. "What are you *really* crying about?"

"I don't know!" The truth is, she has no idea if she's crying about George or Sebastian or me, or the way the whispered innuendoes about her give rise to a resurgence of dirtiness and shame. She cringes at the thought that Carla might know she spent the night at Sebastian's. She can only imagine how disappointed she would be.

"In my forty years with horses, I've learned a couple of things. First, it's almost never the horse's fault. Second, it's almost never about the horse. If your horse isn't cooperating or doing what you've asked, you've either asked him the wrong way or he's simply mirroring whatever you're putting out into the universe." She pulls off her rose-tinted, aviator sunglasses and searches Clarissa's face for a clue.

"Let me ask you something, Claire. What do you want out of this?"

"Out of what?"

Carla points to me. "This journey with your horse."

I step away from the pressure of their stares and stuff my mouth with the spiky, bitter leaves and yellow fluff of rogue dandelions.

"If you want to run away from your life, I suggest you get a bicycle! But if you want to immerse yourself in a true relationship, where Sonny's language is as important as your own, and his needs are more important than yours, and your baggage is your own to carry—then you have half a chance of getting it right and winning the heart of a horse who'll do anything you ask. Sonny's your traveling companion, not a beast of burden. So? Where do you want to go with him?"

Clarissa closes her eyes and ponders the question. There is a place in her mind...it's lush and green and dotted with yellow flowers and there's blue sky and trails to ride and a place to just be...just be...just be...here...now! Yes, my sweet Clarissa, yes! Just be here now! I blow out pleasure and relief.

Clarissa's eyelids flutter open and she glances wide-eyed at her surroundings as though seeing them for the first time.

"I know I say it every day, but it really doesn't get any better than this!" Carla declares with a grand flourish of her hand. Clarissa musters a smile and dabs her eyes with her sleeve.

"Carla?"

"Yes, Claire?"

"I slept over Sebastian's house last night."

"I know, dear."

"Nothing happened."

"Of course not."

"All the show girls know."

"And the hired help, too."

"I feel like such a fool."

"The only opinion of you that should matter around here is *his*." She points to me again.

"Carla."

"Yes, Claire."

"Thank you."

"You're welcome, kid."

She mounts Hershey from the ground and rests in the saddle with the lightness of a butterfly. She thinks forward and so Hershey goes. Clarissa and I linger a bit longer and when she lifts my lead rope and calmly asks me to travel with her to the top of the hill, I'm swayed by her budding confidence and cheerfully oblige. We walk energetically all the way to the arena where Sebastian's lesson with Margaret is winding down. He can't help but turn and follow Clarissa with his eyes. He feels her nearness like the fervent pulse of an Argentine tango that quickens his blood and draws heat to his chest and for a moment, he loses his concentration.

Clarissa allows me to graze outside the ring and stands with her back to Sebastian and Margaret. She vibrates patience and purpose and I nibble a circle around her feet, happy to be near her.

"Sebastian," Margaret coos as she slides down the slab of Dante's side and her tall, elegant boots sink into the sand. "That was an amazing ride! I feel so much better about showing on Saturday." She removes her helmet and her hairnet and lets her shiny, red hair spill over her shoulders.

"Don't overthink it, you're ready."

"I hope so," Margaret says as she takes Dante by the reins and leads him toward the gate. "Are you coming up to the barn?" she tosses behind her with a hopeful smile.

"I have to reset the jumps for Bridget's lesson. Go ahead without me."

"I'll leave a check for you in the lockbox."

Sebastian nods and waves. She glances shyly over her shoulder, wishing he'd change his mind, but he's too busy wishing Clarissa would change hers to notice. I keep one eye on Sebastian as he rebuilds the jump course from one end of the arena to the other. Clarissa pretends to ignore the flurry of activity. She cocks a hip and hums softly. I love when Clarissa hums. The sound oscillates and tickles my ears and makes me feel extra happy to be Clarissa's horse. When the music ends, she shifts her feet and I lift my head from a patch of long grass sprouting around a tree trunk. Something's about to happen. I can feel the subtle change in the rhythm of her breath, followed by a deep, stuttering inhale.

"Sebastian!" she calls out.

He sets the last pole between a pair of jump standards and glances in our direction.

"Come on, Sonny," she murmurs. I turn on my haunches and follow her to the bottom of the fence that hems in the ring. Sebastian meets her there and props his elbows on the top rail, his stance casual and attentive. If he had ears like mine, however, they'd be swiveling, eager as he is to hear what she has to say.

"I made a rash decision. I do want to keep taking lessons with you but I insist on paying you for your services. Furthermore, I want to be treated just like every other student. Like you treat Regina and Margaret, for instance," she says with a firm set to her lips. She drops my lead rope to fold her arms defiantly across her chest.

Sebastian mulls the proposition. "We have an arrangement—your saddle?"

Clarissa rolls her eyes. "You can buy it a hundred times over with the money you make here. I'll give you first dibs, I promise. I just don't want any special treatment, it causes too much drama. Please," she says and lowers her voice to a murmur, "let's forget last night ever happened. I just want to be an ordinary student—okay?"

"But there's nothing ordinary about you, Clarissa," he teases.

Clarissa's crossed arms tighten as though to keep her heart from leaping through her chest.

"Nevertheless, I'll do as you ask."

"Tomorrow morning? Ten o'clock?" Claire proposes.

"You'll not be leaving for Paris anytime soon, then?"

His eyes search hers for a clue.

"I haven't decided," she says and shrugs. "George was probably drunk when he asked."

"Or maybe he wasn't," Sebastian replies as he stands tall and pushes off from the rail. "You said you're a hopeless romantic, why not believe?" He hates himself for saying it, for saying anything that might drive her back into the arms of a man who had callously left her covered in the dust of her life with horses, her life with me. And yet, he can only think of what he would do to preserve the love he once had with Sofía given the chance! He would stop at nothing to save love.

"Correction. I'm only a hopeless romantic on paper," she says with a meager laugh. "In real life, I don't really think love conquers all—at all." Her thoughts drift and she rattles her head in protest. "You don't speak to your other students this way, do you?"

Sebastian grins. "I admit, my musings are only for you."

"We have a deal, remember?"

"Yes, Clarissa, we have a deal. Bring your A-game. You're going to need it."

She balks at his warning but thinks she might need a little extra confidence just the same—perhaps a bit more tread in her stirrups. She leads me back to my barn and settles me in my stall and empties a baggie filled with chopped apples into my feed bin. Before long, she's off to the tack store for whatever cheats she can find. She picks up a pair of summery, crocheted gloves for extra grip, and some new stirrups angled to relieve the pressure on her knees and hips and keep the balls of her feet in their proper place. She even surrenders to the allure of the sparkly belt the show girls wear. She throws in a bag of my favorite horse muffins as additional insurance that I'll be good. There's little I won't do for a horse muffin. But then again, there's *nothing* I won't do for Clarissa when she asks me with conviction.

Later that day and long into the night, she immerses herself in videos and books on the proper forms and techniques of dressage: tempo and frame and half-halts and transitions coupled with suppling and lengthening and bending and yielding... topped off by expositions on the correct aids, proper breath, posture, and centered riding—all to produce a happy, balanced, responsive horse. What a complicated path to a happy, balanced, responsive horse! The world's first and best horsemen achieved harmony with horses through reverence and leadership and respect and humility coupled with softness and lightness and feel. To this, we willingly offer our highest and our best. The mechanics are mere compensation for the unwillingness of humans to do the harder work—the work of the spirit that animates and raises the inner self to freedom from ego and every earthly constraint and offers true unity with the heart of the horse.

Between videos, she Googles with surreptitious fingers...the soft-touch *domador* of the Pampas...the famous trainer of polo ponies for Argentina's most illustrious stud farms...the mysterious woman who was once his wife...Mrs. Sebastian Bergalo...who is she? Surely there are words and images floating somewhere in the worldwide web of secret loves and past lives.

But there's nothing, nothing to be found of the man who fuels her imagination both on and off the page. She shuffles to the bar and pours herself a glass of red wine. Lately, a glass before bed helps her sleep through the night and quiets the disturbing, recurrent dream she has of galloping on my back toward the edge of a cliff, breathless and out of control. She always awakens just before the earth ends and the dark abyss swallows us whole. Her dream disturbs my slumber as well; she is half-horse to my half-human and in our collective consciousness there is no divide. That same connection sustains the fleeting, mental images of hearts and stars she sends me at random times of the day, little reminders that I'm the best horse in the whole world. I feel her like I feel a soft ripple of breeze; I know not from where it comes, or where it goes, but in those soulful and ephemeral moments, I know we are bonded forever.

She sips her wine slowly and closes the lid of her computer. She's done all she can to prepare for the day ahead, to show Sebastian she's as tough and focused and teachable as any other student of dressage, to prove she doesn't need the kind of soft-touch training he offers to her alone. It not only serves to make the show girls resentful but makes her feel like the slow kid in class, less than able and needful of extra patience and understanding.

As she passes through the kitchen on her way to bed, she frowns at the mountain of mail that has piled up since George has been gone. A handsome, brown packet sealed with gold foil and addressed to George begs further inspection. She smirks when she reads the label. Not only had George signed up for monthly deliveries of boutique wines, apparently he had recently joined a cigar-of-the-month club as well. She opens the package and sniffs the cigars. She inhales their earthy, spicy aroma and recalls her father's penchant for expensive, bootlegged Cohiba cigars. When he wasn't smoking them, he'd sneak up behind her and fiddle them up her dress and laugh when she gasped and blushed. She knocks back the rest of her wine and sets the empty glass in the sink. In a moment of magnanimity, she thinks the least she can do for George is put them in the humidor behind the bar where they'll age a for week or a month or longer—until whenever he decides to come home. If he decides to come home!

She shuffles back to the living room and retrieves a sleek, wooden humidor from a shelf below the bar. She raises the burled lid and stares at the damning evidence inside. Dark burgundy lipstick clings to the ivory tip of a slim, half-smoked tiparillo; if she knew George, it was a souvenir of sorts, like the stack of love letters and matchbook covers and ticket stubs he kept of their own storied romance in an old shoebox on the top shelf of his closet. She blinks twice and curses at the wantonness of it all. Her imagination conjures the face of the woman whose full, dark lips drew from the pearly tip. She has glossy, jet-black tresses and a white smile, a vampy slant to her sapphire eyes and a perfect, delicate French nose that tilts at the sight of American farm girls with musty-smelling, mud-brown hair and horse manure on the soles of their shoes and God only knows what under their ragged fingernails.

Clarissa glares at her shabby hands. Maybe George has a point. Maybe he just wants the girly girl he met in Miami and married—maybe he has a right to her. But the horse is already out of the barn and halfway down the road of irreconcilable differences.

Come to Paris.

It was all too much to contemplate! Wine of the Month. Cigar of the Month. If she didn't consent to pack up and go, would Mistress of the Month be next? And if it was, could she blame him? His invitation implies mercy and forgiveness. How can she refuse?

She closes the humidor, shoves it back under the bar, and reminds herself to stay focused, like she's learning to do in the field with me. She resolves not to borrow trouble. Right here, right now, she needs some sleep so that she's refreshed and ready when the sun comes up. She doesn't have an A-game, maybe not even a B-game—but in spite of the sorry end to this day, she's still standing. She's still striving. She's still breathing....

The vivid memory of Sebastian sitting across from her at the table drifts over the inside of her eyelids as he softly utters the words that both console and provoke her. *Hope breathes.* She throws off the sheets and hopes that when the morning comes he's as cold and clinical as a dead man on ice because right now, the recollection of drinking Sebastian's spicy wine and immersing herself in his sultry, dark eyes and sleeping in his warm, cozy bed makes her feel flush with a mortifying mix of humiliation and desire.

She speeds up the overhead fan and nestles her cheek into the coolness of her pillow.

But it's much too *caliente* to sleep.

13

"Okay, let's start with a twenty-meter circle at the walk." Clarissa's doesn't know exactly what twenty meters measures on the ground without orange cones to guide her, but she's watched enough dressage riders to make a close attempt. She clenches the reins and takes up contact in the same manner suggested by nine out of the ten videos she studied last night. I jut my head and try to pull the reins through her hands. To my surprise, nothing gives. She squeezes her legs and sends me forward. I shake my head in protest.

"You have to give to get, Clarissa. What's with the death grip on the reins?"

"I'm taking up contact!"

"That's not contact, that's claustrophobia!" Sebastian reprimands.

"Then what do you want me to do?"

"Relax the inside rein so he can't lean on it and support him with the outside rein. Give him his share of responsibility!"

Clarissa fumbles with the thin, rubber dressage reins that Sebastian has attached to the rings of my snaffle bit. They feel stiff and clumsy in her gloved hands and she fiddles with one and then the other in an ongoing effort to even them out.

"Apply your inside leg at the girth and hold him in with your outside leg. We want to ask him to bend on the circle."

Clarissa compensates for my stiffness and resistance by allowing her inside hand to drift and pull toward the center of the circle. My nose follows her hand.

"No! You're pulling his neck around while his body travels straight. That's not bending that's riding a bicycle! Use your legs and your seat! Your hand is the aid of last resort."

Clarissa and I complete the circle and come to a stop. She pats me on the neck and waits for Sebastian's next command. He strides over from the center of the ring and picks up her leg by the ankle.

"This," he says, moving her inside leg forward an inch, "is at the girth." He presses her leg into me and I step to the right. "Got it?"

"Yes," Clarissa says, "I think so."

"Go ahead and walk the entire ring. I want you to circle in each corner and don't even think about using your hands to steer him." His delivery is cool and mechanical.

Clarissa sucks in breath and cues me to move forward. I offer the marching walk that she wants but my head is high and my back is hollow. She saws the reins to urge me to lower my head. The bit bangs around in my mouth and I can't help but wonder where in the world my sweet Clarissa has gone.

"Exactly where did you learn to do that?" Sebastian chides.

"Do what?"

"Saw the reins like a lumberjack?"

"I learned it on YouTube."

Sebastian groans and removes his hat and runs his fingers through his hair in exasperation.

"When you learn to properly engage your horse from behind and recycle the energy through the reins, he'll naturally assume a collected frame. I don't want to see you do that again. For now, we're simply looking for impulsion and a balanced, steady gait."

Clarissa nods as though she understands every word Sebastian says. As we circle in the corner, I start to spiral in. She leans into the center and makes matters worse.

"Sit up, inside leg!" Sebastian orders.

Clarissa responds with just the right amount of pressure at the girth. I drift back on track and we complete the circle with a respectable finish.

"Good correction!" Sebastian says and nods approvingly.

We repeat the circle exercise in the three remaining corners, then come to a halt at the top of the arena. Sebastian closes the distance between us and strokes me on my neck. "That was better, Clarissa, but you're still too heavy-handed on the reins."

He closes his fingers around Clarissa's inside hand and gently, almost imperceptibly, shifts it forward and back. "Give and take, give and take. A horse's greatest reward is in the release."

"Let's repeat the exercise at a trot. Start with a sitting trot and post when you feel ready."

Clarissa clucks and squeezes and off we go.

"Fix your diagonal," he barks as Clarissa begins to post.

"Got it!" she says and sits a beat. We settle into a steady rhythm and Sebastian follows us with his eyes, but his focus is no longer on me. They're on Clarissa and the way she rises and falls in the saddle with surprising grace. The saddle itself seems to come to life beneath her: the roses vivid and lustrous in the sunlight, the Argentine silver blinding with glory, the polished leather gleaming with pride.

"Sebastian?" Clarissa says as we whiz by for the second time. "Can we stop now? My inside leg feels like a wet noodle."

"Yes, of course, let's change direction."

"No, I mean, can we *stop* now?"

Sebastian glances at his Rolex. "We still have twenty minutes."

Clarissa dismounts and pulls off her crocheted gloves, one finger at a time.

"Don't you want to finish?"

She unbuckles her helmet and shimmies it off her head. Her hair cascades around her shoulders in damp, reckless waves.

"I'm done. I hate taking lessons with you..."

Sebastian's eyebrows shoot up and his jaw grows slack.

"Like this," she adds softly.

He crosses his arms over his chest and plants his feet firmly.

"Did I disappoint you?"

"No, you're a very good teacher."

"Did I not treat you like everyone else?"

"Yes. Yes, you did. And I don't like it—at all."

Sebastian cocks his hip and softens his stance just like a horse at rest. He responds with a thoughtful nod.

"So what would you have me do?"

"Teach me softness, and feel, and connection, like you told me you could...please."

Clarissa's mossy eyes flicker with hope. She inhales deeply and holds her breath.

"Meet me at the trailhead at seven o'clock."

"Should I tack him up?" she says and gestures to me. I hang my head and bask in the warmth of the sun. It feels good on the long muscles of my back that bent around two circles too many.

"Come without him."

She lowers her eyes and gnaws on her bottom lip.

"I cannot teach you if you cannot trust me," he scolds.

Clarissa mentally flashes through every encounter she's ever had with Sebastian, from their first meeting to their intimate dinner together and waking to find herself chastely tucked in his bed. He'd done nothing to prove himself unworthy of her trust. The fact that he so fiercely guarded his personal life wasn't reason enough to doubt his intentions.

"I trust you," she pronounces and levels her gaze to meet his.

"I have just two conditions."

Clarissa's anxiety travels down the reins and I rattle my head to shake it off.

"First, our original agreement stands. My time for your saddle."

Clarissa shrugs. "Okay, what else?"

Sebastian's eyes sweep down to her waist. She squirms at the boldness of his gaze. "Leave the rhinestone belt at home. It hurts my eyes and your natural beauty is dazzling enough." He grins and it shatters the tension between them.

"It's a deal," Clarissa concedes with a demure smile. As Clarissa and I approach the gap in the hedgerow, Sebastian lingers in place and mulls the gift of trust that Clarissa blindly offers. Sofía had trusted him too, trusted him to keep her safe from even her own worst follies and rash adventures. He had done the best that he could and come up short, come up wanting, come up bereaved and alone. She had been lost on his watch. Even if Clarissa trusted him, he could never again trust himself.

"Hey!" Clarissa turns and calls out to Sebastian. He startles from his thoughts. "Thanks for the lesson. It was—horrible!"

"You're welcome," he says and admires the ways she stands a little taller, with her shoulders pinned back and her chin held high—like the leader Sebastian knows I need. It's not that I'm incapable of taking the lead. It's just that any horse, given the chance, would rather relax and graze while the Alpha keeps law and order and assumes responsibility for the security of the herd. There is no ego in the wild. Horses are happiest knowing where they stand in the pecking order. It's ambivalence that creates turmoil in the herd.

It's the same kind of ambivalence that creates turmoil in the human heart. I wish Sebastian and Clarissa would buck or rear or do something physical to work it out. The air between them vibrates with uncertainty and I swish at it with my tail.

Clarissa gets the message and moves us forward. I relax into our easy walk up the hill and anticipate the cool water and tasty hay awaiting me in my stall. Instead, she hoses me off and turns me out into the pasture with Hershey and Merlin and Moose.

"They're calling for storms tonight," she tells me. "Enjoy the grass while you can. I'll come back and put you in your stall," she promises, and sends images of what to expect when darkness falls.

I saunter past Merlin who pins his ears. I'm an old horse, but a smart one. Nothing good can come from physical challenges to improve my standing. After all, there are no mares to be stolen and covered, no lack of food or water, no gain to be had from expending precious energy. A smart horse saves its energy for fights and flights of self-preservation. It's peaceful and calm in our five-acre pasture, and Hershey is a fair and capable leader. I eventually wander to the lowest corner of the field where tall grass grows around a fallen tree trunk that Pedro's too lazy to trim around. I eat for a long time, glad to have this secret stash of sweet grass for myself. But I'm only glad until my muzzle brushes up against a bee's nest tucked in the hollow of the trunk. I squeal and bolt, but not before my face gets bombarded by angry, yellow bees who make it perfectly clear I'm a threat to their existence. Sharp, tingly, throbbing sensations penetrate my skin and even as I gallop to the top of the hill, my field of vision begins to shrink and I feel strangely out of sorts. I cleave to Hershey's side for comfort and protection. My breathing feels labored and I rub my face on my front legs. I put my head down and graze to distract myself from the burning pain and itch. Hershey senses my distress and hovers over me like I'm a newborn colt; I know Clarissa will come for me. Until then, I'm at the mercy of the laws of nature.

Sebastian and Clarissa prepare for their evening lesson in their own ways. He sheds his equestrian uniform and takes an hour-long *siesta*, then showers and dresses in a white tee shirt and jeans that instantly make him feel more relaxed. He prepares a small plate of cheese and olives, followed by freshly brewed *yerba mate* that he consumes in traditional Argentine fashion, served in a mate gourd and sipped through a silver *bombilla*. The potent, tribal mixture invigorates his body and soul with the strength and poetry of the South American rainforest from which the leaves spring forth. In every bittersweet sip, there's nostalgia and rejuvenation. He gazes out over the rolling hills of Crown Ridge, but in his mind's eye, the grassy plains of the Pampas whisper and taunt and beckon him home.

Clarissa steeps in a hot bath seasoned with lavender-scented Epsom salts. Her legs ache from overuse and she lingers until the water turns lukewarm. Reluctantly, she rises and towels herself dry, then stands before racks of clothes in her closet, wondering what to wear. Since she won't be riding, her sleek, black breeches that make her look ten pounds lighter won't do. She settles on a pair of faded Levi jeans tucked into her favorite red boots and a fitted, red-and-blue plaid blouse with pearly, Western-style snaps down the front. At the last minute, she adds a few ringlets to her hair with a curling iron she digs out of the bottom drawer of her vanity. It's twenty years old but it still works and she smiles into the mirror, pleased with the result.

The extra effort steals precious time and she races to the barn to get there by seven. She jams her car in park, furtively glances around, then hurries down the gravel path to the bottom of the hill. I watch her disappear out of the slit of one eye. She promised to come back for me, and I believe her.

Sebastian drums his hands impatiently against his thigh. He glances at his watch—7:03—and ticking. Traces of dappled sunlight sneak through the dense, green canopy and dance on the winding trail ahead. His upturned face receives the last of the day's light and warmth and Clarissa stops in her tracks to behold the sight of him; this man who has emerged from the dog-eared pages of her screenplay covered in warm, sinewy flesh and breathing life and hope. Her own breath stutters in her chest as she realizes what she's about to do—step onto the trail and into some dusky, sultry, leafy unknown. If she was all horse, right about now she'd be spinning and bolting in the other direction. But she's only half-horse, and so she dials in the thinking side of her brain and moves her feet forward. That's it, Clarissa, always forward!

"Hi," she says, softly and shyly. She doesn't mean for it to come out that way, but it does.

"Hi," he says and his generous smile puts her at ease. "I thought maybe you weren't coming." He drinks her in; her eyes, green as the moss on the north side of the pine trees, the bark-colored curls that hug her squared shoulders, her skin, smooth as river stone and tanned by the sun, her curvy body clad in clothing reminiscent of life on *la estancia.* In a moment, the draught of a decade is quenched. "I'm glad you made it."

"Me too. You kicked my butt this morning, I was exhausted."

"Yes, I did. That's precisely why I asked you to meet me here, Clarissa. Forging a partnership with Sonny doesn't have to be so hard. There's a better way—a *softer* way—to get what you so desperately want." He gestures toward the less traveled trail that leads to the river.

"Shall we?"

She merely nods and falls in beside him as shards of sunlight pierce the lowest branches of the trees like golden swords. The shushes of their boots over the trail soon give way to the sound of trickling water. They venture down the gentle slope of an embankment to where the river runs into a stream that swirls and churns over a rubble of rocks before veering into a lively brook of knee-deep water.

Sebastian halts a footstep away from the water's edge. He leans over and pulls off his cowboy boots, then peels off his socks and cuffs his jeans.

"What are you doing?"

"Taking off my boots. I suggest you do the same. I know how much they mean to you."

Her eyes lock on her red boots and he tilts his head with expectation. She groans inside, hoping her last pedicure has held up. She doesn't pay much attention to her feet these days. Gone are the days of wearing flip-flops or sparkly, gold sandals all summer long. That's a sure-fire way to get a broken foot in the barn—no foot, no fun. No hoof, no horse. It's the same thing.

Clarissa grits her teeth and pulls off her boots. She teeters forward and back. Sebastian grasps her by the arm to steady her.

"Thank you," she murmurs as she removes her psychedelic socks and winces at the riot of color against the dark brown earth.

"Is that the secret to never losing one's socks in the wash?" Sebastian teases.

"Apparently not. I lose at least one pair a week," she says.

Sebastian laughs. "Me too."

He keeps his hand on the bottom of her elbow as she rolls up the hem of her jeans, then gingerly takes two footsteps forward into cool, running water. She eyes him skeptically.

"You said you trust me."

She pauses and tiptoes into the water beside him. It ripples around her ankles and her toes spread to welcome the silky mud underfoot. She yelps and giggles at the sensation. He grins at the bubbly, girlish sound and then sinks into a crouch. He gently tugs her down beside him. Her eyes gleam with a dozen questions, but her lips refuse to form the words. Sebastian reaches out and takes her by the hand. He cups his hand under hers, which she holds in a loose fist. With his other hand, he tenderly peels back her fingers, one by one until her hand is a cup, too; a cup that fits neatly and safely within his, like holy communion.

With his free hand, he trickles a scoop of water into her curled palm, where it pools and glints like glass.

"Now, make a fist," he urges.

The water seeps out the sides. Sebastian unfurls her fingers once more and molds her glistening palm into a new vessel with a few strokes of his thumb. He scoops more water from the stream and leisurely, sensually, pours it into her hand where it lingers and catches traces of amber light.

"When you move from a fist...to this..."

He glances at Clarissa's cupped hand and then into her searching eyes.

"...it doesn't mean you've stopped wanting the water, or caring about the water, even desperately. But you can't hold water in a fist, any more than you can hold onto Sonny with a death grip on the reins. He is as alive and free as this water. Only by loosening your grip do you create the space to form a true connection. This is where relationship happens...this is the space of mutual consent."

He gently strokes the palm of her hand with his long, slender fingers and the water displaces and runs in little rivulets down the sides of her hands and she smiles softly in understanding. His dark eyes meld with the dusky brown of the woods just as hers meld with the deep emerald of the leaves and together, steeped in cool water under the last vestiges of daylight they are one with a hushed and sleepy world. He leans over and kisses her on the mouth. He is tentative until she kisses him back and their breath mingles, hope mingles, and neither wants to be the first to pull away. When she finally does, there are no more questions in her eyes. Only wonder—could this really be happening to her? She feels, for the first time, like the heroine in one of her own books and the thought brings a pensive smile to her face.

"I didn't bring you here to kiss you," he assures her.

"But I'm glad you did," she answers boldly.

He helps her stand and as the water swirls around them, he kisses her again, this time without the least bit of hesitation. He pulls her close to his chest and his lips leave her breathless, speechless, and spinning in a whirl of sensations as unpredictable and unruly as her psychedelic socks...

She doesn't even bother to put them back on when they reach dry land. She walks barefoot over the cushion of pine needles and then slips her feet back into her boots when the trail morphs into a manicured walk made of wood chips that leads back to the field. Sebastian does the same, and it's only when they reach the boundary of grass that they let go of each other's hand. They both step tentatively onto the green carpet that leads to another world. To Clarissa, it's a looming page turn, a break in the magic, a twist in the plot that tears lovers apart. She holds her breath and steals a glance at Sebastian, whose eyes have never left her.

"Come back to my cottage. I want to cook for you, if you'll let me."

She nods and knows that there will be more than rich food and spicy Argentine wine to be had; she smiles and knows that there will be a banquet of body and blood and soul and divinity and she is glad at the thought of reclining at table with him, bathed in ineffable light.

"Okay," is all she says as they let go of each other's hand.

They walk across the field in silence as dusk descends. Thunder rumbles in the distance. I know a storm is coming this way, just as surely as I know Clarissa is coming this way. I can feel her giddy joy, her anticipation of seeing me; her atoms fill the air like a burst of lightening. Sebastian glances at the sky uneasily.

"Don't be long out here," he says as they part ways at the top of the hill. "That storm is moving in quickly." His voice is thick with unbidden angst and Clarissa flinches at the intensity of his warning.

"I'll be quick, I just want to get him settled in his stall."

Sebastian nods and can't help but glance behind him as she veers toward the little blue barn. She sprints to the paddock gate where I await her with my head lowered to the ground.

"Hey, Sonny!"

Her warm greeting tunnels into my ears.

"Sonny?"

She unlatches the gate and steps through it, then tugs on my halter until I lift my head. My head is so heavy. It feels like a block of salt, dense and lifeless. She peers at me and her eyes widen and she runs her palm over my swollen eyes and gasps at the spectacle of it all.

"Sebastian! Sebastian!" she shouts.

He turns on his heels and runs toward us, reaching the gate just as the rain starts to fall. It's only a few moments before the raindrops transform from cooling, benevolent droplets to pounding splashes on my inflated face. My pasture mates canter up the hill and head for shelter. I stand by Clarissa, unwilling to leave her in the rain.

"What's wrong with him?" Clarissa whispers. I thought it would be the opposite. I thought she would panic and roar. But she's well past panic and barreling into a quiet shock that tightens her throat at the thought of losing me to whatever has stricken me. It was just a few bees, I long to tell her, and send her images as best I can. But she's shut down and shuts me out and all I can do is sigh and hope that Sebastian knows what to do.

"Let's get him into the barn," he says, and clips the lead rope to my halter. We trot across the gravel drive and into the show barn and arrive at the cool, damp shelter of my stall. I sniff for my hay. I can't really see it, but I know it's there.

Sebastian holds my head between the palms of his hand and inspects me. I can feel his warm breath on my cheeks and the adrenaline that pumps through his pulsing veins. He runs his fingers over my face.

"Ah!" he says knowingly.

"What? What is it?" Clarissa begs to know.

"There's another one...and another...stingers! He got stung by a swarm of bees," Sebastian says and exudes a sigh of relief.

Thanks for noticing, I telegraph with a swish of my tail. How about some hay?

Sebastian continues his ministries until he has removed every stinger from my face.

"There you go, Sonny," he says as he plucks the last one from just above my eyelid.

"My God, his face looks like a bowling ball. Should I call the vet?"

"My guess is that he's over the worst of it. Let's get some baking soda on the stings and give him some antihistamine for the swelling and discomfort. In my country, we'd put some wet tobacco on the welts and they'd practically disappear before your eyes," Sebastian says, and his calm, conversational tone puts Clarissa at ease. "I expect he'll continue to improve. He should be fine by the time we meet tomorrow for a lesson—do you want another lesson, Clarissa?"

Sebastian rubs my ears and I bury my swollen face in his chest. His heartbeat is rapid and strong. Clarissa ponders the question and her heart beats faster too. She doesn't know if he's teasing her but she doesn't care. He takes her shining eyes for consent.

"Let's meet in the ring. I'd like to see you under saddle. Six o'clock?"

"Sure," Clarissa says, feigning nonchalance. "As long as Sonny is up for it." She sits on the little step stool she keeps in my stall and as the rain pommels the roof, she watches Sebastian tend to me with cool cloths and soothing balm, and greater tenderness and intuition than any vet I've ever known. When he's done, he nods with satisfaction.

"There's nothing more we can do for him tonight," he says and extends a hand to help her to her feet. She gazes at his outstretched arm. She shakes her head and refuses his assistance.

"I can't leave him," she says. "I need to know he's going to be okay. This horse is my—world," she chokes out as pent-up tears of relief overflow the banks of her eyes. Sebastian kneels in the shavings beside her and sweeps the tears from her face with the same tender, knowing fingertips that ministered to me.

"Of course you can't," he consoles her as a clap of thunder explodes overhead and makes all of us flinch. "So you will stay and keep watch over him. And I will keep watch over you."

"No, Sebastian! You've already done too much. Go home and get a good night's sleep. I'll take a—rain check?" she says with a forlorn laugh as a fresh torrent unleashes and drowns the sounds of their longing; short, choppy breaths and quickened heartbeats and words that catch in their throats.

Sebastian nods and lightly brushes her tear-stained cheek with his lips. Later that night he returns, not once, but several times to check on us. She doesn't know he's come and gone, curled as she is into a ball in the corner of my stall. Each time he leaves, he stands in the driving rain, under the vault of thunder and lightening, daring the cosmos to strike him twice, to give him the comeuppance he so richly deserves so that he can either die or get on with his life. But the rain tapers off, and the lightening fades, and when the morning finally comes, he remains convicted in his sin, in his intolerable sorrow, and yet—there is the undeniable freshness and renewal that follows the rain. It smells like jasmine and looks like summer, like the lush green of Clarissa's eyes and the fragrance of her skin—and he wakes up happy to be alive.

Clarissa finally stirs at the sound of the feed cart coming down the aisle. I clamber to my feet and shake off the stiffness in my stifle and my aging bones. She rolls onto her side and groans, then remembering where she is and all that has transpired, she clambers to her feet too, and peers at me with intense pressure.

"Sonny! You look so much better!" she coos. I rub my face on her hip. It's still a little itchy, but my eyes are wide open and I can see! Hello? Where's my hay?

She gives me a quick kiss on the muzzle and tells me I'm the best—and bravest!—horse in the whole world. She wants to be gone by the time Miguel reaches my stall with his lusty, brown eyes and traitorous lips. Bridget would never understand why Clarissa would suffer to sleep in a stall. More likely, she'd accuse her of sleeping with the hired help! She slips through my Dutch door and into the pasture, then ducks under the split rail fence. She halts at the sight of Sebastian leading Azul back to the outermost shed row barn from somewhere far afield where they've been since the cusp of dawn. She doesn't have time to ponder the mystery of it all; sunshine breaks and she scurries to her car before it spills her secrets, before anyone knows how she has spent the night. But I know. Her petite impression and flowery scent is pressed into my bedding and I nuzzle the remnants of her with my nose.

My sweet Clarissa. She is ephemeral. She is everything. And she is enough. Clarissa, didn't anyone ever tell you that you are enough?

14

"Mom! It's about time you picked up your phone, I was about to get in my car and hunt you down!"

Clarissa can't blame Gabriella for being mad. She hadn't even looked at her phone until almost noon when she heard it buzzing in her tack bag.

"I'm sorry, sweetie, really I am. But you have to stop worrying about me all the time. Sonny was sick and I slept at the barn. I'm fine. We're both fine. Everything's fine!" she says with an apologetic laugh.

"Maybe right now. But you ride a wild animal and you stay out until all hours of the night with your phone on silent and dad is halfway around the world and you're all alone. You know how that makes me feel? Not fine. I am *not* fine!"

The smile fades from Clarissa's lips. Gabriella sounds like she might actually cry, a major event for a girl who swore off crying when she was ten. She had always been a sensitive child, too sensitive for her own good and Clarissa couldn't help but make it her personal mission to make Gabriella every bit as tough as she herself had learned to be—as she had to be—lest her dirty secret spill out with her tears and her whole world—her mother's and sister's and brother's too—would explode like an atomic bomb and leave them husbandless and fatherless and radioactive with shame.

"I'm sorry," Clarissa repeats, this time with remorse. "I know this is hard on you too."

"Dad says he wants you to come to Paris," she blurts. "Why don't you go?"

Clarissa mulls the question. She can't go because there has been cool, sparkling water in the palm of her hand and space created for something more...because there has been a kiss that forged past her lips and into her soul and it made her feel whole, and holy, and pure and strong...because the promise and power of healing is within her grasp...because as much as she loves Geórgios Stamos for loving her, for being the first to show her that she was lovable and worthy of a gentleman's affection, who benevolently took her into his heart and home, that sleeping giant that is her soul is stirring for the first time since she was seven and first felt the sacred fire of love on her tongue. She can't go to Paris...because she wants to go to Argentina, with its passion and heat and redemption and fierce pulse of life that arouses the drowsy beat of her own body and blood.

"It's complicated," is all Clarissa says.

"I know," Gabriella replies, softening at the regret in her mother's voice. "Hey, what doesn't kill you makes you stronger, right?" she offers brightly, if only to cheer her up, and Clarissa smiles once again.

"Thanks, kid."

"So, when can we get together for lunch or shopping—or both?"

"Soon, maybe sometime this weekend if you're around."

"I'm around. Call me. And don't put your phone on silent anymore—please!"

"I won't, I promise."

"Okay. Love you, mom."

"Love you too, sweetie."

They disconnect and bask in the bond between them. If nothing else, Gabriella is the one thing she and George got right; she has George's common sense and powers of reason and long-legged, Grecian beauty—and Clarissa's impetuosity and creativity and stubborn streak that gives Clarissa the peace of mind of knowing Gabriella can conquer the world if she chooses. *Gabriella*—after the archangel, God's messenger of love. How gloriously she has lived up to her name!

Later, Clarissa showers and dresses in her sleek, black breeches and a bright pink polo shirt and forsakes her sparkly belt for a plain, black leather one stamped with horseshoes and embellished with a heart-shaped silver buckle. She adds some color to her cheeks and curls to her hair and glosses her lips in dusty rose. She nods at her reflection, satisfied with the results. She glances at the clock blinking six o'clock in bold, red numbers that always make her feel like the end is near. George is legally blind without his contacts lenses. Were it not for that, Clarissa would have chucked that ugly, ominous clock out of the window decades ago.

"Ugh!" she yelps, and races out the door. She's bordering on late-to-the-barn, especially with the stop she wants to make in between. She speeds down the winding mountain road to the freeway and swings into the parking lot of the upscale liquor store where George buys most of his finer wines. She bolts in brashly enough to startle the clerk into wondering if he's about to be robbed. Clarissa grins shyly and waves.

"Hey, how's it going?"

The clerk grunts and resumes packing bottles into boxes. Clarissa scans the myriad of signs hanging from the ceiling. She finds the wine section and navigates to the aisle reserved for the hearty reds of Argentina. George would never suffer the Malbec grape in isolation. He always said it was too fruity to stand on its own, and so preferred it only in the rich, deep French Bordeaux blends that he first learned about in class, and then from the dark, velvety lips of his personal sommelier. Clarissa stews in the memory, in the indignity, until she's jarred by the deep, sonorous voice of a man who has cozied up beside her.

"Looks like you're having a hard time choosing."

Clarissa frowns at the gentleman's observation. "You can say that again."

"May I offer my assistance? I'm from Argentina."

Clarissa's frown disappears at the sound of the familiar accent. The stout man standing next to her is in his mid-seventies, with neatly combed, sterling silver hair and a silver mustache that lays over smiling lips and a perfect set of capped, white teeth. He's dressed in a tweedy sports coat over pressed jeans and wears exotic leather loafers without socks. He exudes wealth and privilege and good taste. She decides to accept his recommendations. After all, she wants an extraordinary wine to give to Sebastian as a gesture of thanks for the way he took care of me last night—and of her, by association.

"Where in Argentina?" she asks.

"I have a ranch south and west of Buenos Aires. I breed the world's finest polo ponies and ship them all over the world. Have you heard of polo?"

"Of course, my trainer is from Argentina. In fact, he was a famous *domador* there and from what I understand, polo ponies were his specialty."

"How interesting," the man says and arches a silver brow. "What is his name?"

"Sebastian Bergalo. Perhaps you've heard of him?"

Deep furrows etch the man's forehead and his arched brow flattens.

"Yes, *Señora*, I have heard of him. He is—famous—indeed. But perhaps notorious is a better word," he warns. He gazes at Clarissa with paternal concern and now her forehead is furrowed too.

"Notorious?"

The man plucks a bottle of wine off the shelf and peruses the label. She senses it's a distraction, a way to avoid looking into her eyes. Once he begins to speak, she understands why.

"Rumor has it that he killed his wealthy, young wife—snapped her neck in two. At least that's what some of the gauchos swear to be true. Others say it was a riding accident although they were both exceptionally fine riders. So fine that such an accident is—well, practically implausible."

Clarissa's face blanches. Her knees wobble and she places a hand on a stack of wine crates for support. Is this why Sebastian said he could never return to Argentina?

"It only made him look more guilty when he fled to the United States. He left good money on the table and many important clients in the dust. It is a mystery..." he says and reaches for another bottle with a glossy, black label and fancy, gold script. "The only ones who know the truth are Sebastian, his wife, and the horses they were riding that day. Too bad, he was an exceptional *domador*.

I'd like to meet him someday," he muses. "In any case, this one will do."

He hands Clarissa an expensive bottle of wine. "You look like a sweet girl, perhaps a rich one, too. Be careful, *Señora,* things are not always as they seem. Especially when horses and money meet."

Clarissa's chest tightens and she fights for her next breath. The man seems not to notice, hardened as he is to the harsh realities of the horse world. He nods a gentleman's goodbye and saunters off with a hundred-dollar bottle of wine in each hand. He breaks into a low, melodic whistle as he approaches the checkout counter. The sound is spooky in Clarissa's ears and she studies the particulars of the bottle of Malbec she clutches.

The label is stark; beige and black with a trace of blood red and introduces itself as *Ambrosia* from the *Gualtallary Mendoza*. The irony isn't lost on her, having been married to a Greek for over twenty-five years. Only the immortal Greek gods and goddesses could consume ambrosia. Would she die if she drank of it—like Sebastian's wife? The thought is chilling and sobering and the giddiness she felt earlier in the morning has vanished.

She waits until the Argentine leaves the liquor store, then summons the courage to follow through with her plan. She knows the horse world is notorious for reckless rumors and false accusations. Besides, was it even possible for horses to trust a sinister human being the way they trust Sebastian? If she has learned one thing, it's that we never lie.

She drives to Crown Ridge, shaken but undeterred in her hunt for the truth. When she arrives, she sees Sebastian in the arena working with one of the colts. She lingers at the top of the hill and watches his every stance and pivot and the most subtle gestures that before long cause the colt to enter into a dance that

Sebastian directs with quiet strength and energy and grace. He seems to know Clarissa is near and before long, he tilts his head and offers a nod of acknowledgement. She blushes as she receives it like a caress on her skin, then hurries off in pursuit of me.

I nicker when I see her. I don't nicker lightly. I reserve it for the most appropriate times, such as when there's a fat, molasses cookie at stake, or when I want to let Clarissa know I've grown tired of my stall. Too much of a good thing makes a horse in the wild too soft to stand up to the demands of a nomadic way of life. I am not nomadic but I remain wild at heart. Nice to see you, Clarissa. Now get me out of here!

She greets me in a hushed voice and sets her tack bag on the floor. She vibrates deep anxiety and I perk my ears to pinpoint what troubles her so. I seldom miss a warning, a stalker in the brush, a cue that the feed cart might pass me by. Confusion reigns and I prance in my stall at the prospect of being trapped. She rolls back the door and I stick my head out over her shoulder.

"Easy, Sonny, easy! Let me get your halter on!"

My halter dangles in front of my face and I lower my head to get it on faster. She secures the buckles and attaches my lead rope and at last I am free of my stall. Her anxiety diminishes as she begins to curry me in slow, tender circles that gradually spiral into to an overwhelming sadness. Clarissa has never vibrated such sadness before and I lower my head and sigh, not with contentment but with frustration. It feels all wrong and I wonder where my Clarissa has gone.

She brushes me and picks my hooves and tacks me up without a single word or gesture. No *good boy*, no *there-you-go*, no twirling of my forelock that I like so much. She gently lays the saddle pad on my back and hoists my saddle on top of it, then cinches me up carefully, as though I might break. But I am not breakable. My bones may grow old and fail, but my spirit never will! I blow out and offer her the strength of my will and my being, and she startles from her despondency long enough to smile at the sight of me and my big round eye. That's it, Clarissa! Come on, let's play!

She puts me in my bitless bridle and throws her tack bag over her shoulder, then leads me past a couple of show girls without a waver in her step or a sidelong glance. She doesn't seem to notice them or hear their huffy whispers. Her eyes are focused on Sebastian who awaits us in the arena. He shields his eyes from the sun as we approach and greets us at the gate.

"*Buenos días!*" He tousles my forelock and grins. "I see somebody's feeling better!"

Clarissa's heart trills at his nearness; the sensation travels down her arm and into the lead rope and tickles my chin. I react with a toss of my head.

"Looks like he's ready—are you?" he asks, sensing a hesitation he doesn't understand. He lowers his mirrored sunglasses to hide the creases of concern around his eyes.

"Of course," Clarissa says as she plunks her tack bag on a bench and leads me to the mounting block. She breathes a sigh of relief when she sits in the saddle and plugs into me. The flow between us is synergetic; on good days, we each make up for what the other lacks. On bad days, chaos ensures and we both fall apart. I offer her my willingness. I ask for her try. We depart from the mounting block and she sits up taller. That's it, Clarissa. We'll just keep moving forward until the fear disappears!

"You look good," Sebastian calls out as we finish our first lap. "Pick up the trot at C and when you do, ask with your seat and your legs. Breathe in and give with your hands."

Clarissa tries, but the closer she gets to Sebastian at the top of the ring, the tighter her breath and every muscle in her chest becomes. We whiz by at a respectable trot, but Sebastian still stops us before we round the first corner.

"Whoa, let's take a breather."

"What!" Clarissa sputters as she cues me to halt. "What did I do wrong?"

"I didn't say you did anything wrong, I said let's take a breather."

Sebastian closes the distance between us and puts his hand over hers on the inside rein. "First of all," he says, "create space... remember?" The gentleness in his voice supples her resistance and she finds herself bending to his will. She opens her hand and marvels at the way her breath returns to her as well.

"Second, you must breathe, Clarissa, all the way down to here." He lays his hand on her lightly, just below her navel, and her body electrifies and supercharges our connection. I feel the surge of energy all the way down to my feet and I can't wait to move them. Come on, Clarissa, let's go!

In that moment, she opens her opposite hand as well and breathes deeply and somehow forgets everything but the moment we're in. We ride like we've never ridden before, with grace and rhythm and splendor and ease. It's effortless for both of us. My trot rises higher, rounder, and longer. She keeps her eyes soft, and up, and urges me on with just the right amount of pressure and release. We move in true unity and her joy spills over and we vibrate with a lightness of being that defies the laws of gravity. She doesn't even think of falling; if she did, the magic would disappear, but she doesn't and so we go, around and around, and serpentine through orange cones down the center line and then turn sharply. She barely stifles a giggle at my floaty trot up the long side of the ring.

Sebastian nods at the sight of us from his perch on top of the split rail fence. I feel his admiration and approval spin around us like a cocoon where soon, very soon, if time and nature have their way, Clarissa will burst forth in a dazzling array of unbound energy and glory. I come to a perfectly square halt in front of Sebastian. He laughs aloud at the sight of my balanced stance and proud eye and Clarissa's beaming smile. Cookies for everyone!

"So? How'd I do?"

"Four stars."

"Out of how many?" She's breathless and slightly giddy and she doesn't even know it.

"Three!" Sebastian teases. "So you're teachable after all, my *pequeña mula.*"

"*Mula*?" Clarissa echoes with a twinkle in her eye.

"My little mule! But not so today, well done, Clarissa."

She can't help but grin at his unapologetic explanation. So many endorphins drench the air that she forgets to be suspicious and afraid of the man who was said to have murdered his wife. That is, until now...

"So, about that rain check. Are you free tonight?"

Clarissa stiffens.

"Let's celebrate your spectacular ride with some champagne, shall we?"

"Oh! That reminds me, wait here!" she blurts, glad for the diversion as she dismounts and loops the reins over my head. She sprints over to her tack bag, pulls out a bottle of wine adorned with a red ribbon, and treks back to the top of the arena.

"This is for you," she says, thrusting the bottle forward.

He furrows his brows, grasps the bottle, and stares at the dark, gleaming gift in his hands.

"What for?"

"For helping Sonny last night. I would never have known what to do and you made us both feel better. So—thank you," she finishes awkwardly.

He studies the label and whistles softly.

"This is a very fine Argentine wine. I insist that you share it with me. After all, we got him through it together."

He caresses her with his eyes and she's moved to say yes if only because she can't say no. There are questions that burn and answers only he can supply—if she dares to ask. I stomp at the presence of a fly on my foreleg and break the uneasy silence.

"Sonny insists as well," he adds and smiles. He removes the reins from my neck and hands them to Clarissa. As their fingers brush in the exchange, there's heat and sparks and a surge of excitement that travels upward and buzzes my nose.

"I'll meet you in twenty minutes. Let me untack him and get him settled," Clarissa says. That's human code for cookies. I simply can't wait. I stamp my foot again, this time with real impatience.

"Okay, okay!" Clarissa says but she doesn't scold me. I was too good today to be scolded, even a little bit. I walk between the two of them and Sebastian steals glances at Clarissa between my ears. They travel in silence to the top of the hill where they part ways with tentative smiles and waves. She doesn't notice Margaret begrudging the exchange from the doorway of the outdoor wash stall, or the way her eyes narrow or the way her mouth gapes and issues a sigh as thick and heavy as the sudsy air surrounding her. No, Clarissa only notices Sebastian's cozy cottage looming in the distance and the rakish appearance of his dark, wavy hair when he removes his hat and hangs it on the brass hook outside his front door before disappearing inside.

"This one's for being so awesome today in the ring," Clarissa says as she reaches into a foil pouch and produces a soft, chewy, molasses cookie that tastes every bit as good as it smells. I can smell that smell halfway across the barn, well before the rustle of the bag gives away her intentions. Worse yet, she thinks she can hide bits of cookie from me in her back pocket, but I always know they're stuffed in there, the entire ride I know—and it's all I can do to keep my mind on her ask instead of her ass.

"And this one's for being the best horse in the whole world!" she says with such gusto that I think I might actually get a bonus treat—the core of an apple, a chunk of carrot, maybe a peppermint that comes with a kiss. Yep, that's it. She untacks me and then unwraps a peppermint and holds it in the palm of her hand. I nibble it with my lips and suck it into my mouth and she loudly smooches me on the cheek as I crunch and crunch until my mouth fills with a cool vapor.

"Make good choices," she says as she hastily turns me out in the field for the night.

Horses don't think too much about choices. We simply follow our instincts and let nature take its course. I hope Clarissa will do the same. I lower my head and graze on summer clover as the sound of her swift footsteps fade and a faint knock echoes in the air.

"Welcome back," Sebastian says as he opens the door and the warm glow of candlelight floods Clarissa's face. He's showered and dressed in what Clarissa calls his cowboy clothes and she wishes he looked anything but cowboy rough and tumble. She absently tucks a wayward strand of hair behind her ear and musters the courage to look him in the eye.

"Thanks for the invitation."

She steps over the threshold and follows Sebastian to the living room where he has carefully arranged two fluted glasses, an uncorked bottle of champagne, and the dark bottle of *Ambrosia* on a coffee table inlaid with turquoise Spanish tiles.

"Sit down," he says, gesturing to a rustic, leather sofa trimmed in brass nail heads that feels like butter against Clarissa's skin.

"Thank you," she murmurs as she sinks into the sofa. "Nice couch."

Sebastian grins at her formal posture and the awkward tilt of her head.

"Relax, Clarissa, we're just sharing some wine," he says as he casually pours two glasses of champagne.

"Do I look uptight?"

"Just a little," he teases. "Why?"

"Oh, I don't know. Maybe because there's two bottles of wine and just the two of us and who knows what...could happen," she says in a voice that drifts into a whisper.

"I promise I won't kiss you again," Sebastian says, "unless you want me to."

Clarissa's face infuses with color and warmth and she turns her eyes towards the glass of pale gold wine that bubbles up like her insides. She grasps it and raises it into the air.

"To mutual consent," she says, thinking of her lesson down by the river—of the letting go, of the softness, and the feel, and the perfect harmony she and I experienced in the ring.

"To mutual consent," he replies, interpreting her words in an entirely different way. He runs his fingers through the crown of his hair the way he does every time she rattles his brain. And other places, too.

Their glasses clink and they drink too fast and make small talk about the barn and the show girls and the horses to fill the spaces between breathy sighs and bubbly splashes that leave one bottle empty and one to go.

"*Ambrosia*," Sebastian says, examining the label once more. He offers a devilish grin. "Do we dare?"

Clarissa shrugs. She's not quite drunk but she's a quarter mile around the track; she'll have to make her big move now or fade into oblivion. She searches the cottage for a segue to the past...

"Tell me about the bridle on the wall," she says. "I noticed your work table the last time I was here—and saw a picture of a horse, wearing that same bridle. Did you make it?"

"I did," Sebastian replies, "it belonged to my wife's horse, Rosalita."

"You're very talented. It's beautiful!"

"So was Rosalita," Sebastian says as he pulls the cork from the bottle. He turns his back to Clarissa and strides into the kitchen where he chooses glasses suitable for fine, red wine.

"What happened to her?" Clarissa gently prods.

Clarissa scoots to the edge of the sofa and takes the round bowl filled with dark, ruby wine from Sebastian's outstretched hand. He sits beside her and takes a long, thoughtful sip from his own glass. She fixates on his fingers wrapped around the wine glass—long, slender, powerful, and deft.

"She got hurt. Had to put her down...nice wine."

"Nice couch."

"Touché."

"About the wine..."

Sebastian's jaw ripples with tension at Clarissa's somber tone.

"I met a man at the liquor store who recommended it to me. He was from Argentina."

"Argentina is a big country."

"No, he was from the Pampas."

"Was he?"

"He raised polo ponies there and heard of you—of your work there as a *domador.* He said you had an impressive reputation."

"I see. What else did he say?"

Clarissa raises her wine glass. She drinks slowly until she can drink no more, then presses her lips into a resolute line.

"Did he tell you about my wife—Sofía?"

Clarissa contemplates the name that he utters in a raspy whisper. It sounds exotic and beautiful and tortured and ends abruptly, like a life cut short.

He nods slowly, regretfully, at the condemnation of her silence.

"If you're asking if I'm responsible for her death, the answer is yes. But not in the way that they say."

"How then, Sebastian? Please, I need to know."

"You do not need to know. Either you trust me or you don't!" He rises from the sofa. She watches him pace like a lion caged in a memory.

"I do trust you, but—"

"Then the matter is finished."

"No, it's not. Help me understand who you are and what happened to you. I want to know more about the man I met at the river. I want to know the soft-touch *domador* the horses know. I want to know the truth!"

"What is truth, Clarissa?"

"It's what sets us free," she goads him.

"You're as green out of the saddle as you are in it. Perhaps there's still time to check into that convent. You're hopelessly naïve!" he scoffs.

"Why? Because I believe we don't have be prisoners of the past?" She startles at her own revelation and clambers to her feet. "Hope breathes," she says, straightening her spine. "You said so."

Sebastian sets down his wine glass and closes the distance between them. Clarissa's feet jig and she glances down and wills them to be still. He lifts her chin with the crook of one finger and forces her to look at him.

"Sweet Clarissa." He breathes out her name like incense rising from deep within his soul. "Do you know that in Spanish, your name means light? What has light to do with the darkness?"

"Everything."

Sebastian searches her face and leans down to kiss her. As his lips brush hers, she yields to the ardor that sweeps over her in waves, but only for a moment. She pulls back and traces his lips with her fingertips and questions him with her eyes. He turns his face away and clenches his jaw.

"Tell me your truth," she whispers and rests her head in the cradle of his shoulder. She's prepared to receive it, no matter how bitter it may be. If there's one thing she won't suffer, it's one more secret or lie. She has kept too many secrets, in her heart, in the most intimate gorges of her body. And she has heard too many lies, from every man she ever loved.

But Sebastian doesn't tell her, if only because of the sudden, frantic knocking at the door and the sight of Margaret standing there holding Dante's broken halter with cunning tears in her eyes and a fresh coat of paint on her lips.

"I'm sorry, Sebastian, but I can't find Miguel or Pedro. I was turning out Dante and he spooked and slipped out of his halter! He's heading down the driveway, I'm afraid he'll run into the road! Please, help me!"

"Get a bucket of grain and meet me out front," he orders. Margaret makes haste for the feed room and he bolts out the door after her—but not before tossing Clarissa a look that begs her to stay.

She shrugs and he leaves the door ajar behind him, as though he already knows what she'll choose. He's right. She barely waits until their footfalls fade, then slips out the door into the blue of twilight. She'd given him a chance to redeem himself and he had refused the offer. Could it be that he truly had something to hide, something so awful that he'd rather lose her than confess the truth?

Horses issue refusals all the time. Sometimes it's because we don't understand the question. Other times, it's because we know what's being asked of us is contrary to good sense or our survival. But most of the time, we try. The sensitive human sees and rewards the try. Clarissa asked and Sebastian tried, but she missed it—that subtle downshift in his posture, the grip of his hand on hers, the kiss that begged for mercy and understanding, the look that said, "don't go." For someone always looking for signs, she sure missed a lot of them. She sure missed the try.

She lopes to her car and starts the engine but creeps down the driveway so as not to hinder the hunt for Dante. She doesn't have to worry. He's behind the shed row barn munching on coveted clover, right where Margaret left him. Dante's nobody's fool. He knows it's a rare and splendid day when an expensive performance horse gets to chow down on real grass for more than a minute or two lest their hooves grow sore and warm and render them lame. But Margaret's stake is bigger than that.

Clarissa's dazed and almost halfway home when she realizes she forgot to fly spray me. She winces at the thought of finding me itchy and welted in the morning after all I've just been through and races back to the barn. I hear the tick-tick-hum coming up the driveway and linger by the gate. She turns off her headlights before she reaches the crest of the hill, bolts from her car, then slips into the little blue barn and grabs the first bottle of fly spray she sees. As she approaches our pasture, Merlin snorts a deafening greeting. Clarissa says one of those words and gingerly unfastens the chain that holds the gate shut, making sure it doesn't clang against the metal bars. She hadn't noticed until now that her hands are shaking.

She coats me in fly spray and sends me forth with a scratch on my withers. We both perk our ears at the trill of laughter that pierces the air, and turn our heads toward the distant silhouettes of Margaret and Sebastian dallying on his front porch. Margaret tosses her hair and gestures coyly at the moon. It throws just enough light to expose a rendezvous that makes Clarissa's breath stutter. Sebastian opens the front door and invites Margaret inside with a chivalrous sweep of his hand. The next word Clarissa says is a new one to me. She spits it out like buckshot and flees.

I hear the tick-tick-hum retreat downhill and fade into a choir of crickets that shrieks in the stillness of the night. Moonlight spills over the pasture, creating patches of shadow where predators lie in wait. I huddle and graze close to Hershey and Merlin. Only Moose is young and fast and foolish enough to expose himself to the hungers of the night—the same way that Sebastian knowingly exposes himself to Margaret's wiles. It's the only consolation he knows, only this time, he discovers there's no solace to be found in random wine and women and misspent passion. He's tasted *Ambrosia*, on his own lips and on the lips of a goddess who offered him a chance to confess his guilt and receive absolution and be saved from his own eternal damnation—but he blew it! Within moments, he ushers Margaret out the front door.

"I'm sorry, Margaret, it's been a long day."

She tilts her head and studies Sebastian's face.

"I can see that, you have dark circles under your eyes. Maybe you're working too hard." She reaches out and caresses his forearm. He shoves his hands in his pockets.

"It's not work to be with the horses."

Margaret nods and glances behind her into the bucket of night.

"I should go," she murmurs. "Thanks for the screw!" She fishes in her pocket for the little brass fitting that holds our breakaway halters together. "Oh! That sounded terrible. But there's no other way to say it! At least I won't have to buy Dante new halter," she rambles.

"*Buenos noches*, Margaret."

"*Buenos noches*," she says and sighs and descends the stairs and flings the screw into the hedges the second she's out of his sight. Sebastian stands alone in the moonlight on the front porch and says one of those words too.

Later that night, energies and dreams and urges collide as Sebastian and Clarissa each lie in their own beds and punch down their pillows and toss off their covers in fits of hot and cold. They take turns thrashing like horses stuck in a mud pit. By sunrise they're shocked and thoroughly exhausted. If they were horses, they'd have to be put down. But they're human and so they put their feet on the ground and slog into a brand new day.

When Clarissa finally arrives at the barn, the sun is higher in the sky than usual and her green eyes sport dark circles too. Her energy drags behind her like entrails as she shuffles into the field with my lead rope in hand. I swiftly turn my butt to her. I'm not interested in this version of Clarissa. I want the Clarissa who vibrates like a twelve year old and wants to play games and feed me chewy cookies. She sidles up to me and I bump her with my head. I know it's rude, but I'm the leader today.

"Sonny! That was rude!"

Yup.

"Come on, let's go play," she musters.

Now you're talking, Clarissa! I pivot on my feet and offer her my face. She clips the lead rope onto my halter and we amble toward the gate. I bob my head and charge ahead. She tugs me back to my place near her shoulder. It's going to be one of those days....

She leads me through the gate and offers a faint greeting to Bernie. He still looks at her differently, indelicately, and she avoids making eye contact.

"Have you seen Carla?" he inquires in his viscous, French accent. "She was supposed to meet me an hour ago to go out on trail. She must have forgotten. She has a new boyfriend, you know."

"I didn't know," Clarissa replies dully as she ground ties me under the oak tree and heads into the little blue barn in search of her stick and string.

"Would you like to go out on trail with me?" he bellows into the barn.

"No thanks, I'm not riding today."

"Too bad," he says. "I rather would have liked some company." He finishes tacking up Merlin in silence. Even Bernie catches Clarissa's sullen vibe and keeps his eyes where they belong as Clarissa emerges from the barn with her pockets stuffed with peppermints.

Clarissa's attention darts to the activity in the bottom half of the arena where Sebastian and Margaret have just begun a lesson. Bridget occupies the upper half, where she lunges a young Thoroughbred and makes sure he knows she's the boss mare. As we meander down the gravel path, Clarissa tightens her grip on my rope.

"Let's go play on the grass instead," Clarissa says as we alter our course and aim for the field. She's still hitchy from her last fall in that pasture. She deliberately avoids that particular spot, sure that it's full of bad juju. There's no such thing as bad juju. Only bad thoughts that give rise to bad realities and I swish my tail in protest at the mutterings of her mind.

"Okay, Sonny, this one's for free!" She grins and pops a peppermint into my mouth. I perk up and she laughs at the sight of my round, happy eye. She makes me work for the rest of the treats in her pocket, but it's not work to me. The more we move our feet, the more unified we become until finally we're dancing and for a moment, this blithe moment, all is right in the world.

She doesn't notice the silence in the arena when it eventually falls. It's only when it's broken by Sebastian's voice at her back that she flinches and stops dancing. Clarissa! Let's keep dancing!

"You look stunning. You and Sonny, that is."

Clarissa freezes and holds her breath.

"Thanks," she replies dully. She reels me into her personal space and combs her fingers through my forelock, grateful for the easy distraction I provide.

"About last night—"

"Please, don't. There's nothing more to say."

"There's a lot more, Clarissa, I was up thinking about it all last night."

"Really? You were up thinking?"

She steals a sidelong glance at Sebastian and balks at the plea in his eyes to be heard.

"From what I saw, you were up all last night—with Margaret!"

"Margaret?"

"I came back to fly spray Sonny. I saw you invite her into your cottage."

"Yes, I did, but she wasn't there for long. She just needed a screw."

Clarissa drops her jaw and gapes at him.

"That's not what I mean! I didn't sleep with her!"

Clarissa thrusts her palm into the air between them and turns her face away. Her other hand trembles and sends shock waves toward my chin.

"I don't care what you mean. I don't want to hear it, Sebastian. I'm tired and I'm confused and I can't have this discussion right now. In fact, I need to cancel our lesson tomorrow. Actually, I need to cancel all of them."

"Why?"

"Because I'll be in Paris." She decides it as she says it.

"What about Sonny?"

"I'll arrange for someone to look after him while I'm gone."

"How long will that be?"

"As long as it takes to make things right."

Sebastian's jaw flutters with tension. He clenches his teeth and swallows the truth on his tongue and stuffs his hands in his pockets.

"I can look after him. Please, let me do that for you," he says softly.

"I'm sure Carla won't mind."

"She has a new boyfriend."

"I know! I know!" Clarissa shouts and throws her hands in the air. I nosedive into the grass to escape the sound and fury. Munch, munch, munch.

"Fine, you can take care of Sonny. That would be great," she says and musters a civil smile. If nothing else, she knows I'll be in good hands.

Sebastian pulls his sunglasses down from the top of his head and over his eyes.

"I'm sorry—*Señora*. I presumed too much."

He lingers a split second before he moves his feet, just long enough for Clarissa to soften.

"It's my fault. I was confused," she declares.

Sebastian nods and turns on the heels of his gleaming leather boots. Clarissa hates those haughty boots. Almost as much as she hates his embroidered hat with the emblem that matches the one on his crisp white polo shirt that brands him a cheater and a fraud—and God only knows what else! As far as she's concerned, Sebastian is nothing more than a wily gaucho with wanderlust and a bad reputation. At least that's what she tells herself as she furiously fusses with the knot on my rope halter until he's far enough away that she can safely whisper her darkest secrets in my ears and bury her tears in my chestnut mane like so many twelve year olds before her.

I feel her lean into me and I instinctively give to the pressure. It sets her off balance just enough that she's forced to move her feet. Just keep moving your feet, Clarissa. Don't get stuck in the memories and the mud. Just keep moving forward—always forward!

15

Clarissa's grateful for the 24-hour bustle and din outside of the airport that drowns out the noise in her head. She'd texted George to let him know she'd be taking a pre-dawn flight out of Newark that would land her in Paris in time for dinner.

Coming, she typed.

Hurry!, he replied.

His response had made her smile. He'd always been a man of a few, well chosen words and this was no exception. She drags her overstuffed suitcase over shiny, white tiles that are freshly mopped; the roll of the wheels and the clack of her western boots echo in the vast, nearly empty terminal reserved for international flights. A palpable loneliness hovers in the air like a drone. She veers down a seemingly endless corridor that leads to the checking in of her luggage and the checking out of her stay in Argentina—not a point on a map, but a place in her soul where she'd felt more hopeful and alive than she ever had before.

The walls of the terminal read like a travelogue with posters and signs from every country and port of call, plying their goods and attractions for all the world to see. She whizzes by one poster after another: The ancient artifacts of Rome. The royalty of London. The romance of Paris. The emerald cliffs of Ireland. The turquoise waters of Turks and Caicos. And the toothy grin of a braying mule on a mountaintop, who touts the adventure of a lifetime crossing the Andes and learning "the gaucho way."

She stops in her tracks and reads the Spanish caption with English subtitles:

Harmony. Fullness. Immersion. Persistence. Purity. Argentina!

She pours over the words and each one leads her deeper into Argentina, back to the Pampas where she met a man who inspired all of these things and more—with horses, within herself, and with him—as if there was any distinction at all. She grins back at the mule who symbolizes his homeland and whose likeness—*pequeña mula* —he uses to describe her in tones that are both maddened and tender with affection. How easily she has given way to doubt and fear when perhaps all he needed was more time—more uninterrupted time! What would have happened, what truth would have been told, if Margaret hadn't knocked at the door? Would she not be crossing the Andes in the arms of a man who would teach her the gaucho way of life and love and horses?

She spins her suitcase in a dizzying whorl and bolts in the direction from which she came. Her boots clack louder and faster and barely keep time with the beating of her heart. If ever there was a sign—one sign—meant to change her destiny, surely this was it! She hails a cab and heads west, back into the night sky. Dawn flirts with the skyline behind her. And on the Pampas, it is still dark.

By the time she reaches Crown Ridge, a sliver of amber light cuts across the horizon. She parks her suitcase on Sebastian's porch and raps on the door. She doesn't know what she's going to say when he opens it, but she dares to hope no words are needed. She jigs in place as the seconds tick by, then notices an empty hook on the rack outside his door. If his cowboy hat is gone—so is he!

Azul!

I lift my head and watch Clarissa sprint down the gravel path and into the back field and then disappear into the woods where the trail begins. Adrenaline moves her feet past the fear of the unknown and the noises in the trees and the dimness of her natural vision. It's as though there's a prevailing wind at her back, pushing her off the beaten path onto a smaller, narrower one that she's never noticed before. She descends into a gully and hopscotches over smooth rocks in a stream before climbing a gentle ridge that gives way to a vast, wild, grassy field where the first light of dawn drapes the landscape in gold.

She imagines it's what the Pampas is like, with tall, wavy strands of native grasses and a cloudless sky and the thundering hooves of wild horses pounding the earth. Thundering hooves...she forgets to breathe as Azul gallops across the field with Sebastian on his broad, blue back without the barrier of a saddle between them or the weight of reins in his hands. His eyes are fixed on the thread of gold that forms the horizon and his face is radiant with peace. He looks boyish and handsome and free of the pain that contorts his smiles into polite snarls and his eyes into narrow doorways to the past. They break into a spirited canter and then into an ethereal trot, spiraling in ever-widening circles that make Sebastian grin and Azul blow out with pleasure. No horse will offer such liberty to a human unless he has proven worthy of his unbridled obedience and trust. Horses have built-in lie detectors. What more does she need to know? Clarissa smiles and subtly shifts her weight and as she does, a twig snaps underfoot.

She gasps as Azul tosses his massive head in her direction, deciding if she's worth a spook. Sebastian follows his horse's incriminating stare. His smile fades. He circles and sends Azul forward in her direction, slowly, deliberately, in carefully measured strides. She clutches at her chest and tries to rein in her galloping heart. She's fully immersed in the moment, in each majestic step, until horse and rider arrive at her side.

Sebastian dismounts and grasps her hand. Clarissa takes a stuttering breath and parts her lips to speak. When the words don't come she beseeches him with her eyes to say something, anything, to welcome her home.

"I'm glad you're here."

"Me too."

"Walk with me?"

"Okay."

They leave Azul to graze and he holds her hand tightly, as though fearing she might slip away as quickly as she appeared. They meander through the tall grass and stands of Queen Anne's Lace and he speaks his truth to her in words that make her eyes glisten like the silvery dew that clings to dark green blades of grass.

"...and that's what happened to Sofía, so help me God," he finishes, and begs her understanding with a stoic smile.

"Sebastian, I'm sorry I doubted you."

"I should've told you sooner."

Clarissa pauses and allows his words, his story, to sink into her heart.

"*How strange this mass of ancient treasures, mementoes of past pains and pleasures,*" Clarissa muses as her eyes drift toward the horizon.

"Did you write that?" Sebastian coaxes.

"It's from a poem by Charlotte Brontë. She was a hopeless romantic."

"Just like you."

"Just like me," Clarissa concedes. She steals a glance at Sebastian's chiseled features that soften with amusement at her admission. He nods and cups her face in his hands and his long, tender fingers curl around her jaw like soft, supple, summer vines.

"Tell me, Clarissa—why didn't you go to Paris?"

"I tried. But what I really want is to cross the Andes."

Sebastian cocks his head and ponders her explanation.

"Is that a metaphor?"

"Kind of."

"I know how you can get there from here."

"You do?"

Sebastian kisses her, fully, and deeply, until she's totally immersed in his passion for her and her own passion rises from a lost place of innocence and purity, as though it had never been stolen from her at all. They meld and sink into soft, meadow grass and bask in summer gold and the ground swells beneath them as they rise to heights of glory and communion that leave them breathless and spent and utterly consumed. In that moment they are each other's body and blood and soul and divinity and the love on her tongue is every bit as sacred as the holy host that set her soul on fire when she was seven. She thought she would never be worthy of that kind of love again, and though George had kept her safe, he had never healed her soul.

"Well," Clarissa sighs as she gazes into the pale blue sky and squeezes Sebastian's hand. "The air certainly is purer up here."

Sebastian grins and rolls onto his side and kisses her again. She runs her fingers through his hair and reluctantly pulls away.

"We should get back before the rest of the world wakes up."

"We have nothing to hide."

"We don't?"

Sebastian shakes his head. "I would write it in the sky if I could."

"What would you write?"

"That I'm in love with a mule."

Clarissa bursts out laughing. Sebastian gets half-dressed, hands her bits of clothing, and then saunters off, shirtless, in search of Azul. When he returns on horseback, she gapes at the spectacle of a man who might well have just stepped off the cover of a romance novel. She grins and thinks she just might finish her screenplay after all. Sebastian dismounts, dons his tee shirt, and hoists Clarissa onto Azul's back. He nestles in front of her and she wraps her arms around his waist. Azul steps forward and Clarissa marvels at the sensation of riding bareback. She holds on a little tighter as Azul clambers down the ridge and crosses the stream, but when they reach the familiar trail leading back to the barn, she begins to relax.

"Can you teach me to do this on Sonny?"

"Of course, but what about your saddle?"

"I don't know. I think I could get used to this."

"This?"

"Riding with you. And riding like this."

"You must keep that saddle forever, Clarissa. It was meant for you."

"That's a little dramatic, don't you think? Besides, I thought you wanted it."

"Only with you in it."

"Are all Argentinian men so—poetic?"

"Poetry is a part of every gaucho's heritage. If you like, I can read you some poems from my culture. *El Gaucho Martin Fierro* is a classic."

Clarissa smiles and rests her cheek on Sebastian's shoulder. "I'd like that very much."

I hear Clarissa's voice before I see her. She looks for me in my pasture as they emerge from the woods and waves her hand over her head, her special signal to me from afar. I whinny and turn my nose to the gate, feeling left out and mildly resentful.

"He's mad I'm on another horse," she says. Yep, she got the message.

Sebastian and Clarissa ride to the fence line where Azul's halter and lead rope is draped over a post. Clarissa starts to scramble down.

"Please, allow me to help you."

"I can do it," she protests.

"It's not as easy as it looks without stirrups—and your hip..."

"You know about my hip?"

"Of course, I'm your trainer, I see how you compensate."

"This could get complicated."

"But it won't," he promises as he dismounts. He grasps her by the waist and sets her feet on the ground. "Meet me in the ring with Sonny in twenty minutes. We'll have a little lesson and show him some love."

"You know the way to a woman's heart is through her horse, right?"

"I'm counting on it," he says and turns his attention to haltering Azul.

"Sebastian?"

He pauses and glances at Clarissa intently.

"You already have my heart."

It's all she can do not to speak of love until she's spoken first to George. She figures she owes him that much, even if their *coup de grâce* is a mere technicality.

He smiles with his eyes and walks with Azul back to his pasture. He's an outside horse, as wild on the inside as Sebastian is. A horse like Azul could never be cooped up in a show barn's stall. He'd colic and twist up inside if he was ever deprived of freedom and light. Sebastian knows it and respects it and that's why Azul confers on him the ultimate reward of allowing him to be one with him in body and spirit. It's a gift reserved for the most intimate of friends. It's a gift I gladly give to Clarissa, who has made me her forever horse.

I nicker as she draws near, attracted by the joy she radiates. I don't mind that there's not yet grain in my bucket or a cookie in her hand. I choose joy over creature comforts. I'd choose Clarissa, this radiant, sweet Clarissa, every time!

She leads me under the oak tree outside the little blue barn and tacks me up with the special tenderness that animates a woman in love. She traces her finger over the myriad of scars on the leather of my saddle, hints of hardships that others before her have endured in their journey with horses. There is no shame in them. And for the first time, there is no shame in her, in her own scarred beauty that defines her as a warrior princess in this world and the daughter of a King in the next.

"Okay! Let's go play with Sebastian!" she says. Sebastian? Play? I don't think so. But I'm pleasantly surprised when the ring of death and dull routine turns into a circle of glee as Clarissa and I navigate the makeshift obstacle course Sebastian has arranged for us. We weave through cones and trot over cleverly arranged ground poles and even circle around a rusty barrel that Sebastian found in the shed. I'm still very good at circling barrels and Clarissa squeaks with joy and grabs the horn of her saddle as I lean to the inside and skim the barrel with my hide.

"Ha! Did you see that?" she shouts to Sebastian, who gives her a thumbs-up in reply.

"Now trot to the cavaletti!"

She doesn't know what a cavaletti is, but I capture the image he sends me and head straight for the center of it.

"Keep your head up!" he calls to her as I adjust the length of my stride and my old bones crackle as though waking up from a long sleep. I round my back and sail over the humble little eight-inch jump with scope to spare. My stifle complains on take off, but Clarissa's triumphant laugh is worth the momentary pain. She circles me back to Sebastian and brings me to halt. I stop squarely and completely and Sebastian nods with approval. It just might be my best halt ever.

"That was so much fun!" Clarissa exclaims and leans over and hugs my neck. "Sonny! I didn't know you had that in you!"

Clarissa, my dear, you never asked.

"Heck, I didn't know I had that in myself!" she says and giggles and dismounts.

"I always did," Sebastian says solemnly.

Clarissa turns her eyes toward Sebastian and removes the mirrored sunglasses from his face. She wants to steep in his warm, dark eyes and admiration.

"Of course you did. You're a *domador.* You bring out the best in everything you touch."

She reaches for my cinch to loosen it. Sebastian covers her hand with his own and redirects it to the front flap of the skirt on my saddle.

"Clarissa, there's something else I need to tell you."

Her smile fades at his serious tone.

"Look here," he says, and peels back the flap.

"What am I looking at?" she says, hardly noticing the letters tooled into the leather until her fingers run over them.

"It's the saddle maker's mark."

"Oh, that's kind of cool. The lady at Two Cowgirls didn't really know anything about it. She said she got it on eBay. Maybe I can Google it."

"Clarissa, look closer."

She asks me to pivot on my feet so that the morning sun shines on my shoulders and illuminates the front of the saddle.

"S. Bergalo."

She looks at Sebastian and a quiet panic rises in her chest at the thought that this is all too coincidental. Or all too divine. What if everything that happened was supposed to happen? What if there really was no point in all the worry and sadness and stress and what if what appears to be random chaos is actually all part of a greater wisdom and plan? What if?

"What if I told you that was Sofía's saddle? And that I made it for her as a wedding gift?"

Now she understands the painted roses, symbolic of Rosalita, his wife's beloved horse. She understands the bright, shiny silver of young love and the barbed wire that encircles them so that no one and nothing should ever come between them. But most of all, she understands the scars.

"I would say it is an honor to ride in it. And that you must take it back. It belongs to you."

"It is nothing without you, just leather and metal and wood. Besides," he says, stroking away the tear that escapes from her eye. "Do we not belong to each other?"

"We do," she says, not a mere reply, but a vow that she knows is sacred and true.

They seal it with a kiss and moments later, the barn begins to spring to life with the sound of rolling feed carts and rushing water into buckets and show girls cackling over morning coffee.

Sebastian glances at his watch and sighs.

"I have a lesson in twenty minutes."

"With who?"

"Margaret."

Clarissa nods and shrugs.

"I can cancel it if it bothers you."

Clarissa smiles and takes his hand and entwines his fingers with her own.

"I trust you, Sebastian. I'd trust you with my life."

There are no greater words she could have spoken, none with greater power to heal the guilt and shame and sorrow in his soul. He absorbs their light and peace and mercy and hope and he breathes, really breathes, for the first time in ten years and the darkness takes flight and disappears. He swallows the lump in his throat and smiles.

"Will you join me for dinner?"

"In Argentina?"

"Of course."

"Will there be empanadas and red wine and roses?"

"Is there any other Argentina?"

"Then yes, I will. And for breakfast, too."

Did someone say breakfast? I paw at the sand, eager for mine.

"Okay, okay! I know you're hungry!" she consoles me.

"See you at seven?" Sebastian says.

"Wild horses couldn't stop me," Clarissa replies.

They let go of each other's hands and stifle their longing for one more kiss. He heads to his cottage to change into his training uniform and grins at the sight of Clarissa's suitcase outside his door. She leads me to the little blue barn where she shoos Merlin away from my grain bucket and lets me eat my breakfast in peace under the oak tree. When I finish every last morsel, she wipes my face with a cool washcloth and asks me for a little hack around the farm. I'm sleepy and technically, it's time for bed in my stall, but she vibrates joy and I choose her over sleep.

We meander down the driveway and veer onto the bridle path that borders the farm. As soon as we make the first turn, we come upon a swirling, cackling, black cloud that touches down and takes flight half a dozen times, hopscotching across the paddocks and flashing flamboyant patches of red. Clarissa gasps and I verge on a spook.

"Look, Sonny, red-winged blackbirds! Aren't they magnificent?"

Her wonder and excitement echoes in the chambers of my nine-pound heart and I instantly forgive her for the false alarm. We finish our hack around the farm and she retires me to my stall and feeds me a peppermint and two fat, chewy cookies as a special reward for my bravery and jumping prowess. She kisses me on the muzzle and tells me I'm the best horse in the whole world. I know it's true because I have cool, fresh water, and mounds of tasty, green hay and a shady stall and a pasture in which to run free. Surely I must be the best horse in the whole world, because I am Clarissa's horse.

She promises to come back when the sun goes down and I settle into my fluffy shavings and roll onto my side. The fan spins overhead and creates a breeze that tickles my ears. I lie there for a very long time, nearly until my afternoon grain and hay arrives. Later, Pedro comes to turn me out into my pasture for the night. I graze contentedly as the sun sinks and I anticipate the tick-tick-hum that will bring Clarissa and carrots. But instead, as darkness falls, I'm suddenly struck by a cosmic whorl of chaos and my soul floods with confusion as the sounds and images of screeching brakes and dizzying spins and twisting metal assaults my senses. I run in a blind panic, galloping the length of the pasture and back again and as the tick-tick-hum falls silent, I rear up and scream in one final protest.

It is finished. Darkness hangs like a curtain between us. Later, Sebastian comes looking for me—looking for her. I am no one's horse now. I have come full circle.

16

Blinking red lights and shrill beeps herald the arrival of the big silver box that has come to take me far from this place, the place I've come to call my home. Sebastian stands beside me, clutching my lead rope tightly. His breath catches in his chest as a kindly, old woman reaches out to take the rope from his hand.

"Give me a minute—please," he says as he draws closer to my ear and chokes out words that will be his last to me here.

"I wanted to keep you, Sonny, please believe me, I tried."

I rub my face against his strong, capable hands. I know that if anyone could save me, it would be him. "Be a good horse. She's watching you."

He hands over my lead rope and stiffens his spine. Carla breaks into a sob behind him. I balk at the hollow sound and the shudder of the ramp under my feet.

"Do you want me to get a nose chain?" Bridget says impatiently.

"Please, allow me," Sebastian says stepping forward to reclaim the lead rope from the driver's hand. He strokes my neck and breathes on me, softly and calmly.

"Come on, Sonny," he steps forward and I step with him, one step after another until I'm standing in the big steel box. He secures the bars and hems me in and tousles my forelock like she used to do, then slips out the side door. The engine revs. I rock backward to keep my balance as we descend the driveway of Crown Ridge and eventually settle into the rhythm and sway of winding roads and stops and gos.

It isn't long until we arrive at our destination. The old woman opens the door and allows me to back out. I'm clumsy as my feet search for the end of the ramp and solid ground. I snort with relief when I find it—and again, with even greater relief when I see Gabriella standing there with her mother's round eyes, gazing at me with the same light and love. She reaches out and touches me for the very first time and a single tear spills over her dark lashes. George watches at an arm's length, then draws closer and lays his hand on my neck. He vibrates loss and grief and bewilderment and I stand, stoically, and absorb their pain. I am a conduit to the one they love. In loving me, they love her still, as though she yet lives and breathes in my soul. And she does. We are inseparable in that collective consciousness that only horse and rider can know, in that vast, field of gold where we live and move and have our being.

I feel her in the sun, and in the rain, and in the blades of grass beneath my feet. I feel her kisses on the breeze and hear her breathy sighs in the rustle of the trees. Yes, she is with me still; in Gabriella's shining eyes and in George's generous provision. They lead me to a spacious, run-in shed that smells of fresh paint and sawdust and is set in the corner of a large paddock delineated by pristine, white fencing. Gabriella removes my lead rope, and I wander around and sniff the ground and nibble at little piles of hay spread throughout the pasture. The flies have yet to discover this new place, and I swish my tail with delight.

"I think he needs a friend," Gabriella says. "Maybe a goat. Or a donkey."

George shrugs. "Maybe. But what he needs most right now is time."

Gabriella nods and for a moment, she imagines her mother on my back. She wishes she'd taken the time to observe a lesson or watch her ride in the field. Now, she can only conjure what that looks like—the kind of joy and freedom that was so compelling that she risked her cozy, comfortable life in pursuit of that... that which made her stronger.

Satisfied that I'm settling in, they head back to the house. George pays the old woman for transporting me and I'm glad when the steel box disappears. The next few days reveal my new routine. George brings me grain and fresh water before he leaves for work, and not too much longer after that, Gabriella comes and throws some hay and picks the pasture in hopelessly high heels until she discovers the utility of muck boots. She doesn't even press her fingers to her nose anymore. *What doesn't kill her makes her stronger,* she reminds herself each day. The hours are predictable, with mornings and evenings rolling into one another, punctuated only by short visits from Gabriella or George, who do their best to show me some love. But I miss lip-smacking kisses, and riding, and playing, and fat, chewy cookies, and hearing Clarissa tell me I'm the best horse in the whole world...

That's why I run with excitement at the sight and sound of a black pickup truck that stops at the bottom of the driveway. I know that sound! I know that energy! I race to the back fence and nicker at the sight of Sebastian, who glances around himself furtively as he approaches me. Come on, Sebastian, let's play!

But Sebastian hasn't come to play. He comes to rub my face and feed me my favorite cookies and whisper his secrets into my ear and hide his tears in my chestnut mane. He doesn't stay long, only long enough to commune with Clarissa and me. He leaves four red roses at the bottom of the fence post and ruffles my forelock and takes his leave. I whinny and run the fence line. He turns around and begs my silence with a stern yet tender eye. But it's too late. George is halfway down the driveway and waving his arms.

"Hey!"

Sebastian freezes, lowers his sunglasses, and slowly turns around. George reads the lettering on Sebastian's hat and thrusts out his hand.

"You're Sebastian, Clarissa's trainer, right?"

"Forgive me, I just wanted to visit Sonny. I know I should have called."

"You can come and see him anytime you want," George says. "In fact, I've been meaning to reach out to you. Can you wait here just a minute?"

"Sure," Sebastian says. He scans his surroundings...Clarissa's house...Clarissa's garden...a whirligig that looks like a flying, chestnut Quarter Horse racing in the breeze.

George emerges from the garage, lugging a large carton. He places it at Sebastian's feet and peels back the flaps. Sebastian flinches at the sight of my saddle.

"That tall skinny lady at the barn, Clarissa's friend..."

"Carla?"

"Yeah. Carla. Apparently Clarissa told her that if anything ever happened to her, she wanted you to have this. Please, take it. I have no use for it." George lifts the saddle out of the box and drops it into Sebastian's arms.

Sebastian nods and chokes out a word of thanks and has no choice but to hurry off. His shoulders heave as he approaches his truck and tenderly sets the saddle on the seat beside him. For all appearances, it is empty and wooden and dead—and yet, it is a seat of redemption and a throne of mercy and a tree of salvation that raises his soul to that place where Clarissa is, where Clarissa waits, for both of us.

It's almost as if she knew it couldn't last. In one ephemeral moment, she had reached the summit, she had crossed the Andes, and it was time to move forward, always forward! Just keep moving your feet, Clarissa, and I'll keep moving mine... until we meet again in fields of gold!

About the Author

Andie Andrews is a passionate equestrian, certified equine massage therapist, screenwriter, cowgirl poet, and novelist. She recently moved to a small farm in New Jersey so that Hook, her beloved horse and muse for this project, could live with her happily ever after. She homesteads with her tractor-happy husband, Ed, one silly goat, five quirky hens, her flying chestnut horse, and a gregarious Golden Retriever puppy/farm-dog-in-training.

She is the author of an award-winning historical romance, *The Legacy of Ruby Sanchez*, which was a FaithWords finalist in the American Christian Fiction Writers' Genesis contest. She has also had her work published in the American Kennel Club's *AKC Gazette*, and blogs about her life with horses as a midlife rider at Christiancowgirlpoetry.com.

Other books by Andie include *Saints in the City*, a 2009 triple finalist in the Next Generation Indie Book Awards® competition (Romance, Religious Fiction, and Social Change).

For information, links, and updates on Andie's current and forthcoming titles, please visit andieandrewsauthor.com.

Andie is grateful for your readership and welcomes your honest reviews. Please consider posting a review wherever her books are sold.

Made in the USA
Lexington, KY
28 November 2017